Irresistible Greeks

Unsuitable & Unforgettable

Irresistible Greeks COLLECTION

May 2016

June 2016

July 2016

August 2016

September 2016

October 2016

Irresistible Greeks

Unsuitable & Unforgettable

**MAISEY
YATES**

**JANE
PORTER**

**ABBY
GREEN**

MILLS & BOON

First Published in Great Britain 2016
By Mills & Boon, an imprint of HarperCollins*Publishers*
1 London Bridge Street, London, SE1 9GF

Irresistible Greeks: Unsuitable & Unforgettable © 2016 Harlequin Books S.A.

At His Majesty's Request © 2012 Maisey Yates
The Fallen Greek Bride © 2013 Jane Porter
Forgiven but Not Forgotten? © 2013 Abby Green

ISBN: 978-0-263-92216-5

24-0816

Harlequin (UK) Limited's policy is to use papers that are natural, renewable and recyclable products and made from wood grown in sustainable forests. The logging and manufacturing processes conform to the legal environmental regulations of the country of origin.

Printed and bound in Spain
by CPI, Barcelona

AT HIS MAJESTY'S REQUEST

MAISEY YATES

USA Today bestselling author **Maisey Yates** lives in rural Oregon with her three children and her husband, whose chiselled jaw and arresting features continue to make her swoon. She feels the epic trek she takes several times a day from her office to her coffee maker is a true example of her pioneer spirit. Visit her online at her website www.maiseyyates.com.

CHAPTER ONE

"THERE is a science to matching people." Jessica Carter tucked a lock of blond hair behind her ear and lifted her computer, a flat, all-in-one device shaped like a clipboard, so that it obscured her figure. Pity, Stavros was enjoying the look of her. Even if she was starch and pearls, rather than spandex and diamonds.

She continued, her eyes never leaving the screen. "A matching of social status, values, education and life experience is very important to creating a successful, enduring marriage. I think most match services realize that." She paused and took a breath, pink lips parting slightly, her green eyes locking with his just for a moment before dropping back down. "However, I have taken things a step further. Matching is not just a science. It's an art. The art is in the attraction, and it's not to be underestimated."

Prince Stavros Drakos, second son of the Kyonosian royal family, and named heir to the throne, leaned back in his chair, his hands behind his head. "I am not so much concerned about the art, Ms. Carter. The essentials are general compatibility and suitability for my country. Childbearing hips would help."

Her pale cheeks flushed crimson, her lush mouth tightening. "Isn't that what all men want?"

"I'm not sure. And frankly, I don't care. Most men don't

have to consider the entire populace of their country when they go about selecting a wife."

But it didn't matter what most men did. He wasn't most men. Ever since he'd been forced to step into the place of his older brother, he had been different. It didn't matter what normal was, it didn't matter what he wanted. All that mattered was that he be the best king possible for Kyonos.

His methods might be unorthodox, and they might grieve his father, but what he did, he did for the good of his people. It just wasn't in his nature to be too traditional.

She blew out a breath. "Of course." She smiled, bright and pristine, like a toothpaste commercial. She was so clean and polished she hardly seemed like a real woman, more like a throwback from a 1950s television show. In Technicolor. "I… Not that I'm complaining of course, but why exactly have you hired me to find you a wife? I've read the newspaper articles written about you and you seem perfectly able to attract women on all your own."

"When I want to find a suit for an event, I hire I stylist. When I need to organize a party, I hire an events coordinator. Why should this be any different?"

She tilted her head to the side. Her hair was in a low, neat bun, her dress high-collared, buttoned up and belted at the waist. A place for everything and everything in its place. She all but begged to be disheveled.

Any other time, he might have done so.

"I see you have a…practical outlook on things," she said.

"I have a country to run, I don't have time to deal with peripherals."

"I've compiled a list of candidates, to be refined, of course…"

He took the monitor from her hand and hit the home button, tapping a few icons and not managing to find a list. "What is this?"

She took the device back from him. "It's a tablet computer. Shall I put that technologically savvy women need not apply?"

"Not necessary, but you can put down that women with smart mouths need not apply."

Her full lips curved slightly. "Someone has to keep you in line."

"No one has to keep me in line. I'm going to be king." That hadn't kept Xander in line. In fact, he'd pulled himself straight out of line and put Stavros in front. But Stavros wouldn't falter. He wouldn't quit.

One well-shaped eyebrow lifted upward. "Oh? Is that so." She typed something on her onscreen keyboard.

"What? What did you write?"

"Strong tyrannical tendencies. A possible negative in social interactions, possible positive in BA."

"BA?"

"Bedroom activities. It's shorthand. Don't dwell on it," she said, her tone snappy. "I told you attraction is considered. That said, do you require a virgin bride, Prince Drakos?"

"Stavros will do, and no, I don't." He shouldn't be surprised by her frankness. She had a reputation for being bold, brash even. She also had a reputation for setting up unions that had led to successful mergers and increased fortunes. She was a relationships strategist, more than a matchmaker, and he'd been assured that there was no one better. She knew the rules of society, knew the function a practical marriage served.

His marriage, and securing it, meant nothing to him personally, and being able to pawn off the legwork on Jessica Carter had been too good of an idea to pass up. And if the press happened to pick it up, all the better. He had a reputation for doing things differently. Doing things his way. Turning away from how his father had run the country.

And this was as far from something his father would do as he could think of.

"That's good," she said. "It's always awkward to ask women to submit proof of sexual history."

"Do you do that?"

"I have. Though not just women."

"Who?" he asked.

"Ah, now, if I told you I would have to kill you. I operate on the basis of strict anonymity. Unless those involved are seeking publicity, I don't talk about my clients."

"But word does spread," he said. He'd seen an old school friend three weeks earlier, and the smugness had practically been dripping from him as he stood there with his new fiancée. Oxford educated. And a model. She was everything he'd asked for. Beauty and brains. And who had accomplished the feat?

Jessica Carter.

The woman the media called the World's Most Elite Matchmaker. She catered to billionaires. CEOs, tycoons. Royalty. And she was renowned for making matches that lasted.

That was what he needed. He'd given up on allowing himself any sort of personal interest in the selection of his bride ever since he'd discovered that it was likely he would be assuming the throne for his absentee brother. His wants didn't matter. He needed a woman who could be a princess, an icon for his country, an aide to his rule. Aside from that, he had some of his own ideas. Someone beautiful, of course. Someone smart. Philanthropic. Fertile.

It shouldn't be too hard to find.

"This isn't just about me, Ms. Carter, this is about Kyonos. My family has seen too much tragedy, too much…

upheaval. I have to be the rock. I have to provide a solid foundation for my people to rest on, and establishing a solid marriage is essential to that plan."

The death of his mother, nineteen years ago, had shaken his people to the core. The abandonment of his older brother, the rightful heir, had caused months of instability. Stocks had tanked, trade had stalled, the housing market going into a deep freeze.

Why had the future ruler really left? Would he truly abdicate? What secrets were the Drakos family guarding beneath that veneer of polish and old world sophistication?

He had been determined to undo all of the unrest brought about by his brother. And he had done it. He'd revitalized Thysius, the largest city on the island, with posh hotels and trendy boutiques. He'd brought in new revenue by having the seat of his corporation on the island, a country much too small to house companies the size of his, when the owner wasn't the crown prince.

He'd done much to drag his country back from the brink. From the age of eighteen his entire life had altered so that it revolved around his homeland. He hadn't had the luxury of being a boy. Hadn't had the luxury of feeling fear or sadness. He'd learned early on that feeling had no place in his world. A ruler, an effective ruler, had to be above such things.

"I understand that this is a big deal," she said. "Not just in terms of your country, but for you. She *is* going to be your wife."

He shrugged. "An acquisition I've long known I would make."

Jessica let out a long, slow breath. "Mr....Prince Drakos, will you please stop being so candid? It's remarkably hard to sell a man who clearly has no interest in romantic love."

"Try this for a tagline—marry the jaded prince and receive a title, a small island, a castle and a tiara. That might make up for it."

"Money can't buy love."

"Nice. Trite, overdone, possible copyrighted by The Beatles, but nice. You might consider tacking this onto the end—love doesn't buy happiness."

Something changed in Jessica's eyes, a shard of ice in the deep green that had been warm a moment before. "That's for damn sure, but we're talking about putting together a sales pitch. And you aren't helping."

He shifted. "Can't you put something in my file about my impeccable table manners?"

"I haven't witnessed them, and I don't lie. You're my client, yes, but there is a pool of women I work with on a regular basis, and I have great loyalty to them."

It was intriguing. The way she flashed hot and cold. The way she presented herself, nearly demure, and then she opened that mouth. And such a lovely mouth, too. She was holding it tight. What would it take to make it soften?

The idea made his stomach tighten.

"And you think one of them is my queen?"

"If she isn't, I'll walk through all of Europe beating gold-plated bushes until a member of minor nobility falls out. I won't stop until we get this settled."

"You are supposed to be the best. You did manage to get a confirmed bachelor friend of mine to settle down."

"That's because, in my business, there's no settling. It's all about making the best match possible," she said brightly.

"Somehow, I do not share your enthusiasm."

"That's okay, I have enough for both of us. Now…" She looked back down at her tablet computer. "Your sister's wedding is in just a couple of weeks, and I don't want you going with a date, are we clear?"

He frowned. "I wouldn't have brought a date to a wedding." Weddings were where one picked up women; he didn't see the point of bringing one with him. The thought reminded him that it had been a very, very long time since he'd picked up a woman.

"And no leaving with any of the bridesmaids," she added. "You have to be seen as available, approachable and, oh yes, available."

"You said that already."

"It's important. Obviously, we don't want to put out a call for all eligible women in the kingdom to show up, so we need to go about this subtly."

He frowned. "Why aren't we putting out a call for all eligible women?"

"Look, Prince Charming, unless you want to put a glass slipper on a whole bunch of sweaty feet, you do this my way. That means you behave how I tell you to at Princess Evangelina's wedding."

"I wouldn't have picked up a bridesmaid. My sister's friends are far too young to interest me," he said.

"Ah...so you have an age range," she said, perking up. "That's important."

"Yes, no one as young as Evangelina. I'd say twenty-three at youngest. A ten-year age difference isn't so bad. Maybe cap it at twenty-eight."

She frowned. "Oh. All right." She looked down at her computer, then up, then back down again, her mouth twitching, like she was chewing on something. Her words, he imagined. She looked up at him again. "Why, exactly, is anyone older than twenty-eight too old?"

"I need a wife who can have children. Preferably a few of them. Any older and..."

"Right," she snapped, directing her focus downward again.

"If I ask you how old you are I'll only make this worse won't I?" he asked dryly.

"I have no problem with my age, Prince Stavros, I'm thirty. Not that it's your business."

"It's not personal."

"I get it," she said. "And I'm not applying anyway."

"A pity," he said, noticing the way color bled into her cheeks.

Jessica set her iPad on the ornately carved table to her right and put her hands in her lap, trying like crazy to stop the slight tremble in her fingers. She was saying all the wrong things. Letting her mouth run away with her. Not a huge surprise since she tended to get prickly when she got nervous.

She'd managed to make that little quirk work for her over the years. People found her bold approach refreshing. And that suited her, since it enabled her to keep all shields up and locked, fully protecting her from people getting too close. Without showing vulnerability.

And now, with Prince Stavros Drakos, was not the time to let her guard down. No, most especially not with him.

"I've managed to finagle three wedding invitations," she said. "They will go to three girls that you and I will work at selecting sometime this week. At the wedding, you will speak to them for twenty minutes apiece, no more. And after that, I want you to pick one to advance to a higher tier. I've made a list of questions for you to consider asking."

"I'm not even getting a full date?" he asked, dark eyebrows lifting.

She shifted in her chair. He was so sexy it was unnerving. Because his aesthetic appeal couldn't be observed in the cool detached manner she might use to look at a nice piece of art. That was the way she'd been looking at men for the past few years. As lovely objects, nice to behold, but nothing that invoked feeling.

She'd let that part of herself go and she hadn't missed it. Until now.

Stavros…well, he made a spark catch in her belly. One that had been entirely absent for so long now she'd thought it had gone out permanently. It was a disastrous realization.

She stood up and took a step away from him, hoping distance would bring clarity. Or at least control over her body.

"You don't need a full date. Not at this stage. I've picked out a few candidates based on what we talked about over the phone. And now I've refined some of that, and I've got a number of women I'd like for you to have an initial meet with. You've been matched with them based heavily on compatibility. The kind we can establish from forms, anyway. Attraction," she said, the word sticking in her throat for some reason, "is actually one of the simpler parts of this stage. But it's not simple, not…not really." She felt her stomach tighten. The way Stavros was looking at her was intense, his brown eyes locked with hers. He was gorgeous.

It was sort of ridiculous how hot he was. It was as if he'd splashed around in the finest end of the gene pool, only collecting the good, the bad rolling right off. Square jaw, straight, proud nose and his lips…they changed a lot. Firm and unyielding sometimes. And other times, when he smiled, they looked soft. Soft and…kissable.

She swallowed and tried not to think about how very long it had been since she'd been kissed. She tried even harder to stop thinking about kissing Stavros's lips.

"Anyway," she said, breathing in deeply. She knew what to say next, knew her system by heart. She could explain it in her sleep. And she could take a few more steps away from him while she did it. "We start with that base attraction. What I call 'lightning bolt' attraction—" like the kind she'd felt when she'd walked into Stavros's office this morning "—or what many confuse with love at first sight. You'll feel a stronger pull of that immediate attraction to at least one of the women at the wedding. As we go on, we'll try and figure out which woman you feel a more lasting attraction for. But that's a different phase of the program."

"And you're accusing me of lacking in romance. You have this all worked out to a cold, calculated system. I'm not complaining, but let's be…what was the word you used? *Candid.* Let's be candid, you and I." A smile curved his lips and he rose from his desk, slowly rounding it. "You're no more romantic than I am."

His voice was like warm butter. It flowed over her body, so good, and so very, very bad for her. She cleared her throat. And took a step back. "All right, I'm not a romantic. Not really. I mean I was, at one time. But not so much now. What is romance? Warm fuzzies and the unrealistic ideals we project onto others when we're first beginning a relationship. Romance is an illusion. That's why I believe in matching people based on something concrete. From these basic principles, love can grow. And when the foundation is solid, I believe love can be real and lasting. It's when people go with that lightning attraction only, with nothing to back it up, that's when you have problems."

He lifted his arm and ran his hand over his hair, the action stretching his crisp dress shirt tight over his well-defined chest. She wondered what muscles of that caliber would feel like beneath her hands. She'd never touched a chest that looked quite like that.

Oh, dear. Wandering thoughts again. And redirecting…

"So, is that what you did?" he asked. "Follow one of those flash attractions, or whatever you call them, and have it end in disaster?"

She laughed and turned, hoping to look like she was

starting to pace and not like she was trying to put space between them. "Something like that." A lot more complicated than that, but she wasn't about to get into it. "The point is, I know what works."

"But you aren't married."

She stopped midstep, wobbling slightly on her sky-high stilettoes. "I'm happily divorced, as it happens." Happily might be overselling it, but she was rightfully divorced, that was for sure. "I just celebrated my four-year anniversary of unwedded bliss."

He arched an eyebrow. "And you still believe in marriage?"

"Yes. But the fact that my marriage didn't work helps with what I'm doing. I understand what breaks things down. And I understand how to build a solid foundation. You've heard of the wise man who built his house on the rock, I assume?"

"It's buried somewhere in the ether of my debauched mind. Memories of childhood Sunday school lurk there somewhere." Oh, he did that charming, naughty smile far too well. It was no wonder he had a reputation as the kind of man who could meet a woman and have her taking her clothes off for him five minutes later.

She found her own hand wandering to the top button of her dress and she dropped it quickly, taking another defensive step back. He answered that move by taking three steps forward.

She cleared her throat. "Excellent, well, I'm helping you build a marriage on a rock, rather than sand."

His eyebrows lifted, one side of his mouth quirking into a smile. He took another two steps toward her. "Different than a marriage on the rocks?"

She stepped back. "Much."

"Well, that is good to know," he said.

"You and I will work together to create a strong partnership, for you and your country," she said, with all the confidence she could pull out of her gut. Confidence she didn't really feel.

He closed the distance between them and she took another step in the opposite direction, her back connecting with the wall. She forced a smile, and a step toward him.

He held his hand out, so large and tan and masculine. She just stared at it for a moment, trying to remember what one was supposed to do when they were offered a hand.

Her brain jolted into gear and she stuck her hand out. He gripped it, heat engulfing her as his fingers made contact with her bare skin. She wished now that she'd worn her little white gloves with the pearls. She'd thought them a bit quirky for a business meeting, but the shield against his touch would have been nice.

She just hadn't realized. Sure, she'd seen his picture, but a picture didn't do justice to the man. He was broad, nearly a foot taller than her, and he smelled like heaven. Like clean skin laced with a trace of sandalwood.

He made her feel small and feminine. And like she was losing her mind.

She shook his hand once, then dropped her own back to her side, hiding it behind a fold in her full skirt as she clenched it into a fist, willing the burning sensation to ease.

"I'll hold you to it, Ms. Carter. And I warn you, I can be a tough taskmaster."

Her breath caught. "I'm… I can handle you."

He chuckled, low and dark, like rich coffee. "We'll see."

CHAPTER TWO

"Are you finding the accommodations to your satisfaction, Ms. Carter?"

Jessica whirled around, her heart thudding against her breastbone. Stavros was standing in the hallway of her hotel, a small smile on his face. "I… Yes, very. I didn't expect to see you here. Today. Or ever."

He looked around them, as though checking to see if he was in the right place. "This is one of my hotels."

"Yes, I know, but I assumed…"

"You assumed that I had no real part in the running of my hotels, casinos, et cetera. But I do. In another life I might have been a businessman." His tone took on a strange, hard tinge. "As it is, I divide my time between being a prince and running a corporation. Both are equally important."

She tried to smile and took a step back. "So, to borrow a phrase…of all the hotels you own, on all the island, you walk into mine?"

His sensual lips curved upward. It was hard to call it a smile. "Oh, this was calculated, but I also had a business reason for coming by."

Her stomach fluttered. *Down, girl.* What was wrong with her? A man hadn't made a blip on her personal radar for a long, long time. And Stavros was a client.

Anyway, she wasn't quite through licking her wounds.

The loss of her five-year marriage, and the circumstances surrounding it, had left her feeling far too bruised to jump back into dating. Which had been fine. She'd left her job poured everything into starting her own company and perfecting her system of matchmaking.

Those who can't do, teach, those who can't find a match match others.

That wasn't true. She *could* find a match. Had found one, back when she'd believed in falling in love accidentally with the aid of some sort of magic that might make i stick. As if it were so simple.

And then life had taken her dreams, her hopes, her beliefs and feelings, and it had jumbled them all together until the wreckage was impossible to sift through.

Until it had been much easier to simply walk out of the room and close the door on the mess, than to try and find some sort of order again.

But her ex-husband had no business wiggling into her thoughts. Not now. Not ever, really. That was over. She'd changed.

Her job had always seemed important. At first, being a matchmaker had been all about indulging her romantic streak. She'd been in love with love. With the mystical quality she'd imagined it possessed.

She knew differently now. Knew that relationships were about more than a flutter in your stomach. Now her job seemed essential in new ways. To prove to herself that i could still be real. That people could get married and stay married.

It was almost funny. She created successful relationships successful marriages. And she went to bed alone every night and tried not to dwell on her broken one.

She'd had mixed success with that. But she'd had phe

nomenal success with her business. And that was what she chose to focus on.

"All right, what was your reason?" she asked, taking another step back.

"First off, I had to speak to my manager about handling all of the incoming guests for Mak and Eva's wedding. One of my gifts to them. Putting Mak's family up in the hotel. He could do it himself, and he's argued with me about it no end, but I'm insistent."

"And you do get your way, don't you?" she asked. She had a feeling he never heard the word *no*. That if a command was issued from his royal lips everyone in the vicinity hopped to obey him. It wasn't that he had the manner of a tyrant, but that he had such a presence, a charisma about him. People would do whatever it took to be in his sphere. To get a look from him, a smile.

He was dangerous.

"Always." The liquid heat in his eyes poured into her, his husky smooth tone making her entire body feel like it was melting. She was pretty sure she was blushing.

Oh, yeah, dangerous didn't even begin to cover it.

She cleared her throat, "And the other thing?"

"I came to get you. If you're going to be aiding me in the selection of my future bride, you need to understand me. And in order to do that, you need to understand my country."

"I've done plenty of research on Kyonos and…"

"No. You need to see my country. As I see it."

She really didn't relish the idea of spending more time with him. Because it wasn't really her practice to buddy up to a client, though, knowing them was essential. But mostly because, between yesterday and today, the strange fluttery feeling in her stomach hadn't gone away. The one that seemed to be caused by Stavros's presence.

"Are you offering me a tour?" She should say no. Say she had paperwork. Something.

"Something like that."

"All right." She wasn't quite sure how the agreement slipped out, but it had.

Well, it was best to agree with the one who was signing one's very large check when all was said and done with the marriage business. Yes. Yes, it was the done thing. So she really had no choice but to spend all day in his presence. No choice at all.

"Great. Do you need to get anything?"

"I was ready to go and have some lunch, so I think I'm all set." Her cherry-red pumps weren't the best choice for walking, but she'd packed some black ballet flats in her bag for emergencies. And anyway, they were amazing shoes and worth a little discomfort.

His eyes swept her up and down, a lift in his brow.

"What?" she asked.

"Nothing."

"What?" she repeated.

He turned and started walking down the hall and she clacked after him. "Why did you look at me like that?" she asked.

"Do you always dress like this?"

She looked down at her dress. White with black polka dots, a red, patent leather belt at the waist. It was one of her favorites, especially with the shoes and her bright red bag. "Like what?"

"Like you just stepped off the set of a black-and-white film."

"Oh. Yes. I like vintage. It's a hobby of mine." One her new financial injection allowed her to indulge in in a very serious way. Her bed might be empty, but her closet was full.

"How do clothes become a…hobby?"

"Because you can't just buy clothes like this. Well, you can, but they're reproductions. Which is fine, and I have my share, but to actually get a hold of real vintage stuff is like a game sometimes. I haunt online auctions, charity shops, yard sales. Then there's having them altered."

"Sounds like a lot of trouble for secondhand clothes."

"Possibly fourth- or fifthhand clothes," she said cheerfully. "But I love the history of it. Plus, they just don't make dresses like this anymore."

"No, indeed they don't."

She gritted her teeth. "I don't care if you don't like them. I do."

"I didn't say I didn't."

"Oh, the implication was all there."

He paused, then looked hard at her, his expression scrutinizing. "You know I'm royalty, yes?"

She nodded once. "Yes."

"And yet you still speak to me like this?"

She frowned, a slow trickle of horror filtering through her stomach. She wasn't backing down now, though—pride prevented it. "Sorry, my mouth gets away from me. Sometimes I need someone to restrain me."

He chuckled. "Ms. Carter, you have no idea how interesting that sounds."

Oh, but she did. Especially with the wicked grin crossing his lips. And it had been a very, very long time since she'd been with a man.

Longer since she'd missed it. Longer still since she'd enjoyed it.

"Jessica," she said, her dry throat keeping her from speaking in a voice that transcended a croak. "Just call me Jessica." Because for some reason when he called her Ms. Carter in that sexy, sinful voice of his, that Greek accent adding an irresistible flavor, she pictured him calling her that in bed. And that was just naughty. Naughty and completely out of the blue.

She wasn't interested in sex. Not the responsibility of it, not the repercussions of it. And not the pain that resulted from it.

"Jessica," he said, slowly, like he was tasting it.

Well, that didn't help, either.

"Prince Stavros?"

"Stavros. Please."

Her heart pattered, a sort of irregular beat, like it had tripped. "I don't assume you're in the habit of asking commoners to call you by your first name?"

He shrugged. "Titles are fine. In many regards, they are necessary as they establish one's place in society. I like them for negotiation, for the media. I don't really like them in conversation."

"All right then," she said, "Stavros." She put a lot of effort into the name, taking her time to savor the syllables, as he'd done to hers. She saw a flicker of heat in his dark eyes and fought to ignore an answering flame that ignited in her stomach.

"We'll start here," he said, indicating the halls of the hotel as he began to walk ahead. "This hotel, and many others like it, have been essential to my country. After the death of my mother, my father started neglecting the tourism industry. He neglected a great many things. I was fourteen at the time. My brother, the heir to the throne, was sixteen. He left a few years after that. It became clear that Xander was gone, and that we could not count on him to see to his duties." Stavros didn't bother to hide the hint of bitterness in his voice. "That started rumors of civil unrest. And of course tourists don't want to be somewhere that could possibly be dangerous. As soon as I was able I did what I could to start a revival of the tourism industry. I went abroad for college, established contacts. I studied business, hospitality, economics. Whatever I thought might be helpful in getting my country back to where it needed to be."

"You turned Kyonos into a business."

"Essentially. But not for my own gain. For the gain of my people."

"True," she said, "but by all accounts you have gained quite a bit."

"I have. I won't lie. My own bank account is healthy, in part due to the fact that, at this point, the interest it's collecting on a yearly basis is more than most people will see in a lifetime." He turned to look at her. "Do you need my estimated net worth for your records so you can pass it on to the women you're considering for me?"

"What? Oh, no. I think they'll feel secure enough in your...assets. I doubt they'll need anything so crass as actual net worth. A ballpark figure will do."

"You're very honest."

"Yes, well." She took in a deep breath and tried to ignore the tightening in her stomach. "Hiding from reality doesn't fix anything."

"No. It doesn't," he said.

She could tell, from the icy tone in his voice, the depth to each word, that he was speaking from experience. Just like her.

Interesting that she could fly halfway across the world and meet a prince who seemed to have more common ground with her than anyone in her real life did.

She had friends, at least, the ones Gil hadn't gotten custody of after the divorce. But they were still married. They had children.

A hollow ache filled the empty space where her womb had been. The same one that had plagued her so many times before. When she saw babies. Small children on swings.

Women wiping chocolate stains off of their blouses. And sometimes, it happened for no reason at all. Like now.

"No, reality's one bitch that's pretty hard to ignore," she said.

He chuckled, dark and without humor. "A very true statement. That's why being proactive is important. Sometimes you get problems you didn't make or ask for, but hiding doesn't fix them."

They stopped in front of an elevator and Stavros pushed the button. The gold doors slid open and they stepped inside. The trip down to the lobby was quick, and they breezed through the opulent room quickly, making their way to the front.

There was a limousine waiting for them, black and shiny. Formal. It didn't fit with what she'd seen of Stavros so far. He didn't seem like the type of man who would choose to ride in something so traditional.

He seemed to lurk around the edges of traditional, doing everything a man of his station must do, while keeping one toe firmly over the line of disreputable. It ought to make him obnoxious. It ought to make him less attractive. It didn't.

He opened the door for her and they both slid inside. She sighed, grateful for the air-conditioning. Kyonos was beautiful, but if the breeze from the sea wasn't moving inland it could be hotter than blazes for a girl from North Dakota.

As soon as they settled in and the limo was on the road, she turned to him. "So, why a limo?"

"It's how things are done," he said. He pushed on a panel and it popped open, revealing two bottles of beer on ice. "More or less."

She laughed and held her hand out. "You're about fifteen degrees off unexpected, aren't you?"

He chuckled and handed her a bottle. "Am I?"

"Yes. Hiring a matchmaker to find you a wife and drinking beer in a limo. I'd say you're not exactly what people expect in a prince."

"There are protocols that must be observed, responsibilities that must handled. But there are other things that have a bit more leeway."

"And you take it."

He shrugged. "You have to take hold to the pleasures in life, right?"

"If by pleasures, you mean shoes, then yes."

He laughed and took a bottle opener from a hook on the door and extended his hand, popping the top on the bottle for her. "A true gentleman," she said. "And clearly a professional. Get a lot of practice in college?"

"Like most people."

"Where did you go to school?"

"I did two years in the U.K., two in the U.S."

She nodded. "You would be best suited to a woman who's well traveled, who understands a variety of cultures. Probably someone multilingual."

"Because I'm clearly so cultured?" he asked, raising his bottle. He relaxed his posture, his arm over draped over the back of his seat. There was something so inviting about the pose. The perfect spot for a partner to sit and snuggle against him...

She blinked. "Well, yes, you have to be able to communicate with your spouse. Connect with them on a cerebral level."

"Most of the women I've dated have only connected with me on one level, but it's a level I've found to be very important." The suggestive tone of his voice left no doubt as to just what level he was referring to.

She cleared her throat and tried to banish the heat in her cheeks. For heaven's sake. Talking about sex was normal in her job. It was part of the job, because it was part of relationships. It never made her…blush. She was actually blushing. Really and truly. Like a schoolgirl. Ridiculous.

After enough invasive doctor visits for three lifetimes she thought she'd lost the ability to do that years ago.

"And I consider that important, too," she said, knowing she sounded stiff and a little bit prudish, and she absolutely wasn't either thing, so she had no idea why. "But you will be expected to see each other outside of the bedroom."

"Of course," he said. "But as I said, I have my priorities. Even sexual attraction takes a backseat to a spotless reputation and the ability to produce heirs."

"Right. And how do we establish for certain if she can… produce heirs?"

"Most women can, I assume." He said it with such throwaway carelessness. As though the idea of a woman not being able to have children was almost ridiculous.

She pursed her lips. "And some can't." Why did the subject always make her feel sick? Why did it always make her feel like a failure?

Well, discussing the ability to bear children as an essential trait of a queen, a wife, was never going to be easy, no matter how much peace she imagined she'd made with her lot in life.

"As we get closer to choosing someone, we'll have to undergo a medical screening."

"You'll be required to do the same," she said.

"Will I?"

"Well, yes, I'm not allowing any of the women I might find for you to sleep with you until I establish that you have a clean bill of health."

"You need me to get tested for STDs?"

"Yes. I do. You're planning on having children with the

woman who marries you, which means unprotected sex. And that means a risk to the health of your wife."

"I assume the women will be undergoing the same tests?"

"All of the women who come to me, all of the women and men in my file, are required to submit those test results to me."

"As it happens, I just got tested. Clean. You can have the results if you like."

"I would like them. And I assume you won't be taking on any more sexual partners while we undergo this process?" She felt her cheeks heating again. The topic of sex and Stavros, in the close proximity of the limo, was just a bit too much.

His eyes flickered over her, leaving heat behind. "Naturally not," he said, the words coming slowly. Unconvincingly. "And I haven't had one in quite a while."

"Good. Also, you will not sleep with the women I introduce to you. They know the rules. I don't allow sex between my clients."

"You don't?" he asked, an incredulous laugh in his voice.

"Not until a match is set and I'm not longer involved. Clearly, the relationship can still dissolve, but I'm not a pimp. I'm not prostituting anyone, and I'm not allowing them to prostitute themselves. This is about creating a relationship, a real lasting relationship, not about helping people hook up casually."

"I suppose, running it as a business, you would have to be careful of that," he said.

"Very. When I was starting the business I was really excited, and then I realized what it could quickly turn into if I didn't lay the rules out. Men…well, and women…could use it to find suitable people to…use. And that's not what I want."

"So, you're not a big one for romance, and yet, this is what you choose to do for a living? Why is that?"

She looked out the window, at the crystalline sea and white sand blurring into a wash of color. "It was what I was doing anyway, though not on this level. But after…when I made some changes in life and started my own business, I knew that somehow…I knew relationships could work."

"So you went looking for the formula."

"Yes. And I don't have the only method, though mine has proven highly successful, but I think the way I go about it works. It also helps to have a disinterested party involved who doesn't have their heart in it. That's me. I help people think things through rationally. I set rules so that physical lust doesn't cloud everything else, doesn't create a false euphoria."

"And why don't you apply it to yourself?"

She laughed. "Because. First of all, I can't be my own disinterested party. Second, I don't have the energy or the desire to do it again. I had one big white wedding and I do not intend to do it again."

"Yet you watch other people do it. Get married, I mean."

"Yes. But I find that it…helps. It's restored my faith in humanity a little bit."

The corner of his lip lifted in a sneer. "Was your ex that bad?"

She shook her head slowly. "Sometimes people change, and they change together. Sometimes one person changes. And the other person can't handle it."

It had been her. She'd changed. Her body had changed. And it had altered everything the marriage was built on. Their dreams for the future. It had been too much.

"You're selling the institution so well," he said dryly. He punched the intercom button on the limo divider. "Stop us at Gio's." He let up on the button.

"I'm not trying to sell you the institution. You *have* to get married."

"True."

"And most people who come to me want marriage, or need it for some reason. My personal story, just one of a sad, all too common statistic, will hardly dissuade them. And I'll admit, most of them don't bother to ask about my personal life."

"I find that hard to believe," he said, as the limo slowed and turned onto a narrow road that wound up a hillside.

"Do you?"

"You're interesting. Your clothes for example—interesting. The things that come out of your mouth, also interesting. You beg to have questions asked of you."

"You would be in the minority in that opinion."

"Again, I find it hard to believe."

"I'm very boring. I have a house in North Dakota. I grew up there. Obviously, I don't work with many billionaires, royalty or socialites in North Dakota. I do a lot of work online, and I travel a lot. I'd say my house is empty at least eight months out of the year. I live alone. Can't have a cat because…well, the traveling. So that's me."

"You skipped a lot."

"Did I?"

He leaned in, his head turned to the side. Sort of like how a man looked right before he kissed a woman. If she could even remember back that far, to when she'd experienced anything close to it. "You didn't tell me why you're so prickly."

She leaned in a fraction. "And I don't intend to. Stop flirting with me."

"Am I flirting with you?"

"I think so." If he wasn't that was just too horrifying.

"I can't help it. You're beautiful."

She swallowed. "Look, I know women melt at your feet and all, but I have a job to do, so best you leave me un-melted, okay?"

He leaned back, his lips curving into a smile. "But you're in danger of melting."

She was afraid she might be. "No. Sorry."

He chuckled and settled back in his seat.

The limo stopped in front of a small, whitewashed build-ing that was set into the side of a mountain. The building was tiny, but the deck was expansive, filled with round ta-bles, most occupied by diners. The tables overlooked the beach, with strings of white lights running overhead.

"Ready?" he asked.

She nodded and put her beer in a cupholder. He got out of the car before her and opened her door. "Isn't your driver supposed to do that?" she asked.

He shook his head. "I always open the door when I ac-company a woman."

"Another one for your file," she said.

"I'm not sure whether I'm nervous or aroused at the talk of this file. Makes me feel like I'm in trouble, which leads to the same conflicting feelings."

Heat flooded her cheeks, her stomach. "That's inappro-priate."

"You're the only one who can make jokes?"

"No…but I didn't make any that were that bad."

"BA? Bedroom Activities?"

"That was serious!" she sputtered as they walked into the restaurant.

"Prince Stavros." A maître d' walked to the door quickly, her willingness to serve the prince obvious, as was the blush staining her cheeks. "I wasn't aware you were com-ing today."

He winked. "I'm being spontaneous."

"Of course," the woman said. "Your usual table is available. Shall I bring you your usual dinner? For…two?"

Jessica opened her mouth to correct the woman's assumption, but Stavros cut her off.

"That will do nicely. I can show us to my table."

He led the way through the indoor dining area, and heads turned as they passed. Stavros had a sort of effortless charisma that poured from him, touching everyone who saw him. She could imagine, so easily, the kind of woman he would need.

One who could match his ease. His strength. Someone to create the perfect image for Kyonos. Someone to carry on the bloodline and keep it strong.

She swallowed a strange, unexpected lump in her throat.

They exited the dining room through two glass doors that led out to the deck. There were only a few scattered tables out there, each partly shrouded by draping fabric hung from a wooden frame built over the porch.

Stavros held her chair out for her and she sat, looking out at the view of the ocean, because it was much safer than looking at the man sitting across from her. She wasn't sure why. She had meetings with male clients, and very often they were lunch or dinner meetings, in very nice restaurants.

But being with them didn't evoke this same strange faux-date feel that being with Stavros did. It was that darned attraction.

She opened her purse and pulled out her iPad. "So, I know we were going to talk about specific women to have come to your sister's wedding."

"Were we? Now?" He curled his hands into fists on the table, his knuckles turning white. It was hard for her to look away from his hands, from the obvious strain. His face remained passive, easy, but his manner betrayed him.

"Well, no, but I wasn't expecting to see you until tomorrow, so…no. But we can talk about it now. I've had a chance to think about what you've told me and I've been through my system. I also called two of the three women I'm thinking of and if you're agreeable to them, they're willing to come for consideration."

"This is like an old-fashioned marriage mart."

"Well, these sorts of marriages are," she said. Strangely, she felt like comforting him. She didn't know why. "Granted, you're the first actual prince I've worked with. But I've dealt with lesser royals. Billionaires with an interest in preserving their fortunes. Women with family money who wanted an alliance with businessmen who could help them make the most of their assets. People have all kinds of reasons for choosing to go about things this way. Some of these women have money, but no title, while others have a title but are…low on funds."

"Ah. A title, but no money and a need for a husband with wealth."

"Some of them. Though this one…" She pulled up a picture of a smiling blonde. "Victoria Calder. She's English, from a very well-to-do family. She's not titled but she's wealthy. She's been to the best schools. She has her own money and she donates a lot of it to charities. As far as my research has taken me, and it took me to the far and seedy recesses of the internet, her reputation is as spotless as a sacrificial lamb. So if a prominent title isn't important…"

"As long as you think she would be suitable to the position, she can be considered."

"So basically fertile and scandal-free. And able to handle public appearances with grace and poise, of course."

Stavros took the tablet from Jessica's hand and looked at the photo of the woman on the screen. She was beautiful. More than beautiful, really. He couldn't find fault with her features. A small, pert nose, pretty, well-shaped lips, rosy cheeks, pale blue eyes.

Yet she did nothing for him. She didn't stir his blood. She didn't interest him. More than that, just looking at her made his throat feel like it was tightening. The impression of a noose.

He preferred Jessica's face. Her longer nose, fuller lips, cat green eyes that tilted at the corners. And her figure… she was like a pin-up girl.

He wondered, not too briefly, if she favored old-fashioned undergarments to go with her vintage dresses. Stockings and garters.

That caused a surge of blood to pump south of his belt. She was a distraction. A temptation. A welcome one, in many ways.

"Yes." He shouldn't be allowing distraction now. He had to focus on finding his bride.

Though, Ms. Jessica Carter would make an intriguing lover. She was all soft curves and pale skin. But her eyes… they showed a fire he imagined she set free in the bedroom. She was spicy, her tongue always ready to flay the skin cleanly off the bone if necessary.

Just as she'd pronounced his commanding personality a plus in bedroom activities, he imagined her sharp mind and bold tongue would earn her points in her own BA category.

It would be so sweet. So good. And a welcome distraction from the marriage talk.

"Anyway," Jessica continued, pulling him from his fantasy, "she's one I would like to invite to your sister's wedding."

"And she's aware of just what she'll be invited for?"

Jessica nodded. "Yes. All of the women I'm working with have come to me, seeking out husbands that are suitable to their backgrounds and financial level, just the same as you."

"I see. So invariably my future wife will be after a title and wealth—" he looked at the photo of the blonde again "—just as I am."

"Fair is fair. You both know just what you're getting into. No false expectations. Not if I can help it."

"No false expectations? Then can I assume you're including a list of my faults in the file you'll be sending on to the women involved?"

"Only if they make it past a certain point in the process. Discretion," she said.

"Of course." He looked at her face, illuminated and washed gold by the afternoon sun. She was beautiful. Not due to perfection of features, or from the expertly applied makeup, though. Her features were beautiful, and her makeup was expertly done. But it was something more. Something deeper.

She was captivating. Different.

Sexy.

His stomach tightened. "And the first wave of the process begins at my sister's wedding."

"That's right. Is that okay? Or do you feel it will detract from—"

"It's fine," he interrupted. It was strange to think of Evangelina married. To think of her as a woman rather than a little girl. "My sister is in love," he said.

"That's good. Since she's getting married."

He gave her a look. "But you know that's not really how things work around here. Not necessarily."

"True."

"She was meant to marry for the good of Kyonos. She is marrying her bodyguard instead."

"Are you angry about it?" she asked, her eyes meeting his, the glittering green light in them far too perceptive.

"Not in the least. Anger is a completely unproductive

emotion." As were most emotions. He's witnessed it first-hand. He made sure he didn't have time for them.

"But that leaves only you."

He shrugged. "Doesn't matter. I can do it."

"And your brother…"

"Might as well be dead. He doesn't care for his country. He doesn't care for his family, his people. He might as well have died with our mother." The words tasted bitter on his tongue and he wished he had some ouzo to wash it out with. Bitterness wasn't helpful, either.

As if on command, a waiter appeared with a tray, laden with food and drinks, and set them down on their table. Stavros took the drink first, while Jessica picked up a stuffed grape leaf and turned it in her fingers.

He took a quick hit of the strong alcohol. "I'm happy for Eva. And her husband does bring a lot to the country in terms of assets and security. Mak is a billionaire several times over. She's hardly marrying beneath herself, even if he isn't royalty."

Beneath Stavros's casual manner, Jessica could sense his dark mood. He was very good at playing smooth, very good at coming across as the genial prince. Ready to smile for a photograph. Never caught scowling by a scandal-hungry public, who would latch onto the salacious headline declaring one grumpy expression proof of some sort of national crisis.

And yet, she could feel that something wasn't right. That there was something beneath it.

He was the last man standing. The anchor. How could he not feel it? Of course he would. His sister had abandoned her duty for love, his brother had abandoned it for selfish, personal pleasure. It was only Stavros now.

She felt added pressure. She couldn't imagine that he didn't.

"Well, we'll find you a royal bride who suits the needs of Kyonos, and you, perfectly," she said, injecting a confidence and enthusiasm into her voice she wasn't sure she felt.

A half smile curved his lips, a shaft of sunlight hitting his face, that single moment displaying the breathtaking quality he possessed to its very best effect.

She certainly felt as if her breath had been taken. Ripped straight from her lungs. Why did he have to be so hot? More to the point, why did she have to suddenly care how hot he was?

She looked back down at her iPad, at the picture of Victoria Calder. And for the first time ever, she felt her stomach curl in with jealousy in connection with a client.

It was the first and last time it would happen. She couldn't afford it. Not financially, and most especially not emotionally.

She'd already had everything drained from her in that department. She would never put herself through it again.

CHAPTER THREE

JESSICA tried not to die of despair as she watched one of her favorite potential brides, Dominique Lanphier, standing by the buffet table looking like a deer in the headlights. She was sort of fidgeting, looking as if she was ready to dart away from the table at a moment's notice and grab Stavros from Corinthia, the petite redhead he was currently engaging in approved conversation with.

This wasn't her best idea. She could see that now. It was just a pity she was realizing it far too late to change anything. Her prospective brides, normally so well-behaved, were a bit giddy over the chance to compete for a prince and all of the good manners that had been bred into them seemed to have been knocked from their heads the moment they'd entered the palace.

Jessica was sweating. Actually sweating. And trying not to look like anything more than a guest. Which, in the grand ballroom, filled to maximum capacity with nearly one thousand people, shouldn't be too hard.

Victoria, her best hope for Stavros, had been unavailable for the wedding, which had forced her to bring in Dominique as a last-minute replacement. Something she was bitterly regretting.

"Just stay there," she whispered, begging Dominique to

go with the program, hoping the other woman would absorb the command from across the room.

It just seemed to be getting hotter in the ballroom now, and she could swear the sweetheart neckline of her flirty cocktail dress was about to slip and go from sexy to burlesque. And that would draw far more attention to herself than she wanted.

She gripped the sides of the bodice and tugged at it slightly. Feeling, for a moment, every inch the unsophisticated North Dakota girl she was on the inside. Feeling her persona start to slip.

No. You are not unsophisticated. You are a business-woman. You are in a castle. Own your inner princess!

Yes. Inner princess. She was sure she had one of those.

She took a deep breath and felt a bit of her anxiety ease as Stavros checked his watch and disengaged Corinthia right on time. Any longer and there would be speculation. And now, he would go to the buffet and it would be Dominique's turn.

This sort of brief, public meeting, was, in her experience, the perfect way to open. To see people interact in a social situation, to prevent a feeling of enhanced intimacy too quickly.

She had to remind herself of all the reasons it was a good idea now, since she was on the verge of panicking and eating her weight in wedding cake to try and stave off the anxiety. This was what she did. This was her one area of confidence, of expertise. And watching it go very much not according to plan was crazy-making.

The transition went smoothly and she watched Stavros engage Dominique in conversation. So casual it could have been accidental. He was good.

She watched as he leaned in, his body language indicating interest, the smile on his face warm. Genuine. Her throat tightened a bit, and cut off the flow of air entirely when he brushed Dominique's arm with his hand.

Such a brief touch. And yet, it spoke of attraction.

He hadn't touched her. Not more than a handshake. And that brief touch at the restaurant. She shouldn't have a list of the times his skin had made contact with hers. It shouldn't matter that he was touching someone else.

It shouldn't matter. It didn't. She was here to try and match him with one of these women. This choking jealousy had no place in it. Jealousy was an awful emotion. Consuming. It brought out the worst in people, in her particularly.

When she'd found out Gil was getting married again. When she'd found out his wife was pregnant.

A prickle of shame spread from her scalp through her body.

She shouldn't be jealous of Gil's wife. Of her ability to give birth. It was small and petty. If he couldn't find happiness with her, he should be free to find it with someone else.

The thing that sucked was that he'd found the happiness she'd wanted. He'd been able to move on and get all of the hopes and dreams they'd built their marriage on. He'd been able to leave her.

She couldn't leave herself.

Her body was her body. Her limitations wouldn't change with a new partner. Moving on for her meant something very different than it had for her ex. Moving on meant rebuilding, finding new dreams. She was happy. She had a successful business. She was financially solvent and she was matchmaking for a prince, for heaven's sake.

A prince she should have no feelings for at all. And certainly not any kind of longing type feelings.

Crazy was what it was. Crazy.

Stavros's time with Dominique closed and he made a

polite exit, not lingering for a moment longer. Which suggested he couldn't have gotten too lost in her eyes or anything.

She should not feel satisfied by that.

She felt her stomach free-fall when Stavros changed course suddenly and started walking toward her. His movements easy, his manner approachable. And several people did approach him. He managed to make everyone feel he'd expended attention on them without actually taking much time, barely halting his movement. Every so often, his dark eyes would land on her, leaving her in no doubt that she was his destination.

And, well, he was a prince, and he was a client. So she wasn't going to dodge him.

She stood, rooted to the spot, until Stavros stopped in front of her. "I'd love a word with you in private," he said.

She looked around. "As long as we don't draw attention. I'm hardly the most recognizable face in the world but..."

"Come," he said. Taking her hand and striding toward the ballroom's exit, his gait much more purposeful than it had been a moment ago.

She snagged a glass of champagne off of a passing waiter's tray and followed him out. "Wait. I'm in heels," she said, taking quick, tottering steps out into the corridor. She flashed a passing guest a smile and tried to match Stavros's pace. "Hey, Tarzan. Me not Jane. You no drag me out by the hair."

He ignored her, continuing to walk down the hall until he came to an ornate wood door that she recognized as the entrance to his office. She never would have found it by herself. Not in the maze of halls the Kyonosian palace boasted. He released her hand, entered in a code and pushed the door open. "Come in," he said.

She shot him a look and walked into the room, wiping

ier hand on the tulle skirt of her gown, trying to get rid of
the heated feeling that his touch had left behind. She crossed
ier arms beneath her breasts, pushed her cleavage up into
prominence, then thought better of it when she realized just
iow prominent it was.

She put her hands on her hips. "What's up?"

"None of them were acceptable," he said.

"None?"

"No."

"But…but…" she sputtered. "What about Dominique?
You touched her arm."

He shrugged. "I know how to flirt."

"Well, yeah, I know, I yelled at you for it a while back.
But why flirt if you aren't going to follow up?"

He frowned. "Did you just imply that I am a…tease?"

"Yeah. A marriage tease. Why feign interest if you don't
feel any?"

"I'm not seeking to hurt anyone's feelings," he said dryly.
"I could hardly stand there and act bored. And anyway,
that begs the question why you would send me such dull
women."

"Dull? Dominique is a beauty queen, Corinthia is a doctor, for heaven's sake, and Samantha…"

"Had the most annoying laugh."

"All right. Yes, her laugh is kind of annoying. But it's
sort of endearing."

"No. It's not."

"You're being unkind."

"Maybe. But I don't have forever to find a wife, and you
were supposed to be the best."

"I am," she said. "I can find you a wife. Anyway, I didn't
think your personal preferences came into it."

"I don't want to be…irritated into an early grave by a
woman who laughs at all my jokes, even when they aren't

funny, or by one who can't seem to make conversation about anything other than the weather."

"That's called small talk. It's how people get to know each other," she said.

"Boring." He waved a hand as if dismissing the concept. "Talk about world events. Something other than the 'balmy evening.'"

"So marriage is more to you than you said. Glad to hear it."

"I am not glad that you presented me with unacceptable candidates. This is not about…meaning, or emotions. This is about… I have to be able to stand the woman I marry."

"You really are being ridiculous. They weren't unacceptable. What's the problem? You didn't find them attractive?"

"They were attractive. But I was not attracted *to* any of them."

"You say that like it's my fault."

"It is," he said, whirling around to face her. His dark gaze slid down to her breasts and her own followed.

She looked back up at him. "Elaborate," she said, teeth gritted.

"You expect that you can show up in that dress, and I can focus on other women?"

"What's wrong with my dress?" She gripped the full tulle skirt reflexively.

"Other than the fact that you're showing off much more of your breasts than any straight man could be expected to ignore? It also shows your legs. This was a formal wedding. Every other woman, including the ones I was speaking to, had on long gowns. You…you…"

"This dress comes to my knees. And I didn't realize you were a fourteen-year-old boy masquerading as a prince."

The insult rolled off her tongue, because what he was saying felt far too good. She wanted to turn it over in her mind, to savor it. To pretend that it was for her and that it mattered. To bask in being seen as pretty instead of broken.

The thought made her so annoyed with herself she wanted to scream.

He took a step toward her, and she sucked in a breath, holding her ground. He leaned in, his face close to hers, dark eyes intense. "I can assure you, I am not a boy."

She swallowed, fought the urge to put her hand on his cheek and see if the faint, dark shadow there was rough yet. "I believe it."

"Then do not test me." His eyes held hers, her heart threatening to beat clean through her chest. She pulled away, her breathing shallow.

Stavros turned away from her. She stood in the middle of his office as he paced, each movement languid and deadly. Her heart was pounding, her body shaking. She'd known that he couldn't possibly be so easy, so relaxed. Beneath that charm lurked the soul of a predator. The deadliest sort, because he knew how to portray an air of complete and utter harmlessness.

Stavros Drakos was anything but harmless. How had she not seen it? How had she assumed he was all flirtation and ease?

And had he…had he really just confessed to finding her cleavage distracting? She looked down again and felt a small flush of pride creep into her cheeks. It had been a long time since she'd been able to feel anything overly positive in connection with her body.

It was nice to have a man look at her and simply see a woman.

It might be a facade, a trick, but it didn't really matter. Stavros would never have to get closer. Would never have to know the truth, or deal with the fallout of it.

But that didn't mean she wouldn't enjoy it. Just for a moment.

"I wasn't intending to," she said.

He stopped moving. "You cannot be ignorant of how you look. You outshone the bride."

She couldn't believe that. Not seriously. Princess Evangelina was a great beauty. Olive skin, long dark hair and a slender figure. In her wedding gown, she was unsurpassable. Plus, the princess was only twenty-one. She didn't have the years Jessica had on her body. Didn't have the scars.

"I doubt that," she said.

"My eyes were on you most of the time."

Heat rushed up her neck and into her face, then spread down over her breasts. "We should not be having this conversation."

"We should. Because if you're going to be present at all of my meetings with potential fiancées, you need to dress more suitably."

"I will dress how I please, Prince Stavros," she said, feeling her hackles rise. She really didn't do backed into a corner well, and, at the moment, she felt backed into a corner.

Stavros felt his pulse pounding in his neck, all of his blood rushing south of his belt. He'd been fighting to urge to go and pull Jessica into his arms and kiss her lips, kiss the swells of her breasts where they rose up over that gown. That ridiculous gown that made her look like every man's midnight fantasy.

He'd tried to focus on the women, the bridal candidates. But they'd seemed…insipid. Young. They hadn't interested him. They certainly hadn't stirred his body. Not in the way Jessica did. And that was not part of tonight's plan.

But when she'd walked into the ballroom tonight, it was as though a switch had flipped inside of him.

Lust had ignited in him like fire, the need to see her curves, those gorgeous curves, without a dress covering them. It made him want to press her against the wall and push all that frilly netting aside. To make her scream with the kind of desire that seemed to be actively trying to eat him alive every time she was around.

He was better than this. He mastered his desires. He directed them where he wanted, when he wanted to express them.

"Has anyone ever told you that you are very stubborn?" he growled.

"It's probably been said to me as many times as it's been said to you. Actually, I imagine I've heard it more, since people probably don't stand up to you very often."

That much was true. But she stood up to him, and she did it without compunction. Yes, she had a reputation for being this bullheaded, but he hadn't expected she would truly treat him in the same way she did every other client.

His expectation had been wrong.

"Fair enough then," he said. "But I do expect you to do as I ask."

"Then I expect you might find yourself disappointed."

"You are supposed to be working for me," he said, not sure where this urge to push her was coming from. But that was what he was doing. Pushing her. Daring her.

"If that's how you feel, you can hunt for your own wife. But we both know you don't want that."

"I'm not sure I want this." The closest he'd ever come to voicing the truth to anyone.

"But you will." She was so certain. And she was right. Emotion had no place in this. It had no place in him.

He crossed his arms. "You have other candidates?"

"You still haven't met Victoria. And there are others."

She shifted and so did her cleavage. A flame licked at his body, igniting desire. Arousal.

"We can discuss it further later. Shall we go back to the wedding?"

"Yes."

She pursed her lips and raised an eyebrow. "And will you be civilized?"

A loaded question, and one he was certain applied to more than just tonight. An answer he wasn't certain of. "I suppose you'll have to take your chances. Are you willing to do that?"

He extended his arm and she didn't move for a beat. Then she took a step to him and looped her arm through his. "You don't worry me too much, Stavros."

He felt a kick in his gut, a purely masculine part of himself taking her words as a challenge. He stopped, turning to face her. Her green eyes widened, lips parting.

"You trust me?" he asked, his heart thundering.

Her eyes drifted to his mouth before raising up to meet his. "Yes."

"Ah, but, Ms. Carter, I'm not certain I trust myself. You certainly shouldn't be putting any trust in me."

It was nothing. Just a little lust. Nothing deeper than any other attraction he'd felt. It was a direct result of his long bout of celibacy. He would meet more women. Find the one he was supposed to marry, and then he could focus all of his desire on her.

But *Theos* help him if he could think of marriage without feeling like he was choking. The attraction to Jessica at least made him feel...well, he could breathe.

"I'm going to be in Greece for the next few weeks and I want you to arrange my meetings with prospective brides there. I have business to attend to." Flexible business, but he needed to get out of Kyonos. Now.

Jessica blinked. "I…I can do that. But I have other clients and I…"

"Not right now you don't. I need you to put everything else on hold. I need you with me, organizing meetings and whatever else I might need so we can simply get this done."

"What will people think if we just up and go to Greece the day after your sister's wedding?"

"Perhaps that we're embarking on a wild affair?" The idea made his body harden. The idea certainly had merit. Merit he might have to seriously consider. Just the idea of lowering her dress, revealing those luscious breasts…

She laughed. "Oh, I doubt that. More than likely they'll wonder if you're looking for a Greek wife."

"I'm not opposed." Not any more opposed than he was to the whole idea.

"I guess it doesn't matter if we operate from Greece or Kyonos."

"Good. Then we'll leave for Greece first thing tomorrow." He opened his office door and held it for her. Tomorrow he would get out of Kyonos, get his head on straight.

For now, he was determined to go back to the reception and enjoy the happiest day of his sister's life.

CHAPTER FOUR

WHAT did one wear on a private jet headed to Greece? With a prince as cabin-mate. That last part was important.

That had been the first question in her mind that morning, and it was still plaguing her even as she boarded the private jet, decked out in a yellow halter-top sundress and a matching wide-brimmed hat.

Because seriously, dwelling on anything more important than that might make her head explode. And she didn't want to risk it. Aside from the fact that the interior was far too swanky to chance getting brain matter on it, she had too much work to do and she couldn't function without said organ.

Stavros was already on the plane, lounging in one of the spacious leather seats, hands behind his head. It was like his go-to mess-with-her-composure position. Exposed bulge at the apex of his thighs? Check. Hard, muscular chest on display? Check. Washboard abs on show? Double check.

He was going to drive her insane.

And what would you do about it? Even if you could act on your attraction to him?

Nothing. The answer was an absolutely nothing, because while attraction, flirtation and sexual desire were all fine and fun, going any further than that would only result in pain. Emotional pain if not physical pain.

Probably both.

"Good morning," she said.

He stood, his posture straight as she moved into the cabin and sat down in a chair that was positioned as far from his as was polite. He didn't sit until she had settled herself.

"I like that," she said. "Very chivalrous."

"Etiquette is, of course, important for a prince to learn," he said, humor lacing his tone.

"It's a dying art form these days, trust me. With both men and women."

"I imagine you would have a greater insight into that than most." He buckled his seat belt and she followed suit as the plane readied for take-off.

"Probably. I deal with people on a pretty regular basis. And I have to ask a lot of…intimate questions. But people also tend to be on their best behavior when they're looking for a relationship, or just beginning one. So I see a lot of the polished squeaky clean veneer, too."

He nodded. "I suppose I do, too."

"I'll bet not many people let loose in front of royalty."

"You don't seem that bothered by my position."

The plane started down the runway and a bubble of excitement burst in her stomach. It had taken a while, but she liked flying now. She liked how free it made her feel. If she wasn't happy where she was, she could hop a plane and escape for a while.

It was liberating; providing some of the few real moments of freedom she felt. It was superhuman to fly, and it took her mind off the fact that she really was just human. With all kinds of shortcomings.

"Well, unlike my clients, I don't see the point in hiding who I am." Lies. She absolutely hid who she was. Behind a suit of armor that was a lot tougher than she was. But what was the point of armor if you admitted you had it on?

"Really?"

"Really."

"I don't believe you," he said, his dark eyes far too perceptive for her liking.

What was he? A mind reader? "Why is that?"

"Because you have secrets. You won't tell me why you're prickly."

She bit the inside of her cheek. "I told you not to flirt with me."

"You tell me that when I start to get close to things you don't want to talk about," he said, leaning over slightly. He was still across the aisle from her, but she felt the move. Felt the increased closeness.

She shifted the opposite direction. "Having secrets is normal. I imagine you have them."

"Not one. Every detail of my life is published in the archives and kept in my father's office. My more public exploits are in the news, in tabloids, on royalty stalker websites."

"So that's it then, you're an open book?"

"I have nothing to hide. More to the point, I can't have anything to hide. If I did, it would be put out in the public eye. I'm a public commodity," he ground out, a bitterness tingeing his words. "I exercise discretion in certain areas of my life, naturally. I don't announce when I take a lover, for example, though all tabloids will imply it. You, on the other hand—you have secrets."

"You think you have me figured out?"

A smile curved his lips. Wicked. Dangerous. "No. Not at all."

"Well, that's good. I would hate to be thought of as predictable."

"You aren't predictable in the least. Not down to what you'll wear on a given day," he said, his eyes on her hat.

"That makes you interesting. It makes me wonder." His eyes met hers and she felt a jolt in her system. "It makes me want to discover all of your secrets."

His made goose bumps break out on her arms. Low and husky, with the kind of accent usually only found in her late-night fantasies. And his eyes...dark and rich, like chocolate. A bitter, intense sort of chocolate.

Her favorite.

She swallowed and tried to slow the beating of her heart. "I live in North Dakota when I'm not traveling, as you already know. I don't own pets. I like clothes. And I do a really dorky celebration dance when I beat my own high scores on computer games." She tried to smile. "Open book."

"I would like to see the dance. But I also don't believe you."

"I do the dance. But I won't do it for you."

"No, I believe you do it." His eyes locked with hers, the perception in them, the sudden seriousness, unnerving her. "I just don't believe you're an open book."

"And I can't believe you care. You don't have time to worry about me or my idiosyncrasies, Prince Stavros, you have a wife to find."

"No, *you* have a wife to find. Deliver her to me when you do."

She laughed, trying to dispel the tension. "That's the plan. Although, I have to do a bit more than deliver. You have to agree with my selection."

"I admit I liked the look of...Victoria, was that her name?"

"Um...yes." She bent down and picked her purse up, hunting for her iPad.

"It's fine. You don't need to get her picture out. I remember."

Was that jealousy? That hot, burning sensation in her stomach? Yes. It very likely was. Ridiculous. She wanted him to like Victoria. Victoria was a fabulous candidate. "Victoria would probably like to meet you here in Greece. She was disappointed that work conflicted with the wedding."

"What happened to your speed-dating idea?"

"I'll get a couple of other girls out as well, just to keep the pressure off. But if I—and by I, I mean you—fly them to Greece they deserve more than fifteen minutes of your time."

"Agreed."

"When will you have time?" She looked back down at her bag.

"Get it out if you have to," he said, his tone grudging.

She leaned down and took her tablet out of her purse and opened the flap on the cover. She opened up the calendar and sat poised with her finger at the ready.

"In the evenings. Dinner dates will do."

She typed in a quick note. "Would you like to see photographs of the other women I'll be asking?"

"Not especially."

She let out an exasperated breath. "If I don't show them to you, you'll only accuse me of picking women who aren't attractive again."

"You can't hear a laugh in a picture. And that laugh was unforgivable."

The look she shot him would have been fatal to a lesser man. "You really are being unkind about the laugh."

"She sounded like a nervous mouse. And she even lifted her hands up and wiggled her fingers. Like she was waiting for cheese."

Jessica tried, and failed to suppress a laugh. "That... you...well."

"I'm right."

"You're mean!"

"I'm not mean. It's one of those things that would eat at me. Day in and day out until one day I divorced her over her laugh and that would be a much bigger unkindness than just not pursuing things from the get go."

She expelled a breath. "Fine. I won't push the laugh issue again. You're entitled to your judgmental opinion."

"I am," he said, lowering his hands so that they were gripping the armrests on his chair. He had such big hands. Very big. Oh…dear. What was her problem?

She lowered her head and focused on her computer. "Anyway, I was thinking of asking Cherry Carlisle and Amy Sutton over." She looked at Stavros, who was affecting a bored expression and staring out the window. "Cherry is a brunette. Amy is a redhead. And Victoria's a blonde." He kept his gaze off of her. "It's actually pretty good because it's like the setup to your own, personal joke. A blonde, a brunette and a redhead go to Greece."

He looked at her, the corners of his mouth tipped upward. "To marry the prince. You really are selling this well."

"I try. Once we land in Greece I'll coordinate with them and hopefully we can get them there ASAP."

"You like speaking in acronyms, don't you?"

She shrugged. "It's faster."

"Speaking of, by my very fast math, you'll be involving six women in this so far. And while I'm under no illusion that we'll keep the press out of this entirely, I wonder what might happen if one of them ends up feeling…jilted."

"Oh, they've signed a gag order."

"A gag order?"

"I take my business very seriously and yes, this is tabloid bait. Serious, serious tabloid bait. And I have no interest in feeding you, or me, to the wolves. So I've taken pretty big precautions."

He leaned forward, his interest obviously piqued now. "And what are the consequences if they break the gag order?"

"Their firstborn child. All right, not quite but there are some monetary fees."

"You are quite deceptive, Ms. Carter."

"Am I?" she asked, leaning back in her chair and crossing her arms beneath her breasts.

"Yes. You seem so sunny. Soft," he said, his dark eyes settling on her breasts. "And yet…you are cynical. More so even than I am, I think. Which is really quite something."

She swallowed and angled her face away from him. She could still feel him looking at her. "Call it cynical if you like, I call it realism. Human nature is what human nature is. No matter how much someone thinks they love you, if being with you starts to conflict with their ultimate goals… well, it won't take much for them to start believing that they don't love you anymore. That's why I work to find people who have united goals and interests. Things that are concrete. Much more concrete than love. Whatever that is. I'm a realist, that's all."

"Cynic. Realist. Whatever the case, you certainly aren't soft."

She shook her head. "No. Being soft hurts too much."

She had no idea why she was telling him so much. What was inspiring her to give away any of her tightly guarded self to this man. She only knew that it was easier to talk around him than to hold it in. That was new. Strange.

She'd always found it easier to just keep it all stuffed inside. Locked behind a wall of iron, defended by her sharp wit. Easier to have an off-the-cuff, half-serious response to everything than to let someone see her true self.

And yet, with Stavros, she had shared.

So pointless and silly. Irritating even, because there was no reason for her to choose him as a confidante. No reason at all. She didn't have a confidante. She didn't need one.

So stop it, already.

"You're right about that," he said, his voice different now. Serious. Lacking that mischief that was usually present. "Emotion…it can eat you alive. Steal every good intention. Every concept of responsibility. We'll be staying in my private villa," he said, changing the subject neatly. And she was grateful.

"We? As in…the two of us?"

"What did you imagine might happen, Jessica?" he asked. Her ears pricked and her heart stuttered at the use of her first name. It felt…intimate.

"I thought maybe we'd stay in a hotel and I'd have my own room." Perhaps a floor or twelve away from his.

"I prefer not to stay in hotels, if I can help it, and you may reserve your comments on the irony of that."

She arched an eyebrow. "How did you know I had a comment ready?"

"You always have a comment ready."

"True," she agreed.

"The villa is big. You won't have to run into me at all, unless it's work-related. If you don't want to, that is."

His voice dropped a step when he said that last part, his words a husky invitation that her body was aching to respond to.

"Why…why would I want to?" she asked, her voice a bit shaky.

"You're the only one who can answer that," he said.

She knew what her answer would be. And it would be completely inappropriate. "Well. I won't. Come looking for you, that is. For anything besides work."

He nodded slowly and leaned back in his seat. "Probably a wise decision."

Probably. And she shouldn't regret making it. But she did.

CHAPTER FIVE

The villa was everything a prince's Grecian villa should be. Windows that stretched from floor to ceiling and ran the length of the room, offering views of the Aegean that were incomparable. Everything was washed in white and blue, reflecting the pale sun and glittering sea.

"You have a room on the second floor. Ocean view," he said.

"Are there any non-ocean views available?" she asked.

"Not many. But I like to be near the sea. The product of my island upbringing, I would imagine. I used to…" A strange expression crossed his face. "I used to like watching the ships come into harbor. Or sail out to sea." He cleared his throat. "Until I became a teenager, and just enjoyed watching women walk around in bikini bottoms. Either way, I've always liked the beach."

"North Dakota's not by the ocean. It's landlocked."

"I know. And the idea of it makes me feel claustrophobic. How do you stand it?"

"I leave. A lot." Her hometown made her feel claustrophobic more often than not, in truth. Especially since she always ran the risk of seeing Gil and Sarah if she went grocery shopping. And now it was Gil and Sarah and Aiden.

Suddenly the fresh ocean air seemed too briny, too harsh. Her throat tightened against it.

"That's one solution," he said.

"A temporary one."

"Why not make it permanent?"

Because then she really would have to let go. "I own a house. It's nice. I have...petunias."

"And I have bougainvillea. There are flowers everywhere."

"But they're my flowers." And it was the place she could go and rehash where her dreams had started. And where they had ended.

No. Not ended. Changed. She was just hunting for some new ones now. Well, that was total garbage. She had a bunch of new ones. She was successful. She had awesome shoes. She helped people find...well, lasting marriage if not love.

"You could transplant them."

She sighed. "Oh, come on, Stavros, they're only petunias."

He laughed, the sound rich and genuine, catching her off guard. "Perhaps find me a woman *you* wouldn't mind spending time with."

His suggestion caught her off guard more than his laughter. "What do you mean by that?"

"You're funny. Quick. I imagine you don't hang out with people who bore you."

"I don't hang out with much of anyone these days, outside of a working relationship, but you're right, I don't."

"So, find me someone you would be amused by. Someone who has better things to talk about than the weather."

"The weather here is lovely," she said, unable to resist.

"Things like that," he said, amusement lacing his tone. "Find a woman who does things like that."

"So someone who's like me, but not me."

"Exactly."

He was teasing. And even if he weren't, there was no

way she could be suitable. She wasn't sweet and demure. She didn't know how to do a royal wave. And she wasn't fertile. Not even maybe.

The only requirement she met was being a woman, a broken one. And that just wasn't enough.

Still, when she looked at her ex-husband's curvy, blonde new wife, she felt like he had gone and done that same thing. A woman who was her, but not her. He'd found a replacement model with a working, intact uterus.

It was something that still burned no matter how hard she tried to pretend it didn't. She didn't love Gil anymore. She didn't want him back. But the way it had all gone down… that was the really hard thing to deal with.

That was the part she had to process. So she just had to move forward. Inch by inch, day by day. Breath by breath.

Some days were more successful than others.

"Charming," she said, turning and heading toward the staircase.

"Jessica." Stavros caught her arm and turned her to face him, his dark eye intense. "I'm sorry. That came out… It was a bad joke."

She shrugged and tried to pull away from him. Away from his touch. His heat. "It's nothing. I'm just tired. I'll think about what we talked about today and I'll get back to you, okay?"

He released his hold on her, her skin still burning where his flesh had touched hers. Scorched hers. How long had it been since someone had touched her? And by touch, she didn't mean handshakes. Didn't mean brushes of fingers, or even a proprietary male hand on her back as she was guided into a building.

Really touched her. Personal. Caring, almost.

It had been so long. Even longer since she'd felt a real connection with someone. That was actually worse than not being touched. Being touched, being skin-to-skin with someone, and knowing that there was no connection at all.

This wasn't like that. She didn't want to crave it. She'd let go of those desires and had done her very best to replace them with new ones. He was ruining it.

Reflexively, she brushed her fingers over the spot where his had rested. "It's nothing. I'm fine."

"You don't look fine."

"Stavros, I'm fine," she said, finding it easier to use his first name now. Here in the villa and not in the palace. "I'm not vying for the position of wife to the future king of Kyonos, remember? I'm helping you find her. And I will. Promise."

"Have dinner with me," he said.

"Where?"

"Here, at the villa."

The thought of it made her stomach feel all fluttery. It made her palms sweaty, too. She was seriously out of practice when it came to dealing with men. Except she wasn't, not really, she just never got asked to have dinner with them in a way that went beyond business.

And you think this is more than business?

No. Of course it wasn't. She was here, in the villa, and he was being hospitable to someone who was working to find him a wife. And she was not that wife.

She didn't want to be anyway. Not even tempted.

The only reason she'd forgotten, for a moment, that his invitation wasn't meant to be an intimate one, was because he'd touched her arm. It had caused a momentary short circuit but she was back now.

"That would be lovely. We can discuss some women who might have more advanced conversation skills..."

"Leave your computer in your room."

"B-but..."

"Come on, Jessica, I think we can have a conversation without your piece of technical equipment between us."

Did he? Because she didn't think so. She wasn't sure what she would do with her hands. Or what she would look at when she started to melt into those dark chocolate eyes of his and she needed a reprieve.

"Of course. I don't have a problem with that. None at all."

"Good. See you in a couple of hours. That will give you enough time to unpack and freshen up?"

She frowned and touched her hair. Freshen up? Did she need it?

"Not everything I say is a commentary on you. Or me finding you lacking in some way," he said, his tone sardonic.

"Pfft. Of course not," she said, dropping her hand to her side. "And not everything I do is connected to something you say making me feel like I'm lacking in some way."

One dark eyebrow arched upward. "Touché."

"Oh…which way to my room?"

"Pick any room you want. Top of the stairs and turn left. I'm to the right."

Then she would be picking the room at the very, very far end of the hall. Left as left could be. "Great. Thanks. See you down here at seven?"

He cocked his head to the side, that charming, easy grin curving his lips. "Sounds good to me. I'll have your bags sent up soon."

"All right. See you at dinner."

She turned and started up the stairs, the marble clicking beneath her heels.

She wasn't going to change her dress before dinner. Because that would mean she was treating it like it was special. Like a date.

No. She definitely wasn't changing her dress.

* * *

She'd changed her dress. That was the first thing he noticed when Jessica descended the stairs and stepped into the living area.

She'd traded in the cheery, yellow, low-cut halter-top dress for a slinky, red, low-cut dress, belted at her tiny waist. The skirt hugged her rounded hips and fell just to her knee, showing those shapely, sexy calves that he was starting to fixate on.

Not as much as he was fixated on the creamy swells of her breasts. But close.

"Hello," she said. Her posture was stiff, her elegant neck stretched up as tall and tight as possible. Her cherry-painted lips were thinned. Which was a waste in his mind. If a woman was going to wear red lipstick she should pout a little. Especially this woman.

But it wasn't the sexual feelings she stirred in him that disturbed him. It was the way she'd looked at him earlier... sad, hurt. And how he'd wanted to drop everything, the wall he put between himself and everyone he interacted with, to comfort her.

That feeling, that desire for a true connection, was foreign to him. And if not entirely foreign, connected to the distant past. Back when he'd believed he had a different future ahead of him. Back before he'd realized the importance of erasing any feeling that could root itself inside of him too deeply.

That might control him. Weaken him. As emotion had weakened his father.

"Good evening," he said, inclining his head. "Have you started settling in?"

"Yes. It's lovely here." The corners of her lips turned up slightly. "Very...balmy."

The small talk was too crisp. Too bland. And Jessica Carter was neither of those things. What she was, was

prickly as a porcupine and likely making inane talk to ir-
ritate him. It shouldn't. With women he was all about connecting on a surface level. With people in general. Why did
he want more from her?

Why did she make him want more for himself?

Talking to that woman with the mouse laugh…it had
been grating. Insufferable. Just the thought of being shack-
led to her for the rest of his life… It had seemed personal
in a way it hadn't before. Whether that was due to Jessica
or the wedding being more of a reality, he didn't know.

"Tell me about your dress," he said, because he knew
it would catch her off guard. It would also redirect his
thoughts to her delicious figure, and that was acceptable.
The rest, the feeling, was not.

She blinked rapidly a few times. "My dress?"

He started to walk toward the terrace, where dinner was
waiting for them. "Yes, your dress. What's the story behind
it? A woman who makes clothing her hobby surely has a
story for each item."

"Yes. Well, but I didn't think you would be interested."
She was walking behind him, trying to keep pace in her
spiky black heels.

He hadn't thought he would be interested, either.
Strangely, he was. "I live to surprise." He paused at the
table and pulled her chair out. "Sit. And tell me."

She arched one well-shaped brow. "I don't respond to
one-word commands."

Heat fired through his veins, pooling in his stomach.
His answering remark came easily. And it was welcome as
it served to mask the intense need that gripped him. "I'll
bet there are a few one-word commands I could get you to
respond to."

She sat quickly and picked up the glass of white wine
that was waiting for her, taking a long drink before setting

it down and saying, far too brightly, "I found this dress at a charity shop."

He rounded the table and sat across from her, keeping the chair pushed out a bit. He didn't trust himself to get too close. And clearly, Jessica didn't, either. Her change of topic had been about as clumsy and obvious as they came.

She'd picked up the meaning of his words. And he'd driven her to drink. That was an ego boost.

"Go on," he said.

"It's from the late forties or early fifties. Sort of business attire."

"That was business attire?" It was a wonder any work got done.

"Clothing then was so feminine. It didn't have to be obvious to be sexy, and it didn't have to be boxy to be respectable. That's one reason I like it."

It was certainly that. But then, Jessica would look feminine in a man's suit. She had curves that simply couldn't be ignored or concealed.

"It suits you," he said.

"I'm glad you think so. You looked at me like I had two heads the first couple of days we were together."

"Did I?"

"Yes."

"I hope you like fish," he said, indicating the plate of food. He always opted for simple when he was at the villa. Something from the sea, vegetables from the garden on the property and a basket of bread and olive oil. He had all the formal he could handle in Kyonos. Ceremony and heavy custom, though he'd been born into it, had never seemed to fit him. Just one reason he was always skirting the edge of respectability.

That and a desire—no, a need—to control something about his life.

"I do," she said. "I didn't always, but as we've discussed, my home state is landlocked, so seafood wasn't that fresh. And fish out of the river just tastes like a river and it's not a good experience. Not for me, anyway. Traveling has expanded my horizons in a lot of ways."

"Was your husband from North Dakota?"

A crease appeared between her eyebrows. "Yes."

"Is that why you aren't with him anymore?"

Her mouth dropped open. "No. What's that supposed to mean?"

"Nothing," he said. But he had wondered, when she spoke of travel, of not spending time at her home, if her ambitions had grown bigger than the life of a housewife.

"Are you asking if I traded my husband in for—" she waved her fork over her plate "—for fresh seafood?"

"Not in so many words."

"Well, I didn't." She released a heavy breath. "If only it were that simple."

"It's not simple?"

"It is now," she said, stabbing at the white flesh of the fish on her plate. "Because we're divorced, and he's my *ex*-husband, not my husband. So whatever happened between us doesn't really matter. That's the beauty of divorce."

An unfamiliar twinge of guilt stabbed at him. "You wouldn't be the first person to run from an unhappy situation. To try and find peace somewhere else." He thought of Xander when he spoke those words. Xander, who had been so miserable. Who had been blamed for the death of their mother. By their father, by their people. And sadly, in the end, by Stavros himself.

"I'm the one who left, if that's what you want to know," she said, her voice cold.

His stomach tightened. She'd walked away. He didn't know the story, he didn't know her pain. But still, it was so easy for him to judge her. It was his gut reaction. Because he knew what happened when people walked away just because it was too hard.

"Did he mistreat you?" Stavros asked.

She met his gaze, her green eyes glittering. "That's a loaded question."

"Seems simple to me."

"All right, I think he was an ass, but then, I'm his ex-wife." She looked down. "Really? He's a moral paragon. You know, he could have taken a lot of money from me. I was the main breadwinner. And he didn't. He didn't want it. He just wanted to be free of me. He took the out I gave him and ran." She pushed her plate back. "I'm not hungry." She stood and put her napkin on the table. "Thanks, but I'm going to go to bed now." She turned and walked away, her shoulders stiff.

Stavros wanted to go after her. To grab her arm like he'd done earlier. To soothe her. With a touch. A kiss.

He sucked in long breath, trying to ease the tightness in his chest. To kiss those ruby lips…they would be so soft.

He wanted to offer comfort. To hold her in his arms.

He couldn't do any of those things.

So he let her go, while his body bitterly regretted every step she took away from him.

Jessica flopped onto the bed and growled fiercely into the empty room. "Way to spill your guts there, Jess," she scolded herself.

Why had she told him that? Any of that. Yes, he'd pushed the subject of Gil. And yes, it had gotten her hackles up because she didn't want any judgment from him about her marriage.

But it was hard to talk about it without talking about everything. About the reason things had crumbled. About the pain, the embarrassment. About the bitterness and disappointment laced into every word. About how going to bed at night had been something she'd dreaded. To have to share a bed with someone, maybe even make love with someone, when they were distant at best, disdainful at worst.

About how in the end she'd had to face the hardest, scariest thing she'd ever endured on her own. About how her husband had let her have major surgery without his support, without him there. She'd had to just lie by herself in a hospital bed. Her body had hurt so bad, and her heart had been crumbling into pieces, the victory over her chronic condition costing her her dearest dreams.

And that was when she'd called a lawyer. She hated that. That he'd made her do that. She honestly believed if she hadn't he would have stayed. Would have punished her by making her live with a man who had grown to hate her.

She closed her eyes and blocked out the memory. As much as she could, she just tried to pretend those moments were a part of someone else's life. Sometimes it worked. Just not right now.

She stood up and started pacing the length of the room. She was pathetic. And pitiful. And where was her armor when she needed it?

There was a knock on the door and she paused midstride. "Yes?" she asked.

"It's me."

The very masculine voice was unmistakable. As was the shiver of excitement that raced through her.

She turned and flung the door open, putting her hand on her hip and shifting her weight so that her hip stuck out, exaggerating the roundness of her curves. "What?"

He only looked at her, his dark eyes glittering. A muscle in his jaw ticked, his shoulders flexed.

They stood for a moment and simply looked at each other.

Then Stavros moved, quickly, decisively, and pulled her up against the hard wall of his chest. He dipped his head and his lips met hers. Hot. Hungry.

So good.

She clung to the door with one hand, her other hand extended next to her, balled into a fist as Stavros kissed her, his hands roaming over her back, his tongue tracing the outline of her lips. And when it dipped inside, slid against her tongue, that was when she released her hold on the door and locked her arms around his neck, forking her fingers through his hair.

He turned her so that her back was against the door frame, his hands moving to her waist.

Oh, yes, she wanted this. All of it. More.

She moved her hands to his shoulders, let them roam over his back. He was hot and strong, his muscles shifting beneath her fingertips. His shirt felt too thick, scratchy on her skin. She wanted to pull it off of him. She arched against him, her breasts pressing against his chest, and she became aware of just how present her dress was. How much of an impediment it was.

They needed to get rid of their clothes.

She moved her hands around to his chest, toyed with the first button on his dress shirt. He growled, a masculine, feral sound that she'd never associated with sex, but that made her entire body tighten with need.

Being with Stavros wouldn't be like any experience she'd had before. Not even close. Being with Stavros would be...

A really bad idea.

She froze, their lips still connected, her fingers curled into the fabric on his shirt. "Stop," she said.

He did. Immediately. He moved away from her, his expression as dazed as she felt. "That's not what I came up here for."

"What did you come up here for?" she asked, her words shaky, her entire body shaky.

"I...don't know." He sounded shocked. Dumbfounded. She wasn't sure if it was a comfort or an insult.

"But not for...that?"

He shook his head. "I'd ruled that out as a possibility."

"But you'd...thought about it?"

"Not a good question."

"You're right about that."

He took a step away from her. "It's understandable that we're attracted to each other."

"Totally," she said.

"But that doesn't mean we can act on it."

"No," she said, while her body screamed at her to change her answer.

And what would happen if she did? Professional suicide. And for what?

Sex for her had become all about failure. About shortcomings. All of hers on display when she was literally naked and as vulnerable as she could possibly be. She couldn't get pregnant. She couldn't even orgasm properly. As her husband had told her during one particularly ugly argument, there was literally no point in having sex with her. He'd said at the time his right hand was better company.

"I'm sorry."

"Oh, don't," she said, her lip curling in disgust, her body rebelling. "Don't apologize for kissing me, please, that's just... I'm not going to let you do that. Act like there was something...wrong with it." There was always something wrong.

"It was inappropriate."

Annoyance spiked inside her. "You're acting like you

compromised my maidenly virtue, or something. That's long gone so you don't need to worry."

"You are working for me right now."

"Not exactly."

"No matter what, it was wrong of me to do it. You're trying to help me find a wife, I'm paying you to do it. I have no right to charge in your room and kiss you."

"I kissed you back," she said, crossing her arms beneath her breasts, unwilling, unable to back down. Because she would not be treated like she was a victim in this. She was tired of being a victim. And she would not show him how much she was affected by it, either.

His expression was almost pained. "Don't remind me."

"That good?"

"If you keep talking I'll be tempted to kiss you again simply to quiet you down."

"You say the sweetest things, Prince Stavros. I am pudding at your feet." Oh, she could have cried. She was so relieved to have those sassy words fall out of her mouth. She needed them. Needed the distance and protection they would provide.

His jaw tensed, his lips, so soft and sensual a moment before, thinned. "You are…infuriating."

"And you like it," she said. "Wonder what that says about you?"

For a moment, he looked like he might grab her again. Might pull her up against his hard body and press his lips to hers.

Instead, he turned away from her.

"I'm going to call the girls. See when they can come out here. You're paying, naturally," she said. She didn't know why she'd chosen to tell him that. Only that the temptation to make him stay a bit longer had been stronger than it should have been.

He stopped and turned. "Naturally."

"See you tomorrow then."

"I'll be busy."

"So will I. I have other clients to do consultations with." She was still stalling. Still trying to keep him close.

He ignored her last statement and turned away again, heading down the hall. She let out a breath and walked back into her room, shutting the door behind her.

She picked up her iPad and opened up her file for Stavros. *Good kisser. Amazing body.*

She deleted both as soon as she wrote them. If only she could delete it from her memory so easily.

CHAPTER SIX

THE women had arrived. Victoria, Amy and Cherry. Beautiful, polished and royal. They were wearing sleek, expensive-looking clothing, their hair perfectly coiffed, their makeup expertly applied.

They were perfectly beautiful. Perfectly boring.

Stavros surveyed the three women in their spot on the balcony. He felt like he was being featured on a bad reality television show. It was suddenly hard to breathe.

He'd been around some in his thirty-three years. Some people might call him a playboy, he preferred to think he was taking advantage of the physical while ignoring the emotional. Even so, facing three women who had marriage on their minds was out of his realm of experience.

Jessica was not out there with him, not there to run interference and give him a time limit for how long each woman could speak to him.

Victoria spoke first. "It's nice to meet you," she said. "I apologize if you weren't expecting me...us." He could tell she was irritated to be sharing the terrace with the other two women, who clearly felt the same way she did.

"Of course you were expected," he said, opting for diplomacy. Though he hoped, fervently, that they were staying at a hotel in Piraeus and not in the villa. Two was company, five would be a nightmare.

Especially considering that kiss he'd shared with Jessica and all the options it was making him contemplate. Again.

Victoria smiled, saccharine and a bit false, though, again given the situation, he hardly blamed her. His own smile was just as fake.

Cherry—at least he was assuming she was Cherry based on Jessica's description—spoke next. "I waited down at the airport for quite a while."

"I apologize," he said.

"I didn't have to wait," Victoria said, her expression a bit superior as she looked at the other two women.

"Because your plane landed last," Amy said, sniffing slightly.

He heard the click of high heels behind him and turned, a rush of heat filling him as Jessica came walking out onto the terrace.

"Sorry, ladies, I didn't realize you'd arrived." She smiled widely and he could sense the women in front of him relaxing as Jessica drew closer. She put her hands on her hips, pushing her full skirt in, revealing a bit of those luscious curves. "I had told the driver to bring you to your hotel. I apologize for the confusion."

Efharisto con theo.

He didn't want three women, all vying for position as queen, under the same roof. At least not one he was beneath. Not a very good thought to have, since it was very possible one of the three could be sharing his home, his bed, for the rest of their lives.

They could spend the rest of their lives smiling falsely at each other. He didn't know where the thought came from, and he didn't know why it filled him with an emotion that he could only identify as terror.

He appraised the three sleek women in front of him. All different in coloring, height and shape. He tried, he tried very hard, to find one that appealed to him more than the others.

A blonde, a brunette and a redhead...

He could not find anything especially appealing.

Until Jessica appeared on the balcony. That made fire in his blood, heat pooling in his gut, coursing down to his groin. His lips burned with the memory of her kiss. Just a kiss. Something that, for a man of his experience, should mean nothing. And yet, it had seemed the height of sensuality. The pinnacle of pleasure.

More than that, his heart had burned. And it hadn't hurt. It hadn't been unpleasant at all. He didn't know what that meant.

"Since you're here, I think we should have a drink before you're taken back into the city." Jessica was in control, her smile unshakable, her composure solid. "Does that suit?"

Amy looked like she might protest, about the drink or being taken back into the city, but instead, she nodded along with the others. Jessica turned and went back into the villa, undoubtedly to give the order for drinks to be served.

The three women stared at him, doe-eyed. An indistinct blur of beauty that meant nothing more to him than the scenery. Possibly less. "Excuse me for a moment," he said, turning and following Jessica. "Jessica…"

She whirled around, hands on her head. "I am so sorry."

"You are?"

"Yes. I don't really like all the three of the women to be together and…this…all right, this isn't really going according to my system. But it's okay. We'll improvise. We'll all have a drink, we'll chat, tomorrow you can choose one to go on a dinner date with. Does that work?"

"Fine," he said, amused by how quickly her composure had evaporated once they were out of sight of the other women.

"Really, this just makes it all seem a bit…"

"Like a reality television show?"

"Yes. And also a bit crass. And I'm sorry. But they all know the drill, so while it's awkward, they knew that they weren't the only people who had put in to be considered for this match."

He leaned against the wall. "So how exactly do women find you?"

"I advertise. In a discreet manner of course, but I've managed to put together a select group of men and women. When someone comes to me looking for a match, I let those who meet the qualifications know, and then they respond and let me know if they're interested. Simple."

"In a complex sort of way."

She raised both eyebrows, her expression haughty. "Well, it works anyway."

"So how many of these women you've shown me haven't made the final cut with other men?"

She sniffed. "Almost all of them. Where is the wine?"

"Which ones?"

"Only Victoria has never asked to be entered in for consideration yet. You were the first one she showed interest in."

"Setting her sights high?"

She kept her focus on her hunt for beverages. "Wine?"

"I mean that as far as status goes, not really saying I surpass the other men in terms of other qualities."

"Right. Where is the wine?"

He chuckled and reached behind her, pulling a bottle from the built in rack above her head. "Will a merlot do?" He took glasses from the rack as well, holding them by the stems.

"Fine." She reached up and took the bottle from his hand, then tilted it in his direction. "We should…" She gestured in the direction of the terrace. "Because I don't want them to scratch each other's eyes out or anything."

"Remind me again why you thought this would be a good idea?"

She frowned. "Well, it seemed logical. It sort of followed how I do things…it's just…it not being a big event sort of closes everything in a bit more."

"Yeah."

He took the bottle from her hand and led the way back out onto the terrace. Victoria, Cherry and Amy were standing at the far end of the terrace, a healthy bit of distance between each them so that they didn't have to engage in conversation with one another.

He set the glasses down on a small round bistro table and opened the bottle, pouring a substantial portion into each glass.

"Drinks," he said, lifting one for himself. They would need them.

The women advanced and each took their wine. The silence was awkward, oppressive. He hated this, he was starting to realize. It was the first thing he could remember hating in a long time. He hadn't had an emotion so strong in…years.

He hadn't thought he would mind this situation. Because he didn't want a wife, not in a particular sense. Marriage for him would be something he did for his country. A distant affair, and that was how it had to be. He knew—he'd seen—that love, emotional attachment, could overpower strong men. Bring them to their knees. And if those men were in control of the country, they could bring the country down with them.

That was why he had to do it this way. That was why he had to keep everyone at a distance. Why he had to find a wife who would matter to the country, not to him.

Still, even with that in mind, being in the middle of the matchmaking process was as enjoyable as being boiled alive. His flirtatious manner was harder to hold on to than he could ever remember it being before.

Ultimately, it was Jessica, her quick wit and sparkling laugh, that saved the night. She engaged everyone in conversation and managed to make things seem easy. Easier at least.

By the time his marriage candidates had been sent off in the limo, the knot in his gut had eased. Though, it could have been due to the wine and not just Jessica's lightning-quick wit.

As soon as the women were out of sight Jessica let out a loud breath and lifted her wineglass to her lips, tilting her head back and knocking the rest of the contents in. "That was vile. Worse than vile."

"You're good at covering up how you feel."

"So are you," she said. "Image. It's important to both of us, right?"

"I have to put on a good front for my people." Except he hadn't thought of it as a front before. He'd simply thought of himself as empty of anything but confidence. Empty of anything unimportant. If something needed to be done, he saw it done.

"And I have to put on a calm front for my clients."

"Then why is it you're letting me in on just how stressed out that made you?"

She grimaced. "Well, for all intents and purposes, we're roommates at the moment and I have to let my hair down at some point in the day, so to speak. For another, you've licked my lips and that puts you slightly over the line of 'usual client.' Slightly."

"You don't let all your clients lick your lips?" he asked. A strange tightness invaded his chest, his stomach. Jealousy.

Possessiveness. The image of all of her clients getting the sort of special treatment he had been on the receiving end of made him want to pull her to him again, to make sure she didn't forget what it was like to be kissed by him. To make sure she never forgot.

That was as foreign as all the other emotions she'd brought out in him over the past few days. Jealousy implied some sort of special connection, and a fear of that connection being threatened.

He gritted his teeth, fought against the tightness in his chest. Flirting. That would put the distance back between them. Something light. Sexual.

"Hardly," she said. Unable to read his mood, she kept her tone casual. "Indulge me, though, since I've now confessed that I don't kiss my other clients. What exactly are you hiding?" She tilted her head, her green eyes assessing. Far too assessing for his taste. Too sincere.

It made it impossible to find that false front. Made him feel something shift deep inside himself.

"No skeletons in my closet," he said. "But of course I have to live a certain way, conduct myself in a certain way."

"You aren't exactly a traditional ruler."

"It's not just tradition. It's about instilling confidence. Showing stability. Emotion…that has no place. I must be charming, confident, at ease at all times."

"I've never heard a whispered rumor that you were anything but."

He looked out into the darkness, at the black ocean, moonlight glittering across the choppy surface. "I know. Because I don't slip up. Ever."

He had, though. He had slipped up with her. He had let go of his control, control he'd been forced to cultivate when he'd been named heir to the throne. He'd let go of it completely in those moments his lips had touched hers. Not control against physical desire, but the control he kept so tightly over his feelings.

Jessica laughed, a sad, hollow sound. "I'm certain I do. Sometimes."

"What about you, Ms. Carter?" he said. "What are you hiding?" He turned to her, studying her face in the dim light. It seemed imperative to know her secrets. And he wasn't certain why it would be. But just like last night, he was going to let his guard drop. Just for a moment. Just to follow that heavy, aching feeling in his chest. To give it some satisfaction.

The corners of her mouth twitched slightly. "If I told you, I'd have to kill you."

Warmth spread through him. In him. An alien feeling. One he was compelled to chase for the moment. "And that would create an international incident."

"It would prick my conscience as well, so maybe I should keep it to myself," she said, a small curve in her lips. It wasn't really a smile, though. It was too sad for that. "Better question, if you could be anything, I mean, if the whole world was open to you, what would you be?"

He frowned. "If I wasn't in line to rule Kyonos?"

"If you weren't royal at all. If you could have anything you desired, without obligation, what would you do?"

It was the thing he never let himself wonder. The alternate reality that wasn't even allowed in his dreams. But he was cheating now. Cheating on his own standards for himself.

For a fleeting moment, he had a vision of a life that was his own. A life with a woman of his choosing, in a home of his choosing. With children who wouldn't know the pain, the responsibility of a royal lineage depending on them. With love.

He shoved the image aside. "I would run my corporation," he said. He had a sudden image of sailing a ship around the world and wondered if he'd told the truth.

"Would you get married?" she asked, a strange tone to her voice.

"Yes," he said, the answer almost surprising him. But in that little, warm hint of fantasy, there had been a wife. There had been kids. And it wasn't hard to breathe. "Yes," he said again.

"Hmm." She turned and walked to the end of the terrace, resting her hands on the railing.

He followed her, standing behind her, watching the sea breeze tug wisps of hair from her updo, letting them fall around her neck. He wanted to brush them aside. To kiss her shoulder. Her neck. Not just because he wanted her, but to feel connected to her.

A deadly desire.

"Why do you do it?" she asked. "Why is this so important?"

She was asking for more honesty. For answers he wasn't sure he had. "I… When my mother died things fell apart. And the one thing that seemed real, that seemed to matter, was Kyonos. It was the one thing I could fix. The one place I could…matter."

As he spoke the words, he realized that they were true. That every change he'd made, every effort he'd put forth, had been not just about helping his country, but about finding new purpose for himself.

"What about you?" he asked, ready to shift the spotlight off of himself.

She didn't speak for a long time. When she did, she spoke slowly, cautiously. "In this scenario, reality isn't playing a part, right?"

"Right," he said, voice rough. He waited for her next words, anticipated them like a man submerged beneath the waves anticipated breaking the surface, desperate to take a breath.

She lowered her head, her eyes on her hands. "I would be a wife. A mother…" Her voice broke on the last word. "And maybe I would still do this, or maybe not. I don't know if I would…need it. But…I would be a mother."

She pushed off from the railing. "Back to reality," she said, trying to smile. Failing. "I'm going to bed."

He nodded, watching as she walked past him.

I would be a mother.

There was something so sad, so defeated in the admission. It made his chest tighten, and he couldn't pinpoint why. He'd never had someone else's feelings inhabit his body in this way. But he was certain that's what was happening. That the oppressive weight that had just invaded him was the same sadness that filled her.

Maybe Jessica wasn't as happily divorced as she appeared to be. And maybe she wasn't quite as hard as she appeared to be, either.

She was running interference for Stavros and his harem today, and she wasn't all that thrilled about it. It was getting harder to chuck other women in his direction when she just wanted to throw herself at him.

Not happening, but still. She was so envious of her clients that she was developing a twitch.

And for heaven's sake, she never should have said all that about being a mother. Should never have asked him what he wanted. Should never have tried to get to know him. Because it didn't matter. It just didn't. There was no point in suspending reality, even for a moment.

There was no escaping reality. You couldn't outrun it. You could try but eventually it would bite you in the ass. She knew that. She knew it really, really well. She'd tried to ignore how often she and her husband went to their separate corners of the house. She'd tried to ignore his touch at night, and when she couldn't, she tried to ignore his total disregard for her pain. She'd even tried to ignore his outright berating of her. The screaming and anger and hateful words.

No, there was no point in ignoring that kind of thing. The facts were simple. Stavros needed certain things, she didn't have any of them.

Why was she even thinking about that crap? She didn't have time for it. She had a gaggle of women to manage for the whole day.

She blew out a breath and slipped her oversize sunglasses onto her face, tightening her hold on her latte. She had gotten them all booked into a luxury salon in Piraeus, and they were all safely getting massaged and waxed as she stood out on the crowded, narrow streets drinking her coffee.

Stavros was coming soon. He was meeting the group of them for a quick lunch and tour around the city, and then he would be selecting the woman who would accompany him on a private date for the evening.

And it would be up to Jessica to send the other two off without making them feel like it really was some low-rent reality television show.

Jessica wasn't used to feeling like things were out of her control. Not since that moment four years ago when she'd taken back the reins of her life. She liked to feel like she had everything managed. Like her little universe was in the palm of her hand.

It was an illusion, and she knew it, but she still liked it. Since Stavros, she didn't even have her illusion.

What was it about him that reminded her…that reminded her she was a woman? Not just on the surface, but really and truly. With a woman's desires, no matter how hard life had tried to wring them out of her.

Oh, dear…right on time. The master of her rekindled sexual needs was striding toward her. Cream-colored jacket and trousers, shirt open at the collar. She did love a man who knew how to dress. A Mediterranean sex god with very expensive taste.

He also had two dark-suited members of security flanking him and discreetly parting the crowd so that His Majesty wouldn't be jostled.

Not that Stavros ever behaved that way. He didn't act like a spoiled prince who would be able to feel a pea through fifty mattresses, not even close. He acted like a man who carried the weight of a nation on his shoulders.

More than that, he acted like a man who intended to support the weight of that nation for the rest of his life. A man prepared to tailor his every decision to suit that responsibility.

"Hello, Jessica," he said, a smile curving his lips.

"Prince Stavros," she said, reverting because last night had gotten a bit too intimate and she had no desire to go there again. Well, that was a lie. She did want to go there again. But she couldn't.

"Demoted, I see."

"What?"

"Back to a title."

"Oh…" Why did he have to notice all these little things about her? Why did he have to care at all? "Sorry."

"How are things going?"

"Good. Great. Looking forward to you thinning the herd tonight."

"You make it sound like there are a lot more than three."

She sighed. "They feel like more than three. In my experience, the women haven't been so catty. But then, I normally don't do this with them in such close proximity to each other. I've also never tried to match a crown prince."

He looked past her, into the spa. "Let's leave them in there."

"What?" She looked behind her.

"If we hurry, they won't know I was here."

She laughed. "You're not serious."

He frowned. "No. I'm not. Things are getting... I need to make a decision."

"Because of Eva?" she asked, remembering his mood at his sister's wedding.

"Everyone in Kyonos was happy for Eva. They love to see their princess in love. But I have to be sure that I make them feel like there's stability."

"You've been the rock for Kyonos for a long time," she said, not quite sure why she felt compelled to offer him... not comfort...support, maybe.

"And I will continue to do it. With a wife by my side."

"A most suitable wife."

"Yes." He looked back in the spa. "Will they be done soon?"

"Soon. ·

"It's not too late to go another route," she said, not sure why she was offering her client an out from a program she publicly professed, and privately believed, to be the best way to find a mate.

He shrugged. "Why would I?"

"You could still fall in love." She wrapped both hands around her paper cup and hugged it close to her body.

"No. I can't."

"I'm sure you could. What if you met the perfect woman and she was wholly suitable?"

He shook his head. "It isn't that I don't think it's possible. It's that I won't. Love weakens a leader. You know of Achilles and his heel, I assume?"

"Of course."

He frowned, his expression intense. "One weakness is all it takes to crumble a man who is strong in all other areas. And a weak leader can destroy what was a strong nation. I will never have part in that."

He was serious again. Like last night. Not a hint of flirtation. She was starting to wonder if that was really him at all. Or if it was who he thought he was supposed to be.

"Is that really what you think?"

"I know it. I saw it happen, in my family, in Kyonos. When my mother died everything fell apart. My father could not function. He… We made Xander the scapegoat for it, all because grief could only give way to anger. I had to set it aside. I had to move on for the good of the country. It took my father years to do it. He is a king, he did not have the luxury of grief, or pain. It's different for us."

She studied his face, so hard and impassive, as though it were carved from marble. "Feeling pain is the only way I know to deal with it." Sometimes she wondered if she clung to pain. If she turned it over and dissected more than she needed to. If she used it to protect herself.

"I have gotten to the point where I don't feel it at all. Kyonos comes first, and everything else comes second. That will include a wife. She'll have to understand that. She'll have to understand that her role is not to love me, but to love my country."

Bone deep sadness assaulted her. He deserved more than that. More than this.

Her phone buzzed and she pulled up her text messages.

We're done. Where are you?

The message was from Victoria.
Out front. She typed out the note and then hit Send.
"They're done," she said. "Brace yourself."

He straightened his shoulders, his expression changing, that wicked charm back in place. She had to work hard to suppress a smile.

As if on cue the three women walked out of the spa, sunglasses fixed firmly on flawless faces. Victoria was the first to spot Stavros, the first to smile widely. "Prince Stavros. How lovely."

Like she was surprised. Like she hadn't been briefed by Jessica early that morning.

"Lovely to see you, Victoria," he said, inclining his head. "Cherry, Amy."

Cherry and Amy didn't look thrilled at being afterthoughts, but they managed to smile, too, and offer platitudes about what a lovely day it was.

"I've made reservations at a café down by the water," he said.

"Sounds lovely," Amy said, taking her chance to be the first to speak.

"My car is just this way," he said, leading down the narrow street and to a black limo idling at the curb. The security detail opened the back doors on both sides. The women slid in and took their positions on the bench seats that ran the length of the car.

Jessica got in and sat on the bench facing them, and Stavros slid in beside her. The doors closed and the air-conditioning provided immediate relief from the heat. Or, rather, it would have, if Stavros himself wasn't so hot.

A thick, awkward silence settled into the air and Jessica worked to find her social ease. She was good with people. It was one of her strengths. But Stavros had her in the throes of her first sexual attraction in years and his potential brides were sitting a foot away.

It was more awkward than any situation had the right to be.

"I…" She cleared her throat. "I'm really looking forward to lunch."

"I'm looking forward to dinner," said Cherry, flashing Stavros a smile.

From awkwardness to greater awkwardness.

"I imagine everyone will be eating dinner tonight," Jessica said, a bit too brightly. *Some will be eating alone, though.*

Stavros laughed…easy, charming. False. He did that so well. No matter the situation he seemed to be in control. More than that, he seemed to distance himself. The flirtier and friendlier he seemed, the less present he actually was. And that seemed to be his default setting.

Not always. Her mind flashed back to the kiss. That hadn't been emotionless at all. Or distant. That had been… amazing. And wild. She sneaked a peek at him from the corner of her eyes, her line of sight connecting her with the strong column of his throat. She was willing to bet he tasted like salt. Clean skin and man.

"I'm certain everyone will," he said, earning a delicate blush from Cherry.

The limo stopped and Jessica nearly said a prayer of thanks out loud. "We're here!"

The doors opened and they filed out. The restaurant was at the harbor, the seating area extending over the pier. Boats, ranging in size from dinghies to yachts, filled the horizon. Seagulls screeched nearby, landing near tables, fighting over crumbs, showing no respect for their otherwise elegant surroundings.

Jessica made sure everyone ordered wine with their

lunch. Heaven knew they would need it to get through the afternoon.

They made appropriate small talk while they waited for their orders to be filled and Jessica cringed inside as she watched the patented disinterest in Stavros's eyes grow more and more pronounced.

She wanted to pinch him. She couldn't fix him up if he didn't even try to like the women she introduced him to.

She caught his gaze and treated him to a hard stare. A glimmer of amusement appeared in the depths of his dark eyes. She didn't even want to know what he was thinking.

When everyone had their food, Stavros leaned in, his very best charming-politician smile on his face. How had she not noticed before? How fake it was. How much it wasn't him at all. "I know this is a bit unusual. But I think it's best to think of it as a job interview. I hope no one finds that offensive. We have all signed up to have Jessica's help finding a suitable spouse, have we not?"

Jessica wanted to hit him. Except none of the women seemed offended at all. They should have been. His mercenary assessment should have made them all angry. They should have poured wine in his lap.

They didn't, they simply nodded.

"The reality is, my country needs very specific things from a queen. That's my top priority."

"Naturally," Victoria said. "We're all far too practical to think this is going to be a love match."

Cherry nodded, and Amy only stared into her glass.

"Then the rejection should not be personal, either," he said, his charm never slipping. He was firm, yet still perfectly engaging. She didn't understand how he did it. She didn't understand what he was doing, and yet, he was doing it.

"This is really lovely," Jessica said, looking around them. "Isn't it lovely?"

Amy nodded. "It really is."

She chattered on about the scenery and the food, anything to dispel the lingering scent of that horrible honesty of Stavros's. They managed to make it through the meal and get the women deposited at their hotel without it appearing again.

That left just the two of them alone in the limo for the ride back to the villa.

"And what was that?" she asked.

"What was what?" He was positioned across from her, and he still felt too close, because now there was no one in the back with them to help diffuse the tension.

"That. The whole thing about it being a job interview. Didn't I tell you to keep your candor to yourself? Or just tell me if you have something so honest to say."

"They didn't seem to mind. Anyway, I had to make a choice about tonight, about which one of the three to continue seeing. If that, the clinical nature of this, is going to bother them, they should leave now. I'm not doing this for romance."

"I know…"

"And now so do they. If any one of them wants to leave they better do it now, I don't have time to mess around with the future of my country. I told you already, I need a queen who understands that her loyalty will be to Kyonos."

"Still…geez. Don't underestimate the power of a little sweet talk."

"I of all people know about sweet talk, as you should know. I do have a reputation. But I'm not going to deceive anyone that's involved in this."

"I appreciate that. I wasn't talking deceit. Just…sugar-coating."

"I didn't think you did sugarcoating," he said, his dark eyes locked with hers.

"Um…well, I don't…I mean not with you, but you have to know how to talk to women."

"You think you know how to talk to women better than I do? How many women have you dated?"

She crossed her arms beneath her breasts. "Zero, but I *am* a woman so I win."

"This isn't about tricking someone into marrying me because they want to be a princess and live in a castle and have their happily-ever-after. They can want a title, but they have to be worthy of it. They have to know what it means. They have to realize I'm a busy man and that love isn't high on my list of priorities. It's not even on the list of options. For that reason, I thought it was important I spelled it out."

She looked out the window, her throat tightening. For one moment, just for a moment, she pictured Stavros without the obligations. What would it be like for him? If he could have been free to do what he wanted? If he could have had that wife and the children that he'd seen in his mind's eye last night while they were talking? Would his expectations be different?

Would he have loved that wife? If he didn't feel like a nation was dependent on his emotional strength, would he have given himself over to love? Would he have focused his fearsome loyalty on his family?

The thought of it, of what it would be like to be the woman on the receiving end of all that intensity, filled her with a kind of bone-deep longing.

Get a grip, Jess. Even if he was free, she wouldn't be the woman for him. He had goals, dreams and desires that weren't about his wife, or who she was, but what she could offer. And they were things she couldn't offer. She knew all about trying to be perfect for someone when she fell so far short of it. She could never do it again.

"I respect that," she said.

"Victoria."

"What?"

"It's Victoria. She's the one I want to see again." His voice didn't hold any particular enthusiasm.

She felt like she'd been sucker punched. And she wasn't sure why. "Did you…have a lightning-attraction thing?"

A muscle in his cheek jumped. "She's lovely. More than that, I think she's a bit…well, she seemed unemotional." He didn't sound too enthusiastic and she hated the small, ridiculous part of herself that liked that. The part that wanted Stavros to be dwelling on their kiss, and not on his attraction to another woman.

Even if that other woman was the one he might potentially marry.

"Victoria is… She's very smart. And I'm certain she would do a lot of good as queen." Victoria wasn't just smart, she was brilliant. And, Stavros was right, a bit on the unemotional end of things. She was looking for an opportunity to better herself, and to make an impact on the world.

Jessica had been trying to talk Victoria into considering a few of her previous clients, but Victoria hadn't been interested. Because she'd clearly been holding out for better. And had found it in Stavros.

Well, nice for some.

For you, too, she tried to remind herself, but herself wasn't listening. Herself was sulking a little bit.

"Great, I'll call down to the hotel later."

"I'll do it," he said. "If you give me her room number."

"Can't," she said, the word escaping before she could think better of it.

"Why?"

Her stomach tightened to a painful degree. "No sex, remember?"

"I'm not going to have sex with her, not at this point. I'm going to call and ask her to dinner."

She cleared her throat, ignoring the little surge her heart had taken when he'd said the word *sex*. Because when he said it was so…evocative. Husky male tones wrapped in an exotic accent. It made her think of tangled limbs and heavy breathing and…

And what? Like she was some great sensual goddess? Like she would be able to enjoy being with him? Like he would enjoy being with her? Her throat ached and she couldn't fathom the sudden onslaught of emotion. What was wrong with her?

"Yeah, I'll call Amy and Cherry then and just let them know that…I'll let them know they can return home."

"At their leisure. They can stay in the city for a few more days if they wish. I'll continue to pay their expenses for as long they remain here. An extended holiday doesn't seem too unreasonable."

"Ah, so you'll ask Victoria out but I have to break it off with the other two?"

"As I said earlier, it's just a job interview. And only one candidate can get hired, so to speak."

"Right." She leaned back in the chair and flexed her fingers, curling them into fists and letting her manicured nails dig into her palms.

There was no reason at all the thought of Stavros going on a date with Victoria should make her feel like she might be sick.

But it did. She couldn't deny that it did.

She was seriously losing it.

"Well, if I don't see you again before your date…break a leg."

He smiled, but his eyes held a strange, unreadable expression. "I'll see you. After at least."

No. "See you then."

CHAPTER SEVEN

THERE was nothing wrong with Victoria. She was beautiful, she was pleasant. Smart. She would make a wonderful queen. Over dinner she'd talked at great length concerning how passionate she was about charities, starting foundations and visiting hospitals.

She possessed all the qualities he required for a bride.

Yet as he thought of binding himself to her, he felt nothing. No matter how hard he tried. He felt like he was being suffocated. As if the weight of the crown would physically crush him.

Don't think of marriage. Think of sex.

If he could find a connection with her on that level, then maybe nothing else would matter. If he could flirt and put them both at ease, put a wall between them, maybe the tightness in his throat would abate.

When the limo stopped in front of the hotel she looked at him from beneath her lashes, her open, friendly expression changing. Seduction, he decided, was her intent. Good. He knew the game. Often, he relished the game.

So, why didn't he feel anything? Nothing. Not even the slightest twinge of interest in his stomach. When she cocked her head to the side and licked her lips, there was no answering tug in his groin. Indeed, there was no signal coming from south of his belt at all. It was as though that member of his body hadn't registered her existence.

He was a man, a man with a healthy appetite for sex. And she was, on paper, a sexually attractive woman. What he should be doing was pressing her back against the soft leather seat and claiming her soft pink lips.

His body rejected the idea while his mind replaced the image of a rosy pink mouth with one painted in temptation red. And with that image came a tightness in his chest, his heart pounding harder, his mind suddenly filled with Jessica.

"I had a nice time at dinner," he said.

"So did I," she said, cocking her head to the side even farther. Why was it that some women thought affecting the mannerisms of a cocker spaniel was sexy?

Except, usually, he would find this sexy. He just didn't now. No use pretending he didn't know why.

"Good night," he said, opening the door to the limo and stepping out into the cool night. He held the door for her, giving as strong of a hint as he could.

She frowned and slid out, her body on the opposite side of the door to his. "I had a…a really nice time." Her blue eyes were locked with his, her intentions obvious.

"So you said."

"I appreciate you taking me out."

"We'll go out again. When I'm through with my business here." Where was the flirtation? Why couldn't he even pretend that he was interested? Whatever he felt for Jessica, it shouldn't have the power to reach him here and now. It shouldn't be able to control his thoughts and actions. That was the sort of thing he'd spent most of his adult life fighting.

"Oh…okay." She smiled. "That's good, right?"

It should have been. But he didn't have any sort of positive feeling about it. "You're a…nice woman, Victoria."

Nice? Where the hell had his seduction skills gone?

"Thank you. You're a nice man, Stavros." She cleared her throat. "Good night, then?"

"Good night," he said.

She stepped out of the way of the door and he closed it firmly. He would walk her into the hotel, as was the appropriate thing to do, but that was all.

She looked at him one more time in the lobby of the hotel, requesting a kiss, and when he took a step back he could have sworn he saw a fleeting hint of relief in her eyes.

"Hopefully we'll see each other again soon," she said.

"Hopefully," he said, turning and leaving her in the lobby.

He felt no such hope. He would see her again though. Just because something in him was off at the moment didn't mean she wasn't the right candidate for the job. For the marriage.

He grimaced, lifted his hand to loosen his tie, which suddenly felt like a hangman's noose.

Victoria was a sound choice.

He gritted his teeth. Yes, she was a sound choice. It didn't matter that he desired someone else. Desire, no matter how strong, did not have a say in the future of his country. Desire could not shake his resolve.

He closed his eyes for a moment, clenched his hands into fists to disguise the unsteadiness in his fingers. It was only lust. Nothing special. Nothing important. A picture of Jessica flashed through his mind and there was an answering kick in his gut.

In spite of his intentions, desire seemed to be shaking

him from the inside out. And what he really didn't want to believe was that a whole lot more than desire was making him tremble.

Jessica wrapped her arms around herself and turned away from the view of the ocean, leaning against the rail of the terrace, the salted breeze blowing at her back, tangling in her hair. She wondered what Stavros was doing. If his date with Victoria has been successful.

Part of her hoped that it had been. He could marry her and they could have gorgeous, royal babies that could inherit the throne of Kyonos. They could be all sexy and royal together and she could go back to her empty house and contemplate the merit of getting a cat.

Yes, that was a good plan. A solid plan. She could name her cat Mittens.

"And how was your evening?"

She turned and her breath caught in her throat, forcing a sharp, gasping sound. Stavros was in the doorway, his black tie draped over his shoulder, the first three buttons of his shirt undone, the sleeves pushed up to his elbows.

He looked like he'd been undressed. She tried to smile while her stomach sank slowly into her toes, jealousy an acrid thing that ate at her insides, working its way out.

"I think that's my line," she said. Her words scraped over her dry throat.

"Lovely. Not nearly as lovely as you are. But lovely." A smile curved his lips and he stepped fully onto the deck, closing some of the distance between them.

There was something strange about his manner. Something too slack. Too easy. "Have you been drinking?"

"Not even a little. But you do make me feel a bit lightheaded."

"Seriously. What the heck, Stavros?"

"Careful, *agápe,* you'll make me think I've lost my touch."

"What did I tell you about not flirting with me?" Rather than the sort of shaky, sexy unease she usually felt when he flirted with her, she only felt anger. He had no right to do this to her. No right at all. He had been on a date with another woman. A date that, ideally, would be the beginning of a 'til-death sort of relationship.

"You told me not to." He stepped closer to her, his movements lithe. Graceful. Like a panther. "But I find I can't help myself."

"Then get some help from an outside source," she growled, tightening her arms around herself.

"You are upset with me?" he asked, a boyish, teasing glint in his eye.

"Yes, I am upset with you. I don't understand you. You kiss me, you act mad about it, you apologize, you go on a date with another woman and now you're flirting."

"Victoria was fine."

"Fine?"

"Adequate. I should like to see her again."

"What? That's all?"

"I would like to marry her," he said between clenched teeth.

"And you came out here flirting with me?"

He shrugged. "I told you why I'm doing this. It has nothing to do with personal feelings or excitement on my part and everything to do with getting things in order for Kyonos."

"Great," she said, annoyance deserting her, replaced by a sadness she had no business feeling.

"I prefer it when you smile," he said, injecting a playful note to his voice.

"I don't feel like smiling." She turned away from him, her focus pinned decidedly onto the scenery.

"Why do you do this?"

"Why do I do what?" she asked, not looking at him as she responded.

"Why do you make it impossible for me to reach you?"

"Why are you trying?"

"Because I can't take a breath without thinking of you," he said, his voice suddenly real. Raw.

"I don't…"

"Jessica," he said, regaining some of his composure, "you know my situation. My obligations. But that doesn't mean we can't see where our attraction takes us."

"Yes, Stavros, yes, it does mean that," she said, panic fluttering in her chest. Panic and a desperate desire to believe the words he'd just spoken.

His dark brows locked together. "That kiss…it haunts me. It's eating at me. I need…" He sucked in a sharp breath. "I need you. Tell me you need me, too."

"I…" She shook her head. "It doesn't matter if I do."

His expression shifted, a veil dropping, revealing unguarded hunger. Stark and nearly painful to witness. "Let's pretend that it does." The desperation in his tone, the raw need, was beyond her. And yet it called to her, echoed inside of her. "Let's pretend, like we did the other night, that none of the other stuff exists. That I am just a man. And you are just a woman. A woman I desire above all else."

She sucked in a breath that tore at her lungs, leaving her raw and bleeding inside, and tried to keep the tears from falling. How could he tempt her like this? "Stavros…that's the problem, all of that, that stuff we tried to ignore? It is real. And we can't pretend it's not. It won't change anything."

"Tonight it doesn't have to be real," he said, his voice dark, tortured.

"I am not your best bet for a last-minute, commitment-phobic fling," she admonished. "I am the last woman you should want for that."

"Why? The attraction between us is real. And you said yourself, it isn't as though you're a virgin. You're an experienced woman who knows what she wants."

There was no ease now. No flirtation. And he was harder to resist now because of it. Because this was real. What she'd witnessed when he'd first come out onto the terrace, that had been the fake. This was her evidence that he really did want her.

It was unfair. It was too much.

Anger, unreasonable and not entirely directed at Stavros, spilled over. "I'm pointless, don't you know? Can't you tell? I can't have a baby. I am a testosterone killer. I make a man feel like he isn't really a man. I can't be pleased sexually. Don't I know what that does to a man?" She knew she sounded crazy, hysterical. She didn't care. "I am cold. And frigid. A bitch who cares more for her own comfort than the dreams of her husband, than the hope of a family. Does that sound like the sort of woman you should have a fling with?"

She stood, her hands clenched at her sides, her breathing harsh. Speaking those words, giving voice to every terrible thing she'd been called, every horrible feeling that lived in her, made her feel powerful. It made her feel a little sick, too.

"Jessica...who said those things to you?" he asked, his voice rough.

"Who do you think?"

"Your husband?"

"Ex," she said, the word never tasting so sweet.

"He was wrong," he said.

"You don't know that. I just turned you down, didn't I?"

"And my ego remains intact."

"Just go."

"No. Help me understand," he said. It was a quiet statement, a simple gesture. It was more than anyone else had ever asked from her or offered her.

"This is one of those things men don't like to hear about. And by that I mean it contains the word *uterus* and pertains to that particular 'time of the month' that means a man can't get any action."

"Try me," he said, his dark eyes never leaving hers, his jaw tense. "Scare me, Jess. I dare you."

She forced a laugh. "Fine. I'll give it a shot. I had endometriosis. I might have it again someday, since it's still possible to have a flare-up. I don't know if you really know what that is but it's incredibly painful. I was one of the lucky ones for whom it was especially bad. It causes bleeding and…pain. Lots of pain. Lots of blood. For me it caused pain during sex. After orgasm. It could last for days for me. And…I started just not wanting to have desire anymore. I didn't even want to want sex. The reward was too fleeting for what I had to go through and…I rejected my husband. Often. I made him feel undesired. And you know what? He was."

She was sure that had to have done the trick. That had to have scared him. "I think that's your cue to turn and run."

He crossed his arms over his chest, his eyes never leaving hers. "I'm not a runner. Did it hurt you all the time?"

"Most of the time. I've had…" She always tripped over the word *hysterectomy* because there was something so defeating about it. "I had a procedure done to help, and it has, but…I haven't tested how well it worked in terms of… it still scares me."

"Jess…"

She was the one to take a step back. She shook her head. "It's not worth it, Stavros. For one night? It's not worth it. I'm way too much trouble. If you want one more fling before you get married make it with someone who's easy. And I don't mean that in the general sense. Make it with someone who actually wants sex."

The idea of trying it again, of failing again, destroyed her. It was more than just what it might mean to him. It was that she wanted it so much, and the thought of desiring yet one more thing that remained out of her reach was too painful to even consider.

She'd made success. She'd left her failures behind. There was no point repeating the same mistakes.

"I'm tired." She turned away from him and headed back to the house.

Stavros watched Jessica walk back into the villa, her arms wrapped around her body as though she were holding herself together with her own strength.

He felt numb. Numb and in pain all at once. He'd come out with the express purpose of seducing her. Of finding a way to put her in a category he was comfortable with. To embrace his sexual need and ignore the strange ache in his chest that seemed to appear whenever she was around.

It hadn't worked. She hadn't allowed the distance, and he certainly hadn't been able to retreat behind the security of flirtation, not after that admission.

What an ass he was for making her confess something like that.

She was right, he should run. He should take her advice and focus on his upcoming marriage. Or find a woman to help him burn through his pent-up sexual desire.

He took a heavy breath and walked into the house, heading for his office. He closed the door behind him and sat at his computer desk. He ought to email his father, at the very least, to let him know he was almost certain he was close to finding the future queen of Kyonos.

Instead he opened his internet browser and stared at the blinking cursor in the text box of the search engine.

Then he typed in *endometriosis*.

She wanted to cry, and she couldn't. She'd spent so long forcing herself to keep it together that now she actually wanted to take a moment to fall apart, she couldn't.

It was impossible to force tears.

She just lay on her bed and stared out the window at the moon glimmering on the surface of the ocean. It was the perfection of nature, beautiful and unspoiled. She would never understand why some things were fashioned so perfectly when she wasn't.

Why her body seemed to have been put together wrong when so many other people were made just right. Why she hadn't been able to just buck up and deal with it. Why the shame and failure still ate at her like a parasite.

And she wanted Stavros so much she could hardly stand living in her skin. She wanted to touch him, wanted to taste him. She wanted to kiss him again, to have all that passion directed at her. Mostly she wished she could go back and not tell him about her endometriosis. It had been so nice to have a man look at her like she was beautiful. To have him not see her as different from other women, not in a bad way, but in a way that made her seem special rather than damaged.

When he said she was different, he hadn't meant broken. He hadn't meant pointless. Worthless as a woman or a partner.

His perception of her had been a lie, sure. But it was one she would have been happy to live in for just a little while.

She closed her eyes and let their kiss play through her mind again. Allowed herself to relive what it had been like to feel the pressure of his hard body against hers. To feel his lips against hers, so hot and demanding. So unlike any man she'd ever kissed.

Desire coiled in her stomach, her heart beating faster, her body begging her for some sort of release. Release she'd denied herself for so long. Too long, maybe.

She sat up and balled her hands into fists, pushing against her closed eyes. Without thinking, she stood, her heart hammering as she slipped out into the hall and looked in the direction of Stavros's room. He would be in there by now, asleep.

And he wanted her. He'd said he did. It was such a rush. Such a shot of adrenaline. Pure, feminine pleasure. To be wanted. To want someone.

Her hands trembled and she shook them out, trying to steady them. Trying to steady herself. Easier said than done. She breathed in, then out again.

What if she could have a little bit of it? Something guaranteed. Something she couldn't fail at. She tried to swallow but the motion stuck in her dry throat. The idea of sleeping with Stavros was the most elating and terrifying thing she could imagine. To be so vulnerable to a man who was so perfect. To take a chance at failing again. At being revealed as not good enough.

Blood roared in her ears as she made her way to his room. She stopped and wiped her hands, damp with sweat, on her skirt. She knocked lightly on the door, not pausing to think because, if she did, she would have just turned and scurried back to the safety of her bed.

"Yes?" She heard Stavros's sleep-roughened voice from the other side of the door and she pushed it open.

He was propped up on his elbows, the sheets riding low

around his waist, revealing his chest. The moon glanced off the hard ridges of muscle, the valleys cast into shadow, giving his body the impression of cut stone.

He was utter perfection. Just as she thought, that was not the sort of chest she'd ever touched before. And she was dying to touch him. Aching for it. His beauty drew her in, but it also intimidated.

"I couldn't sleep," she said. So lame. "Obviously *you* could so maybe I shouldn't have come."

"I wasn't sleeping well," he said.

"That's good, I…" She took a step forward. "Can I?"

"Please," he said, his face half-hidden in shadow, his voice strained.

She sat on the edge of the bed and held her hand out in front of her, curling it into a fist, then flexing her fingers as she fought against indecision. Then she placed her palm on his chest and her breath caught as a shock of fire streaked through her veins.

He was so hot, his hair rough on her skin, his muscles hard, his skin smooth. She let her fingers drift down over his sculpted muscles, lightly skimming, following the ripple of his body.

She leaned in and kissed his lips. He remained frozen beneath her, his stomach rock-hard beneath her hand, his body wound tight. She could feel his tension, flowing from every tendon and into her fingertips. Hers to command. Hers to enjoy.

Maybe she couldn't have everything she wanted. But she could have some of it. He wanted her. And she could satisfy him. Without having to give up any power. Without being vulnerable. Without failing.

"What are you doing?" he asked, his forehead resting against hers, his lips a whisper away.

"If you have to ask, I must not be doing it right. It has

been a while, maybe protocol has changed?" She kissed his neck, tasted salt and sweat on his skin.

She let her hands slide down beneath the sheet, where she found him hard for her, a whole lot bigger than she'd anticipated. An involuntary rush of air hissed through her teeth, matching time with Stavros's sharp intake of breath as she curled her fingers around his erection.

In this, she was certain. Giving a man pleasure without taking any for herself had been a necessity in the latter days of her marriage. A desperate attempt to hold things together. A way to keep intimacy without having to deal with any physical discomfort.

She could do the same now, with Stavros. A way to have him without risking anything. It seemed so easy.

Except she was getting a lot hotter than she'd anticipated, and it made the thought of leaving his bed unsatisfied a lot less…satisfying than it had seemed a few moments earlier. Still, even without an orgasm she was enjoying this. Enjoying wanting him. Enjoying exploring his body.

It was a slice of what she wanted, and she'd learned to accept that that was how life was for her. Little tastes here and there of true pleasure, while the full experience stayed out of her reach. It would be enough, because it had to be.

She pressed a kiss to his pectoral muscle and down to his nipple, sliding her tongue over it, feeling it tighten beneath her touch.

His hand came up to the back of her head, fingers sifting through her hair. She smiled against his skin and continued to pepper kisses over his body. "You have the most incredible chest," she said, "among other things." She squeezed his shaft lightly. "I have never, ever, seen a man like you. Much less been close enough to have a taste. And I was really looking forward to it. You do not disappoint." She lifted her head and tugged the sheet down, exposing him. "Oh, no, you don't disappoint at all."

Her heart beat hard, echoing in her temples, at the apex of her thighs. He was amazing. Everything she'd imagined and so much more. She leaned in and trailed her tongue over his stomach muscles, then flicked it over the head of his shaft. He jerked beneath her tongue, a rough groan escaping his lips as he tightened his hold on her hair.

She felt like she'd been let loose in a candy store. Every delight she could imagine spread before her. And she wasn't planning on employing restraint.

She slipped her hand lower, took as much of him into her mouth as she could, reveling in the taste, the feel of him. She could feel the muscles in his thighs shaking, feel the tension in his body as he tried to maintain control.

She didn't want his control. She wanted him to lose it. She wanted him to lose it in a way that she couldn't. She wanted him to do it for her. She more than wanted it, she needed it. Needed his strength to dissolve beneath her, needed to be a part of his undoing. She wanted to exercise the power she had over him. And she did have it. She could feel it. Could feel just how close he was to losing it completely.

That was what she wanted. Needed. Craved. To have victory tonight, in his bed. To be perfection for him. For herself.

"Jessica," he said, and he tugged lightly, trying to move her away from him.

She didn't stop. She ran her tongue along his heavy length and she felt his ab muscles contract sharply beneath her hand.

"Jess," he said again. His tone a warning.

She lifted her head, her eyes locking with his. His gaze was clouded, sweat beaded on his forehead. A surge of power rushed through her. "This is for me," she said. "I want you like this. And I intend to have you."

She leaned in again and his fingers tightened, tangling deep in her hair, the slight sting of pain heightening the pleasure that created a hollow ache between her thighs.

A shaky laugh escaped his lips. "Doesn't it matter what I want?"

"Not in the least. But you like this, don't you?" She traced the head of his shaft with her tongue. "Don't you?"

"*Theos,* yes," he breathed his consent.

She continued to pleasure him with her lips and tongue. And she took everything. His ecstasy, every broken breath and trembling muscle, every curse, every word of praise.

This was her moment. Her pleasure. Her power.

Her taste of what she truly wanted. A hint of the feast she couldn't have.

She didn't stop until he found his pleasure, his body shaking, his skin slicked with sweat, every vestige of control stripped of him as he found his release.

He lay on his back after, stroking her cheek. She rested her head on his stomach and closed her eyes. Just for a moment.

She felt him stir beneath her. He sat up and brought her with him, kissing her on the lips. The kiss intensified, his tongue sweeping across her bottom lip, arousal pouring through her.

When she felt like she was on the edge, she pulled away. Her body trembled, her breath shaky and uneven. She had meant to push him to the brink. She hadn't realized that she would go with him. She needed sanctuary. Needed escape.

"That was it," she said, her voice choked. "I mean…I'm going back to bed now."

He frowned. "What do you mean 'that's it'?"

"Just what I said. Most men would be pretty happy with that."

His face was hidden in shadow, his tone dark. "Then why did you come to me tonight?"

"Because I wanted you. And I got to have you."

"You didn't have an orgasm," he said, his words blunt in the quiet of the room.

"I know, but that wasn't what I came for. I got to have a taste, no pun intended." She slid off the bed and crossed her arms beneath her breasts. "We can talk more tomorrow about how we're going to handle all this."

"This?" he said, indicating the bed.

She shook her head, heat prickling her cheeks. Not embarrassed heat, but anger. She was so mad at…everything. At her body, at Stavros, at herself. At the fear that lived inside of her. A tenant she couldn't seem to evict. "No. About Victoria and where we intend to go from here with that part of our arrangement. You wanted a night. This was a good night. Let's not ruin it now."

"I wanted more," he said. "I still want more."

She nodded. "I know." She wanted more, too. But any more would be far too much. She would have to be too vulnerable. She would have to give too much. Far more than she'd given tonight.

"Stay with me. Just sleep," he said.

That was tempting. Beyond. To sleep in his arms with her head on his chest. To listen to his breathing all night… it surpassed almost every other desire that lived in her.

Which meant she had to say no. "I need to go to bed."

His expression changed, hardened. "We'll talk tomorrow," he said.

"Okay."

She had a feeling that he wasn't going to stay on the topic she wanted to stay on. If there was one thing she'd learned about Stavros it was that beneath all that charm lay a stubbornness that rivaled her own.

Stavros's body still burned. It had been six hours since his late-night visit from Jessica and he couldn't get it, or her, out of his mind. The way she'd taken him, so confident, so bold and sexy. And the way she'd retreated, arms wrapped around her middle, looking like she wanted to disappear.

His feelings on the matter didn't make sense. He'd wanted her to stay. Even if it just meant holding her all night. He'd wanted...he wasn't sure what he'd wanted.

Her actions didn't make sense to him, either. Sex was all about pleasure and release, and she'd taken none for herself. She hadn't removed any of her clothes, he'd barely touched her, and yet, she'd acted as though it was what she wanted.

And then she'd acted like they weren't going to talk about it. She was so very wrong on that count.

His housekeeper refilled his mug of coffee and retreated from the terrace as he lifted the cup to his lips. There was another mug placed across from him and the contents were getting cold, but they were ready for Jessica, when she decided to show herself.

"Morning." He turned and saw Jessica, buttoned up into a yellow dress that covered her from knee to throat, a white belt spanning her tiny waist. She was clutching her little computer in her hands. Her tiny electronic shield.

"Good morning," he said, not bothering to be discreet in his appraisal of her. Her cheeks flushed as she sat down across from him.

She took a sip of her coffee and frowned, not swallowing, not spitting it back out, either.

"Cold?" he asked. She nodded, her frown intensifying. "Bitter?" She nodded again. A smile tugged at the corner of his mouth.

She swallowed slowly, her lip curling into a grimace. "I'll need fresh coffee."

"Leda will be back soon," he said.

"So, things went well last night?"

He said nothing, simply looked at her until the double meaning of her words hit her. He could tell when they did, because she blushed, her lips pulling into a pucker.

"With Victoria," she said sharply.

"Very well." He leaned back in his chair. His heart was beating faster than usual, and that surprised him. He was always in control of himself. Although, Jessica tested that, at every turn she did, and right in this moment, what he had to say to her made him feel...nervous. What her reaction might be made him nervous. "But there is a problem."

"What's that?"

"The same problem we discussed last night. I am currently...obsessed—" he hated the word, but it was the only one that fit "—with another woman, and I can't possibly get engaged to Victoria, much less marry her, while I'm still wrestling with it."

Her face paled, her green eyes looking more vivid set against waxen skin. "Me? This is me you're talking about? Good grief, Stavros, what does it take for a woman to scare you off?"

"A blow job at midnight might not be the best way to go about scaring a man off."

"Granted," she said tightly, some of her color returning.

"I did some reading on endometriosis last night."

Her mouth dropped open, a perfect, crimson O. "You did what?"

"I wanted to understand it more. To understand what you were telling me. I'm embarrassed to say I didn't know anything about it."

"I... Why should you?" The utter confusion on her face puzzled him.

"Because it...it seems like it's not uncommon and like I should. But now, I especially wanted to know about it because of you."

"I don't really have it anymore, like I said. At least I'm not symptomatic."

"You mentioned that, but you still don't want to have sex?"

"It's not that I don't want to. I do, I just...don't. I'm aware that that sounds stupid. But it's...complicated. It's wrapped up in a lot of little problems that you really don't want me to get into." Her green eyes chilled, hardened. "Like I said. I'm not fling material. Too many issues."

"It's understandable. But you also said you had a procedure that fixed most everything for you. Maybe it won't hurt now. Maybe..."

"You know, if it was only physical pain it wouldn't bother me. I've been through hell and back with physical pain. A little more would hardly wreck me. But the point is, I don't know if I can deal with that kind of relationship again. I don't know if I can deal with a man looking at me like I'm the living embodiment of his every crushed dream."

"Jessica, I am not your ex. I don't want anything from you but..."

"Sex. You want sex. And I suck at that, too. My own pain was offensive to him," she said, her words coming out harsh, bitter. "I just had to bite my lip and deal with it because it hurt his feelings. Because crying when it hurt made him feel bad. I had to hide anything I bled on because it disgusted him. And then even when I took steps to fix the pain, when I couldn't take it anymore, that was a failure in his eyes, too. I can't do this right now..."

Stavros felt sick. He pushed his coffee back into the middle of the table. "Tell me."

She looked away from him. "The bottom line is that he wanted kids, I can't have them."

She'd said as much last night. "I saw that endometriosis can effect fertility," he said.

A smile curved her lips. "Yes. It can. But not for everyone. And it doesn't mean it can't happen. But I can't. Because in order to try and fix my endometriosis, I opted to get a hysterectomy. He didn't want me to. He wanted to keep trying to conceive first and I...I couldn't take it anymore. In his mind, I gave up. Can't very well get pregnant if you haven't got an oven to put the bun in, right? To him, I gave up on kids. I gave up on us. I killed our dreams for my own comfort. I'm a selfish bitch. I told you that, remember?" She stood up. "Sorry. I have to go."

She turned and walked back into the house, her expression pale and set as marble. His stomach burned, acid, anger, eating away at him.

Not at her. Never at her.

He stood, and looked out at the ocean for a moment before walking back into the villa. He was more determined now than he'd been a few moments ago.

He needed Jessica. And she needed him. Even if it was only for a while, he was determined to have her. Determined to heal some of the wounds her husband had left behind.

Determined to have a stolen moment of time that belonged solely to him.

He had not been born to be the king. He had taken hold of it when it became clear that Xander would not. He had let go of so many things. So many desires he wouldn't let himself remember now. He had consigned himself to a marriage that was to be little more than a business arrangement.

He had given it all. Would continue to give it all for the

rest of his life. He would embrace the hollowness he had carved out inside of himself, let it fill with all the duty and honor he could possibly stand.

Just now, he was filled with Jessica. With whatever it was she made him feel. Something foreign, all-consuming. Something he wanted to embrace with a desperation he couldn't put into words.

For now, for just a little while, he would. If only she would allow it.

CHAPTER EIGHT

IF POUNDING her head against a wall and repeating the "you are an idiot" mantra would have made any difference to the outcome of her morning conversation with Stavros, she would have done it. Unfortunately, no amount of self-recrimination would fix the fact that she'd vomited her emotional guts up for him to dissect whether he wanted to or not.

Yes, he'd asked. But he hadn't known what he was asking.

I did some research on endometriosis.

Replaying those words in her mind made her eyes sting, made her skin feel tight. When had anyone in her life done that for her? Her mother, her husband, her friends? When had anyone cared enough? Or been brave enough? As far as everyone in her life was concerned her condition only mattered in terms of how it affected them.

Only Stavros had asked. Only he had made that extra effort. Why? Why did he care for her at all? It didn't make sense.

The commanding knock on her door could only come from Stavros. She knew it by now.

"Come in," she said. There was no point in avoiding him. He wouldn't go away. He was like that.

The door opened and Stavros walked in, closing it behind him. "Why don't you let me decide what's too much work?"

She blinked. "What?"

"Can I be the one to decide if you're too much work? Because you keep telling me you are, and that I don't want to deal with you but…the thing is, I do."

He looked so sincere, so deadly serious, and she couldn't help but laugh. "Why? It doesn't make sense. Go…have a fling if that's what you need before you get married. There's a whole lot of women in bikinis down on the public beaches. Or hurry up and marry Victoria, so you can get to your wedding night. But why would you want to waste your time with me?"

"I want you. And if you don't want me, that's fine, but I'm pretty sure your actions last night mean that you do. So if you want me, take some time with me."

"I…I don't think I understand."

"Four weeks. Four weeks and I'll ask Victoria to marry me, and until then, I want you." He looked down. "I understand it's not the world's most romantic proposition, but it's all I can offer."

Her stomach seemed to be cold inside, and she knew that wasn't possible. "Yes, I know. I'm over twenty-eight, I can't have children, I probably have an annoying laugh. The reasons why I'm wrong for you are many and varied. Those are just the obvious ones."

"Yes," he said, the word flat, honest. "But that hasn't stopped me from wanting you."

"I…I don't know whether I'm flattered or insulted. Actually, scratch that, I don't know if I'm supposed to be flattered or insulted. I think I'm flattered, I'm just not certain I should be."

"Because it's a temporary offer?"

She lifted her thumb to her lips and gnawed the corner of her nail, nodding.

"I would never insult you by pretending I could offer something I couldn't. My responsibilities won't change. They are what they are. But I can't get you out of my head. I can't force myself to want Victoria when it's you that I see every time I close my eyes."

"No one's ever said things like this to me," she said, looking up at him, trying to see some hint in his expression that he was joking because…it didn't seem real.

"Not even your husband?"

"No. He uh…he was a college student when we got together. So was I. Young and stupid and very sincere, but not very poetic." She cleared her throat. "It didn't last, either, for all that we thought it would."

"Neither will this," he said.

She nodded. "But we won't pretend otherwise, will we?"

"No. I won't pretend with you, ever. Promise to do the same with me?"

"Yes," she whispered, not sure if she was agreeing to his last request, or his request for the four weeks. She was lost anyway. No matter how much she pretended she was undecided, she was lost to him. To her desire for him. Her curiosity. Yes, she was afraid, but she wanted him more than she wanted to keep hiding.

Because that's what it really was. She wasn't afraid of the pain of sex. She wasn't even as afraid of failing as she'd thought. She was more afraid that she would have sex, and that it would be good. And then she would lose her excuse to hold men at arm's length. She would lose that thing that kept her from seeking out another relationship.

She swallowed, trying to push her fear down. Fear she didn't want. Not now.

"I need you," he said, the words raw, lacking charm,

flirtation, any kind of artifice. "I'm not sure if you realize how much. I'm not sure you could, as it's something I don't entirely understand. But I need...you. This. I hope you want me."

She did understand. She needed him, too. As much as she needed to escape from the confines she'd put herself into, as much as she needed to move on. He felt like a necessity.

She hadn't ever thought of herself as a temporary kind of woman. But then, when sex was such an ordeal it was hard to think of it as something she might do recreationally. Still...Stavros made her want a taste of the illicit.

Of something she'd never really had, first because she'd met her husband at such a young age, and then because she'd developed endometriosis. And after that, because clinging to the past, wrapping herself in the memories of the pain, had become a shield against any sort of future hurt.

It also kept her tied to her old life. Tied to who she'd been.

She needed to be free of it. She finally felt ready to be free of it. It was all well and good to wish she could fully embrace her new reality. But she wasn't. And that was no one's fault but hers.

"Yes," she said again. "I want you, too. And now that you've given up on that fake flirting business I actually find you a lot more irresistible."

"What fake flirting business?"

"You know. That's not you, Stavros. This is. This is the man I can't resist."

He swallowed visibly, a muscle in his jaw twitching. "As long as you can't resist me."

"I could. But I'm not going to anymore."

He laughed, the sound as raw and ragged as his expression. "I couldn't resist you. That's why I'm here."

Her stomach contracted, her heart pounding faster. To

have such a big, strong man admitting he couldn't fight his attraction to her was…it was beyond her. And it restored something in her. Something she'd thought was so mangled beyond recognition it could never be fixed.

"This is stupid," she said, laughing, because if she didn't she thought she might cry.

"I know," he said, taking a step toward her, cupping her cheek in his palm. "I know." He rested his forehead against hers, his eyes closed.

She tilted her face and touched her lips to his, a gentle kiss, a question. One he answered with his own kiss, stronger, more certain. His tongue teased her, and she parted her mouth for him, sliding her tongue against his, the friction igniting a wave of heat in her stomach that spread to her breasts, down to her core.

"Wow. You really are an amazing kisser," she said, a shiver sliding down through her.

"And you are very honest."

She shook her head. "I'm not usually. I just do my very best to seem tough all the time and no one questions what I do or say too closely. They don't want me to kill them with snark. And that way I don't have to be honest. But for some reason, I am honest with you. I'm not sure why."

"You have the same effect on me," he said. "I can't fathom it."

"It's the lust thing. It's scrambling our brains."

A smile turned up the corners of his mouth. "Is that it?"

She nodded. "I'm not familiar with it on quite this level, but I remember feeling this way in college a couple of times."

"Yes, that sounds about right. You'd think at our age we would be impervious." He smiled slightly and it made her knees feel a little weak.

"Hey, watch it. No age jokes."

He kissed her again. "You are a beautiful woman. I cannot imagine you being any more attractive to me. Your dress today is lethal."

She looked down at her demure yellow dress. "This?"

"It has buttons," he growled. "And all I can think of is undoing all of those buttons."

Her face heated. "Really?"

"Oh, yes, really. I want to do it now, but I don't want to move too quickly."

"It's not even noon."

"So?"

"Isn't there a no-sex-before-noon rule?"

He laughed. "Sex isn't like alcohol. And if that's been your experience with it, I can tell you, you need your experience broadened."

She swallowed. "I'm a little nervous. A lot nervous." She wasn't sure what he would do to her, and that fear wasn't rooted in the fear of physical pain, but over how complete the loss of control might be. Over whether or not she would be able to hold onto her defenses.

He smoothed his thumb over her cheek. "Tell me, is there a specific act that causes worse pain?"

She nodded, finding that focusing on the physical was helpful. "Orgasm can cause pain, which…sucks." She breathed the last word with a shaky laugh. "The worst of it always came from…penetration. In the end at least."

He nodded slowly. "No sex. Not now. I want to take your dress off. I want to touch your breasts. Taste them, too. Nothing more. Nothing more until you're ready."

She could hardly breathe. His promises, so husky and sensual and perfect, had her body wound so tight she was certain she would break. "You really do have a way with words."

"Funny you should say that. My speechwriters usually

handle my words. I pride myself on being a man of action. What are words if you can't back them up?" He slid his hands down to the first button on her dress and slowly slid the little fabric-covered bead through the hole, letting the neck of the dress gap.

She wished she could capture the bravado she'd felt last night. But then, last night had been her game. She'd been in control, in her element. She'd been giving pleasure and feeding off of the residual. Here and now, Stavros had command of her. A reverse on last night, and she found she actually liked it.

He moved to the next button, then the next, pressing a kiss to her neck for each button. When he reached the button just beneath her breasts, he slid his tongue along the line of her collarbone, then down a fraction. He paused at her belt, sliding it through the buckle slowly, then letting it drop. He continued down, until her dress hung open, until his tongue was curving around the line of her bra, teasing her sensitive flesh.

She shivered as he pushed the dress from her shoulders and let it fall to the floor, leaving her in her white pumps and matching bra and panties.

"You are amazing," he said, dropping to his knees to press a kiss to her stomach. Tears filled her eyes and she couldn't stop them. She didn't want him to take her panties off, not this time. He would see her scars and she wasn't ready. Not yet.

She tugged on his shoulders, urging him up, and he complied, his hand on her back, toying with the catch on her bra, teasing them both. He took a step, his arms wrapped around her still. She stepped backward. They made a slow, smooth dance to the bed and he undid her bra as he laid her down, pulling it off and casting it aside.

He was half over her, his breathing harsh, his eyes on

her bare breasts. Thankfully, she knew they were one of her best features, so this was the easy part. It was made even easier when she caught the feral light in his dark eyes. "You are so much more beautiful than I imagined. Much more beautiful than I *could* have imagined. I have never seen a woman as exquisite as you." He cupped her, slid his fingers gently over her tightened nipples.

She arched into him, pleasure making her breath catch.

"Tell me if I do something you don't like," he said. "Tell me, and I'll stop."

She didn't want him to stop. Not ever. She reveled in his touch, in the feel of his rough, masculine hands on her tender skin. And when he replaced his fingers with his mouth, with the slick friction of his tongue, she felt a sharp tightening in her core, waves of pleasure, of pending release, rippling through her.

She gripped his hair, arched her body. She was close. She'd never been so close, so fast. She couldn't remember ever wanting anyone this badly, either.

"Oh, yes." She sighed, letting her head fall back.

He raised his head. "More?"

She nodded, biting her bottom lip. "Yes."

He moved his hand down her stomach and she was certain he would feel the line of scar tissue that ran just below the waistband of her underwear, but she was past caring. Past caring about anything. About the future. About possible pain. Even about the loss of control.

How could something that felt so amazing end in pain? Any kind of pain was worth it, surely.

He slipped his fingers beneath her panties, grazed the scar and continued down to where she was wet and ready for him. He teased the entrance to her body with his fingers, before sliding them over her clitoris. The sensation was like fire, burning heat from there throughout her body.

She gritted her teeth, her breath getting sharper, uneven. She curled her fingers into the sheets as he continued to touch her there. Soft, even strokes that brought her closer and closer to the edge.

He leaned in and kissed her mouth as he increased the pressure of his touch, and everything in her seemed to release at once, a flood of pleasure roaring through her, drowning out thought and sound. She cried out, not caring if she was loud, not caring that it was daylight, not caring that their relationship would only last a month.

Because there was nothing else. Not in that moment. There was Stavros. And there was what he made her feel.

Only when reality started piecing itself back together, did fear assault her. But there hadn't been any pain yet. Still, she waited. Waited for the low, dragging sensation that rivaled stories she'd heard about childbirth to begin.

And there was nothing. Nothing but a feeling of being replete. Nothing but a feeling of total bliss and satisfaction. She didn't feel as though she'd given her body away, didn't feel as though she was lost. She felt as though she'd gained a part of herself back.

A sob shook her body and she felt a tear slide down her cheek. The tears she couldn't find earlier. Tears she hadn't been able to find for a long time. Something in her shifted, changed. Like a dam had been broken inside of her, one she'd walled up to protect herself. One she felt she didn't need. Not now.

Stavros cupped her face, his expression fierce. "Did I hurt you?"

She bit her lip and shook her head. "No. You didn't. I can't…I can't remember the last time… Thank you."

He wrapped his arms around her and pulled her to him so that her head was rested on his chest. "Don't thank me.

I can't accept thanks for that. I took far too much pleasure from it for that."

"Realistically," she said, trying to escape from some of the moment's intimacy, impossible when she was mostly naked and cradled in his arms, but worth a try, "you have to see Victoria a couple more times before you propose."

He nodded. "All right."

"I know that will run during our...relationship. But I suppose as long as you don't..."

"I will be faithful to you, you don't have to worry about that. And I will be faithful when I am married," he said.

She swallowed. It was the right thing for him to say, the right thing for him to do. He should keep his vows. She believed in marriage, respected it. For all that she and Gil had screwed up their marriage, neither of them had cheated.

Still, a part of her died when he said it. "I'm glad. For all of that."

"This might not be the best idea. But I don't regret it."

"I can't, either," she said. It was the absolute truth. How could she regret what had passed between them? How could she regret the loss of a fear? There were others, of course. But she was free of one, too. And that wasn't a small thing.

"So, tell me," she said, attempting a subject change, in a bid keep things from getting too heavy, "what does a woman expect when she signs on to be your temporary companion?"

"I'm not sure. I've never had a relationship quite like this. Of course, I've never met a woman quite like you."

"What do you normally do?"

"There's that sort of coyness to it that one employs in a sexual relationships. Gifts, shallow conversation, references only to the here and now, nothing said of the future one way or the other. And with you, there's no coyness, that's for sure."

She smiled. "I don't do coy."

"I noticed." He tightened his hold on her. "All of my life has been devoted to fulfilling the needs of others. Right now, just now, I want to meet my own."

So this was for him, as much as for her. She liked knowing that. Felt empowered by it. Because there was something he needed to, and maybe she could provide it. Maybe she could be the one to give him moments of bliss. Moments that were purely his own, so that he would have the memories years later when his life was no longer his at all.

"What do you want?" she asked.

He sifted his fingers through her hair. "I want to sleep with you tonight. Just sleep, if that's all you want."

"That's too easy. What else?"

"To go to the beach. Which should be easy, since we're on an island. I am a man with the world at my fingertips in terms of the material. The thing I often find myself lacking in is a companion who makes life interesting. Who makes it fun. You be you, and I will simply enjoy it."

"Really, you're too nice. I feel outmatched."

"I like your prickles," he said. "Even more now that I understand them."

She sat up and wrapped her arms around herself. "I should get dressed."

"I'm in no hurry."

"I have some work to check on, just real quick, and then…and then we can do whatever we want. Because that's what we've decided to do, isn't it? Whatever we want for the next month."

He smiled at her and her heart felt like it tightened in on itself. She could do a month. A month was short enough. Short enough that he wouldn't start wishing she could be a million things she could never be.

CHAPTER NINE

ANYTHING he wanted turned out to be much more low-key and much less in bed than she'd imagined it might be.

Stavros took her on a tour of the ruins just outside the city, and then down to the open-air markets to shop. The market ran just outside the boundaries of the packed harbor, small stalls crammed between buildings, the ocean just beyond them.

Stavros could have taken her anywhere in Piraeus. To the more modern quadrants of the city, to exclusive boutiques with cutting-edge fashion.

But he'd taken her here. Because he knew what she liked. He understood what she enjoyed. She did her best to ignore her constricted lungs and turn her focus to the items for sale.

There was an eclectic mix of trash and truly exquisite treasure on offer. Things she would have found at an average yard sale in her home town, fresh seafood and antiques all mingled together. She bought a necklace fashioned from fishing line and glass beads, and earrings made from old coins.

"It's certainly vintage," Stavros said, eyeing her purchases later at an outdoor restaurant.

"Yes, most definitely."

"You need a *pallas* to go with it."

She pulled her necklace out of the bag and held it up so

that the afternoon sun filtered through the glass beads. "All right, what's that?"

"The traditional draped dress. It would look beautiful on you."

"Not my typical style though, draped clothes."

"No. Not at all." Today she was in a full white skirt that went down past her knees and a red button-up top. All very crisp and tailored.

"It makes for an intriguing thought."

"Yes, but you don't like my clothes."

"No, I like your clothes very much, it's just that I find them a distraction. And now that I have permission to be distracted...well, I like them even more."

Her cheeks heated. He made her feel...he made her feel so new. Like this was fresh. Flirting, and eating together. The anticipation of sex. And she was anticipating it. Big-time. She smiled and looked down at her plate.

She ignored the little hint of fear that pooled in her stomach. If she felt so close to him now, what would happen after? She really hadn't ever been a fling girl. She'd been one and done. She'd met her husband right out of high school, and he was the man she'd married.

"What is it?" he asked.

"Nothing."

He reached over and took her chin between his thumb and forefinger, tilting her face up. "What?"

It was hard meeting his eyes. Intimate, suddenly. "I'm happy. I haven't...enjoyed anything like this in a long time."

"I haven't, either."

"Stavros, why is this marriage so important to you?" She wasn't sure where the question came from, only that it seemed essential, suddenly. "I mean, I know why you need to do it eventually. But it's more than that, I can tell. I just...want to know why."

He frowned. "I'm the only one, Jessica."

"I know."

"When Xander left, everything was chaos. My father was a wreck, my mother was gone. Eva was just a child. There was only me. My willingness to step in. I was a teenager, but just that show of strength and solidarity, and the years I spent after building up the economy, that made the difference. I need everything to be as it should be. I need it to have balance and order. I want it to."

"And Victoria will help with that."

"Victoria is only a piece of the puzzle. I've been setting all of this in place for years."

"I know," she said, looking away from him again. "Plans…I wish sometimes that some of mine had worked out. And sometimes…I'm glad they didn't."

Really, today was the first time she was honestly glad to be in a different place. With a different man. She hadn't loved her ex for years. But very often she'd longed to go back to a time when she did love him.

A time when her life had been full of possibilities. Instead of a time when so many of her dreams had died.

"Mine have to work out," he said. "For my people."

"Has Xander officially abdicated?"

"No. And he won't until after my father dies, which doesn't look like it will be soon. I am thankful for that."

"But you're playing chess," she said.

"What do you mean?"

"I actually suck at chess, but I have a brother who plays very well, and he used to talk me into playing when we were younger. I could never win, because I was always responding to his moves. He knew all of his moves from the beginning. And he had back-up maneuvers just in case I failed to be predictable, but mostly, he just followed the strategy he'd had since the opening move. You already know your checkmate."

He laughed and placed his hand over hers, his thumb blazing a trail of heat over her skin as he moved it back and forth. "But this is a move I did not see making."

"Do you regret it? Because we haven't done anything we can't take back."

He shook his head. "I don't. I should, I'm certain of that. This is unfair to you."

It was her turn to laugh. "How? I'm not some young, inexperienced girl. I've been married, I've been divorced. I've done love and loss. I'm a bit too cynical to get hurt by a temporary affair." She hoped that was true. She'd certainly believed it of herself before she'd met Stavros. Before she'd started caring for him.

How had that happened? He was so far removed from her. A prince, for heaven's sake. And a client. They shouldn't connect on any level. Yet, she felt like he was the one person who had a hope of understanding her. She felt she understood him. How had he started to matter so much?

He nodded. "I know. But your husband hurt you. I don't want any part of that. Of hurting you."

She forced out a laugh and lifted her wineglass to her lips. "By that logic, you should worry about yourself. Yes, he hurt me. But I hurt him, too. Marriage is a two-way street, and very rarely is everything the fault of one person. I'm capable of breaking a man's heart, Stavros, so perhaps it's me who should be giving you an out."

"I don't have a heart to break, Jess."

"I don't believe that."

"When have I had time to worry about my feelings? I have to take care of Kyonos. While my father took his rage and grief out on Xander, while Xander wallowed in his guilt, someone had to push it aside and stand up. I have made it my mission to never allow emotion to dictate what I do. It has no place in me." His eyes met hers, the blankness in them frightening. She was so used to his charming glimmer that seeing him now, flat, empty, made her feel cold. The problem was that it rang far truer than the charismatic charm ever had. As though this was really him. The real depth of him. "It is what I must do, to be the best king I can be. To be better than my father."

"I get that." If she hadn't been able to hide behind her wall of snark, she could never have done her job. Could never have gone on matching other couples, trying to help them find their happily ever after. She couldn't have done it if she'd allowed the wound from the loss of her own to keep on bleeding.

She'd learned to shut it off. To protect herself. That was all deserting her now.

Not the time.

The darkness in his eyes changed, warmed. "But for a while, I'm going to focus on this." He leaned over and pressed a light kiss to her lips. He'd barely touched her since their encounter in the morning, and it was so very welcome.

"I appreciate your focus," she said, her breath coming in shorter bursts now. She tried not to be so obvious, tried to regain control.

But she could tell, from the expression on Stavros's face, that he didn't have any more control than she did. And that made it all seem a little bit more acceptable. Made it feel better that she couldn't stop her stomach from fluttering and her heart from thundering, hard and fast.

Neither of them had command of the attraction. The fact she was a part of it, that she was able to drive a man to this point, it did wonders for her completely squished ego.

It affected more than that, but she didn't really want to ponder it on a deeper level.

"I can't focus on anything else when you're around," he said, sliding his fingers through her hair.

"It's hard to believe you needed my help finding a wife. You seem to have the romance thing down."

He shook his head. "Romance is an area I've always found myself lacking in. Not in seduction, or flirting, but that's a different matter, isn't it? It requires no sincerity. And the matter of my marriage…that's separate from either of those. You know that."

His eyes were intense on hers, desperation evident in their depths. Desperation for her to understand. She didn't know why, and she was willing to bet he didn't, either. Only that she felt it echo inside of her.

"I know," she said, covering his hand with hers. "But we aren't worrying about that, right?"

"I see you've finally gotten on board with the denial tactic."

"Reality has its place. But it's not here."

"Normally, I would disagree. I would disagree with the entire concept of this relationship. But I don't have the strength right now." The words were rough, a hard admission for a man who lived his life by his strength. Who had based every action on being stronger than those around him.

He was Atlas, with the world on his shoulders. Or at least a country.

He deserved to set it down for a second. To have some relief.

"The only reason you don't have the strength right now, is because you've had to be stronger than any man should have to be. You've given up too much." she said.

"Maybe. But until now I hadn't missed anything. But if I passed up the chance to be with you…I think I would miss it for all of my life."

His words hung between them, thick and serious. And

far too true. They'd always spoken with honesty, it seemed like they couldn't help speaking with honesty. But this was a hard truth to take. Mostly because it was true for her, too, and admitting he was that important, that essential, scared her.

She swallowed, blinking to try and dispel the stinging in her eyes. "I would certainly hate to miss this." She looked at the view, at the sun glinting off the crystalline water. It was easy to look at the scenery and say it. Easy to let him think she might mean something else.

Far too difficult for her to let herself be vulnerable to him. To let him know how much he was starting to mean to her. It was almost harder to admit to herself how much he was starting to mean to her. Because she was tired of wanting the impossible.

"Jess." He whispered her name and he turned to look at him. His expression stopped her heart. He looked so hungry, so sad. And just as quickly as the emotions became evident on his face, they disappeared. "I do have some work to complete today, and then I would like to see you again. After dinner?"

She nodded. "Yes." She was grateful for a break, a reprieve. Because her chest felt so tight, far too tight, and she was finding it difficult to breathe.

This was supposed to be about her. About reclaiming a part of herself she thought was lost. About letting go of her past, not clinging to someone else. And she couldn't lie and say Stavros meant nothing to her. Of course he did. She liked him. She wanted him to have this, this last thing that he desired, before he gave himself over to his country.

But she was going to try to lie and say that was the end of it. She was going to try and do that for as long as she could.

She would use the time apart to try and get a grip on the other emotions, the unwelcome ones.

"Then I'll see you back to the villa."

She nodded, trying to ignore the fullness inside of her that was keeping her lungs from expanding all the way. "That sounds good."

Yes, she needed to get a grip, and she needed to get it badly.

She'd gone into her marriage a naive idiot, and she'd learned a lot about the reality of life since then. That, coupled with the fact that she knew her relationship with Stavros wouldn't last, should be enough to keep her head on straight.

Sadly, she wasn't certain it was.

"Jessica?" The villa was empty when Stavros returned later that evening. It was later than he'd intended. Mainly because he'd spent the evening sitting in his Piraeus office, staring out at the ocean and trying to get a grip on his rioting libido.

And the strange twinge in his heart that seemed to hit him hard and radiate down to his stomach whenever he pictured Jessica's face.

He was much later than he should have been, and he half expected her to be in bed. He prowled the halls for a few moments, opened the door to her room and confirmed that it was empty. He'd known right away.

He could feel that she wasn't here. A strange sensation, an impossible one, and yet, he had complete certainty in it. Strange how she'd done that. How she'd opened him back up to feeling.

Stranger that he wasn't fighting it.

Just for this month. Just a little while.

He walked out onto the terrace and looked down at the beach below. He could see her by the shore, her silhouette outlined by the silver moon. He walked down the terrace stairs, and out to the beach, pulling the knot on his tie and letting it fall somewhere in the sand. He discarded his jacket and kept moving to her.

No matter where she was, he felt compelled to find her. To go to her. He could feel her absence nearly as keenly as he could feel her presence. And he wasn't certain what that meant. Only that he had to be near her. And that if the force of his physical desire weren't so powerful, weren't so all-consuming, the need that came with it, the need to be with her, would be frightening. At least with the lust there, he had something else to focus on. Something to take the edge off the unfiltered emotion she called up in him with so much ease.

He walked soundlessly on the sand, discarding his shoes, not caring about their fate. Jessica turned sharply, and he wondered if she could feel him, too.

"Hi," she said, her voice barely audible above the sound of the waves on the shore.

"Sorry I'm late."

"You didn't give me a time. It's okay."

"Still, it's pretty late."

She shrugged. "It's okay. I had a nice evening. I called Victoria and told her to expect an invitation to an event in Kyonos. I hope that was okay."

"It was the right thing to do. No matter how I feel about it."

"It's not exactly ignoring it, I admit. But we both know you can't just not contact her at all over the next month."

His stomach tightened. "I know."

"Don't you have a celebration ball coming up for when Eva and Makhail return from their honeymoon? It's on the copy of your schedule I received and I thought it would be the perfect opportunity for you to be seen with Victoria."

"Oh, yes. I had forgotten."

"She should go to that. With you. Give a hint as to your

developing relationship. That way your people can really look forward to the engagement announcement."

His people. That was what all of this was about. His country. His heart. He had thrown himself into it, completely, into planning what he would do to make it better, to heal it. And that was why he was marrying Victoria.

He couldn't lose sight of it. But it was so easy to do when Jessica filled his vision. So easy to simply let his desire for her color everything. That was emotion. That was weakness. He could not afford it.

Just right now, it was okay though. Just for this moment in time. He moved to her, unable to stand apart from her any longer. Unable to be so close yet not touching her.

He sifted his fingers through silken strands of blond hair. "I missed you," he said. He wasn't sure why he said it, even though it was true.

He wasn't certain that level of honesty had a place in their arrangement. But he wasn't sure what else he should say, either. Wasn't sure what to hold back and what to give.

Holding anything back when Jessica was around seemed an impossibility. He wasn't sure he wanted to, and that was a new feeling entirely.

Lust he'd dealt with. He'd put it aside when he had to, embraced it when it was convenient. He'd never been controlled by it. But it had never before been accompanied by this strange…ache. An ache that seemed to spread through his body, sink down deep into his bones, beyond, down into his soul.

Wanting Jessica was painful. And it was more real than anything in his recent memory. He craved it. Because it was better than not being near her. Than not wanting her. He wasn't sure what kind of madness it was, only that for now he wanted to drink it in.

"Jessica, I want to kiss you."

She nodded, her gaze level with his. "I'm game. I like it when you kiss me." She had a bit of her false bravado in place, but it was all right. One of them needed to keep their guard up, and he wasn't certain he could.

When his mother had died, he had been the only one to hold himself together. He had been the one to pick up and move forward. He hadn't been allowed to grieve. Hadn't had time to feel. He had closed down.

But he couldn't shut these feelings off. Couldn't staunch the flow of emotion that seemed to bleed inside of him like a hidden wound. When he looked at Jessica, he had no control.

"I want to do more than that. I want to make love with you tonight. But you tell me, if it hurts. And I'll stop. I don't care how hard it is for me to stop, I will. I would never hurt you." Even as he said the words he feared they weren't true. Not that he wouldn't stop making love with her if it hurt, he was confident he would do that.

But he feared he might hurt her emotionally. That he might have a part in causing her further pain that way. He didn't want to, but to avoid it he would have to turn back. And at this point, even that would hurt her.

More than that, he feared what would happen to himself. Selfish, maybe. But he felt like he was standing at the edge of a fire, toying with the idea of touching the flame. Then throwing himself into it.

They were in too deep to escape unscathed. But then, maybe they had been from the beginning. That connection—instant, seemingly physical—had been more from the moment they'd met.

She nodded slowly. "I want that. And I'm not even nervous. Which is crazy but I just…know it will be good. That I'll be good."

"Something I have no doubt about," he said, forcing words through his tightened throat.

She laughed. "I'm glad."

"Oh, Jess, you are the most beautiful woman. The most fascinating. Bewitching." He kissed her. Her lips were so soft, so warm. They heated him, all the way through his body, his blood burning in his veins, his body getting hard.

She parted her lips and angled her head, her hand pressed to his cheek. He took advantage of the move and slid his tongue into her mouth, sliding it against hers, the intimate action sending a hard kick of lust through him.

It roared in him like a beast, one that demanded satisfaction. That demanded he lay her down in the sand and take what he needed. That he use her to fill the emptiness inside of him. Because she could. She was the only one who could.

He put his hands on her hips, braced her. Braced him. He curled his fingers in, gripped the full skirt of her dress tightly in his palms. He wouldn't do that to her. He wouldn't make this hard and fast, he wouldn't make it about his satisfaction.

He would give to her. He would control his own need. He would master it.

It was Jessica who changed the game. Jessica who moved her hands over his chest, down to where he was hard and ready for her. She was a mass of contradictions, his Jessica. So confident in giving pleasure. So hesitant to receive it.

So afraid to release control.

She cupped him and he nearly lost his head then and there, her palm sweet and knowing on his erection, sliding over the length of him.

"Oh, yes," she whispered against his lips. "I'm so ready for this."

He took her hand and moved it away from him, his body

protesting. He lifted it to his lips and kissed her palm. "Not like that, Jess. Not this time."

"Stavros…"

"You aren't in charge. I know you don't like to hear that. But that's the way it's going to be."

Her eyes rounded and he wondered if he'd taken her a step to far. But she didn't move away. She moistened her lips and slid her hand around to the back of his neck, her fingers sifting through his hair. She kissed his jaw, his ear.

He chuckled when he felt her teeth scrape against his earlobe. "I see how it's going to be," he said.

"Do you?" she said, her voice trembling, betraying a hint of nerves.

"Well, that isn't entirely true. I can't really guess how it's going to be. Because I have never felt this way about a woman before." As he said it, he realized how true it was. "I have never wanted a woman as I want you."

"Glad we're on the same page there. I've never felt like this, either, not even before…not even before…not ever."

"Then we're both equal. And for that I'm glad. I would hate to be standing here, ready to lose my mind with wanting you, with you feeling completely calm and certain."

"Oh, no sweat there, Stavros. I'm shaking," she whispered.

He swore. "Sorry, I'm losing my finesse."

"Good. I don't need your finesse. You're a very charming man, Stavros, and you seem to come by it effortlessly, no matter how you really feel. I would much rather have something real."

"You have it." He kissed her again, through with talking. Words were too difficult now. He just had to show her. Because it was the absolute truth. With her there was no artifice. He had tried to put distance between them with his charming persona, and he hadn't been able to. She made him real.

She made him real in a way he could never remember being before.

He wrapped his arms around her and pulled her flush against his body, sighing when her full breasts made contact with his chest. She was soft and perfect, everything a woman should be. He ran his hands over her curves, the indent of her waist, the fullness of her hips, the round curve of her butt. He palmed her, his body shuddering.

"Buttons," he growled, taking his hands from her backside and turning his focus to the front of her dress. Most of her dresses had buttons, but he was half convinced she'd chosen this one to torment him thanks to his earlier comments.

Her wicked smile confirmed it. He moved slowly, pushing each button through the hole at half the speed he could have done it in. Teasing them both. It was worth it. She bit her lip and watched him work. Even in the dim light, he could see the color mounting in her cheeks. He could feel her breath shorten, her breasts rising up against his fingers as he worked at the buttons there.

He was hard, burning with the need to take her, to join with her.

He pushed the top of the dress down, letting it fall around her waist. She had a lace bra on beneath it, thin and sexy. He slid his thumb over one breast, felt her nipple harden beneath his touch.

He moved to the next set of buttons on until the skirt loosened enough to fall down her hips and pool in the sand.

She was barefoot already, and now she was wearing nothing more than a pair of lace underwear and bra. He'd had her this undressed before, but not all the way. He unhooked her bra in one deft movement and consigned it to the sand with the dress.

"You're perfection," he said, cupping her breasts, teasing her nipples. She closed her eyes, her lips parted slightly. He took advantage of the moment and kissed her, then moved to her neck, her collarbone, before drawing one tightened bud between his lips and sliding his tongue over it. "And you taste amazing," he said.

She shivered beneath him, and he felt an answering tremor echo in his own body. He'd never felt so connected to a lover before. He'd always been committed to giving pleasure, because sex was only satisfying if all involved got what they needed. But he'd never felt dependent on his partner's response. Had never needed to draw the pleasure out like this, to be sure it was superior to his own. To be sure it was superior to any she'd had before.

He got on his knees in the sand, not caring about his suit, not caring about anything but the need to taste her everywhere. He slid his tongue along the waistband of her panties and he felt her stiffen.

"Come on now, Jessica, don't get shy on me."

She gripped his shoulders, the cold from her fingertips seeping through his shirt. She didn't stop him. He hooked his fingers into the sides of her underwear and tugged them down her legs.

She stepped out of them, her movements unsteady. He looked up at her and saw a shimmer of tears in her eyes. When he looked back down, it wasn't simply the gorgeous triangle of curls at the apex of her thighs that caught his attention. It was the scar that ran just above it. A thin line, an imperfection that meant very little to him in terms of how it looked.

But one he knew held a wealth of pain. Her pain. He could not remain unaffected by that. He was grateful he was on his knees, because the hard punch it delivered to his stomach might have taken him there had he not been down already.

He could hear her teeth chattering. "Stavros…"

"Oh, Jess." He leaned in and pressed his face to her stomach, kissing her there, just beneath her belly button. "You are amazing to me."

He lowered his head and traced the same line the surgeon's knife had followed, pressing kisses to the depressed section of skin. He didn't give her a chance to protest. He moved lower and flicked the tip of his tongue over her clitoris. A raw sound escaped her lips and she clung more tightly to him, her nails digging sharply into his shoulders.

He held her hips tightly and continued his exploration of her body with his lips and tongue. He could feel her shaking beneath his touch, and that was good, because he was shaking, too. He couldn't remember wanting a woman more, couldn't remember if the taste of woman had ever been essential. He was certain it never had been before.

Jessica was utterly unique. Comparing her to other experiences, comparing this moment to other experiences, was an impossibility.

He slipped his hand between her thighs and pressed a finger slowly inside her body, she froze for a moment, her hands gripping at his shirt and he felt her muscles contract around him as she found her release. It was her orgasm, her pleasure, and yet he felt spent. Satisfied.

But still in need of more. He was so hard his body burned.

She slid down to her knees, kissing him, her body pressed against him, her hands tearing at the buttons on his shirt. He was sure more than one was made a casualty in her haste, but he didn't care. Nothing mattered now. Nothing but being joined to Jessica. Nothing but finding some solace from the ache. From the emptiness he'd never been cognizant of until she'd walked into his life.

He helped her with his pants, shucking them off as quickly as possible. She pressed lightly on his shoulders, pushing him back into the sand. She slid her hands down his chest, his torso, along the side of his erection, teasing but not touching.

"Careful," he groaned.

She smiled, a sassy, sleepy smile of a woman who'd been satisfied, but who was still hungry for more. The big difference between the two of them right now was that she'd had the edge taken off, and she had the time to tease. He feared he did not.

She moved over him, and he put his hands on her waist, tilting his face up to pull one nipple into his mouth. She arched into him and he slid one hand down her back, guiding her so that his erection was pressing against her slick entrance.

"It's up to you now," he said, words nearly impossible to force through his tightened throat.

She bit her lip, her eyes on his. He could see her fear and he wished there was something he could to ease it. He kept his hold on her steady, kept his body still, gave the control back to her. He didn't want to move too quickly, didn't want to do anything to ruin the moment.

She lowered herself onto him, taking him inside an inch at a time. It took all of his strength not to thrust up into her. He kept his focus on her face. Her lips parted, her expression intense. And when she had him inside all the way, she let her head fall back, a slow breath escaping her lips.

"Oh, yes," she whispered.

"Good?" he asked.

She looked down at him, a smile touching her lips. "So good. And not enough."

She tilted her hips and pleasure flashed through him like a flood, pouring over him, taking over him. She set the pace, but he moved with her, thrusting up into her body, encouraged by the sounds of ecstasy coming from her lips. She planted her hands on his chest, her face tilted down, her hair covering them both, shielding them.

He could feel his orgasm building, taking him to the edge. He clung to it, every ounce of his willpower channeled into keeping his control. He had to give her more. One more. One more graceful movement and she tossed her head back, her breasts thrust forward. He captured one with his lips and she froze, her mouth open on a silent scream.

And then he let go. He was falling, lost, unsure if he would ever come back to earth. Back to himself. But Jessica was there. And that meant nothing else mattered. Nothing but the pleasure that bound them together, nothing but the all-consuming sensation that was washing over him like a wave, drawing him farther and farther away from shore.

She collapsed over his chest, her breath hot on his skin, her breasts pressed against his stomach. He wrapped his arms around her and smoothed his hand over her hair.

He could feel her tears on him, dampening his skin. "Jess…don't cry."

"It's good crying," she said, sniffing.

"No pain?"

She shook her head. "No pain. You're amazing, by the way."

"That was all you."

"I don't think so," she said. "It's never been quite like that for me before."

He wound a silken strand of her hair around his finger, then released it, watching as the ocean breeze caught it. "Well, it hasn't ever been quite like that for me, either."

"You've never had to deal with a neurotic woman who had mass amounts of sexual hang-ups and cried afterward?"

He laughed, so strange because he had her naked body pressed to his front and he was becoming increasingly aware of the sticky, itchy sand at his back. And he couldn't remember ever wanting to laugh after sex. Sleep. Go back to his own bed, yes. But not laugh.

He sat up and brought her with him, holding her on his lap. "You are truly unique." He kissed her, drank her in. Would he ever feel like he wasn't starving for her?

He stood and swept her into his arms, looking out at the waves, the breeze warm on his bare skin. "Hang on," he said.

He ran toward the water and she tightened her hold around his neck, making a sharp, squeaking sound as they hit the waves, the water spraying around them. He walked out into the surf and spun them around. He set her down gently, the water lapping around her hips. She was laughing, breathless. He was shocked to discover that he was laughing and breathless, too.

She didn't just make him feel. She made him feel everything. All at once. And in such a big way he was sure he would burst with it.

"You're crazy," she said, kissing his mouth, her lips tasting of salt water and Jessica.

"Maybe a little." He looked at her face, so pale and lovely in the moonlight. "Yeah, maybe a little." He couldn't stop the smile from spreading over his face, couldn't fight against the strange, expanding feeling in his chest.

She wrapped her arms around his waist. "You're like Prince Charming's hot cousin. Prince Sexy."

"No nicknames," he said.

She laughed against his chest. "All right, fine. No nicknames." She smoothed her hands over his back. "You've got sand all over your back, Prince Sexy."

"I wonder whose fault that is?"

She looked up at him, the expression on her face impish. "No clue."

Something in his chest seemed to break, causing a release. Like a bird escaping the confines of a cage. A strange sensation assaulted him. Happiness. Freedom. Things he didn't have a lot of experience with.

If only he could hold on to it forever.

This month would have to do. Four weeks to carry him through the rest of his life.

CHAPTER TEN

"STAY in bed with me tonight." Stavros tightened his hold on her hand when they reached the top of the stairs back at the villa.

"You want me to sleep with you?"

"Eventually." A wicked smile spread over his lips and her heart expanded. Sex, lovemaking, whatever it had been, with him was like a whole new experience.

She should feel...some sort of awkwardness. It was their first time together after all. Walking back from the beach with him completely naked, her beautiful 1950s-secretary dress discarded and uncared for, should have left her blushing.

The memory of what it had been like to ride him, to be filled with him, to lose her mind completely when she orgasmed, rushed over her. How vocal she'd been both when he'd gone down on her and when he'd been in her, should have made her want to hide under the covers.

But she felt...surprisingly relaxed. And also still turned on.

She'd never experienced this sort of comfort in her own skin before. Even when she'd been younger with nothing medically wrong with her, she'd had insecurities. Her hips were a little wide for her body, her stomach not perfectly flat.

It had taken her a long time to let Gil make love with her with the lights on. And earlier she'd let Stavros touch her with the sunlight filtering through the window. Maybe it was her age. Maybe she'd finally hit that point where she just didn't care. With Gil she'd been an eighteen-year-old virgin, after all. A couple years later and they'd gotten married. Then things had started going wrong with her body.

And now things were so much better. The sex had been so good she didn't think she could have felt anything but good about it if she'd tried. His pleasure had been obvious. He'd had no insecurities, no anger to project onto her. And she'd just basked in her own pleasure, in the way they'd been connected, like one person. She hadn't had to wonder if she'd been right, because she could feel that she had been. That they'd been in perfect sync.

And that was a new experience. She didn't feel like there were ghosts hovering in the background anymore. She hadn't realized how much of herself had still be wrapped up in things from the past. How afraid she'd been of letting it go. Because clinging to it had been less scary than moving on.

"I just want you to know, that really was the best ever," she said.

He smiled. "You're very good for my ego."

"As if your ego needed inflating."

"It may not have needed it. At least not from just any woman. From you it means a lot more than that. So much more than empty flattery."

She cleared her throat, tried to deny the tender feelings that were swirling in her stomach. "I'm definitely staying in your bed tonight."

"Good." They walked down the hall hand in hand and he pushed the door open to his room, scooping her into his arms again as he had at the beach. "Shower first though. I'm still sandy."

He carried her into the bathroom and set her down on the bright white marble floor before turning on the water in the shower.

She turned and caught her reflection in the mirror. There were red splotches on her body, from sand and Stavros's whiskers. Her cheeks were pink from the sun, her hair tumbled beyond reason, stringy from the salt water. Her scar was still there. Still impossible to ignore.

But her eyes…they looked so happy.

She lowered her hand and ran her fingertips across the line that ran below her belly button.

"It's nothing to worry about," he said, wrapping his arms around her from behind and lowering her hand. "You're beautiful."

"Do you know…you're the first person besides my doctor to see me since I've had that scar."

"I didn't know," he said.

"Well, that was… This," she said, moving her hand back to the scar, "was the end of my marriage."

"He divorced you because you got a hysterectomy?"

She but her lip and shook her head. "No. I divorced him after he wouldn't come to the hospital to see me. To sit with me. After I came home and all he would do was look at me like…like I'd betrayed him."

"Bastard."

She shook her head. "I don't know. Maybe not. Maybe… maybe I did the wrong thing. Maybe if we would have kept trying it would have worked. Maybe the first four years of trying weren't enough. Maybe if there would have been four more years, or IVF or something…it would have worked. I was the one who couldn't take it anymore. My doctor told me the hysterectomy would make my pain go away and so I jumped at the chance."

"What about adoption? Why wouldn't he adopt a child?"

She swallowed. "It wasn't the same to him. It...wasn't what he wanted." She would have done it. Gladly. Happily.

"Jessica—" he turned her so that she was facing him "—how can you think you made a bad decision? And what business did he have making you feel bad for dealing with pain the way you had to? It wasn't his pain. It wasn't his right to make the decision. You said yourself he did his best to ignore your pain. It wasn't his right to make you suffer for trying to make it stop."

"Sometimes I think so, too," she said, her voice breaking. "A lot of the time I do. For the last couple months before the procedure I was on a steady pain-pill diet. That made me feel a bit happier, but it also made me sleepy. Made my brain foggy and made me unable to do my job."

"That's unacceptable. I can't believe you were in so much pain. I can't believe he didn't care." He shook his head. "That's too much," he said, his voice rough.

"I know," she whispered. "And he never...he never wanted to know how bad it was. He just didn't...he didn't want things to change. He didn't want a sick wife that couldn't stand to be touched. Didn't want a woman who was broken. It wasn't what he signed on for."

"He *never* asked you how badly you hurt?" Stavros touched her cheek. "He didn't care?"

"I don't know. I don't...I was so convinced he loved me. He was my husband. But on this side of it, I get angry. I wonder how you could watch someone suffer and only care about how it made you feel. I... And he said I was a bitch. But I wasn't." Her voice caught a sob sticking in her chest. "I wasn't. He was a bastard. And he didn't love me.

He didn't even have the decency to divorce me. He made me do it so he could hate me for that, too."

"And you did what you had to do. For yourself. And it was right. You know that, don't you?" His expression was so earnest, so impossibly sincere. It made her heart ache.

"I do. But then sometimes I think I gave up too quickly." *I would be a mother.* Her own words echoed in her head. "I'll never know if I could have conceived if..."

"And then you would have stayed with a man who loved the ideal better than he loved you. You don't deserve that."

She laughed. "Funny you should say that. About the ideal. I always think his new wife looks too much like me for comfort."

"He's remarried?"

"Yes. And they have a baby. The sad part? I cried for two days when I found out she was pregnant. I hated her. I hated her so much. And that was so stupid. So wrong."

He shook his head. "Not wrong. You're human."

"Yeah. I am. Too human. But you're right. I do deserve better than him. Better than being the vehicle for his dreams. Better than being his failed dream. He was able to move on and have the exact same thing. I can't. I am who I am. I have the body I have."

"You say that, that you can't leave yourself, but that he can move on, but you overlook something."

"What?" she whispered.

He cupped her face, his thumbs moving over her cheekbones. "He can't leave himself. He's a sad, selfish person. And that's who he is. He won't grow or change. He'll never understand what he lost. His punishment is living with himself. And living without you."

"Oh," she breathed, words failing her completely.

"Come here." He took her hand and led her into the shower. His hands slid over her curves, the water making his touch slick. It wasn't sexual, even though it did arouse her. His touch was comforting.

She had him turn around so she could rinse the sand from his skin. Kiss the place a rock had bit into his flesh while they'd made love. They helped dry each other off, and then they got into bed.

He pulled her against the curve of his body, his arms so strong, his heat warming her.

It was so intimate. It felt far more intimate than anything she'd ever experienced. Because for the first time she felt like the man in her bed understood her. That there wasn't a secret thought in her mind she knew he wouldn't approve of.

Stavros felt like her ally. Sadly, most of the time her husband had felt like an enemy.

Her pain had caused him pain, so he hadn't allowed her to talk about it. Her escape from pain had been unacceptable to him, so he hadn't supported it. His words had wounded her. Flayed the skin from her bones.

But Stavros's words were healing.

"He really let you go through that by yourself?" His fingers grazed her scar.

"Yes. He didn't want me to do it."

He swore, a truly foul word in Greek that she knew roughly translated to something that would be physically impossible for her ex to do to himself. She laughed. "I appreciate how strongly you feel about it. But I've been my own champion for long enough that I don't need your anger." Was it so wrong that she wanted it? That it soothed her?

He turned her so she was facing him. "I need to be angry at him. For me."

Her throat tightened and tears stung her eyes. "Oh."

"He should have been there for you."

"He couldn't do it. He couldn't stand that I was killing our dreams. And without those dreams…there was no point."

"I don't believe that, Jess. You're enough to fulfill a man's dreams all on your own."

His words hung between them. She couldn't speak. She didn't bother to wipe away the tears that were falling down her cheeks. Tears it felt so good to finally be able to cry.

When Stavros woke up the next morning, Jessica was lying across the end of the bed, playing a game on her iPad. Her lips were pursed in concentration, her focus on the screen. She must have gone back to her room to get both the computer and a set of pajamas that consisted of a thin T-shirt and some very short shorts.

But she'd come back to his room. That thought brought him more pleasure than it ought to. "What are you doing?" He sat up and leaned over to get a good view of the screen.

"Oh." She turned and looked at him, the impact of her smile carrying all the force of a prize fighter's right hook. "Waiting for you to wake up."

"How do you play the game?"

"You shoot these little birds out of the slingshot and try to hit the pigs." She demonstrated by drawing one slender finger over the touch screen and aiming her feathered bullet at its target. "Yes!" She sat up after she hit her target, pumping her fist.

He laughed, this moment, this one where she was so happy, so relaxed, where he felt the same things, was one he would cling to always. One he would hold inside of him to keep. To treasure.

You are weak. You find it too easy to grow attached to this woman.

He had always feared as much. That he was as weak, as

governed by his emotions as his father, as his brother. That it would be his ruin, the ruin of his country.

But he didn't see how it could be. Looking at Jessica now, being with her, he felt strong. Stronger than he had in his life. More vulnerable in some ways too, but he wondered if it was good.

Then he wondered about his sanity.

"High score!" she said.

He smiled. "Don't you do a dance when you get high scores?"

She treated him to a bland look. "I told you, you don't get to see my dance."

"So, I can see you naked, but I can't see you dance?"

She stood on the bed and looked over her shoulder. "Don't tell anyone about this."

"I wouldn't dare."

She swayed her hips from side to side, her arms moving in time, her lips pulled to the left. She twirled in a circle, continuing in the same motion. He felt, for a moment, like he was watching himself from a distant place. An observer rather than a participant. Like it couldn't be real. This snatch of happiness, this moment of pure connection and silliness with another person. He had never felt anything like it.

His heart seemed to draw tight around itself and squeeze hard. The same heart he had professed not to have.

She plopped back down onto her knees in front of him. "There. Now I've done it."

He leaned in and kissed her. "Amazing."

She was amazing. What she made him feel was amazing. He felt different. He wanted to fight against it. He wanted to embrace it, and all the changes he could feel her making inside of him.

Just take this time. Just this time.

He put everything into the kiss, into losing himself in it. In her.

For once, he didn't want to think. He only wanted to feel.

They spent the next week in Greece. Jessica handled clients remotely, and Stavros went to work in the city, or worked from his office in the villa. And mostly they had a lot of sex.

Jessica was pretty sure she had a perma-grin from all the ecstasy she'd been exposed to over the past seven days. She was a little worried, though, because she didn't seem to be getting tired of him. Worse, she missed him a lot when he was working, or when she was working. And if he got up to work on his computer at night, she would wake up, feeling his absence almost immediately.

She'd been sleeping in her own bed since well before her divorce, but it had been so easy to get used to having someone again. No, not just someone. Because even after eight years of sharing a bed with Gil he hogged the covers and pushed her to the edge of the bed.

Stavros hogged the covers sometimes. And he certainly took up more than his half of the king-size bed. But she was content to curl around him and let him hold her. And she didn't really mind that he kept most of the blankets. Because she liked having him there. Liked waking up and seeing his face first thing. Liked having him be the last thing she saw before she went to sleep.

That was a bit of a problem. Because this was temporary. They had three weeks left.

That sucked big-time.

They were also going to have to figure out how to make it work in Kyonos, which would be its own problem.

She walked into Stavros's—now their—bedroom just in time to see him walking out of the bathroom with a white towel slung low on his lean hips, his muscles shifting pleasantly as he ran his fingers through his dark, damp hair.

"Hey, stranger," she said.

He turned and looked at her, his smile making her heart stop beating for a moment. "Did you get any work done?"

"Uh…yeah. I had a woman from India contact me. She's from a very wealthy family and she wants to use my contacts to find someone better than the guy her parents are pushing her toward. She seems fun. I'm looking forward to it."

She was looking forward to matching anyone except Stavros, really.

"You sound excited."

"I am."

"I understand if you have to travel once we're back in Kyonos," he said. "If you need to go and meet this client."

"I probably will." She didn't really like to think about it. To consider wasting nights away from him when their time was already so limited.

"You can use my plane."

"Oh, no, I don't want to do that."

He put his hands on his hips and her eyes were drawn to the cut lines that ran down beneath the towel, an arrow to an even more interesting part of his anatomy. "Jessica, don't be difficult."

Annoyance coursed through her, battling against the arousal being near him all damp, fresh and half-naked had caused. "Tough luck, Prince Sexy, I am difficult, if you hadn't noticed. And I'm not going to take advantage of you. My expenses are all worked into the fees I charge my clients. I'm a businesswoman. A very successful one. Maybe not quite on your level, but I do very well for myself."

"I know that. But if you use airports, it will all take longer. I can have you flown any time, day or night, in superior comfort in half the time."

"Well. Yes. But still, it's not my plane."

"Then I'll sell you a ticket."

She narrowed her eyes. "For?"

"If I say sexual favors will you knee me in the groin?"

She bit the inside of her cheek to keep from smiling and offered him a deadly glare. "Yes."

He named an insultingly low figure.

"No dice," she said. "I'll be flying out of Kyonos International. Deal with it."

He reached out and grabbed her around the waist and tugged her to him. "You are a pain."

"Yeah, so? You like it." She grabbed his towel and tugged it, letting it fall to his feet.

He smiled down at her, then kissed her nose. "Maybe."

"What time are we headed back to Kyonos?"

"This afternoon." His tone said what his words didn't. That it was too soon. That even though they still had time together, the real world would be intruding. That he didn't want that.

She didn't, either. She wanted to freeze time and live in the bubble for a while. Where reality wasn't such an intrusive force. Where chemistry was enough of a reason to be with someone. Where her ability to produce children, to be a figurehead and not just be Jessica, wouldn't be essential to her being with Stavros.

But that wasn't real. That couldn't last. And they both just had to buck up and deal with it.

"All right. I guess I should get packed then."

He kissed her lips. "Later." He kissed her neck, her shoulder.

"Yes. Later."

Reality could have a turn later. She'd spend another hour in the fantasy.

CHAPTER ELEVEN

STAVROS idly wished he felt a sense of homecoming when he walked into the Kyonosian palace. He didn't. It felt like the walls had started to close in. A sensation he wasn't very fond of. Somehow, even the high ceiling seemed to reach down to him, as though it was trying to crush him.

Apt indeed.

He walked down the empty corridor and to his father's office. He pushed the door open. "Your Highness," he said, inclining his head.

"Stavros." His father stood, his hands clasped behind his back. "How was Greece?"

"Everything is in order. My hotels there are doing well."

"And your marriage?"

"Have I arranged it? Is that what you mean?"

"For all the money you've spent on that matchmaker I should think it would be settled by now," his father said, his voice gruff, his focus turned back to the papers spread over his desk.

Ah, yes, his matchmaker. His lover. The woman who held his body and his soul captive. The woman who made him feel more than any one person had ever made him feel in his life. The woman who made him question the core of his existence. That matchmaker.

He tightened his jaw. "Ms. Carter introduced me to several outstanding candidates."

"And?"

"And I've selected one." The words threatened to strangle him.

"Name?"

"Victoria Calder. She's English. Beautiful."

"Fertile?"

That made his stomach clench. "According to all of her paperwork, yes. That's part of why I hired Jessica. She handled that unpleasant pre-screening process for me. No potential scandals. No nasty medical surprises." It galled him to say the words. Because it made him feel no better than Jessica's ex. A man looking for a woman who met his terms. A man choosing a woman who was a mere placeholder, rather than a person.

Was that what he was? What he was doing?

Yes. It was.

"Excellent. When do you announce?"

"Not for a while." Not until he had to. Not until he'd taken the chance to draw out every possible moment with Jessica. "We'll make an appearance at Eva and Mak's ball."

"Excellent. I'm looking forward to it. This will be a good thing for, Kyonos. I'm certain of it."

"Yes," Stavros said, feeling no certainty at all.

Stavros nodded and exited the office. And fought the urge to punch the stone wall. Of course he was the only one to never disappoint his father. To never dishonor the Drakos name.

No, but his father had. His father had given up. Receded behind a veil of grief after his wife died. After he drove his oldest son away.

Stavros had never had the option of letting anyone down. He'd had to fix everything. Had had to pretend that everything in him was fixed because someone had to stand firm. He'd never had the luxury of feeling. Of falling apart.

He wanted to now. He wanted to give in to himself. He wanted to follow the emotions Jessica had brought back to him. Wanted to hold on to them forever.

He strode out of the palace and got into his car. He liked to drive himself whenever he could. He needed it. Because it was one of the few times he was able to be alone. When he was able to stop putting on a show.

Alone and with Jessica. Those were the only times that was possible. He shook his head and started the engine.

The streets in Thysius were crowded, but it didn't take long for him to get to his penthouse apartment. It was fortified with security, of course, but for the most part he didn't worry. Kyonos was a small country, and he'd always felt safe there.

He parked his car in the underground garage and touched his fingerprints to the scanner on the elevator. He would have to move into the palace eventually. But for now he would relish his freedom.

The doors to the lift slid open and revealed his penthouse, open and stark. It was a man's home, for sure. And it was modern in the extreme, his rebellion against the ultra old-fashioned stylings of the castle. One of his many small rebellions. Rebellions that, he could see now, were the lingering bits of a man he'd thought long banished. The man Jessica made him feel like again.

He looked on the couch and saw a cream-colored chenille blanket draped over the black leather. He smiled and picked it up, running his fingers over the soft fabric. There was a romance novel on the glass coffee table. He picked it up and flipped through a few pages, careful to save the spot it had been left open to.

"You're home."

He looked up and saw Jessica standing in the entryway of the living room and his breath stopped for a moment. She was so beautiful. She added something to his home, something soft and feminine, something it had been lacking. Something he'd certainly never thought it lacked before.

"Yes. How was your day?"

"Great. I spoke with Harneet on the phone for a while, and that was nice. Got an idea of the type of man she was looking for. I think I'm going to fly out and have lunch with her sometime during the weekend."

"The ball for Mak and Eva is coming up in a couple of weeks."

She nodded. "I know."

"Will you be there?"

"I... Probably not."

He nodded. "I wish you could be."

"Gee, not to hurt your feelings or anything, Stavros, but watching you make your public debut with Victoria ranks right up there with shoving glass under my fingernails for fun." She crossed her arms beneath her breasts and cocked her hip to the side.

"That isn't why I want you there."

"No? But that's what you'll be doing there. I know...I know that's what's going to happen. We both know. But that doesn't mean I want to watch it."

She turned away from him and he caught her arm. "Why are you suddenly mad at me?"

"For having all the sensitivity of a bull elk."

"I want you with me. If I could, I would fly to India with you and hover around the lunch table while you talked to Harneet. But I can't do that, can I? Because that's when the press would wonder, and since I am about to try and show that I'm making a move toward marriage we both know that can't happen."

"I know. So what do you want me to do at the ball? Hover around the edges and stare longingly at you?"

"No, I want you to hover around the edges so I can stare longingly at you."

She frowned. "That doesn't make any sense."

"None of this does. None of it. It hasn't from the moment I met you. You make me want things, Jessica. And I can't have any of them."

She closed her eyes. "Neither can I, Stavros."

"Jessica…"

"You know? I think I'm going to call Harneet and ask if I can meet with her earlier. I might leave tomorrow. I should be back in to help arrange any future endeavors with Victoria." She opened her eyes, her resolve clearly set, her chin pushed out at a stubborn angle.

"You're still helping me with Victoria?"

"It's my job, Stavros. And nothing changes that. Because nothing changes what has to happen."

"True enough." She was right. No matter what, he had to marry. And really, given her qualifications, Victoria was the woman he needed to marry. "I have to work early."

He knew what she was doing. Getting them both some distance. And they desperately needed it. They'd been in each other's pockets during their time in Greece, and she was staying in his home now. They needed space.

She nodded. "I'll probably be gone when you get home." She took a deep breath. "And I should probably sleep in my own room tonight."

He shook his head. "No. Sleep with me." Because even if they needed that kind of distance he wasn't sure he could stand it. "Please."

She nodded. "Okay."

Tomorrow they would take a break. He could clear his head.

He could set his focus back on what had to be done, and not on the insidious little fantasy that had burrowed beneath his skin over the past few weeks.

A fantasy that was simply impossible, no matter how badly he might want it.

Jessica felt like something that had washed up on the beach back at their Grecian villa by the time she got back from India a few days later. Definitely more bedraggled seagull than mermaid.

Their Grecian villa. What a silly way to think of it. It was Stavros's Grecian villa. She had simply shared his bed there for a while.

And now the idea was for her to share his penthouse for the next few weeks. She sighed. She'd done a lot of thinking on her out-of-town days, about whether or not what they were doing was a good idea.

The conclusion she'd come to was that it was a very bad idea, but then, she'd known it was a bad idea from moment one. They both had. They just hadn't been stronger than the desire.

She closed her eyes as she lifted her hand to the finger-print reader on his elevator, one he'd programmed to accept her touch, and she knew that no amount of realization about the badness of their arrangement had made her any stronger.

She had a feeling Stavros was just as aware of the folly of it as she was. And that he was just as unlikely to stop.

She stepped inside and leaned her head against the metal wall as the doors slid closed and the lift carried her up the penthouse.

She'd strongly considered staying over in India for a while longer, if only to miss the ball. She didn't want to see Stavros with Victoria. She couldn't play disinterested party anymore. She couldn't separate Stavros her lover from Stavros her client. It was impossible.

Everything inside of her seemed to be tangled around him, and he seemed to be completely tangled up in her life.

The doors to the lift opened and she stepped out into his immaculate living room. She knew the housekeeper had been in, because if there was one thing she'd learned about Stavros, it was that his neat-as-a-pin modern-looking homes weren't kept in that fashion by him.

He left his clothes on the floor. And very often he left dishes in the sink.

He's not perfect.

No, he very much wasn't perfect, but she wasn't sure she cared about that, either. The reminder meant nothing, because if anything, being so aware that he wasn't perfect only gave validity to the feelings that were eating her from the inside out.

She stalked over to the fridge and pulled out a bottle of milk. It was nearly empty. She could add that to his list of sins. Putting a nearly empty milk bottle back into the fridge. And he'd probably forgotten to tell his housekeeper that he needed milk.

She padded down the hall and pushed open the door to his office. It was empty. He wasn't here.

It was easy to pretend, standing in his house, walking around as thought she belonged. Like they belonged together. But she'd had a lot of time to think while she'd been away. Even if she could have him, if he gave it all up for her...she couldn't let him.

Because she'd been the broken dreams of one man already. Stavros would only grow to resent her, too, as she tried, once again, to fit into a position she simply wasn't made for.

She took her phone out of her pocket and saw that she

had three new text messages. She'd put it on silent and forgotten about it.

She opened the first one.

Will you be back in time for dinner?

It was long past dinner so the answer to that was no.
She opened the next message.

Call me when you land so I know you're safe.

A smile curved her lips and she ran her fingers over the
screen of her phone. Why did he have to do things like that?
She scrolled to the next one.

Jess, I miss you.

A tear slid down her cheek. Had she really mourned
how hard it was for her to cry only a few weeks ago? Now
it seemed so easy. What had he done to her?

She curled her fingers around her phone and thought
about calling. She wasn't sure it was a good idea. In fact,
she was almost certain it was a bad idea. She would probably cry all over him. Maybe blurt out things she had no
business thinking, much less saying to him.

She hit the reply button and typed in: I miss you, too.
She deleted it. And took a breath.

I'm here. Where are you?

Her phone pinged a second later.

Can I send a car for you in an hour? I want to show you
something.

She'd wanted to rest for a while, but that didn't seem important anymore for some reason. The only thing that mattered was seeing him.

Sure. Give me time to get the travel grime off.

His return message came quickly. I'll be waiting for you.

She'll wonder where Hattie is. Hattie, too, was expendable, a necessary sacrifice. Throbbing thing that manacled her aching arm.

I am more sore today than I was yesterday, or perhaps I just feel pain more deeply today.

CHAPTER TWELVE

THE car stopped in front of a lighthouse. The tower was dark, no signs of life anywhere in the small stone house. Jessica gathered up the skirt of her white, flowing gown, the one she'd purchased in Greece with Stavros in mind, and stepped out into the warm evening.

She looked up and saw Stavros, standing in front of the whitewashed building, his hands in his pockets, the top button of his shirt undone. He looked different. And so wonderfully the same. She had the strangest sense of being home. A feeling she hadn't had in so long she hadn't realized the absence of it.

"What's this?" she asked.

"A place I'd almost forgotten about. The palace is there," he said, pointing to glimmering lights on a hill. "Technically, this is part of the grounds. It hasn't been used for years. I used to come here whenever I could sneak away. I wanted to see it again and then, when I did...I wanted to show it to you."

"Why?" she asked, the tightness in her chest spreading, climbing into her throat, making it hard to breathe.

"Because you... Come with me, maybe then I can explain." He held his hand out and she took it, his fingers warm and strong as they closed around hers. He led her into the house. It was cool inside, the thick stone walls providing protection from the heat that still lingered in the air.

There was no furniture in the house. Not even a chair. "No one lives here?" she asked. "Well, that's actually obvious."

"No one has lived here in years. It's been vacant since I was a kid. Come with me." He led her through to the back of the house, to a small, rounded doorway with a steep set of stairs. She followed him up the curving staircase, her fingers laced with his.

They ended at the top of the tower, a small, clean room with a lantern at the center. Here there was a chair. And blankets laid across the floor.

"I used to come here and watch the ships," he said. "Imagine where they had been. Where they were going. Dream I was here, keeping them from hitting the rocks. Keeping watch."

"You've always been protecting people, haven't you?" she whispered.

He walked over to the lantern, pressing his hand against the glass case. "It was different. It wasn't real, first of all. And second…I remember caring more then for imaginary ships and dangers, feeling more for created peril, than I've cared about anything since. It was a child's game. Silly. But I had a passion for it. I felt something. I…I lost that. I lost it very purposefully. I…I wanted to show you, because I thought you might understand."

"If I ask what I'm supposed to understand does that mean I fail?" she asked, her heart pounding, her stomach weighted down. With desire. Fear. Longing.

"I want to feel again, Jess. For the first time since I was a child…I want it back. I want to care. You brought it back to me. Passion. I hadn't felt a passion for anything in so long…."

"Sure you have. I know you've had a lot of lovers besides me," she said, trying to steer the conversation away from where she feared it was going.

"Lust isn't the same as passion. It's not the same as… It's not the same as this. I used to think…I have thought for so long…that emotion was weakness. That caring for something, for someone, made you weak. And then I kept thinking of this place. Of how much I cared. Of how seriously I took even an imagined responsibility…because of love, really."

"Stavros…"

He moved to her, his eyes locked with hers. "You look like a goddess," he said, reverting to the physical. And she was so very glad he had.

"I had a layover in Greece and I remembered you saying… I remembered you saying I should wear a *pallas*. It's really vintage," she said, trying to force a smile. "Nearly a hundred years old, or so I was told."

He closed his eyes and leaned in, pressing his forehead to hers. She thought her heart might burst. "I need…I need you. Now."

His body was shaking with desire and that was something she could handle. This was what they both needed. The physical. To remember that this was about desire, mutual lust that they were both trying to satisfy.

It had been the reclamation of her sexuality. Of her body. A release of the things in her past, letting go of any remaining desire to be the person she had been. And she could never regret that. She wouldn't let herself.

She also wouldn't let it be more. There were so many things Stavros needed. So many responsibilities he needed a wife to help him fulfill. Things she couldn't possibly do.

"Are we… No one will come up here, right?"

"I told your driver he could leave. I drove myself." He

moved his hand to her hip, then slid it around to her lower back, to the curve of her bottom. "This dress is not fit for public. It's far too erotic."

"There isn't a single button on this dress to fuel your fantasies."

A strange expression crossed his face. "No. But I don't think it was ever the buttons." There was a heavy undertone to the statement, a meaning she didn't want to search for. Because there was no point. "I think it's been you all along."

She sucked in a sharp breath, ignoring the pain that lodge in her chest. This had to be about sex. Only sex.

If she let it be more…she just couldn't let it be more. Because it had to end.

"*You* have buttons, on the other hand." She put her hands on his chest and started working at the buttons of his dress shirt, revealing teasing hints of his perfect chest. She parted the fabric and slid her hands over his bronzed skin. "Oh, Stavros, I don't think I could ever get tired of this." The words were far too candid, far too honest, but she couldn't have held them back if she'd tried.

They were true. She could never tire of him. Not of his body, not of his humor, or his drive. Not of that spark of rebellion in him. That glorious bit of himself that could never be fully tamed.

She swallowed and pushed his shirt and jacket from his shoulders, leaving him nothing more than a pair of dark slacks.

He leaned in and pressed a kiss to her bare shoulder, his hand searching for where her dress was held together, at the waistband, taking the end of the fabric and tugging it from its secure place. He let it fall and she felt the top of the dress loosen.

He stepped back, his eyes appraising.

She put her hand on her shoulder and pushed the large

swath of fabric that crossed her body down, exposing her breasts to him. She watched his face as she slowly unwrapped herself, memorized the agony and ecstasy she saw there. No one had ever looked at her like that before. No one had ever made her feel so vulnerable and so powerful at the same time.

Stavros did it as effortlessly as most people drew breath.

He removed his pants and underwear quickly and shoved them to the side, naked and aroused for her enjoyment. And she did enjoy him. He was a sensual feast, amazing for all of her senses. To touch, to taste, to see. Stavros never disappointed.

She was about to go to him, to wrap her hand around his erection, but he moved first, dropping to his knees before her. He kissed her stomach, pushed her panties down and slid his finger through her slick folds, drawing the moisture from her body over her clitoris.

"You're so very good at that," she said, holding tightly to his shoulders. It was so much more than sexual skill, and she knew it.

Because her response to him went well beyond a basic physical reaction. It grabbed her, low and deep, and held her in thrall, no matter what was happening. Whether they were naked, alone on a beach, or fully clothed in a crowded ballroom, Stavros held her. All of her.

"The pleasure is mine," he said, rising back to his feet and kissing her mouth. "You have no idea."

He walked her backward to the blankets that had been spread on the floor, and held her tightly as he lowered them both to the soft surface.

"I've been expertly seduced," she said. "You planned this."

"I very much did," he said, not a hint of apology in his tone.

"One of the things I…" She stopped herself before she could say the words that were ringing inside of her head, her heart. "You and I think alike," she said. No feelings. No love. Oh, please not that.

He cupped her face and kissed her again while his other hand teased her breasts.

"You don't get to have all the fun," she said, sliding her hand down so that she could cup his erection.

He closed his eyes, the expression on his face one of a man completely given over to pleasure, completely lost in it. She memorized that, too. Watched him until her own pleasure became so intense she had to close her eyes.

She clung to the image of his face. Made sure it stayed in the forefront of her mind.

She clung to his shoulders, wrapped her leg around his hips, and he angled himself so that he slid inside of her. She bit her lip to keep from crying out. To keep from crying period.

He rolled her to her back and she parted her legs. He pushed in deeper and she arched into him, rocking her body in time with each of his thrusts.

There was no sound in the room beyond fractured gasps and short breaths, echoing from the stone walls. She dug her fingernails into his shoulders, trying to find something solid to keep her on earth. To keep her from losing herself completely.

If it wasn't already too late.

A sob climbed in her throat and burst from her as she fell over the edge, her orgasm stealing control of everything, drowning her in pleasure. She couldn't think, she could only cling to Stavros as wave after wave of bliss crashed down over her.

"Stavros," she said, tears spilling from her eyes.

He shuddered his own release, his muscles tight, her name on his lips.

After he pulled her against him, pressed kisses to her cheeks, her forehead, her mouth. His hands, hands that had been demanding in their pursuit and deliverance of pleasure, were gentle as he smoothed them over her curves.

She rested her head on his chest, tears drying on her cheeks, her eyes getting heavy in the aftermath of her release.

"I love you, Jess."

The words hit like a blow. She closed her eyes against the pain. Against the regret. Against the desire to turn and say them back to him. She couldn't. And he didn't mean it. He couldn't. He had responsibilities, responsibilities that far surpassed getting imaginary ships to the shore, and she knew that fulfilling those obligations meant the world to him.

And if he tried to put her in that position of being the one to fulfill them with...she could do nothing but fail. Could do nothing but watch the sweet tenderness in his eyes flatten into a cold, bitter hatred.

You're such a selfish bitch, Jessica. The words were always there. So easy to hear. So easy to remember.

She wouldn't be. Not now. No matter how much she wished she could. Tonight, though...she had to let herself have tonight.

She curled tighter into Stavros's embrace and hoped he wouldn't notice the tears that fell onto his chest.

Stavros knew the revelation should terrify him. But it didn't. Not even hours later, after he drove them back to his penthouse. After he laid her down in his bed and made love with her again. And now, as he lay in bed with Jessica curled up at his side.

He loved her.

He waited for something in him to crumble, for it to break and reveal his weakness. But it didn't. He felt reinforced. As though everything in Jessica, as though loving her, was shoring up his strength. Fueling it.

Love was different than he'd imagined. But then, Jessica was a different woman than he ever could have imagined.

He stroked her silky blond hair and watched her sleep, her cheek pillowed on his chest, and he wondered how he would ever face a future without her.

And he knew that if he was truly going to be the king, the man, he was meant to be, he needed her to be the one at his side.

CHAPTER THIRTEEN

IT WAS the coward's way out. To sneak out while he was sleeping. While the first edges of light were peeking over the mountains. But men did it all the time, didn't they? And wasn't it supposed to save everyone from a big emotional scene? She certainly needed to be saved from it.

Because he'd said he loved her. Loving her, being with her, would stop him from finding everything he'd said he wanted. She would never, ever allow herself to be blamed for a man's ruined life and broken dreams.

Never again.

She held her suitcase tightly to her body and walked across the apartment, heading for the elevator.

"What are doing?"

She turned and saw Stavros, still naked, his pants in his hand.

"I'm…I'm going."

"Why?"

She let out a breath. "Because it was now or in a few weeks, and I decided it should be now. We both knew this wasn't permanent, and the four-week time frame no longer works for me."

"Put your suitcase down." He tugged his pants on quickly, leaving the belt undone.

She shook her head. "No. I'm leaving."

"I love you."

"You don't want love. You told me that already. You don't believe in it…you don't."

"I love you," he repeated, the words breaking.

"Stop it," she said, her voice shaking. "Just stop."

"It's true, I do. I love you, Jessica." He sounded tormented, his voice raw and pained. And she had caused it.

"It doesn't matter, don't say it like it does. Like it ever could. So you love me? What does that mean?"

"What does it mean? You want to know what it means? It means that my world stops turning when you aren't in it, and when I see you I feel like I can breathe again. That's what it means. It means I've found my passion again. That I'm not hollow anymore."

She dropped the suitcase then, pressing her hand to her chest. "No. What does it mean? Practically. In the real world. Because we both know that loving me doesn't make me able to have your royal babies, which means I'm not good enough to wear the royal crown. We both know it, so what's the point in any of this?"

"The point," he said, taking a step toward her, his expression deadly, "was to make me forget you. To make me get over this…need that I feel for you. To make it so the thought of a future without you didn't make me feel like my guts were being torn from my body. That was the point. We failed on all counts. I have…feelings, Jessica. I was so dead for so long and then you came into my life. And I couldn't put you at a distance, and I couldn't stop myself from being me when I was with you. I love you, and it's not simple, but it is so damned important because it changed me."

"You just think that, Stavros. Because of the sex. Because you love skirting the edge of convention as much as you possibly can and oh, how shocking would a divorced infertile queen be? But it's not real. It's temporary. Victoria is real. She can be your princess, your queen. And she can give you everything that you need. I can't."

"That is unfair, Jessica. Don't tell me what I feel."

"You would hate me in the end, Stavros. You would."

He stood there, his dark eyes pinned on her. "Tell me you love me, too."

She shook her head, the words tearing at her throat, struggling to escape. She wouldn't let them. She wouldn't make it worse.

He crossed the room in three strides, cupped her face, his hands so gentle, his expression so dark and fierce. "Tell me."

"No," she whispered, taking a step back and picking up her suitcase again. "I'm glad that you…found yourself with me, or whatever you want to call it. But you don't need me to feel passion. You don't need me to have emotions. I hope that things with Victoria go well. I hope you…I hope you love her some day." She didn't. She never wanted him to love her. She wanted his love forever, and if that made her small, she didn't care. But she would lie now. She would preserve what pride she had left now. "Please don't pay me. Not for any of it."

He didn't say anything, he only stood there, his body tense. He looked like he might try to physically stop her from leaving. But he didn't. He only watched her as she turned away. And she didn't look back. She couldn't.

Stavros could only watch as Jessica walked into the elevator, as the doors closed behind her. He could only concentrate on taking breaths, each one causing raw, physical pain.

She was wrong. She was wrong about everything. At least as far as he was concerned. He did need her. He needed her more than he needed air. She had brought something back to him. Something he'd long thought dead. Something he'd been glad was gone.

He hadn't allowed himself to feel the pain of his mother's

death. There had been too much to do. The people around him had fallen apart and his country had fallen into chaos. He had vowed he would never let that happen again.

But now…now he felt as though his insides had broken apart, that each breath dug a shard of the destroyed pieces into his flesh.

He looked at the wineglass sitting on the counter. Something Jessica must have had earlier. He walked to the kitchen area and released a growl as he picked up the glass and hurled it at the wall. It exploded into a million unfixable pieces.

And it didn't heal anything inside of him.

He feared nothing ever would.

CHAPTER FOURTEEN

Stavros stood in front of his father's desk and looked down at the ring, nestled in a velvet box, glittering at him. The old-world vintage style of the piece mocked him. Made his heart feel as if it was shattering. Which should be impossible since it had shattered days ago.

"You have chosen then?" his father asked, looking at him from his seated position, his grey brows raised.

"Victoria is a wonderful choice for Kyonos. She will be a good queen." He reached out and curled his fingers around the box, lifting it from the desk. He raised it to his eyes, studied it.

"Your mother's ring," his father said. "She loved the unusual antique setting."

He laughed, a bitter sound. "I know a woman like that."

"I get the feeling she is not the woman you will be offering the ring to?"

Stavros shook his head. "Jessica Carter is not fit to be queen of Kyonos. Not by the standards set out for me. If I were to marry her, it would cause great scandal." Something in his chest burned, spread through his blood like fire. The thought of life without her, day after day, faded and brittle, devoid of color, of beauty.

"And if you weren't going to be king, Stavros?"

Stavros looked at his father. "But I am going to be king. And that means I have to think of more than just myself."

King Stephanos paused for a moment, his expression grave. "If you care for nothing, you'll never be able to care for your people. Not as you should."

"Love makes you weak," Stavros said. "I've seen it." He'd never condemned his father to his face. For some reason, now it poured from him. His renewed passion came with a renewal of every emotion. Happiness, and anger. Deep and hopeless sadness.

"What made me weak was the absence of love," his father said slowly. "I cared for nothing after your mother died. Not the country. Not even my children. And so I left it all abandoned. Which is easy to do when you no longer care."

Stavros had never seen it that way before. And yet, it rang true in his soul. Jessica made him feel real again. In touch as he hadn't been for years. She brought passion out in him, to be better, do better.

He looked at the ring again and an image flashed into his mind. One of him sliding the ring onto Jessica's finger. He tried to make the image turn into Victoria. He couldn't. There was only one vision for his future. Only one woman he could have at his side.

"If I marry Jessica there will be scandal," he said, his voice rough. "We will not have an heir. Her past will be fodder for the papers." He raised his focus to his father, who was regarding him silently. "And I don't give a damn. I love her. That's all that matters."

He turned away, his heart pounding hard.

"And that is why you will be twice the king that I have been, Stavros. You are a man who should follow his heart. Because your heart is strong."

He curled his fingers more tightly around the ring box. "It is now. Because of her."

* * *

"Jessica." She heard Stavros's voice through her hotel room door and she froze.

Why was he here? Why was he tormenting her? She'd been miserable for the past forty-eight hours. And she was planning on being miserable on the plane ride home. And then she was planning on being a sopping, miserable mess in North Dakota, so really, she didn't need his help.

Her entire body was heavy. The effort of dragging herself out of bed that morning had been nearly not worth it. Putting on pajamas last night hadn't been worth it, and she was still in yesterday's clothes because dressing hadn't seemed like it was worth it, either.

And now he was here. And she wanted to run to him and ignore reality so much it was nearly impossible to stop herself from flinging to door open and huddling against him.

"What do you want?" she said, knowing she sounded whiny and not caring. She felt whiny. She felt crushed.

"You. Open the door."

Her heart slammed against her breastbone. "Why?"

"Because I can tell you what it means now."

She swallowed and walked to the door, turning the dead bolt and unlinking the chain before pulling it open. "What?"

He gripped the edge of the door and the door frame. "I'm not marrying Victoria."

"What?" she asked again, taking a step back.

"I can't. I can't because you are the only woman that I want. I see you in my dreams, I see you when I'm awake and I close my eyes. I can't forget you. I don't want to forget you. I want you."

"But you...Victoria is perfect for you. She...she..." Jessica reached for her tablet computer, sitting on the arm of the couch, and swiped through a few screens until she found Victoria's file. "She is graceful, and wonderful and she can have your babies. She's beautiful and she does charities for homeless children. She's *perfect*."

"Yes, she is. There—" he pointed at her computer "—in writing, yes, she's perfect for my country. But you, Jessica Carter, you are perfect for me. And I don't care what you can't do, I only care what you do for me, what you give me. I care that when I'm with you I'm a better man. I have been closed off for years. What does it matter if I can give my people charm, an empty smile if I can give them nothing deeper than that? It doesn't matter. But you...you make me feel. You have forced me to find something in myself that's...real. To be more than a shell. I can't go back. I won't."

"Stavros, I... You can't do this. You can't. You have to have these things," she said, pointing to her computer again. "You have to. And if you don't..."

"If I don't, I'll be a better man for it. For pursuing what I want. For finding real passion. For ruling with everything I have in me. You, you helped me find it. Yes, I am expected to have a wife who can have heirs...but I won't. And that will have to be fine, it will be perfect, because my wife will be you. Unless you don't want me. Then...well, I'm not sure what I'll do then."

"Stavros—" her voice broke "—I want you. But I'm not going to be the cause of your unfulfilled vision. You want this so much. To be this perfect figurehead for your people. And I can't be the one to stop you from doing it. I've been that. I have been a man's broken dreams and I won't do it again. I can't. I can't watch love turn into resentment, and anger. I can't be more than I am. I am in this body, and I can only give so much."

A tear slid down her cheek, then another. Tears she realized had been stored up for the past few years of her life.

Anger and pain, and the anguish of being limited. Of not being enough.

Stavros moved to her, brushed her tears away with his thumb. "You are *everything*," he said, his voice rough. "You have given me everything. I didn't want love. Because I was so afraid of it, so afraid of the pain it could cause. Losing my mother devastated me. I just...shut down rather than dealing with it. I shut it all down. But you brought me back, you brought a part of me back and you restored it. I talked to my father. He told me the reason he let things fall apart was that he didn't care anymore. Not about anything. I wanted so badly not to be like him, not to lose myself to love, and I didn't realize I was him. Caring for nothing, going through the motions. But not now. Not since I met you."

He kissed her cheek. "Maybe on paper this doesn't work. But I don't think marriage is as simple as I believed it was. I can't just hire a wife the way I'd hire an assistant. I need a woman who will challenge me, who will push me, to be better, to do better. I know you are that woman. Most of all, I need the woman I love by my side."

"I love you," she said, letting the words come out. Finally. They felt like balm on her soul, healing old wounds that had never truly gone away. Until now. Until Stavros.

"I told you that once that you were enough of a dream for any man, and I stand by that statement now. I want nothing else. I want you."

She bit her lip. "I'm afraid you'll regret it. That you'll look at me every day and see...holes in me. All of the things I'm missing."

"Jessica, there are holes in me," he said, pressing his hand flat to his chest. "I am not perfect. But I believe you're the one who can fill the holes. The one who can make me stronger. Certainly the one who brings me joy."

She let out a sob. "I…I'm afraid you'll regret not having children."

"We can adopt children."

Shock bloomed in her stomach, making it hard to breathe. "But…adopted children couldn't take the throne, it doesn't solve the problem of heirs, it doesn't…"

"I'm not trying to solve a *problem* with adoption. If we want children, if we want to expand our family, we can adopt. We won't be the ones to produce the heirs. That's all right. I don't want another woman's children, I want yours. And by that I mean you're the one I want by my side raising my children. That's what matters anyway." He rested his forehead against hers. "That and if you love me. Because if you really love me, then nothing else matters."

"I do. I really do love you. But when we met you told me all the things you wanted and…"

"Because I was scared. A coward. I was trying to make things easier on myself. Going through life without caring is vain, but it's simple. I was going to marry a woman who would have been a placeholder, and you'll never be that. You make me want to be the king, the man, I didn't know I could be. You make me strong. Be my wife, Jessica. Please."

Every word, every line in his face, spoke of his sincerity. And if she thought back to their time, to the moment they'd first met, she knew it had started then. That every look, every touch, every kiss, had brought them to this point.

That every bit of pain before they met, had made them strong enough to stand here. Made them strong enough to make marriage work. To have love that lasted.

"I… Yes." Her heart lifted, happiness, true happiness, filling her, flooding her. Every place inside of her that had felt empty, incomplete, seemed filled now, with love.

"Don't ever feel like you aren't enough for me. You fill me. All the empty places in me."

She nodded. "I believe you."

"Jessica, this life won't always be easy. There will be press to deal with, and there are big responsibilities, long work hours and a lot of traveling. But I want you by my side for all of it. My queen, my lover, my partner."

"Yes," she said again, her voice stronger this time. "Stavros, I've loved before. But this is different. Because I feel like you're a part of me. I feel like you want me, and not me wrapped up as part of a dream, a fantasy. I truly believe that you love me, and not who you wish I was."

"I do. You aren't a dream. Far from it."

"Hey!" she said, laughing through her tears.

"What I mean is, you are too special, too unique for me to ever have dreamed up. I wrote down all the things I thought I needed in a wife, and I was delivered something completely different. I didn't truly know myself at all, or what I needed. Not until I met you."

"I must be the worst matchmaker in the world. I matched a woman to a prince and then…and then I got engaged to him. We are engaged, right?"

"Yes, we are. In fact—" he reached into his pocket and pulled out a white satin box "—this was my mother's." He opened the box and revealed a platinum, pear-cut diamond with intricate detail etched into the band. "It's been in our family for hundreds of years. When I saw it…when I saw it I knew there was only one woman I could give it to. It's perfect for you."

"You're right," she said. "You're so very right."

He took her hand in his and slid the ring onto her third finger. "It's like it was made for you."

She shook her head. "No, I think you were made for me."

Jessica leaned in and kissed him, pouring all of her love into the kiss. Now that she had Stavros, she didn't feel like she was missing anything.

"You fill all those places inside me that used to feel empty," she whispered.

He stoked her hair, his touch so warm and perfect. Even more perfect now that she knew she would have him forever. "As you do for me. I think you must have been my missing piece."

She closed her eyes and leaned into him. "For so long I felt like I was made wrong."

"No, *agápe mou,* you weren't made wrong. You were made for me."

* * * * *

THE FALLEN
GREEK BRIDE

JANE PORTER

For Randall Toye—thank you for
the friendship and support.

Jane Porter grew up on a diet of Mills & Boon
romances, reading late at night under the covers so
her mother wouldn't see! She wrote her first book
at age eight, and spent many of her high school and
college years living abroad, immersing herself in
other cultures and continuing to read voraciously.
Now Jane splits her time between rugged Seattle,
Washington, and the beautiful beaches of Hawaii,
with her sexy surfer and three very active sons.
Jane loves to hear from her readers. You can write
to her at PO Box 524, Bellevue, WA 98009, USA.
Or visit her website at www.janeporter.com

CHAPTER ONE

"WELCOME HOME, MY WIFE."

Morgan froze inside Villa Angelica's expansive marble and limestone living room with its spectacular floor-to-ceiling view of blue sky and sea, but saw none of the view, and only Drakon's face.

It had been five years since she'd last seen him. Five and a half years since their extravagant two-million-dollar wedding, for a marriage that had lasted just six months.

She'd dreaded this moment. Feared it. And yet Drakon sounded so relaxed and warm, so *normal,* as if he were welcoming her back from a little holiday instead of her walking out on him.

"Not your wife, Drakon," she said softly, huskily, because they both knew she hadn't been his anything for years. There had been nothing, no word, no contact, not after the flurry of legal missives that followed her filing for divorce.

He'd refused to grant her the divorce and she'd spent a fortune fighting him. But no attorney, no lawsuit, no amount of money could persuade him to let her go. Marriage vows, he'd said, were sacred and binding. She was his. And apparently the courts in Greece agreed with him. Or were bought by him. Probably the latter.

"You are most definitely still my wife, but that's not a conversation I want to have across a room this size. Do come in,

Morgan. Don't be a stranger. What would you like to drink? Champagne? A Bellini? Something a little stronger?"

But her feet didn't move. Her legs wouldn't carry her. Not when her heart was beating so fast. She was shocked by Drakon's appearance and wondered for a moment if it really was Drakon. Unnerved, she looked away, past his broad shoulders to the wall of window behind him, with that breathtaking blue sky and jagged cliffs and azure sea.

So blue and beautiful today. A perfect spring day on the Amalfi Coast.

"I don't want anything," she said, her gaze jerking back to him, although truthfully, a glass of cool water would taste like heaven right now. Her mouth was so dry, her pulse too quick. Her head was spinning, making her dizzy from nerves and anxiety. Who *was* this man before her?

The Drakon Xanthis she'd married had been honed, sleek and polished, a man of taut, gleaming lines and angles.

This tall intimidating man in front of the picture window was broader in the shoulders and chest than Drakon had ever been, and his thick, inky brown and black hair hung in loose curls to almost his shoulders, while his hard fierce features were hidden by a dark beard. The wild hair and beard should have obscured his sensual beauty, rendered him reckless, powerless. Instead the tangle of hair highlighted his bronzed brow, the long straight nose, the firm mouth, the piercing amber gold eyes.

His hair was still damp and his skin gleamed as if he'd just risen from the sea, the Greek god Poseidon come to life from ancient myth.

She didn't like it. Didn't like any of this. She'd prepared herself for one thing, but not this....

"You look pale," he said, his voice so deep it was almost a caress.

She steeled herself against it. Against him. "It was a long trip."

"Even more reason for you to come sit."

Her hands clenched into fists at her sides. She hated being here. Hated him for only seeing her here at Villa Angelica, the place where they'd honeymooned for a month following their spectacular wedding. It'd been the happiest month of her life. When the honeymoon was over, they had left the villa and flown to Greece, and nothing was ever the same between them again. "I'm fine here," she said.

"I won't hurt you," he replied softly.

Her nails pierced her skin. Her eyes stung. If her legs would function, she'd run. Protect herself. Save herself. If only she had someone else to go to, someone else who would help her, but there was no one. Just Drakon. Just the man who had destroyed her, making her question her own sanity. "You already did that."

"You say that, my love, and yet you've never told me how—"

"As you said, that isn't something to discuss across a room of this size. And we both know, I didn't come here to discuss us. Didn't come to rehash the past, bring up old ghosts, old pain. I came for your help. You know what I need. You know what's at stake. Will you do it? Will you help me?"

"Six million dollars is a lot of money."

"Not to you."

"Things have changed. Your father lost over four hundred million dollars of what I gave him."

"It wasn't his fault." She met his gaze and held it, knowing that if she didn't stand up to him now, he'd crush her. Just as he'd crushed her all those years ago.

Drakon, like her father, played by no rules but his own.

A Greek shipping tycoon, Drakon Sebastian Xanthis was a man obsessed with control and power. A man obsessed with amassing wealth and growing his empire. A man obsessed with a woman who wasn't his wife. Bronwyn. The stunning Australian who ran his Southeast Asia business.

Her eyes burned and her jaw ached.

But no. She wouldn't think of Bronwyn now. Wouldn't wonder if the willowy blonde still worked for him. It wasn't important. Morgan wasn't part of Drakon's life anymore. She didn't care whom Drakon employed or how he interacted with his female vice presidents or where they stayed on their business trips or what they discussed over their long dinners together.

"Is that what you really believe?" he asked now, voice almost silky. "That your father is blameless?"

"Absolutely. He was completely misled—"

"As you have been. Your father is one of the biggest players in one of the biggest Ponzi schemes ever. Twenty-five billion dollars is missing, and your father funneled five billion of that to Michael Amery, earning himself ten percent interest."

"He never saw that kind of money—"

"For God's sake, Morgan, you're talking to me, Drakon, your husband. I know your father. I know exactly who and what he is. Do not play me for a fool!"

Morgan ground her teeth together harder, holding back the words, the tears, the anger, the shame. Her father wasn't a monster. He didn't steal from his clients. He was just as deceived as they were and yet no one would give him an opportunity to explain, or defend himself. The media had tried and convicted him and everyone believed the press. Everyone believed the wild accusations. "He's innocent, Drakon. He had no idea Michael Amery was running a pyramid scheme. Had no idea all those numbers and profits were a lie."

"Then if he's so innocent, why did he flee the country? Why didn't he stay, like Amery's sons and cousins, and fight instead of setting sail to avoid prosecution?"

"He panicked. He was frightened—"

"Absolute rubbish. If that's the case, your father is a coward and deserves his fate."

She shook her head in silent protest, her gaze pinned to Drakon's features. He might not look like Drakon, but it was definitely him. She knew his deep, smooth voice. And those eyes. His eyes. She'd fallen in love with his eyes first. She'd met him at the annual Life ball in Vienna, and they hadn't danced—Drakon didn't dance—but he'd watched her all evening and at first she'd been discomfited by the intensity of his gaze, and then she'd come to like it. Want it. Crave it.

In those early weeks and months when he'd pursued her, Drakon had seduced her with his eyes, examining her, holding her, possessing her long before he'd laid a single finger on her. And, of course, by the time he did, she was his, completely.

The last five years had been brutal. Beyond brutal. And just when Morgan had found herself again, and felt hopeful and excited about her future, her world came crashing down with the revelation that her beloved, brilliant financier father, Daniel Copeland, was part of Michael Amery's horrific Ponzi scheme. And instead of her father handling the crisis with his usual aplomb, he'd cracked and run, creating an even bigger international scandal.

She drew a slow, unsteady breath. "I can't leave him in Somalia to die, Drakon. The pirates will kill him if they don't get the ransom money—"

"It would serve him right."

"He's my father!"

"You'll put yourself in debt for the rest of your life, just to buy his freedom, even though you know that his freedom will be short-lived?"

"Yes."

"You do understand that he'll be arrested the moment he tries to enter any North American or European country?"

"Yes."

"He's never going to be free again. He's going to spend

the rest of his life in prison, just like Michael Amery will, once he's caught, too."

"I understand. But far better for my father to be in an American prison than held by Somali pirates. At least in the United States he could get medical care if he's sick, or medicine for his blood pressure. At least he could have visitors and letters and contact with the outside world. God knows what his conditions are like in Somalia—"

"I'm sure they're not luxurious. But why should the American taxpayer have to support your father? Let him stay where he is. It's what he deserves."

"Do you say this to hurt me, or is it because he lost so much of your money?"

"I'm a businessman. I don't like to lose money. But I was only in four hundred million of the five billion he gave to Amery. What about those others? The majority were regular people. People who trusted your father with their retirement money…their life savings. And what did he do? He wiped them out. Left them with nothing. No retirement, no security, no way to pay the bills now that they're older and frailer and unemployable."

Morgan blinked hard to clear her vision. "Michael Amery was my father's best friend. He was like family. Dad trusted him implicitly." Her voice cracked and she struggled to regain her composure. "I grew up calling him Uncle Michael. I thought of him as my family."

"Yes, that's what you told me. Just before I gave your father four hundred million dollars to invest for me. I nearly gave him more. Your father wanted more. Twice as much, as a matter of fact."

"I am so sorry."

"I trusted your father." His gaze met hers and held. "Trusted you. I know better now."

She exhaled slowly. "Does that mean you won't help me?"

"It means…" His voice faded, and his gaze narrowed as

he looked at her, closely, carefully, studying her intently. "Probably not."

"Probably?" she repeated hoarsely, aware that if Drakon wouldn't help her, no one would. The world hated her father, and wanted him gone. They all hoped he was dead. And they all hoped he'd suffered before he died, too.

"Surely you must realize I'm no fan of your father's, *glykia mou*."

"You don't have to be a fan of my father's to loan me the money. We'll draft a contract, a legal document that is between you and me, and I will pay you back in regular installments. It will take time, but it'll happen. My business is growing, building. I've got hundreds of thousands of dollars of orders coming in. I promise—"

"Just like you promised to love me? Honor me? Be true to me for better or worse, in sickness and in health?"

She winced. He made it sound as if she hadn't ever cared for him, when nothing could be further from the truth. The truth was, she'd cared too much. She'd loved him without reservation. And by loving him so much, she'd lost herself entirely. "So why haven't you divorced me then? If you despise me so much, why not let me go? Set me free?"

"Because I'm not like you. I don't make commitments and run from them. I don't make promises and then break them. I promised five and a half years ago to be loyal to you, and I have been."

His deep gravelly voice was making her insides wobble while his focused gaze rested on her, examining her, as if she were a prized pet that had been lost and found.

"Those are just words, Drakon. They mean nothing to me. Not when your actions speak so much louder."

"My actions?"

"Yes, your actions. Or your lack of action. You only do something if it benefits you. You married me because it benefited you…or you thought it would. And then when times were difficult…when I became difficult…you disappeared. You wouldn't grant me a divorce but you certainly didn't come after me, fight for me. And then when the world turned against us, where were you again? Nowhere. God knows you wouldn't want your name sullied by connection with the Copeland family!"

He studied her for an endless moment. "Interesting how you put things together. But not entirely surprising. You've inherited your mother's flair for the dramatic—"

"I hate you! I do." Her voice shook and her eyes burned, but she wouldn't cry, wouldn't give him the satisfaction. He'd taken everything from her, but not anymore. "I knew you'd mock me, humiliate me. I knew when I flew here, you'd make it difficult, but I came anyway, determined to do whatever I had to do to help my father. You'll let me plead with you, you'll let me beg—"

"That was a very passionate speech, so please forgive my interruption, but I'd like to clarify something. I don't believe you've begged. You've asked for money. You've demanded money. You've explained why you needed money. But there's been very little pleading, and absolutely no begging, at all."

A pulse beat wildly in her throat. She could feel the same wild flutter in her wrists and behind her ears. Everything in her was racing, raging. "Is that what you want? You'd like for me to beg you to help me?"

His head cocked, and he studied her, his gaze penetrating. "It'd certainly be a little more conciliatory, and far less antagonistic."

"Conciliatory." She repeated the word, rolling it over in her mouth, finding it sharp and bitter.

He said nothing, just watched her, and she felt almost breathless at the scrutiny, remembering how it had been between them during their four weeks here on their honeymoon. It was in this villa she'd learned about love and lust, sex and pleasure, as well as pain and control, and the loss of control.

Drakon never lost control. But he'd made sure she did at least once a day, sometimes two or three times.

Their sex life had been hot. Explosive. Erotic. She'd been a virgin when she'd married him and their first time together had been uncomfortable. He was large and it had hurt when he entered her fully. He'd tried to make it pleasurable for her but she'd been so overwhelmed and emotional, as well as let down. She couldn't respond properly, couldn't climax, and she knew she was supposed to. Knew he wanted her to.

He'd showered with her afterward, and kissed her, and beneath the pulsing spray of the shower, he lavished attention on her breasts and nipples, the curve of her buttocks and the cleft between her thighs, lightly playing with her clit until he finally accomplished what he hadn't in bed—she came. One of his arms held her up since her legs were too weak to do the job, and then he'd kissed her deeply, possessively, and when she could catch her breath, he'd assured her that the next time he entered her, it wouldn't hurt. That sex would never hurt again.

It hadn't.

But that didn't mean sex was always easy or comfortable.

Drakon liked it hot. Intense. Sensual. Raw. Unpredictable.

He loved to stand across the room from her—just as he was doing now—and he'd tell her what to do. Tell her what he wanted. Sometimes he wanted her to strip and then walk naked to him. Sometimes he wanted her to strip to just her panties and crawl to him. Sometimes he wanted her to wear nothing but her elegant heels and bend over...or put a foot on a chair and he'd tell her where to touch herself.

Each time Morgan would protest, but he'd look at her from beneath his black lashes, his amber gaze lazy, his full mouth curved, and he'd tell her how beautiful she was and how much he enjoyed looking at her, that it gave him so much pleasure to see her, and to have her trust him....

Obey him...

She hated those words, hated the element of dominance, but it was part of the foreplay. They had good sex in bed, but then they had this other kind of sex—the sex where they played erotic games that pushed her out of her comfort zone. It had been confusing, but inevitably she did what he asked, and then somewhere along the way, he'd join her, and his mouth would be on her, between her legs, and his hands would hold her, fingers tight on her butt, or in her hair, or gripping her thighs, holding them apart, and he'd make love to her with his mouth and his fingers and his body and he'd arouse her so slowly that she feared she wouldn't ever come, and then just when the desire turned sharp and hurt, he'd relent. He'd flick the tip of his tongue across that small sensitive nub, or suck on her, or stroke her, or enter her and she'd break. Shatter. And the orgasms were so intense they seemed to go on forever. Maybe because he made sure they went on forever. And by the time he was finished, she was finished. There was nothing left. She was drained, spent, but also quiet. Compliant.

He loved her flushed and warm, quiet and compliant. Loved her physically that is, as long as she made no emotional demands. No conversation. No time, energy or patience. Required no attention.

Morgan's chest ached. Her heart hurt. She'd been so young then, so trusting and naive. She'd been determined to please him, her beautiful, sensual Greek husband.

Their honeymoon here, those thirty days of erotic lovemaking, had changed her forever. She couldn't even think of this villa without remembering how he'd made love to her in every single room, in every way imaginable. Taking her on chairs and beds, window seats and stairs. Pressing her naked back or breasts to priceless carpets, the marble floor, the cool emerald-green Italian tiles in the hall...

She wanted to throw up. He hadn't just taken her. He'd broken her.

"Help me out if you would, Drakon," she said, her voice pitched low, hoarse. "I'm not sure I understand you, and I don't know if it's cultural, personal or a language issue. But do you *want* me to beg? Is that what you're asking me to do?" Her chin lifted and tears sparkled in her eyes even as her heart burned as if it had been torched with fire. "Am I to go onto my knees in front of you, and plead my case? Is that what it would take to win your assistance?"

He didn't move a muscle and yet the vast living room suddenly felt very small. "I do like you on your knees," he said cordially, because they both knew that on her knees she could take him in her mouth, or he could touch her or take her from behind.

She drew a ragged breath, locked her knees, praying for strength. "I haven't forgotten," she said, aware that she was in trouble here, aware that she ought to go. Now. While she could. While she still had some self-respect left. "Although God knows, I've tried."

"Why would you want to forget it? We had an incredible sex life. It was amazing between us."

She could only look at him, intrigued by his memory of them, as well as appalled. Their sex life had been hot, but their marriage had been empty and shallow.

Obviously that didn't trouble him. It probably didn't even cross his mind that his bride had feelings. Emotions. Needs. Why should it? Drakon's desires were so much simpler. He just needed her available and willing, as if she were an American porn star in a rented Italian villa.

"So on my knees it is," she said mockingly, lifting the hem of her pale blue skirt to kneel on his limestone floor.

"Get up," he growled sharply.

"But this *is* what you want?"

"No. It's not what I want, not like this, not because you need something, want something. It's one thing if we're making love and there's pleasure involved, but there's no pleasure in seeing you beg, especially to me. The very suggestion disgusts me."

"And yet you seemed so charmed by the memory of me on my knees."

"Because that was different. That was sex. This is…" He shook his head, features tight, full mouth thinned. For a moment he just breathed, and the silence stretched.

Morgan welcomed the silence. She needed it. Her mind was whirling, her insides churning. She felt sick, dizzy and off balance by the contradictions and the intensity and her own desperation.

He had to help her.

He had to.

If he didn't, her father was forever lost to her.

"I've no desire to ever see my wife degrade herself," Drakon added quietly, "not even on behalf of her father. It actually sickens me to think you'd do that for him—"

"He's my father!"

"And he failed you! And it makes me physically ill that you'd beg for a man who refused to protect you and your sisters and your mother. A man is to provide for his family, not rob them blind."

"How nice it must be, Drakon Xanthis, to live, untouched and superior, in your ivory tower." Her voice deepened and her jaw ached and everything in her chest felt so raw and hot. "But I don't have the luxury of having an ivory tower. I don't have any luxuries anymore. Everything's gone in my family, Drakon. The money, the security, the houses, the cars, the name…our reputation. And I can lose the lifestyle, it's just a lifestyle. But I've lost far more than that. My family's shattered. Broken. We live in chaos—"

She broke off, dragged in a breath, feeling wild and unhinged. But losing control with Drakon wouldn't help her. It would hurt her. He didn't like strong emotions. He pulled away when voices got louder, stronger, preferring calm, rational, unemotional conversation.

And, of course, that's what she'd think about now. What Drakon wanted. How he liked things. How ironic that even after five years, she was still worrying about him, still turning herself inside out to please him, to be what *he* needed, to handle things the way *he* handled them.

What about her?

What about what she needed? What she wanted? What about her emotions or her comfort?

The back of her eyes burned and she jerked her chin higher. "Well, I'm sorry you don't like seeing me like this, but this is who I am. Desperate. And I'm willing to take desperate measures to help my family. You don't understand what it's like for us. My family is in pain. Everyone is hurting, heartsick with guilt and shame and confusion—how could my father do what he did? How could he not know Amery wasn't investing legitimately? How could he not protect his clients…his friends…his family? My sisters and brother—we can't even see each other anymore, Drakon. We don't speak to each other. We can't handle the shame of it all. We're outcasts now. Bottom feeders. Scum. So fine, stand there and mock me with your principles. I'm just trying to save what I can. Starting with my father's life."

"Your father isn't worth it. But you are. Stop worrying about him, Morgan, and save yourself."

"And how do I do that, Drakon? Have you any advice for me there?"

"Yes. Come home."

"Home?"

"Yes, home to me—"

"You're not home, Drakon. You were never home."

She saw him flinch and she didn't like it, but it was time he knew the truth. Time he heard the truth. "You asked me a little bit ago why I'd want to forget our sex life, and I'll tell you. I don't like remembering. It hurts remembering."

"Why? It was good. No, it was great. We were unbelievable together—"

"Yes, yes, the sex was hot. And erotic. You were an incredibly skillful lover. You could make me come over and over, several times a day. But that's all you gave me. Your name, a million-dollar diamond wedding ring and orgasms. Lots and lots of orgasms. But there was no relationship, no communication, no connection. I didn't marry you to just have sex. I married you to have a life, a home. Happiness. But after six months of being married to you, all I felt was empty, isolated and deeply unhappy."

She held his gaze, glad she'd at last said what she'd wanted to say all those years ago, and yet fully aware that these revelations changed nothing. They were just the final nail in a coffin that had been needing to be sealed shut. "I was so unhappy I could barely function, and yet there you were, touching me, kissing me, making me come. I'd cry after I came. I'd cry because it hurt me so much that you could love my body and not love me."

"I loved you."

"You didn't."

"You can accuse me of being a bad husband, of being cold, of being insensitive, but don't tell me how I felt, because I know how I felt. And I did love you. Maybe I didn't say it often—"

"Or ever."

"But I thought you knew."

"Clearly, I didn't."

He stared at her from across the room, his features so hard they looked chiseled from stone. "Why didn't you tell me?" he said finally.

"Because you hated me talking to you." Her throat ached and she swallowed around the lump with difficulty. "Every

time I opened my mouth to say anything you'd roll your eyes
or sigh or turn away—"

"Not true, either."

"It is true. For me, it's true. And maybe you were raised in
a culture where women are happy to be seen and not heard,
but I'm an American. I come from a big family. I have three
sisters and a brother and am used to conversation and laughter and activity and the only activity I got from you was sex,
and even then it wasn't mutual. You were the boss, you were
in control, dictating to me how it'd be. Strip, crawl, come—"
She broke off, gasping for air, and shoved a trembling hand
across her eyes, wiping them dry before any tears could fall.
"So don't act so shocked that I'd beg you to help me save my
father. Don't say it's degrading and beneath me. I know what
degrading is. I know what degrading does. And I've been
there, in our marriage, with you."

And then she was done, gone.

Morgan raced to the door, her heels clicking on the polished marble, her purse on the antique console in the grand
hall close to the front door, her travel bag in the trunk of her
hired car.

She'd flown to Naples this morning from London, and
yesterday to London from Los Angeles, almost twenty hours
of traveling just to get here, never mind the tortuous winding drive to the villa perched high on the cliffs of the coast
between Positano and Ravello. She was exhausted and flattened. Finished. But she wasn't broken. Wasn't shattered, not
the way she'd been leaving him the first time.

Count it as a victory, she told herself, wrenching open the
front door and stepping outside into the blinding sunshine.
*You came, you saw him and you're leaving in one piece. You
did it. You faced your dragon and you survived him.*

CHAPTER TWO

DRAKON WATCHED MORGAN spin and race from the living room, her cheeks pale, her long dark hair swinging. He could hear her high-heeled sandals clicking against the gleaming floor as she ran, and then heard the front door open and slam shut behind her.

He slowly exhaled and focused on the silence, letting the stillness and quiet wash over him, calm him.

In a moment he'd go after her, but first he needed to gather his thoughts, check his emotions. It wouldn't do to follow her in a fury—and he was furious. Beyond furious.

So he'd wait. He'd wait until his famous control was firmly in check. He prided himself on his control. Prided himself for not taking out his frustrations on others.

He could afford to give Morgan a few minutes, too. It's not as if she would be able to go anywhere. Her hired car and driver were gone, paid off, dispensed with, and the villa was set off the main road, private and remote. There would be no taxis nearby. She wasn't the sort to stomp away on foot.

And so Drakon used the quiet and the silence to reflect on everything she'd said. She'd said quite a bit. Much of it uncomfortable, and some of it downright shocking, as well as infuriating.

She'd felt degraded in their marriage?

Absolute rubbish. And the fact that she'd dare say such

a thing to his face after all these years made him want to throttle her, which seriously worried him.

He wasn't a violent man. He didn't lose his temper. Didn't even recognize the marriage she described. He had loved her, and he'd spoiled her. Pampered her. Worshipped her body. How was that degrading?

And how dare she accuse him of being a bad husband? He'd given her everything, had done everything for her, determined to make her happy. Her feelings had been important to him. He'd been a respectful husband, a kind husband, having far too many memories of an unhappy childhood, a childhood filled with tense, angry people—namely his mother—to want his wife to be anything but satisfied and content.

His mother, Maria, wasn't a bad woman, she was a good woman, a godly woman, and she tried to be fair, just, but that hadn't made her affectionate. Or gentle.

Widowed at thirty-five when Drakon's father died of a heart attack at sea, Maria had found raising five children on her own overwhelming. The Xanthis family was wealthy and she didn't have to worry about money, but that didn't seem to give her much relief, not when she was so angry that Drakon's father, Sebastian, had died leaving her with all these children, children she wasn't sure she'd ever wanted. One child might have been fine, but five was four too many.

Drakon, being the second eldest, and the oldest son, tried to be philosophical about her anger and resentment. She came from a wealthy family herself and had grown up comfortable. He told himself that her lack of affection and attention wasn't personal, but rather a result of grief, and too many pregnancies too close together. And so he learned by watching her, that she was most comfortable around her children if they asked for nothing, revealed no emotion or expressed no need. Drakon internalized the lesson well, and by thirteen and fourteen, he became the perfect son, by having no needs, or emotions.

But that didn't mean he didn't enjoy pleasing others. Throughout his twenties he had taken tremendous pride in spoiling his girlfriends, beautiful glamorous women who enjoyed being pampered and showered with pretty gifts and extravagant nights out. The women in his life quickly came to understand that he didn't show emotion and they didn't expect him to. It wasn't that he didn't feel, but it wasn't easy to feel. There were emotions in him somewhere, just not accessible. His girlfriends enjoyed his lifestyle, and his ability to please them, and they accepted him for who he was, and that he expressed himself best through action—doing or buying something for someone.

So he bought gifts and whisked his love interests to romantic getaways. And he became a skilled lover, a patient and gifted lover who understood the importance of foreplay.

Women needed to be turned on mentally before they were turned on physically. The brain was their largest erogenous zone, with their skin coming in second. And so Drakon loved to seduce his partner slowly, teasing her, playing with her, whetting the appetite and creating anticipation, because sex was how he bonded. It's how he felt close to his woman. It was how he felt safe expressing himself.

And yet she hadn't felt safe with him. She hadn't even enjoyed being with him. Their lovemaking had disgusted her. He had disgusted her. He'd turned off Morgan.

Drakon's stomach heaved. He swallowed the bitter taste in his mouth.

How stupid he'd been. Moronic.

No wonder she'd left him. No wonder she'd waited until he had flown to London for the day. He had only been away for the day, having flown out early on his jet, returning for a late dinner. But when he had entered their villa in Ekali, a northern suburb of Athens, the villa had been dark. No staff. No dinner. No welcome. No Morgan.

He remembered being blindsided that night. Remembered

thinking, he could go without dinner, could live without food, but he couldn't live without Morgan.

He'd called her that night, but she didn't answer. He'd left a message. Left another. Had flown to see her. She wasn't to be found.

He'd called again, left another message, asking her to come home. She didn't. She wouldn't even speak to him, forcing him instead to interact with her trio of attorneys as they informed him that their client was filing for divorce and moving on with her life, without him.

His surprise gave way to frustration and fury, but he never lost his temper with her. He tried to remain cool, focused, pragmatic. Things had a way of working out. He needed to be patient, and he refused to divorce her, insisting he wouldn't agree to a divorce until she met with him. Sat down and talked with him. In person.

She wouldn't. And so for two years her attorneys had battled on her behalf, while Drakon had battled back. His wife would not leave him without giving him a proper explanation. His wife could not just walk away on a whim.

While the Copeland attorneys filed their lawsuits and counter lawsuits, Drakon had made repeated attempts to see Morgan. But every attempt to reach her was stymied. Her cell phone was disconnected. He had no idea where she was living. Her family would only say she'd gone away indefinitely. Drakon had hired private investigators to find her, but they couldn't. Morgan had vanished.

For two and a half years she'd vanished into thin air.

And then in October she had reappeared, emerging again on the New York social scene.

The private investigators sent Drakon her address, a high-rent loft in SoHo, paid for by her father. She'd started her own business as a jewelry designer and had opened a small shop down the street from her loft, locating her little store close to big hitters.

Drakon immediately flew to New York to see her, going straight from the airport to her boutique, hoping that's where he'd find her at 11:00 a.m. on a Wednesday morning. Before he even stepped from his limousine, she walked out the shop's front door with her youngest sister, Jemma. At first glance they looked like any glamorous girls about town, slim and chic, with long gleaming hair and their skin lightly golden from expensive spray-on tans, but after that first impression of beauty and glamour, he saw how extremely thin Morgan was, dangerously thin. She looked like a skeleton in her silk tunic and low-waisted trousers. Wide gold bangles covered her forearms, and Drakon wondered if it was an attempt to hide her extreme slenderness, or perhaps accent her physique?

He didn't know, wasn't sure he wanted to know. The only thing he knew for certain was that she didn't look well and he was baffled by the change in her.

He let her go, leaving her with Jemma, and had his driver take him to her father's building on 53rd and Third Avenue. Daniel Copeland could barely hide his shock at seeing Drakon Xanthis in his office, but welcomed him cordially—he was, after all, taking care of Drakon's investment—and asked him to have a seat.

"I saw Morgan today," Drakon had said bluntly, choosing not to sit. "What's wrong with her? She doesn't look well."

"She hasn't been well," Daniel answered just as bluntly.

"So what's wrong with her?" he repeated.

"That's her business."

"She's my wife."

"Only because you won't let her go."

"I don't believe in divorce."

"She's not happy with you, Drakon. You need to let her go."

"Then she needs to come tell me that herself." He'd left Daniel's office after that, and for several weeks he'd expected a call from Morgan, expected an email, something to say she was ready to meet with him.

But she didn't contact him. And he didn't reach out to her. And the impasse had continued until three days ago when Morgan had called him, and requested a meeting. She'd told him up front why she wanted to see him. She made it clear that this had nothing to do with them, or their marriage, but her need for a loan, adding that she was only coming to him because no one else would help her.

You are my last resort, she'd said. *If you don't help me, no one will.*

He'd agreed to see her, telling her to meet him here, at Villa Angelica. He'd thought perhaps by meeting here, where they'd embarked on their married life, they could come to an understanding and heal the breach. Perhaps face-to-face here, where they had been happy, he could persuade Morgan to return to Athens. It was time. He wanted children, a family. He wanted his wife back where she was supposed to be—in his home, at his side.

Now he realized there was no hope, there never had been, and he felt stupid and angry.

Worse, he felt betrayed. Betrayed by the woman he'd vowed to love and protect, a woman he'd continued to love these past five years, because it was his duty to love her. To be faithful to her. To provide for her.

But he was done with his duty. Done with his loyalty. Done with her.

He wanted her gone.

It was time to give her what she wanted. Time to give them both what they needed—freedom.

Drakon ran a hand over his jaw, feeling the dense beard, a beard he'd started growing that day he'd learned she intended to end their marriage without uttering a single word, or explanation, or apology to him.

He'd vowed he'd grow his beard until his wife returned home, or until he'd understood what had happened between them.

It had been an emotional, impulsive vow, but he'd kept it. Just as he'd kept hope that one day Morgan, his wife, would return to him.

And she had returned, but only to tell him how much she hated him. How much she despised him. How degrading she'd found their marriage.

Drakon exhaled slowly, trying to control the hot rush of emotion that made his chest ache and burn. He wasn't used to feeling such strong emotions. But he was feeling them now.

He headed into the small sitting room, which opened off the living room to his laptop and his briefcase. He took a checkbook to his personal account out of his briefcase and quickly scrawled her name on a check and filled in the amount, before dating it and signing it. He studied the check for a moment, the anger bubbling up, threatening to consume him, and it took all of his control to push it back down, suppressing it with ruthless intent.

He wasn't a failure. She was the failure. She was the one who had walked out on him, not the other way around. He was the one who had fought to save their marriage, who had honored their vows, who had honored her by thinking of no other woman but his wife, wanting no other woman than Morgan.

But now he was done with Morgan. He'd give her the money she wanted and let her go and once she left, he wouldn't waste another moment of his life thinking or worrying about her. She wanted her freedom? Well, she was about to get it.

Morgan was standing on the villa's front steps gazing out at the sweeping drive, with the stunning view of the dark green mountains that dropped steeply and dramatically into the sapphire sea, anxiously rubbing her nails back and forth against her linen skirt, when she heard the front door open behind her.

Her skin prickled and the fine hair at her nape lifted. She knew without even turning around it was Drakon. She could feel his warmth, that magnetic energy of his that drew everything toward him, including her.

But she wouldn't allow herself to be drawn back into his life. Wouldn't give him power over her ever again.

She quickly moved down the front steps, putting distance between them. She refused to look at him, was unable to look at him when she was filled with so much anger and loathing.

"You had no right to send away my car," she said coolly, her gaze resolutely fixed on the dazzling blue and green colors of the coast, but unable to appreciate them, or the lushness of the dark pink bougainvillea blooming profusely along the stone wall bordering the private drive. Panic flooded her limbs. He was so close to her she could barely breathe, much less think.

"I didn't think you'd need it," he said.

She looked sharply at him then, surprised by his audacity, his arrogance. "Did you imagine I was going to stay?"

"I'd hoped," he answered simply.

She sucked in a breath, hating him anew. He could be so charming when he wanted to be. So endearing and real. And then he could take it all away again, just like that. "You really thought I'd take one look at you and forget my unhappiness? Forget why I wanted the divorce?"

"I thought you'd at least sit down and talk to me. Have a real conversation with me."

"You don't like conversation, Drakon. You only want information in bullet form. Brief, concise and to the point."

He was silent a moment, and then he nodded once, a short, decisive nod. "Then I'll be brief in return. The helicopter is on the way for you. Should be here soon. And I have this for you." He handed her a folded piece of paper.

Morgan took it from him, opened it. It was a check for seven million dollars. She looked up at Drakon in surprise. "What's this?"

"The money you begged for."

She flinched. "The pirates are only asking for six."

"There will be other expenses. Travel and rescue logistics. You'll want to hire an expert to help you. Someone with the right negotiation skills. There are several excellent firms out there, like Dunamas Maritime Intelligence—"

"I'm familiar with them."

"They won't be cheap."

"I'm familiar with their fees."

"Don't try to do it on your own, thinking you can. Better to pay for their expertise and their relationships. They know what they're doing, and they'll help you avoid a trap. The Somali pirates sound like they're a ragtag organization, but in truth, they're being funded by some of the wealthiest, most powerful people in the world."

She nodded, because she couldn't speak, not with her throat swelling closed. For the first time in a long, long time, she was grateful for Drakon Xanthis, grateful he had not just the means to help her, but knowledge and power. There weren't many people like Drakon in the world, and she was suddenly so very glad he had been part of her life.

"Use whatever is left after you pay your management fee to pay your father's travel expenses home. There should be enough. If there isn't, let me know immediately," he added.

"Thank you," she whispered huskily.

His jaw tightened. "Go to London before you return to New York, cash the check at the London branch of my bank. There won't be any problems. They'll give you the six million in cash you need for the ransom. You must have it in cash, and not new bills, remember that. But I'm sure your contact told you that?"

"Yes."

His lashes dropped, concealing his expression. "They're very particular, *agapi mou*. Follow the instructions exactly. If you don't, things could turn unpleasant."

"As if storming my father's yacht off the Horn of Africa, and killing his captain, wasn't unpleasant enough—" She broke off, hearing the distinctive hum of the helicopter. It was still a distance from them, but it would be here soon.

For a moment neither said anything, both listening to the whir of the helicopter blades.

"Why have you kept the news of your father's kidnapping private?" he asked her. "I would have thought this was something you'd share with the world…using the kidnapping to garner sympathy."

"Because it wouldn't garner sympathy. The American public hates him. Loathes him. And if they discovered he was kidnapped by Somali pirates, they'd be glad. They'd be dancing in the streets, celebrating, posting all kinds of horrible comments all over the internet, hoping he'll starve, or be killed, saying it's karma—"

"Isn't it?"

She acted as though Drakon hadn't spoken. "But he's my father, not theirs, and I'm not using their money. Not spending government funds, public funds or trust funds. We haven't gone to the police or the FBI, haven't asked for help from anyone. We're keeping this in the family, handling it on our own, and since my brother and sisters don't have the means, I'm using my money—"

"You mean my money."

She flushed, and bit hard into her lower lip, embarrassed. His money. Right. They weren't married, not really, and she had no right to spend his money, just because she had nothing left of her own.

"I stand corrected," she whispered. "Your money. I'm using your money. But I will pay you back. Every penny. Even if it takes me the rest of my life."

A small muscle popped in his jaw. "There is no need for that—" He paused, glancing up at the dark speck overhead. The helicopter.

One of the reasons Drakon had chosen this villa for their honeymoon five and a half years ago was that the outdoor pool had a special cover that converted it into a heli landing pad, making the remote villa far more appealing for a man who needed to come and go for meetings in Naples, Athens and London.

"No need to pay me back," Drakon said, picking up his broken train of thought, "because I'm calling my attorney this afternoon and asking him to process the paperwork for the divorce. He will make sure the dissolution is expedited. By the end of the month, it will be over."

It will be over. For a moment Morgan couldn't take this last bit in. What was he saying? He'd finally agreed to the divorce?

He was giving her the money *and* granting her the divorce?

She just looked up at him, eyes burning, too overwhelmed to speak.

He dipped his head and raised his voice in order to be heard over the hum of the helicopter, which had begun to descend. "You will receive your full settlement once the dissolution occurs. With the current state of affairs, I'd suggest you allow me to open a personal account for you in London or Geneva and I can deposit the funds directly into the account without fear of your government freezing it. I know they've frozen all your family accounts in the United States—"

"I don't want your money."

"Yes, you do. You came here for my money. So take what you came for—"

"I came to see you for my father, and that was the only reason I came here today."

"A point you made abundantly clear." He smiled at her

but his amber gaze looked icy, the golden depths tinged with frost. "So I am giving you what you wanted, freedom and financial security, which fulfills my obligation to you."

She shivered at the hardness in his voice. She had never heard him speak to her with so much coldness and disdain and it crushed her to think they were ending it like this— with contempt and anger.

"I'm sorry," she whispered, her heart beating too fast and aching far too much.

He didn't answer her, his gaze fixed on the helicopter slowly descending. Morgan watched him and not the helicopter, aware that this just might be the last time she would see Drakon and was drinking him in, trying to memorize every detail, trying to remember him. This.

"Thank you," she added, wanting him to just look at her, acknowledge her, without this new terrible coldness.

But he didn't. He wouldn't. "I'll walk you to the landing pad," he said, putting his hand out to gesture the way without touching her or looking at her.

Perhaps it was better this way, she told herself, forcing herself to move. It was hard enough being near him without wanting to be closer to him. Perhaps if he'd been kind or gentle, she'd just want more of him, because she'd always wanted more of him, never less. The doctors had said she was addicted to him, and her addiction wasn't healthy. He wasn't the sun, they lectured her, and Drakon, despite his intense charisma and chemistry, couldn't warm her, nor could he actually give her strength. She was the only one who could give herself strength, and the only way she could do that was by leaving him, putting him behind her.

And so here she was again, leaving him. Putting him behind her.

So be strong, she told herself. *Prove that you're strong on your own.*

Morgan blinked to clear her vision, fighting panic as they

rounded the villa and walked across the lawn for the open pool terrace where the helicopter waited, balancing like a peculiar moth on the high-tech titanium cover concealing the pool. The roar from the helicopter's spinning blades made conversation impossible, not that Drakon wanted to talk to her.

One of the household staff met them at the helicopter with Morgan's travel bag and Drakon set it inside the helicopter, then spoke briefly to the pilot before putting out his hand to assist Morgan inside.

She glanced down at his outstretched hand, and then up into his face, into those unique amber eyes that had captivated her from the start. "Thank you again, Drakon, and I hope you'll be happy."

His lips curved, but his eyes glittered with silent fury. "Is that a joke? Am I supposed to be amused?"

She drew back, stunned by his flash of temper. For a moment she could only stare at him, surprised, bewildered, by this fierce man. This was a different Drakon than the man she'd married. This was a Drakon of intense emotions and yet after they'd married she'd become convinced that Drakon felt no emotion. "I'm serious. I want you to be happy. You deserve to be happy—"

"As you said I'm not one for meaningless conversation, so I'm going to walk away now to save us from an embarrassing and uncomfortable goodbye," he said brusquely, cutting her short, to propel her into the helicopter. Once he had her inside, he leaned in, his features harsh, and shouted to her, "Don't try to cut corners, Morgan, and save money by handling the pirates yourself. Get help. Call Dunamas, or Blue Sea, or one of the other maritime intelligence companies. Understand me?"

His fierce gaze held hers, and she nodded jerkily, even as her stomach rose up, and her heart fell. If he only knew...

If he only knew what she had done....

And for a split second she nearly blurted the truth, how she had been negotiating with the pirates on her own, and how she'd thought she was in control, until it had all gone terribly wrong, which was why she was here…which was why she needed Drakon so much. But before she could say any of it, Drakon had turned around and was walking away from the helicopter.

Walking away from her.

Her eyes burned and her throat sealed closed as the pilot handed Morgan a set of headphones, but she couldn't focus on the pilot's instructions, not when she was watching Drakon stride toward the villa.

He was walking quickly, passing the rose-covered balustrade on the lower terrace then climbing the staircase to the upper terrace, and the entire time she prayed he'd turn around, pray he'd acknowledge her, pray he'd wave or smile, or just *look* at her.

He didn't.

He crossed the terrace to the old ballroom and disappeared into the great stone house without a backward glance.

So that was it. Done. Over. She was finally free to move on, find happiness, find love elsewhere.

She should be happy. She should feel at peace. But as the helicopter lifted off the pad, straight into the air, Morgan didn't feel any relief, just panic. Because she didn't get the help she needed, and she'd lost him completely.

It wasn't supposed to have gone like this. The meeting today…as well as their marriage. Because she had loved him. She'd loved him with everything she was, everything she had, and it hadn't been enough. It should have been enough. Why wasn't it enough? In the beginning she'd thought he was perfect. In the beginning she'd thought she'd found her soul mate. But she was wrong.

Seconds passed, becoming one minute and then another as the helicopter rose higher and higher, straight up so that the villa fell away and the world was all blue and green, with the sea on one side and the sharp, steep mountains on the other and the villa with its famous garden clinging to that bit of space on the rock.

Fighting tears, her gaze fell on the check she still clutched in her hand. Seven million dollars. Just like that.

And she'd known that he'd help her if she went to him. She'd known he'd come through for her, too, because he'd never refused her anything. Drakon might not have given her much of his time or patience, but he'd never withheld anything material from her.

Guilt pummeled her, guilt and fear and anxiety, because she hadn't accomplished everything she'd come to Villa Angelica to accomplish. She needed more from Drakon than just a check. She needed not just financial assistance, but his help, too. There were few men in the world who had his knowledge of piracy and its impact on the shipping industry. Indeed, Drakon was considered one of the world's leading experts in counter piracy, and he'd know the safest, quickest method for securing her father's release, as well as the right people to help her.

Morgan exhaled in a rush, heart beating too hard.

She had to go back. Had to face Drakon again. Had to convince him to help her. Not that he'd want to help her now, not after everything that was said.

But this wasn't about pride or her ego. This was life and death, her father's life, specifically, and she couldn't turn her back on him.

Swallowing her fear and misgivings, Morgan grabbed at her seat belt as if throwing on brakes. "Stop, wait," she said to the pilot through the small microphone attached to her headphones. "We have to go back. I've forgotten something."

The pilot was too well-trained, and too well-paid, to question her. For a moment nothing seemed to happen and then he shifted and the helicopter began to slowly descend.

* * *

Drakon didn't wait for the helicopter to leave. There was no point. She was gone, and he was glad. While climbing the stairs to his bedroom suite, he heard the helicopter lift, the throbbing of the rotary blades vibrating all the way through the old stone walls.

In his bathroom, Drakon stripped his clothes off and showered, and then dried off, wrapping the towel around his hips and prepared to shave. It would take a while. There was a lot of beard.

He gathered his small scissors and his razor and shaving cream, and as he laid everything out, he tried not to think, particularly not of Morgan, but that was impossible. He was so upset. So angry.

What a piece of work she was. To think he'd wanted her back. To think he'd loved her. But how could he have loved her? She was shallow and superficial and so incredibly self-centered. It was always about her...what she wanted, what she needed, with no regard for anyone else's needs.

As he changed the blade on his razor, he felt a heaviness inside, a dull ache in his chest, as if he'd cut his heart. And then Drakon took the razor to his beard.

He had loved her, and he had wanted her back. Wanted her home with him. But that was before he understood how disgusted she was with him, how disgusted she'd been by their marriage.

Disgust.

He knew that word, and knew disgust produced shame. His mother used to be disgusted by emotion, and as a young child, Drakon had felt constant shame in her presence, shame that he had such strong emotions, emotions she found appalling. He still remembered how wild he'd felt on the inside as a little boy, how desperate and confused he'd felt by her rejection, and how determined he'd been to win her affection, even if it meant destroying part of himself. And so that became the goal, his sole objective as a child. To master his hideous emotions. To master want and need, to stifle them, suppress them, thereby winning his mother's approval and love.

He succeeded.

Drakon rinsed the shaving cream from his face and studied his smooth, clean jaw in the mirror. He'd forgotten what his face looked like without a beard, had forgotten how lean his cheeks were above his jutting chin. He had a hard chin, a stubborn chin, which was fitting since he knew he'd become a very hard, stubborn man.

A knock sounded on the outer door of his suite. Drakon mopped his damp face, grabbed a robe and crossed his room to open the door, expecting one of the villa staff.

It wasn't one of the staff. It was Morgan.

Something surged in his chest, hot and fierce, and then it was gone, replaced by coldness. Why was she back? What game was she playing now? He leaned against the door frame, and looked her up and down, coolly, unkindly. "Need more money already?"

Color stained her cheeks, making her blue eyes even deeper, brighter. "You…shaved."

"I did."

"We need to talk."

He arched an eyebrow. "Thank you, but no. I've heard more than enough from you already. Now if you'd be so good as to see yourself out, and get back into the helicopter—"

"The helicopter is gone. I sent him away."

"That was foolish of you. How are you getting back home?"

"We'll figure that out later."

"You mean, you can figure that out later. There is no more we. I'm done with you, and done helping you. You've got your check, and in a month's time you'll receive your settlement, but that's it. That's all there is. I've nothing more for you. Now if you'll excuse me, I have things to do."

Her eyebrows lifted and she walked past him, into his room, glancing around the impressive bedroom where they'd spent the first month of their marriage. "Looks just as I remembered," she said, turning to face him. "But you don't. You've changed."

"Yes, I grew a beard, I know."

"It's not just the beard and hair. It's you. You're different."

"Perhaps you weren't aware. My wife left me. It wasn't an easy thing."

She gave him a long, level look. "You could have come after me."

"I did."

"You did not."

"I *did.*"

"I'm not talking about phone calls, or emails or texts. Those don't count."

"No, they don't, and they don't work, either, not once you turned your phone off. Which is why I flew repeatedly to New York, drove up to Greenwich—"

"You didn't!"

His hands clenched at his sides. "Good God, if you contradict me one more time, I will throttle you, Morgan, I will. Because I did go after you, I wanted you back, I wanted you home and I did everything I could to save our marriage. I visited your father at work. I appeared on your parents' doorstep. I spoke—repeatedly—to each of your siblings—"

"I can't believe it," she whispered.

"Believe it," he said grimly, moving toward her, stepping so close he could smell the hint of fragrance from her shampoo, and the sweet clean scent of her perfume on her skin. He loved her smell. Loved her softness. Loved everything about his woman.

But that was then, and this was now, and he was so done with the craziness and the chaos that had followed their marriage.

His gaze caught hers, held, and he stared down into her eyes, drinking in that intense blue that always made him think of the sea around his home in Greece. Tiny purple and gold flecks shimmered against the deep blue irises…like the glimmer of sun on the surface of water. He used to think her eyes perfectly expressed who she was…a woman of magic and mystery and natural beauty.

Now he knew he'd been tricked. Tricked and deceived by a beautiful face, by stunning blue eyes.

Bitterness rolled through him and his gut clenched, his jaw hardening, anger roiling. He really didn't like remembering, and he really didn't like feeling the fury and rejection again, but it was what it was. They were what they were. Such was life.

"And if you don't believe me, make some enquiries. Ask your brother, or your sister Tori, or Logan, or Jemma. Ask them all. Ask why no one would tell me anything. Demand answers, if not for you, then for me. Find out why the entire Copeland family turned their backs on me. I still don't know why. Just as I don't know why you disappeared, or where you went, but you were gone. I even hired private investigators, but you were nowhere to be found."

Morgan bundled her arms across her chest and drew a slow, unsteady breath. A small pulse beat wildly at the base of her throat. "You really came after me?"

"Of course I came after you! You were my wife. You think I just let you go? You think I'd just let you leave?"

She swallowed hard, her blue eyes shining. "Yes."

He swore softly, and walked away from her, putting distance between them. "I don't know what kind of man you think you married, but I am not he. In fact, you, my wife, know nothing about me!"

She followed him, her footsteps echoing on the tiled floor. "Maybe that's because you never gave me a chance to get to know you, Drakon."

He turned abruptly to face her, and she nearly bumped into him. "Or maybe it's because you didn't stay long enough to get to know me, *Morgan*."

Morgan took a swift step backward, stunned by his blistering wrath. She squeezed her hands into fists, crumpling the check in her right hand.

The check.

She'd forgotten all about it. Her heart ached as she glanced down at the paper, creased and crumpled in her hand. "If that is truly the case," she said, voice husky, "I'm sorry."

"If," he echoed bitterly, his upper lip lifting. "I find it so ironic that you don't believe a word I say, and yet when you need something, you'll come running to me—"

"I didn't want to come to you."

"Oh, I'm quite sure of that." He made a rough sound and turned away, running a hand over his newly shaven jaw. "My God, what a joke. I can't believe I waited five years for this."

"What does that mean?"

"Forget it. I don't want to do this." He turned and looked at her, cheekbones jutting against his bronzed skin, his amber gaze hard. "I have finally come to the same realization you did five years ago. That we don't work. That we never worked. That there is no future. And since there is no future, I've nothing to say to you. You have the money, you have what you came for—"

"I didn't just come for money. I need your help."

"That's too bad, then, because the check is all you're getting from me."

She inhaled sharply. He sounded so angry, so bitter, so unlike her husband. "Drakon, please. You know how the pirates operate. You've dealt with them before—"

"No. Sorry. I'm not trying to be ugly, just honest. I'm done. Done with you. Done with your family. Done with your father—my God, there's a piece of work—but he's not my problem anymore, because I'm not his son-in-law anymore, either. And I never thought I'd say this, but I'm actually glad to be done…glad to have a complete break. You've exhausted every one of my resources, and I've nothing more to give. To you, or the rest of the Copeland family."

She winced and looked away, hoping he didn't see the tears that filled her eyes. "No one told me you came after me," she said faintly, her gaze fixed on the view of the sea beyond the window. "But then, in that first year after I left you, no one told me anything."

"I don't see how that is relevant now."

"It probably won't mean anything to you now, but it's relevant to me. It's a revelation, and a comfort—"

"A *comfort?*" he repeated sarcastically.

She lifted her chin a fraction, squared her shoulders. "Yes, a comfort, knowing you didn't give up on me quickly, or easily."

"Unlike you, who gave up so quickly and easily."

"I'm sorry."

"I'm sure you are, now that the privileged Copelands are broke."

She laughed to keep from crying. He was so very, very changed. "We're broke," she agreed, "every last one of us, and struggling, but my brother and sisters, they're smart. They'll be fine. They'll come out of this okay. Me…I'm in trouble. I'm stupid—"

"If this is a play for my sympathy, it's not working."

"No. I'm just telling you the truth. I'm stupid. Very, very stupid. You see, I didn't come to you first. I tried to handle the pirates on my own. And I've already given them money—"

"What?"

She licked her lower lip. "We didn't want it known about my father, and so we kept the details to ourselves, and I tried to manage freeing my father on my own, and I gave them money. But they didn't free my father."

Drakon just looked at her, his jaw clenched, his lips a hard flat line. She could see the pulse beating at the base of his throat. His amber gaze burned. He was furious.

Furious.

Morgan exhaled slowly, trying to calm herself, trying to steady her nerves, but it wasn't easy when her heart raced and the blood roared in her ears. "I didn't want to have to bother you, Drakon. I thought I could manage things better than I did."

He just kept staring at her, his spine stiff, his muscles tensed. He was clearly at war within himself and Morgan felt his anger and frustration. He wanted to kick her out of the villa but he didn't run from responsibilities, or from providing for his family.

He was Greek. Family was everything to him. Even if he didn't enjoy his family.

His tone was icy cold as he spoke. "You should have never tried to handle the pirates on your own. You should have gone to Dunamas or Blue Sea immediately—"

"I didn't have the money to pay for outside help or expertise," she said softly, cutting him short, unable to endure another lecture. "I didn't even have enough to pay the three million ransom. You see, that's what they asked for in the beginning. Three million. But I couldn't come up with exactly three million, and I'd run out of time, so I made the sea drop with what I had, thinking that almost three million was better than nothing, but I was wrong. The pirates were really angry, and accused me of playing games, and they were now doubling the ransom to six million and I had just two weeks or they'd execute Dad."

"How much were you short?"

"A hundred thousand."

"But you dropped two-point-nine million?"

She nodded. "I was so close to three million, and to get it I emptied my savings, sold my loft, liquidated everything I had, but I couldn't get more. I tried taking out personal loans from family and friends but no one was able to come up with a hundred thousand cash in the amount of time we had."

"You didn't come to me for the hundred thousand."

"I didn't want to involve you."

"You have now."

"Because there was no one else who would help me. No other way to come up with six million without my father's situation becoming public knowledge."

"One hundred thousand would have been a hell of a lot cheaper than six million."

"I know." Her stomach heaved. She felt so terribly queasy. "But then, I told you I was stupid. I was afraid to come to you, afraid to face you—"

"I wouldn't have hurt you."

"No, but I have my pride. And then there were all those feelings—" she broke off, and gulped air, thinking she might just throw up "—because I did have feelings for you, and they confused me, but in the end, I had to come. Had to ask you for help…help and money, because the pirates are playing games. They're toying with me and I'm scared. Scared of botching this, scared of never seeing my father again, scared that they have all the power and I have none."

She opened her fist, smoothed the creased check, studied the number and sum it represented. "I know you're angry with me, and I know you owe me nothing. I know it's I that owe you, but I need your help, Drakon. At the very least, I need your advice. What do I do now? How do I make sure that they will release my father this time?" Her gaze lifted, met his. "Who is to say that they will ever release him? Who is to say that he's even…he's even…" Her voice drifted off, and she gazed at him, unable to finish the thought.

But she didn't have to finish the thought. "You're afraid he might not be alive," Drakon said, brutally blunt.

She nodded, eyes stinging. "What if he isn't?"

"That's a good question."

"So you see why I need you. I've already given them three million. I can't give them another six without proof, but they refuse to let me speak to him, and I don't know what to do. I'm frightened, Drakon. And overwhelmed. I've been trying to keep it together, but I don't know how to do this—"

"You and your father sing the same tune, don't you?"

She just stared at him, confused. "What does that mean?"

"The only time I hear from you, or your father, is when one of the Copelands needs money. But I'm not a bank, or an ATM machine, and I'm tired of being used."

Morgan struggled to speak. "I never meant to use you, Drakon. And I certainly didn't marry you for money, and I'm ashamed my father asked you to invest in his company, ashamed that he'd put you in that position. I didn't agree with it then, and I'm shattered now that he lost so much of your personal wealth, but he is my father, and I can't leave him in Somalia. It might be acceptable…even fiscally responsible, but it's not morally responsible, not to me. And so I'm here, begging for your help because you are the only one who can help me."

She paused, swallowed, her gaze searching his face, trying to see a hint of softening on his part. "You might not want to hear this right now, Drakon, but you'd do the same if it were your family. I know you…I know who you are, and I know you'd sacrifice everything if you had to."

Drakon looked at her hard, his features harsh, expression shuttered, and then turned away, and walked to the window where he put his hand on the glass, his gaze fixed on the blue horizon. Silence stretched. Morgan waited for him to speak, not wanting to say more, or rush him to a decision, because she knew in her heart, he couldn't tell her no…it'd go against his values, go against his ethics as a man, and a protective Greek male.

But it was hard to wait, and her jaw ached from biting down

so hard, and her stomach churned and her head throbbed, but she had to wait. The ball was in Drakon's court now.

It was a long time before he spoke, and when he did, his voice was pitched so low she had to strain to hear. "I have sacrificed everything for my family," he said roughly. "And it taught me that no good deed goes unpunished."

Her eyes burned, gritty, and her chest squeezed tight with hot emotion. "Please tell me I wasn't the one who taught you that!"

His hand turned into a fist on the window.

Morgan closed her eyes, held her breath, her heart livid with pain. She had loved him…so much…too much….

"I need to think, and want some time," Drakon said, still staring out the window, after another long, tense silence. "Go downstairs. Wait for me there."

CHAPTER THREE

DRAKON WAITED FOR the bedroom door to close behind Morgan before turning around.

His gut churned with acid and every breath he drew hurt.

He wasn't going to do it. There was no way in hell he'd actually help her free her father. For one—he *hated* her father. For another—Drakon had washed his hands of her. The beard was gone. The vigil was over. Time to move forward.

There was no reason he needed to be involved. No reason to do more than he had. As it was, he'd gone above and beyond the call of duty. He'd given her the money, he'd told her what to do, he'd made it clear that there were those who knew exactly what to do, he'd named the people to call... he'd done everything for her, short of actually dialing Dunamas on his cell phone, and good God, he would not do that.

Drakon stalked back to the bathroom, stared at his reflection, seeing the grim features, the cold, dead eyes, and then suddenly his face dissolved in the mirror and he saw Morgan's instead.

He saw that perfect pale oval with its fine, elegant features, but her loveliness was overshadowed by the worry in her blue eyes, and the dark purple smudges beneath her eyes, and her unnatural pallor. Worse, even here, in the expansive marble bathroom, he could still feel her exhaustion and fatigue.

She'd practically trembled while talking to him, her thin arms and legs still too frail for his liking and he flashed back

to that day in New York where he'd spotted her walking out
of her shop with Jemma. Morgan might not be sick now, but
she didn't look well.

Someone, somewhere should be helping her. Not him…
she wasn't his to protect anymore…but there should be someone who could assist her. In an ideal world, there would be
someone.

He shook his head, not comfortable with the direction
his thoughts were taking him. She's not your problem, he
told himself. She's not your responsibility. Not your woman.

Drakon groaned, turned away from the mirror, walked
out of the bathroom, to retrieve his phone. He'd make a few
calls, check on a few facts, see if he couldn't find someone
to work with her, because she'd need someone at her side.
Not him, of course, but someone who could offer advice and
assistance, or just be a source of support.

Standing outside on his balcony he made a few calls, and
then he made a few more, and a few more, and each call was
worse than the last.

Morgan Copeland was in trouble.

She'd lost her home, her company, her friends, her reputation. She was a social outcast, *and* she was broke. She was
overdrawn in her checking account and she'd maxed out
every credit card she owned.

Drakon hung up from his last call and tossed the phone
onto the bed.

Dammit.

Dammit.

He was so angry with her.…

And so angry with her rarified world for turning on her.

She had lost everything. She hadn't been exaggerating.

Morgan was standing in the living room by the enormous
wall of windows when Drakon appeared, almost an hour after
she'd left him in his bedroom. He'd dressed once again in

the off white cashmere V-neck sweater he'd worn earlier, his legs long in the pressed khaki trousers, the sweater smooth over his muscular chest. He'd always had an amazing body, and his perfect build allowed him to wear anything and now with the beard gone she could see his face again and she couldn't look away.

She couldn't call him beautiful, his features were so strong, and his coloring so dark, but he had a sensuality and vitality about him that fascinated her, captivated her. "How long had you been growing that beard?" she asked.

"A long time."

"Years?"

"I'm not here to discuss my beard," he said curtly, crossing the room, walking toward her. "While upstairs I did some research, made a few phone calls, and you did sell your loft. Along with your boutique in SoHo."

Energy crackled around him and Morgan felt her insides jump, tumble. He was so physical, always had been, and the closer he got, the more the tension shifted, growing, building, changing, binding them together the way it always had. The way it always did. "I had to," she said breathlessly, "it was the only way to come up with the money."

"You should have told me immediately that you'd given the Somali pirates ransom money and that they'd failed to release your father."

"I thought you might not have helped me, if you knew…." Her voice faded as Drakon closed the distance between them. He was so alive, so electric, she could almost see little sparks shooting off him. Her heart pounded. Her tummy did another nervous, panicked flip.

She shouldn't have sent away the helicopter. She should have gone while she could. Now it was too late to run. Too late to save herself, and so she stared at him, waited for him, feeling the energy, his energy, that dizzying combination of warmth and heat, light and sparks. This was inevitable. He was inevitable. She could run and run and run, but part of her knew she'd never escape him. She'd run before and yet here she was. Right back where they'd honeymooned, Villa Angelica.

She'd known that coming here, to him, would change everything. Would change her.

It always did.

It already had.

Her legs trembled beneath her. Her heart pounded. Even now, after all these years, she felt almost sick with awareness, need. This chemistry and energy between them was so overwhelming. So consuming. She didn't understand it, and she'd wanted to understand it, if only to help her exorcise him from her heart and her mind.

But all the counselors and doctors and therapists in the world hadn't erased this…him.

Why was Drakon so alive? Why was he more real to her than any other man she'd ever met? After Drakon, after loving Drakon, there could be no one else…he made it impossible for her to even look at anyone else.

He'd reached her, was standing before her, his gaze fierce, intense, as it traveled across her face, making her feel so bare, and naked. Heat bloomed in her skin, blood surging from his close inspection.

"What did you do, Morgan?"

"I don't understand."

"You've sold everything," he added harshly. "You have nothing and even if you get your father back to the United States, you'll still have nothing."

"Not true," she said, locking her knees, afraid she'd collapse, overwhelmed by emotion and memories, overwhelmed by him. She'd been up for two days straight. Hadn't eaten more than a mouthful in that time. She couldn't, knowing she would soon be here, with him again. "I'd have peace of mind."

"Peace of mind?" he demanded. "How can you have peace of mind when you have no home?"

He could mock her, because he didn't know what it was like to lose one's mind. He didn't know that after leaving him, she'd ended up in the hospital and had remained there for far too long. It had been the lowest point in her life, and by far, the darkest part. But she didn't want to think about McLean Hospital now, that was the past, and she had to live in the present, had to stay focused on what was important, like her father. "I did what I had to do."

"You sacrificed your future for your father's, and he doesn't have a future. Your father—*if* alive, *if* released—will be going to prison for the rest of his life. But what will you do while he's in his comfortable, minimum security prison cell, getting three square meals a day? Where will you sleep? What will you eat? How will you get by?"

"I'll figure it out."

"You are so brave and yet foolhardy. Do you ever look before you leap?"

She flashed to Vienna and their wedding and the four weeks of honeymoon, remembering the intense love and need, the hot brilliant desire that had consumed her night and day. She hated to be away from him, hated to wake up without him, hated to breathe without him.

She'd lost herself completely in him. And no, she hadn't looked, hadn't analyzed, hadn't imagined anything beyond that moment when she'd married him and became his.

"No," she answered huskily, lips curving and heart aching. "I just leap, Drakon. Leap and hope I can fly."

If she'd hoped to provoke him, she'd failed. His expression was impassive and he studied her for a long moment from beneath his thick black lashes. "How long has it been since you've spoken to your father?"

"I actually haven't ever spoken to him. My mother did, and just that first day, when they called her to say they had him. Mother summoned us, and told us what had happened, and what the pirates wanted for a ransom."

"How long did she speak to your father?"

"Not long. Just a few words, not much more than that."

"What did he say to her?"

"That his yacht had been seized, his captain killed and he had been abducted, and then the pirates got back on the phone, told her their demands and hung up."

"Has anyone spoken with your father since?"

She shook her head. "No."

"Why not?"

"They won't let us. They say we haven't earned the right."

"But you've given them three million."

Her lips curved bitterly and her gaze lifted to meet his. "I can't sleep at night, knowing I was so stupid and so wasteful. Three million dollars gone! Three million lost forever. It would have been fine if we'd saved my father, but we didn't. I didn't. Instead it's all gone and now I must start over and worse, the ransom has doubled. I'm sick about it, sick that I made such a critical error. I didn't mind liquidating everything to save my father, but it turns out I liquidated everything for nothing—"

"Stop."

"You are right to despise me. I am stupid, stupid, stupid—"

He caught her by the shoulders and gave her a hard shake. "Enough. You didn't know. You didn't understand how the pirates operated, how mercurial they are, how difficult, how unpredictable. You had no way of knowing. There is no handbook on dealing with pirates, so stop torturing yourself."

With every sentence he gave her a little shake until she was thoroughly undone and tears filled her eyes, ridiculous tears that stung and she swiped at them, annoyed, knowing they were from fatigue, not sadness, aware that she was exhausted beyond reason, knowing that what she wanted was

Drakon to kiss her, not shake her, but just because you wanted something didn't mean it was good for you. And Drakon wasn't good for her. She had to remember that.

He saw her tears. His features darkened. "We'll get your father back," he said, his deep voice rumbling through her, his voice as carnal as the rest of him, drawing her into his arms and holding her against his chest, comforting her.

For a moment.

Morgan pulled back, slipping from Drakon's arms, and took several quick steps away to keep from being tempted to return. He'd been so warm. He'd smelled so good. His hard chest, covered in cashmere, had made her want to burrow closer. She'd felt safe there, secure, and yet it was an illusion.

Drakon wasn't safe. He was anything but safe for her.

He watched her make her escape. His jaw jutted, his brow lowered, expression brooding. "We'll get your father back," he said, repeating his promise from a few moments ago. "And we'll do it without giving them another dollar."

She looked up at him, surprised. "How?"

"I know people."

She blinked at him. Of course he knew people—Drakon knew everyone—but could he really free her father without giving the pirates more money? "Is that possible?"

"There are companies...services...that exist just for this purpose."

"I've looked into those companies. They cost millions, and they won't help me. They loathe my father. He represents everything they detest—"

"But they'll work with me."

"Not when they hear who they are to rescue—"

"I own one of the largest shipping companies in the world. No maritime agency would refuse me."

Hope rose up within her, but she didn't trust it, didn't trust anyone or anything anymore. "But you said...you said you wouldn't help me. You said since you'd given me the check—"

"I was wrong. I was being petty. But I can't be petty. You're my wife—" he saw her start to protest and overrode her "—and as long as you are my wife, it's my duty to care for you and your family. It is the vow I made, and a vow I will keep."

"Even though I left you?"

"You left me. I didn't leave you."

Pain flickered through her. "You owe me nothing. I know that. You must know that, too."

"Marriage isn't about keeping score. Life is uneven and frequently unjust and I did not marry you, anticipating only fun and games. I expected there would be challenges, and there have been, far more than I anticipated, but until we are divorced, you are my wife, and the law is the law, and it is my duty to provide for you, to protect you, and I can see I have failed to do both."

She closed her eyes, shattered by his honesty, as well as his sense of responsibility. Drakon was a good man, a fair man, and he deserved a good wife, a wife less highly strung and sensitive…a wife who craved him less, a wife who could live and breathe without him at her side.…

Morgan wasn't that woman. Even now she wanted to be back in his arms, to have his mouth on hers, to have him parting her lips, tasting her, filling her, possessing her so completely that the world fell away, leaving just the two of them.

That was her idea of life.

And it was mad and beautiful and impossible and bewitching.

"It's not your fault," she whispered, wrapping her arms around her, wishing she'd needed less talk and tenderness and reassurance. "It's mine. Maybe even my father's. He spoiled me, you know, and it infuriated my mother."

"Your mother did say at our wedding that you were your daddy's little girl."

Morgan's breath caught in her throat and she bit into her bottom lip. "Mother had Tori and Branson and Logan, and yes, I was Daddy's girl, but they were Mother's darlings, and you'd think since she had them living with her, choosing her, she wouldn't mind that I chose to live with Father, but she did."

"What do you mean, they lived with her, and you lived with Daniel? Didn't you all live together?"

Morgan shook her head. "Mother and Father lived apart most of the time. They'd put on a show for everyone else—united front for the public, always throwing big parties for the holidays or special occasions…Christmas party, New Year's party, birthdays and anniversaries. But behind closed doors, they could barely tolerate each other and were almost never in the same place at the same time, unless there was a photo shoot, or reporter about. Mother loved being in the society columns, loved having our lavish, privileged lifestyle featured in glossy magazines. She liked being envied, enjoyed her place in the sun. Father was different. He hadn't grown up with money like Mother, and wasn't comfortable in the spotlight. He lived far more quietly…he and I, and Jemma, when she joined us. We'd go to these small neighborhood restaurants and they weren't trendy in the least. We loved our Mexican food and Greek food and Indian food and maybe once every week or two, we'd send out for Chinese food. After dinner, once my homework was done, we'd watch television in the evening…we had our favorite show. We had our routines. It was lovely. He was lovely. And ordinary." She looked up at Drakon, sorrow in her eyes. "But the world now won't ever know that man, or allow him to be that man. In their eyes, he's a greedy selfish hateful man, but he wasn't. He really wasn't—" She broke off, drew a deep breath and then another.

"Mother used to say I was a demanding little girl, and she hated that Father humored me. She said he spoiled me by taking me everywhere with him, and turning me into his shadow. Apparently that's why I became so clingy with you. I shifted my attachment from my father onto you. But what a horrible thing for you...to be saddled with a wife who can't be happy on her own—"

"You're talking nonsense, Morgan—"

"No, it's true."

"Well, I don't buy it. I was never saddled with you, nor did I ever feel encumbered by you. I'm a man. I do as I please and I married you because I chose you, and I stayed married to you because I chose to, and that's all there is to it."

She looked away, giving him her profile. It was such a beautiful profile. Delicate. Elegant. The long, black eyelashes, the sweep of cheekbone, the small straight nose, the strong chin, above an impossibly long neck. The Copeland girls were all stunning young women, but there was something ethereal about Morgan...something mysterious.

"You're exhausted," he added. "I can see you're not eating or sleeping and that must change. I will not have you become skin and bones again. While you're here, you will sit and eat real meals, and rest, and allow me to worry about things. I may not have been the patient and affectionate husband you wanted, but I'm good at managing chaos, and I'm damn good at dealing with pirates."

He didn't know what he expected, but he didn't expect her to suddenly smile at him, the first smile he'd seen from her since she arrived, and it was radiant, angelic, starting in her stunning blue eyes and curving her lips and making her lovely face come alive.

For a moment he could only look at her, and appreciate her. She was like the sun and she glowed, vital, beautiful, and he remembered that first night in Vienna when she'd turned and looked at him, her blue eyes dancing, mischief playing at her mouth, and then she'd spotted him, her eyes meeting his, and her smile had faded, and she'd become shy.

She'd blushed and turned away but then she'd peek over her shoulder at him again and again and by the end of the ball he knew he would have her. She was his. She would always be his. Thank God she'd felt the same way. It would have created an international scandal if he'd had to kidnap her and drag her off to Greece, an unwilling bride.

"I am happy to allow you to take the lead when it comes to the pirates," she said, her smile slowly dying, "and you may manage them, but Drakon, you mustn't try to manage me. I won't be managed. I've had enough of that these past five years."

Drakon frowned, sensing that there was a great deal she wasn't saying, a great deal he wouldn't like hearing, and he wanted to ask her questions, hard questions, but now wasn't the time, not when she was so fragile and fatigued. There would be time for all his questions later, time to learn just what had dismantled his marriage, and who and what had been managing her, but he could do that when she wasn't trembling with exhaustion and with dark purple circles shadowing her eyes.

"I'm concerned about you," he said flatly.

"There's been a lot of stress lately."

He didn't doubt that, and it crossed his mind that if he'd been a real husband, and a more selfless man, he would have gone to Morgan, and offered her support or assistance before it'd come to this. Instead, he, like the rest of the world, had followed the Copeland family crisis from afar, reading about the latest humiliation or legal move in the media, and doing nothing.

"I can see that, but you'll be of no use to your father, if you fall apart yourself," he said. "I'll make some calls and the staff can prepare us a late lunch—"

"Do we really need lunch?"

"Yes, we do. And while I understand time is of the essence, not eating will only make things worse. We need clear heads and fierce resolve, and that won't happen if we're faint-ing on our feet."

Morgan suddenly laughed and she shook her head, once again giving him a glimpse of the Morgan he'd married... young and vivacious and full of laughter and passion. "You keep using 'we,' when we both know you mean me." She paused and her gaze lifted, her eyes meeting his. "But I do rather like the image of you fainting on your feet."

His gaze met hers and held and it was all he could do to keep from reaching for her. He wanted her. Still wanted her more than he'd wanted anyone or anything. "Of course you would," he said roughly. "You're a wicked woman and you deserve to be——"

Drakon broke off abruptly, balling his hands into fists and he realized how close he'd come to teasing her the way he'd once teased her, promising her punishment, which was merely foreplay to make her hot, to make her wet, to make her shudder with pleasure.

It used to give him such pleasure that he brought her plea-sure. He wasn't good at saying all the right words, so he used his body to say how much he adored her, how much he desired her, how much he cherished her and would always cherish her.

But only now did he know she'd hated the way he'd plea-sured her.

That she'd been disgusted——

"Don't," she whispered, reaching out to him, her hand set-tling on his arm. "Don't do that, don't. I know what you're thinking, and I'm sorry. I shouldn't have said what I did, shouldn't have said it how I did. It was wrong. I was wrong. I was upset."

His body hardened instantly at her touch, and he glanced down at her hand where it clung to his forearm. He could feel her warmth through the softness of the cashmere, and the press of her fingers, and it was nothing at all, and yet it was everything, too. Nothing and everything at the same time.

He looked away from her hand, up into her eyes, angry with her all over again, but also angry with himself. How could he have not known how she felt? How could he have not realized that she didn't enjoy...him...them?

"Rest assured that I will not take advantage of you while you are here," he said, trying to ease some of the tension rippling through him. "You are safe in the villa," he continued, hating that he suddenly felt like a monster. He wasn't a monster. Not even close. It's true he could be ruthless in business, and he had a reputation for being a fierce negotiator, a brilliant strategist, an analytical executive, as well as a demanding boss, but that didn't make him an ogre and he'd never knowingly hurt a woman, much less his wife. "You are safe from me."

"Drakon."

"I'll have your bag taken up to the Angelica Suite," he said. "It's the second master suite, on the third floor, the suite one with the frescoed ceiling."

"I remember it."

"It's in the opposite wing of where I'm staying but it should give you privacy and I think you'll find it quite comfortable. I can show you the way now."

"There's no need to take me there," she said hoarsely. "I remember the suite."

"Fine. Then I'll let you find your way, and as I have quite a few things to do, I'll eat as I work, and I'll have a light lunch sent to you in your room, but we'll need to meet later so I can fill you in on the arrangements I've been able to make for your father."

Morgan was glad to escape to her room, desperate to get away from Drakon and that intense physical awareness of him....

She'd hurt him. What she'd said earlier, about their sex

life, about their marriage, it'd hurt him terribly and she felt guilty and sorry. So very sorry since she knew Drakon would never do anything to hurt her. He'd always been so protective of her but he was also so very physical, so carnal and sexual and she was a little afraid of it. And him. Not when she was with him, making love to him, but later, when he was gone, separated from her. It was then that she analyzed their relationship, and what they did and how they did it and how little control she had with him.

It frightened her that she lost control with him.

Frightened her that he had so much power and she had so little.

It had niggled at her during their honeymoon, but their picnics and dinners out and the afternoon trips on his yacht were so fun and romantic that she could almost forget how fierce and shattering the sex was when he was charming and attentive and affectionate. But in Athens when he disappeared into his work life, his real life, the raw nature of their sex life struck her as ugly, and she became ugly and it all began to unravel, very, very quickly.

Upstairs in her suite, Morgan barely had time to open the two sets of French doors before a knock sounded on the outer bedroom door, letting her know her overnight bag had arrived. She thanked the housemaid and then returned to the first of the two generous balconies with the stunning view.

She had never tired of this view. She couldn't imagine how anyone could tire of it.

The Amalfi Coast's intense blues and greens contrasted by rugged rock had inspired her very first jewelry collection. She'd worked with polished labradorite, blue chalcedony, pāua shell, lapis lazuli and Chinese turquoise, stones she'd acquired on two extensive shopping trips through Southeast Asia, from Hong Kong to Singapore to Bali.

It'd been a three-month shopping expedition that big sister

Tori had accompanied her on for the first month, and then Logan came for the second month, and Jemma for the third.

By the time Morgan returned to New York, she'd filled two enormous trunks of stones and had a briefcase and laptop full of sketches and the first orders from Neiman Marcus and Bergdorf Goodman. The designs were pure fantasy—a stunning collection of statement-making collars, cuffs and drop earrings—and had cost her a fortune in stone. It had tested her ability to execute her ideas, but had ended up being worth every stress and struggle as the Amalfi Collection turned out to be a huge success, generating significant media attention, as well as the attention of every fashion designer and fashion publicist of note, never mind the starlets, celebrities and socialites who all wanted a Morgan Copeland statement piece.

Morgan's second collection, Jasper Ice, had been inspired by her love of the Canadian Rockies and ski trips to Banff and Lake Louise. The collection was something that an ice princess in a frozen tundra would wear—frosty and shimmering pieces in white, silver, blush, beige and pale gold. The second collection did almost as well as the first, and garnered even more media with mentions in virtually every fashion magazine in North America, Europe and Australia, and then photographed on celebrities and young royals, like the Saudi princess who had worn a gorgeous pink diamond cuff for her wedding.

Morgan was glad Jasper Ice did well, but the cool, frozen beauty of the collection was too much like her numb emotional state, when she'd been so fiercely, frantically alive and in love with Drakon Xanthis.

Drakon, though, was the last person she wanted to think of, especially when she was enjoying the heady rush of success, and for a while she had been very good at blocking him out of her mind, but then one October day, she had been walking with Jemma to lunch and she had spotted a man in a limousine. He'd had a beard and his hair was long but his eyes reminded her so much of Drakon that for a moment she thought it was him.

She had kept walking, thinking she'd escaped, but then a block away from her shop, she'd had to stop, lean against a building and fight for air.

She'd felt like she was having a heart attack. Her chest hurt, the muscles seizing, and she couldn't breathe, couldn't get air, couldn't even speak. She opened her mouth, stared at Jemma, wanting, needing help, but she couldn't make a sound. Then everything went black.

When she woke up, she'd been in an ambulance, and then when she woke again, she was in a bed in the emergency room. She'd spent the next ten days in the hospital, six in ICU, being seen by cardiac specialists. The specialists explained that her extreme weight loss had damaged her heart, and they warned her that if she didn't make immediate and drastic changes, she could die of heart failure.

But Morgan hadn't been dieting. She didn't want to lose weight. She had just found it impossible to eat when her heart was broken. But she wasn't a fool, she understood the gravity of her situation, and recognized she was in trouble.

During the day they'd fed her special shakes and meals and at night she'd dreamed of Drakon, and the dreams had been so vivid and intense that she'd woke desperate each morning to actually see him. She made the mistake of telling Logan that she was dreaming about Drakon every night, and Logan had told their mother, who then told the doctors, and before Morgan knew it, the psychiatrists were back with their pills and questions and notepads.

Did she understand the difference between reality and fantasy?

Did she understand the meaning of wish fulfillment?

Did she want to die?

It would have been puzzling if she hadn't been through all this before at McLean Hospital in Massachusetts, and then at the Wallace Home for a year after that. But she had been through it before so she found the doctors with their clipboards and questions and colorful assortment of pills annoying and even somewhat amusing.

She'd refused the pills. She'd answered some questions. She'd refused to answer others.

She wasn't sick or crazy this time. She was just pushing herself too hard, working too many hours, not eating and sleeping enough.

Morgan had promised her medical team and her family she'd slow down, and eat better, and sleep more and enjoy life more, and for the next two plus years she did. She began to take vacations, joining her sisters for long holidays at the family's Caribbean island, or skiing in Sun Valley or Chamonix, and sometimes she just went off on her own, visiting exotic locations for inspiration for her jewelry designs.

She'd also learned her lesson. She couldn't, wouldn't, mention Drakon again.

Those ten days in the hospital, and her vivid, shattering dreams at night, had inspired her third collection, the Black Prince, a glamorous, dramatic collection built of ruby hues—garnets, red spinels, pink sapphires, diamonds, pave garnets, watermelon tourmaline, pink tourmaline. The collection was a tribute to her brief marriage and the years that followed, mad love, accompanied by mad grief. In her imagination, the Black Prince was Drakon, and the bloodred jewels represented her heart, which she'd cut and handed to him, while the pink sapphires and delicate tourmalines were the tears she'd cried leaving him.

But, of course, she had to keep that inspiration to herself, and so she came up with a more acceptable story for the public, claiming that her newest collection was inspired by the Black Prince's ruby, a 170-carat red spinel once worn in Henry V's battle helmet.

The collection was romantic and over-the-top and wildly

passionate, and early feedback had seemed promising with orders pouring in for the large rings, and jeweled cuffs, and stunning pendulum necklaces made of eye-popping pale pink tourmaline—but then a week before the official launch of her collection, news of the Michael Amery scandal broke and she knew she was in trouble. It was too late to pull any of her ads, or change the focus of the marketing for her latest Morgan Copeland collection.

It was absolutely the wrong collection to be launched in the middle of a scandal implicating Daniel Copeland, and thereby tarnishing the Copeland name. The Black Prince Collection had been over-the-top even at conception, and the finished pieces were sensual and emotional, extravagant and dramatic, and at any other time, the press and fashion darlings would have embraced her boldness, but in the wake of the scandal where hundreds of thousands of people had been robbed by Michael Amery and Daniel Copeland, the media turned on her, criticizing her for being insensitive and hopelessly out of touch with mainstream America. One critic went so far as to compare her to Marie Antoinette, saying that the Black Prince Collection was as "frivolous and useless" as Morgan Copeland herself.

Morgan had tried to prepare herself for the worst, but the viciousness of the criticism, and the weeks of vitriolic attacks, had been unending. Her brother, Branson, a media magnate residing in London, had sent her an email early on, advising her to avoid the press, and to not read the things being written about her. But she did read them. She couldn't seem to help herself.

In the fallout following the Amery Ponzi scandal, the orders that had been placed for her lush Black Prince Collection were canceled, and stores that had trumpeted her earlier collections quietly returned her remaining pieces and closed their accounts with her. No one wanted to carry anything

with the Copeland name. No one wanted to have an asso-
ciation with her.

It was crushing, financially and psychologically. She'd
invested hundreds of thousands of dollars into the stones,
as well as thousands and thousands into the labor, and thousands more into the marketing and sales. The entire collection was a bust, as was her business.

Fortunately, there was no time to wallow in self-pity. The
phone call from Northern Africa, alerting her that her father
had been kidnapped, had forced her to prioritize issues. She
could grieve the loss of her business later. Now, she had to
focus on her father.

And yet…standing here, on the balcony, with the bright
sun glittering on the sapphire water, Morgan knew she
wouldn't have had any success as a designer, or any confidence in her creative ability, if it hadn't been for her honeymoon here in this villa.

And Drakon.

But that went without saying.

CHAPTER FOUR

MORGAN HAD ONLY packed her traveling clothes and the one blue linen top and skirt she'd changed into after arriving in Naples, and so before lunch arrived, she slipped into her comfortable tracksuit to eat her lunch on the balcony before taking a nap. She hadn't meant to sleep the afternoon away but she loved the breeze from the open doors and how it fluttered the long linen curtains and carried the scents of wisteria and roses and lemon blossoms.

She slept for hours in the large bed with the fluffy duvet and the down pillows all covered in the softest of linens. The Italians knew how to make decadent linens and it was here on her honeymoon that she'd come to appreciate cool, smooth sheets and lazy afternoon naps. She'd fall asleep in Drakon's arms after making love and wake in his arms and make love yet again and it was all so sensual, so indulgent. It had been pure fantasy.

She'd dreamed of Drakon while she slept, dreamed they were still together, still happy, and parents of a beautiful baby girl. Waking, Morgan reached for Drakon, her hand slipping sleepily across the duvet, only to discover that the other side of her big bed was empty, cool, the covers undisturbed. Rolling onto her side, she realized it was just a dream. Yet more fantasy.

Tears stung her eyes and her heart felt wrenched, and the heartbreak of losing Drakon felt as real as it had five years ago, when her family had insisted she go to McLean Hospital instead of return to Drakon in Greece.

You're not well. This isn't healthy. You're not healthy. You're too desperate. This is insanity. You're losing your mind....

Her throat swelled closed and her chest ached and she bit into her lip to keep the memories at bay.

If she hadn't left Drakon they probably would have children now. Babies...toddlers...little boys and girls...

She'd wanted a family with him, but once in Greece Drakon had become a stranger and she had feared they were turning into her own parents: distant, silent, destined to live separate lives.

She couldn't do it. Couldn't be like her parents. Wouldn't raise children in such an unhealthy, unsuitable environment.

Stop thinking about it, she told herself, flipping the covers back and leaving the bed to bathe before dinner. In her grand bathroom with the soaring frescoed ceiling and the warm cream-and-terra-cotta marble, she took a long soak in the deep tub before returning to the bedroom to put her tired linen skirt and blouse back on. But in the bedroom the crumpled blue skirt and blouse were gone and in their place was a huge open Louis Vuitton trunk sitting on the bench at the foot of the bed.

She recognized the elegant taupe-and-cream trunk—it was part of the luggage set her father had given her before her wedding and it was filled with clothes. Her clothes, her shoes, her jewelry, all from the Athens villa. Drakon must have sent for them. It was a thoughtful gesture and she was grateful for clean clothes and something fresh to wear, but it was painful seeing her beautiful wardrobe...so very extravagant, so much couture. So much money invested in a couple dozen dresses and blouses and trousers. Thousands more in shoes and purses.

Morgan sorted through the sundresses and evening dresses

and chic tunics and caftans. Her sisters were far more fash-
ionable than she was, and constantly pushing her to be a bit
more trendy, but Morgan liked to be comfortable and loved
floaty dresses that skimmed her body rather than hug every
curve, but she needed something more fitted tonight, something to keep her together because she was so close to falling apart.

She settled on a white eyelet dress with a boned corset and
small puffy sleeves that made her feel like a Gypsy, and she
added gold hoop earrings and a coral red shawl worn loosely
around her shoulders. Morgan didn't wear a lot of makeup
and applied just a hint of color to her cheeks and lips, a little
concealer to soften the circles that remained beneath her eyes
and then a bit of mascara because it gave her confidence.

The sun was just starting to set as she headed downstairs.
She remembered her way to the dining room, but one of the
villa staff was on hand at the foot of the stairs to escort her
there. Before she'd even entered the dining room she spotted Drakon on the patio, through the dining room's open
doors. He was outside, leaning against the iron railing, talking on the phone.

She hesitated before joining him, content for a moment to
just look at him while he was preoccupied.

He'd changed from the cashmere sweater to a white linen
shirt and a pair of jeans for dinner. His choice in wardrobe
surprised her.

Jeans.

She'd never seen him wear jeans before, and these weren't
fancy European denim jeans, but the faded American Levi's
style and they looked amazing on him. The jeans were old
and worn and they outlined Drakon's strong thighs and
hugged his hard butt and made her look a little too long at
the button fly that covered his impressive masculine parts.

How odd this new Drakon was, so different from the sophisticated, polished man she'd remembered all these years

ago. His beard and long hair might be gone, but he still wasn't the Drakon of old. He was someone else, someone new, and that kept taking her by surprise.

The Drakon she'd married had been an incredibly successful man aware of his power, his wealth, his stature. He'd liked Morgan to dress up, to wear beautiful clothes, to be seen in the best of everything, and Drakon himself dressed accordingly. He wouldn't have ever worn a simple white linen shirt halfway unbuttoned to show off his bronze muscular chest. He'd been too controlled, too tightly wound, while this man…he oozed recklessness. And sex.

Drakon had always had an amazing body, but this new one was even stronger and more fit now and Morgan swallowed hard, hating to admit it, but she was fascinated by him. Fascinated and a little bit turned on, which wasn't at all appropriate given the situation, especially considering how Drakon had promised not to touch her….

Drakon suddenly turned, and looked straight at her, his amber gaze meeting hers through the open door. Despite everything, heat flickered in his eyes and she swallowed hard again, even as she blushed hotly, aware that she'd been caught staring.

Nervous, she squared her shoulders and briskly crossed the dining room before stepping outside onto the patio. Drakon had just ended his call as she joined him outside and he slipped the phone into the front pocket of his jeans.

Those damn faded jeans that lovingly outlined his very male body.

There was no reason a Greek shipping magnate needed a body like that. It was decadent for a man who already had so much. His body was beautiful. Sexual. Sinful. He knew how to use it, too, especially those lean hard hips. Never mind his skillful fingers, lips and tongue.

"Hope I didn't keep you waiting long," he said.

Cheeks hot, insides flip-flopping, she reluctantly dragged

her gaze from his button fly up to his face with its newly shaven jaw and square chin. "No," she murmured, almost missing the dark thick beard and long hair. When she'd first arrived, he'd looked so primitive and primal. So undeniably male that she wouldn't have been surprised if he'd pushed her up against the wall and taken her there.

Perhaps a little part of her wished he had.

Instead he'd vowed to stay away from her, and she knew Drakon took his vows seriously. Was it so wrong of her to wish he'd kissed her properly before he'd made that vow? Was it wrong to crave his skin even though he'd made the vow already?

Just thinking of his skin made her glance at his chest, at that broad expanse of hard muscle, and her body reacted, her inner thighs tightening, clenching, while her lower belly ached with emptiness. She hadn't been honest with him. She had loved to make love with him, loved the way he felt inside of her, his body buried deeply between her thighs and how he'd draw back before thrusting back in, over and over until she raked her nails across his shoulders and gripped his arms and arched under him, crying his name.

And just remembering, she could almost feel the weight of him now, his arms stretching her arms above her head, his hands circling her wrists, his chest pressed to her breasts. He'd thrust his tongue into her mouth even as his hard, hot body thrust into hers, burying himself so deeply she couldn't think, feel, want anything but Drakon.

Drakon.

And now she was here with him. Finally. After all these years.

Morgan, it's not going to happen, she told herself. He's letting you go. You're moving on. There will be no sex against the wall, or sex on the floor, or sex on the small dining table painted gold and rose with the lush sunset.

But wouldn't it feel good? another little voice whispered.

Of course it'd feel good. Everything with Drakon had felt good. Sex wasn't the problem. It was the distance after the sex that was.

"Something to drink?" he asked, gesturing to the bar set up in the corner and filled with dozens of bottles with colorful labels. "I can make you a mixed drink, or pour you a glass of wine."

"A glass of wine," she said, as a breeze blew in from the sea, and caught at her hair, teasing a dark tendril.

"Red or white?"

"Doesn't matter. You choose."

He poured her a glass of red wine. "Were you able to sleep?" he asked, handing her the goblet, and their fingers brushed.

A frisson of pleasure rushed through her at the brief touch. Her pulse quickened and she had to exhale slowly, needing to calm herself, settle herself. She couldn't lose focus, had to remember why she was here. Her father. Her father, who was in so much danger. "Yes," she said, her voice pitched low, husky with a desire she could barely master, never mind hide.

Drakon stiffened at the sudden spike of awareness. Morgan practically hummed with tension, her slim figure taut, energy snapping and crackling around her. It was hot and electric, she was hot and electric, and he knew if he reached for her, touched her, she'd let him. She wanted him. Morgan had been right about the physical side of their relationship. There was plenty of heat…intense chemistry…but she'd been the one that brought the fire to their relationship. She'd brought it out in him. He'd enjoyed sex with other women, but with her, it wasn't just sex. It was love. And he'd never loved a woman before her. He'd liked them, admired them, enjoyed them…but had never loved, not the way he loved her, and he was quite sure he would never love any woman this way again.

"For hours," she added, blushing, her voice still husky. "It was lovely. But then, I always sleep well here."

"It's the air, I think," he said. "You look beautiful, by the way," he said.

Her cheeks turned pink and her blue eyes glowed with pleasure. She looked surprised, touched. His beautiful woman. Part of him wanted to shake her, kiss her, make her his again, and another part of him wanted to send her away forever.

"Thank you for sending for my clothes," she said, fighting the same tendril of hair, the one the breeze loved to tease. "That was very kind of you."

"Not kind, just practical," he answered. "Since you're not returning to Ekali, there's no point keeping your things at the villa there anymore. Which reminds me, I have another trunk with your winter clothes and ski things ready to go home with you when you leave for New York. It's in one of the storage rooms downstairs. Didn't see any reason to drag it up three flights of stairs only to drag it down again in a few days.

A shadow passed across her face. "Is that how long you think I need to be here?"

"We'll know better once Rowan arrives. I expect him in late tonight or early tomorrow."

"Rowan?"

"Rowan Argyros, from Dunamas Maritime Intelligence. He's the one I work with when my ships have been seized. His headquarters are in London, but when I phoned him this afternoon I learned that he's in Los Angeles and he's promised to fly out this afternoon."

"But if you are a maritime piracy expert, why do you need outside help?"

"Because while I know shipping, and I've becoming quite knowledgeable about counter-piracy, it takes more than money to free a seized ship, or crew being held hostage. It takes a team of experts, as well as information, strategy and decisive action, and in your father's case, it will take extraordinary action. As you can imagine, it's crucial to do everything exactly right. There is no room for error in something like this. Even a small mistake could cost his life."

She paled. "Perhaps it's too dangerous."

"Rowan won't act unless he's sure of a positive outcome."

He watched her bite nervously into her lower lip and his gaze focused on that soft bottom lip. For a few seconds, he could think of nothing but her mouth. He loved the shape, the color, the softness of it. Always had. Her lips were full and a tender pink that made him think of lush, ripe summer fruit—sweet strawberries and cherries and juicy watermelon.

"We don't even know if my father is alive," she said after a moment, looking up into his eyes.

He knew from her expression that she was looking for re-assurance, but he couldn't give it, not yet, not until Rowan had finished his intelligence work. And yet at the same time, there was no reason to alarm her. Information would be coming soon. Until then, they had to be positive. "We don't know very much about his condition at the moment, but I think it's important to focus on the best outcome, not the worst."

"When do you think this…Rowan…will have news for us?"

"I expect he'll have information when he arrives."

Morgan's eyes searched his again and her worry and fear were tangible and he fought the impulse to reach for her, comfort her, especially when she was so close he could feel her warmth and smell her light, delicate fragrance, a heady mix of perfume and her skin.

"It's difficult waiting," she said softly, the tip of her tongue touching her upper lip. "Difficult to be calm and patient in the face of so much unknown."

The glimpse of her pink tongue made him instantly hard. He wanted her so much, couldn't imagine not wanting her. It was torture being this close and yet not being able to kiss her, hold her, and he hardened all over again at the thought of kissing her, and tasting her and running his tongue across the seam of her lips.

He'd been with no one since Morgan left. For five years he'd gone without a woman, gone without closeness, intimacy, gone without even a kiss, and he suddenly felt starved. Ravenous. Like a man possessed. He needed her. She was his. His wife, his woman—

Drakon stopped himself. He couldn't go there, couldn't think of her like that. She might be his legally, but the relationship itself was over. "But that is life," he said grimly. "It is nothing but the unknown."

His staff appeared on the patio, lighting candles and sconces, including the heavy silver candelabra on the round white-linen covered table. "It appears dinner is ready," he added, glad for the diversion. "Shall we sit?"

Morgan realized with a start that the sun had dropped significantly and now hung just above the sea, streaking the horizon red, rose and gold. It would be a stunning sunset and they'd be here on the patio to see it. "Yes, please," she said, moving toward the table, but Drakon was already there, holding a chair for her.

She felt the electric shock as she sat down, her shoulder briefly touching his chest, and then his fingers brushing across the back of her bare arm. Her shawl had slipped into the crook of her elbow and the unexpected sensation of his skin on hers made her breath catch in her throat and she held the air bottled in her lungs as she pressed her knees tightly together, feeling the hot lick of desire and knowing she had to fight it.

"It will be a gorgeous sunset," she said, determined to think of other things than the useless dampness between her thighs and the coiling in her belly that made her feel so empty and achy.

His amber gaze met hers, and the warm tawny depths were piercing, penetrating, and it crossed her mind that he *knew*.

He knew how she felt, he knew she wanted him, and it was suddenly too much…being here, alone with him.

"Must grab my camera," she said, leaping to her feet. "Such an incredible sunset."

She rushed off, up to her room, where she dug through her things and located her phone, which was also her camera, but didn't return to the dining room immediately, needing the time to calm herself and pull her frayed nerves back together.

He's always done this to you, she lectured herself. *He seduced you with his eyes long before he ever touched you, but that doesn't mean anything. It's lust. He's good at sex. That doesn't mean he should be your husband.*

Morgan returned downstairs, head high. As she approached the patio through the dining room, the sunset bathed the patio in soft golden light. The small, round dining table seemed to float above the shimmering green tiles on the patio. The same green tiles extended all the way into the dining room and from the kitchen she caught a whiff of the most delicious aromas—tomato and onion, garlic, olive oil, herbs—even as the breeze rustled her skirts, tugging at her air, whispering over her skin.

So much light and color and sound.

So much sensation. So much emotion. It was wonderful and terrible…bittersweet. Drakon and Villa Angelica had made her feel alive again.

Drakon rose as she stepped out onto the patio. "The sun is almost gone," he said, holding her chair for her.

She glanced out at the sea, and he was right. The bright red ball of sun had disappeared into the water. "I did miss it," she said, hoping she sounded properly regretful as she sat back down.

"Maybe next time," he said, with mock sympathy.

She looked up at him and then away, aware that he was playing her game with her. Pretending she'd wanted a photo when they both knew she just needed to escape him.

"I'll have to keep my phone close by," she said, reaching for her water glass and taking a quick sip.

His gaze collided with hers and then held, his expression one of lazy amusement. "Photos really help one remember things."

She felt herself grow warm. "I have a purely professional interest in the scenery."

"Is that so?"

She hated the way one of his black eyebrows lifted. Hated that curl of his lips. It was sardonic, but also quite sexy, and she was sure he knew it. "I use them for inspiration, not souvenirs," she said coolly, wanting to squash him, and his amusement. There was no reason for him to take pleasure in her discomfiture. No reason for him to act superior.

"Interesting," he drawled, and Morgan had to restrain herself from kicking him beneath the table because she knew he didn't mean it. And he didn't believe her. He probably was sitting there arrogantly thinking she was completely hung up on him...and imagining she was obsessing about having great sex with him...which was ludicrous because she wasn't thinking about having great sex with him anymore. At least not when she was talking about the scenery and inspiration.

"I use the inspiration for my work," she said defiantly, not even sure why she was getting so upset. "But you probably don't consider it work. You probably think it's silly. Superficial."

"I never said that."

"Perhaps you didn't say it, but you think it. You know you do."

"I find it interesting that you feel compelled to put words into my mouth."

His ability to be so calm and detached when she was feeling so emotional made her even more emotional. She leaned toward him. "Surely you've wondered what drove you to marry a flighty woman like me...a woman so preoccupied with frivolous things."

"Are you flighty?"

"You must think so."

He leaned forward, too, closing the distance between them. "I'm not asking you to tell me what I think. I'm asking you—are you flighty?"

Her chin jerked up. "No."

"Are you preoccupied with frivolous things?" he persisted.

Her cheeks burned hot and her eyes felt gritty. "No."

"So you're not flighty or frivolous?"

"No."

His eyes narrowed. "Then why would I think you are?"

She had to close her eyes, overwhelmed by pain and the wave of grief that swept over her.

"Morgan?"

She gave her head a small shake, refusing to open her eyes until she was sure they were perfectly dry. "I am sorry," she said huskily. "You deserved better than me."

"And I'd like to hear more about your jewelry and your ideas, unless you're determined to hold onto this bizarre fantasy of yours that I don't care for you or what's going on inside that beautiful, but complicated head."

She suddenly seethed with anger. Why was he so interested in her thoughts now, when he hadn't been interested in anything but her body when they'd lived together? "I loved what I did," she said shortly. "I was really proud of my work, and I am still proud of those three collections."

She glared at him, waiting for him to speak, but he simply sat back in his chair and looked at her, and let the silence grow, expand and threaten to take over.

The silence was beginning to feel uncomfortable and he was examining her a little too closely. She felt herself grow warm, too warm. "They were jewelry, yes," she said, rushing now to fill the silence, "but they were also miniature works of art, and each collection had a theme and each individual piece told a story."

"And what were those stories?"

"Life and death, love and loss, hope and despair…" Her voice faded, and she looked away, heart aching, because the collections had really been about him, them, their brief fierce love that became so very dangerous and destructive.

"I liked them all, but my favorite collection was your last one. The one you called a failure."

Her head jerked up and she had to blink hard to keep tears from welling up. "You're familiar with my three collections?"

"But of course."

"And you liked my designs?"

"You have such a unique vision. I admired your work very much."

She exhaled slowly, surprised, touched, grateful. "Thank you."

"I was proud of you, my wife. I still am."

The tears she'd been fighting filled her eyes and she didn't know what affected her more—his words or his touch. "My short-lived career," she said, struggling to speak, trying to sound light, mocking, but it had hurt, closing her business. She'd truly loved her work. Had found so much joy in her work and designs.

He caught one of her tears before it could fall. "I don't think it's over. I think you're in the middle of a transition period, and it may feel like death, but it's just change."

"Well, death certainly is a change," she answered, deadpan, flashing him a crooked smile, thinking she liked it when Drakon talked to her. She'd always liked his perspective on things. She found it—him—reassuring, and for her, this is how she connected to him. Through words. Language. Ideas.

If only they'd had more of this—time and conversation— perhaps she wouldn't have felt so lost in Greece. Perhaps they'd still be together now.

He suddenly reached out and stroked her cheek with his thumb, making her heart turn over once again.

"I liked it when you smiled a moment ago," he said gruffly, his amber gaze warm as he looked at her. "I have a feeling you don't smile much anymore."

For a moment she didn't speak, she couldn't, her heart in her mouth and her chest filled with hot emotion.

She was still so drawn to him, still so in love with him. But there was no relationship anymore. They were mostly definitely done—finished. No turning back.

He was helping her because she needed help, but that was all. She had to remember what was important—her father and securing his release—and not let herself get caught up in the physical again because the physical was maddening, disorienting and so incredibly addictive. She hadn't known she had such an addictive personality, not until she'd fell for Drakon.

"There hasn't been a great deal to smile about in the past few months," she said quietly. "Everything has been so grim and overwhelming, but just being here, having your support, gives me hope. If you hadn't agreed to help me, I don't know what I would have done. I'm so very grateful—"

"Your father's not home yet."

"But with your help, he soon will be."

"Careful, my love. You can't say that. You don't know that."

She averted her head and blinked hard, gazing out across the water that had darkened to purple beneath a lavender sky. The first stars were appearing and the moon was far away, just a little crescent of white.

"I'm not saying that it's hopeless," Drakon said. "Just that there is still a great deal we do not know yet."

"I understand. I do."

CHAPTER FIVE

MORGAN PASSED ON coffee and returned to her room, finding it far too painful to sit across from Drakon and look at him, and be so close to him, and yet not be part of his life anymore. Better to return to her suite and pace the floor in privacy, where he couldn't read her face or know how confused she felt.

How could she still want him so much even now? How could she want him when she knew how dangerous he was for her?

She needed to go home, back to New York, back to her family. There was no reason to remain here. Surely this man, Rowan whatever-his-name-was, from Dunamas Intelligence, didn't need her here for his work. He could email her, or call, when he had news....

Morgan nearly returned downstairs to tell Drakon she wanted to leave tonight, that she insisted on leaving tonight, but as she opened her door she realized how ridiculous she'd sound, demanding to go just when Rowan was set to arrive. No, she needed to calm down. She was being foolish. As well as irrational. Drakon wouldn't hurt her. He wasn't going to destroy her. She just needed to keep her head, and not let him anywhere close to her body.

Morgan went to bed, thinking she'd be too wound up to sleep, but she did finally sleep and then woke up early, her room filled with dazzling morning sunlight. After showering, she dressed simply in slim white slacks and one of her favorite colorful tunics and headed downstairs to see if she could get a coffee.

One of the maids gestured to the breakfast room, which was already set for two. Morgan shook her head. "Just coffee," she said, unable to stomach the idea of another meal with Drakon. "An Americano with milk. Latte," she added. "But nothing to eat."

The maid didn't understand and gestured again to the pretty table with its cheerful yellow and blue linens and smiled winningly.

"No, no. Just coffee. Take away." Morgan frowned, wondering why she couldn't seem to remember a single word of Italian. She used to know a little bit, but her brain wasn't working this morning. She was drawing a total blank.

The maid smiled. "Coffee. Americano, *si. Prego.*" And she gestured to the table once more.

Morgan gave up and sat down at the table, needing coffee more than argument. She ended up having breakfast alone and enjoyed her warm pastries and juice and strong hot coffee, which she laced with milk.

The sun poured in through the tall leaded windows, and light dappled the table, shining on the blue water glasses and casting prisms of delicate blue on the white plaster walls.

Morgan studied the patches of blue glazing the walls. She loved the color blue, particularly this cobalt-blue glass one found on the Amalfi coast, and could imagine beautiful jewelry made from the same blue glass, round beads and square knots mixed with gold and shells and bits of wood and other things that caught her fancy.

Her fingers suddenly itched to pick up a pencil and sketch some designs, not the extravagant gold cuffs and collars from her Amalfi collection, but something lighter, simpler. These pieces would be more affordable, perhaps a little bit of a splurge for younger girls, but within reach if they'd saved their pennies. Morgan could imagine the trendy jet-setters buying up strands of different colors and textures and pairing them with easy bracelets, perfect to wear to dinner, or out shopping on a weekend, or on a beach in Greece.

"What are you thinking about?" Drakon asked from the doorway.

Startled, she gazed blankly at him, having forgotten for a moment where she was. "Jewelry," she said, feeling as if she'd been caught doing something naughty. "Why?"

"You were smiling a little…as if you were daydreaming."

"I suppose I was. It helps me to imagine designing things. Makes the loss of my company less painful."

"You'll have another store again."

"It'd be fiscally irresponsible. My last collection nearly bankrupted me."

One of the kitchen staff appeared with an espresso for Drakon and handed it to him. He nodded toward the table. "May I join you?"

"Of course you may, but I was just about to leave," she said.

"Then don't let me keep you," he answered.

His voice didn't change—it remained deep, smooth, even—but she saw something in his face, a shadow in his eyes, and she suddenly felt vile. Here he was, helping her, supporting her, extending himself emotionally and financially, and she couldn't even be bothered to sit with him while he had breakfast?

"But if you don't mind my company," she added quickly, "I'll have another coffee and stay."

There was another flicker in his eyes, this one harder to read, and after sitting down across from her, he rang the bell and ordered another coffee for her, along with his breakfast.

They talked about trivial things over breakfast like the weather and movies and books they'd read lately. Morgan was grateful their talk was light and impersonal. She was finding it hard to concentrate in the first place, never mind carry on a conversation. Drakon was so beautiful this morning with his dark hair still slightly damp from his shower and his jaw freshly shaven. The morning light gilded him, with the sun playing across his strong, handsome features, illuminating his broad brow, his straight Greek nose, his firm full mouth.

It was impossible to believe this gorgeous, gorgeous man had been her husband. She was mad to leave him. But then, living with him had made her insane.

Drakon's black brows tugged. "It's going to be all right. Rowan should be here in the next hour. We'll soon have information about your father."

"Thank you," she said quietly.

"Last night after you'd gone to bed I was thinking about everything you said yesterday—" He broke off, frowning. "Am I really such an ogre, Morgan? Why do you think I would judge you…and judge you so harshly?"

His gaze, so direct, so piercing, unnerved her. She smoothed the edge of the yellow square cloth where it met the blue underskirt. "Your corporation is worth billions of dollars and your work is vital to Greece and world's economy. I'm nothing. I do nothing. I add little value—"

"Life isn't just about drudgery. It is also about beauty, and you bring beauty into the world." The heat in his eyes reminded her of their courtship, where he'd watched her across ballrooms with that lazy, sensual gleam in his eyes, his expression one of pride and pleasure as well as possession. She'd felt powerful with his eyes on her. Beautiful and important.

"But I don't think important thoughts. I don't discuss relevant topics."

"Relevant to whom?"

"To you! I bore you—"

"Where do you get these ideas from?"

"From you." She swallowed hard and forced herself to hold

his gaze even though it was so incredibly uncomfortable. "I annoyed you when we lived together. And I don't blame you. I know you find people like me irritating."

His black eyebrows pulled and his jaw jutted. "People like you? What does that mean?"

She shrugged uneasily, wishing she hadn't said anything. She hadn't meant anything by it.

No, not true. She had. She still remembered how he had shut down her attempts at conversation once their honeymoon had ended and they'd returned to Greece, remembered their silent lonely evenings in their sprawling modern white marble villa. Drakon would arrive home from work and they'd sit in the dining room, but it'd been a silent meal, with Drakon often reviewing papers or something on his tablet and then afterward he'd retreat to a chair in the living room and continue reading until bed. Once in the bedroom, things changed. Behind the closed door, he'd want hot, erotic sex, and for twenty minutes or sixty, or even longer depending on the night, he'd be alive, and sensual, utterly engrossed with her body and pleasure, and then when it was over, he'd fall asleep, and in the morning when she woke, he'd be gone, back to his office.

"People like me who don't read the business section of the newspaper. People like me who don't care passionately about politics. People like me who don't make money but spend it." She lifted her chin and smiled at him, a hard dazzling smile to hide how much those memories still hurt. "People who can only talk about fashion and shopping and which restaurants are considered trendy."

He tapped his finger on the table. "I do not understand the way you say, 'people like you.' I've never met anyone like you. For me, there is you, and only you."

She leaned forward, her gaze locking with his. "Why did you marry me, Drakon?"

"Because I wanted you. You were made for me. Meant for me."

"What did you like about me?"

"Everything."

"That's not true."

"It is true. I loved your beauty, your intelligence, your warmth, your passion, your smile, your laugh."

She noticed he said *loved,* past tense, and it hurt, a hot lance of pain straight through her heart. Perhaps it was merely a slip, or possibly, a grammatical error, but both were unlikely. Drakon didn't make mistakes.

"But you know that," he added brusquely.

"No," she said equally roughly, "I didn't know that. I had no idea why you cared about me, or if you even cared for me—"

"How can you say such a thing?"

"Because you never talked to me!" she cried. "After our honeymoon ended, you disappeared."

"I merely went back to work, Morgan."

"Yes, but you worked twelve- and fourteen-hour days, which would have been fine, but when you came home, you were utterly silent."

"I was tired. I work long days."

"And I was home alone all day with servants who didn't speak English."

"You promised me you were going to learn Greek."

"I did, I took lessons at the language school in Athens, but when you came home at night, you were irritated by my attempts to speak Greek, insisting we converse in English—" She compressed her lips, feeling the resentment and frustration bubble up. "And then when I tried to make friends, I kept bumping into your old girlfriends and lovers. Athens is full of them. How many women have you been with, Drakon?"

"You make it sound like you met dozens of exes, but you bumped into just three."

"You're right, just three, and in hindsight, they were actually much nicer than the Greek socialites I met who were furious that I'd stolen Greece's most eligible bachelor from under their noses." Morgan's eyes sparkled dangerously. "How could I, a trashy American, take one of Greece's national treasures?"

"It wasn't that bad."

"It was that bad! Everybody hated me before I even arrived!" She leaned across the table. "You should have warned me, Drakon. Prepared me for my new married life."

"I didn't know...hadn't realized...that some of the ladies would be so catty, but I always came home to you every night."

"No, I didn't have you. That was the problem."

"What do you mean?"

Morgan laughed coolly. "You came home to dinner, a bed and sex, but you didn't come home to me, because if you had, you would have talked to me, and tried to speak Greek to me, and you would have helped me meet people, instead of getting annoyed with me for caring what Greek women thought of me."

He swore violently and got up from the table, pacing the floor once before turning to look at her. "I can't believe this is why you left me. I can't believe you'd walk out on me, and our marriage, because I'm not one for conversation. I've never been a big talker, but coming home to you was my favorite part of the day. It's what I looked forward to all day long, from the moment I left for my office."

She swallowed around the lump filling her throat. "And yet when Bronwyn called you at home, you'd talk to her for hours."

"Not for hours."

"For thirty minutes at a time. Over and over every night."

"We had business to discuss."

"And could nothing wait until the morning? Was everything really a crisis? Or could she just not make a decision without you?"

"Is that why you left me? Because of Bronwyn?"

Yes, she wanted to say. Yes, yes, yes. But in her heart she knew Bronwyn Harper was only part of the issue. Drakon's close relationship with his Australian vice president only emphasized how lonely and empty Morgan felt with him. "Bronwyn's constant presence in our lives didn't help matters. Every time I turned around, she was there, and you did talk to her, whereas you didn't talk to me."

The fight abruptly left her, and once her anger deserted her, she was exhausted and flattened, depressed by a specter of what they had been, and the illusion of what she'd hoped they'd be. "But it's a moot point now. It doesn't matter—" She broke off. "My God! You're doing it now. Rolling your eyes! Looking utterly bored and annoyed."

"I'm frustrated, Morgan, and yes, I do find this entire conversation annoying because you're putting words in my mouth, telling me how I felt, and I'm telling you I didn't feel that way when we were married."

"Don't you remember telling me repeatedly that you had people—*women*—talking at you at work, and that you didn't need me talking at you at home? Don't you remember telling me, you preferred silence—"

"I remember telling you that *once,* because I did come home one day needing quiet, and I wanted you to know it wasn't personal, and that I wasn't upset with you, that it had simply been a long day with a lot of people talking at me." He walked toward her, his gaze hard, his expression forbidding. "And instead of you being understanding, you went into hysterics, crying and raging—"

"I wasn't hysterical."

"You had no right to be upset, though." He was standing before her now. "I'd just lost two members of my crew from a hijacked ship and I'd had to tell the families that their loved ones were gone and it was a bad, bad day. A truly awful day."

"Then tell me next time that something horrific has happened, and I'll understand, but don't just disappear into your office and give me the silent treatment."

"I shouldn't have to talk if I don't want to talk."

"I was your wife. If something important happens in your world, I'd like to know."

"It's not as if you could do anything."

"But I could care, Drakon, and I would at least know what's happening in your life and I could grieve for the families of your crew, too, because I would have grieved, and I would have wanted to comfort you—"

"I don't need comforting."

"Clearly." Hot, sharp emotions rushed through her, one after the other, and she gave her head a fierce, decisive shake. "Just as you clearly didn't need me, either, because you don't need anything, Drakon Xanthis. You're perfect and complete just the way you are!"

She brushed past him and walked out, not quickly, or tearfully, but resolutely, reassured all over again that she had done the right thing in leaving him. He really didn't want a wife, or a partner, someone that was equal and valuable. He only wanted a woman for physical release. In his mind, that was all a woman was good for, and thank God she'd left when she had or he would have destroyed her completely.

Drakon caught up with her in the narrow stairway at the back of the villa. It had once been the staircase for the servants and was quite simple with plain plaster walls and steep, small stairs, but it saved Morgan traversing the long hallway.

He clasped her elbow, stopping her midstep. "You are so very good at running away, Morgan."

She shook him off and turned to face him. He was standing two steps down but that still put them on eye level and she stared into his eyes, so very full of anger and pain. "And you are so good at shutting people out!"

"I don't need to report to you, Morgan. You are my wife, not my colleague."

"And funny enough, I would rather have been your colleague than your wife. At least you would have talked to me!"

"But then there would have been no lovemaking."

"Perhaps it will surprise you to know that I'm actually far more interested in what's in your brain than what's in your trousers." She saw his incredulous expression and drew a ragged breath, horrified all over again that their entire relationship had been based on sex and chemistry. Horrified that she'd married a man who only wanted her for her body. "It's true. Lovemaking is empty without friendship, and we had no friendship, Drakon. We just had sex—"

"Not this again!"

"Yes, this again."

"You're being absurd."

"Thank God we'll both soon be free so we can find someone that suits us both better. You can go get another pretty girl and give her an orgasm once or twice a day and feel like a real man, and I'll find a man who has warmth and compassion, a man who cares about what I think and feel, a man who wants to know *me,* and not just my body!"

He came up one step, and then another until they were on the same narrow stair, crowding her so that her back was against the plaster of the stairwell, and his big body was almost touching hers.

A dangerous light shone in his eyes, making her blood hum in her veins and her nerves dance. "Is that all I'm interested in? Your body?" he growled, a small muscle popping in his jaw.

She stared at his jaw, fascinated by that telling display of temper. He was angry and this was all so new…his temper and emotion. She'd always thought of him as supremely controlled but his tension was palpable now. He practically seethed with frustration and it made her skin tingle, particularly her lips, which suddenly felt unbearably sensitive. "Apparently so."

He stepped even closer, his eyes glittering down at her. "I wish I'd known that before I married you. It would have saved me half a billion dollars, never mind years of trouble."

"We all make mistakes," she taunted, deliberately provoking him, but unable to help herself. Drakon Xanthis's famous icy control was cracking and she wondered what would happen when it shattered completely. "Best thing you can do now is forgive yourself for making such a dreadful mistake and move forward."

Fire flashed in his eyes and he leaned in, closing the gap between them so that his broad chest just grazed the swell of her breasts and she could feel the tantalizing heat of his hips so close to hers.

"Such an interesting way to view things," he said, his head dropping, his voice deepening. "With you as my mistake."

His lips were so close now and her lower back tingled and her belly tightened, and desire coursed through her veins, making her ache everywhere.

She could feel his need, feel the desire and her mouth dried, her heart hammering harder. He was going to kiss her. And she wanted the kiss, craved his kiss, even as a little voice of reason inside her head sounded the alarm....

Stop. Wait. Think.

She had to remember...remember the past...remember what had happened last time...this wasn't just a kiss, but an inferno. If she gave in to this kiss, it'd be all over. Drakon was so dangerous for her. He did something to her. He, like his name, Drakon, Greek for dragon, was powerful and potent and destructive.

But he was also beautiful and physical and sensual and

he made her *feel*. My God, he made her feel and she wanted that intensity now. Wanted him now.

"My beautiful, expensive mistake," he murmured, his lips brushing across the shell of her ear, making her breath catch in her throat and sending hot darts of delicious sensation throughout her body, making her aware of every sensitive spot.

"Next time, don't marry the girl," she said, trying to sound brazen and cavalier, but failing miserably as just then he pushed his thigh between her legs. The heat of his hard body scalded her, and the unexpected pressure and pleasure was so intense she gasped, making her head spin.

"Would you have been happier just being my mistress?" he asked, his tongue tracing the curve of her ear even as his muscular thigh pressed up, his knee against her core, teasing her senses, making her shiver with need.

She was wet and hot, too hot, and her skin felt too tight. She wanted relief, needed relief, and it didn't help that she couldn't catch her breath. She was breathing shallowly, her chest rising and falling while her mouth dried.

"Would you have been able to let go more? Enjoyed the sex without guilt?" he added, biting her tender earlobe, his teeth sharp, even as he wedged his thigh deeper between her knees, parting her thighs wider so that she felt like a butterfly pinned against the wall.

"There was no guilt," she choked, eyes closing as he worked his thigh against her in a slow maddening circle. He was so warm and she was so wet and she knew it was wrong, but she wanted more, not less.

His teeth scraped across that hollow beneath her ear and she shuddered against him, thinking he remembered how sensitive she was, how her body responded to every little touch and bite and caress.

"Liar." He leaned in closer, his knee grinding and his hips pressing down against her hips, making her pelvis feel hot and yet hollow, and the muscles inside her womb clench. "You liked it hot. You liked it when I made you fall apart."

And it was true, she thought, her body so tight and hot and aching that she arched against him, absolutely wanton. There was no satisfaction like this, though, and she wanted satisfaction. Wanted him. Wanted him here and now. Wanted him to lift her tunic and expose her breasts and knead and roll the tight, aching nipples between his fingers. He'd made her come that way before, just by playing with her nipples, and he'd watched her face as she came, watched every flicker of emotion that crossed her face as he broke her control....

If only he'd peel her clothes off now, if only she could feel his skin on her skin, feel him in her, needing the heat and fullness of him inside her, craving the pleasure of being taken, owned, possessed—

Morgan's eyes flew open.

Owned?

Owned? My God. She *was* insane.

Visions of her months at McLean Hospital filled her head and it dragged her abruptly back to reality. She had to be smart. Couldn't destroy herself again. Never wanted to go back to McLean Hospital again.

The very memory of McLean was enough for her to put her hands on his chest and push him back, and she pushed hard, but he didn't budge and all she felt was the warm dense plane of muscle that banded his ribs, and the softness of his cashmere sweater over the dense carved muscle.

"Get off," she panted, pushing harder, putting all of her weight into the shove but Drakon was solid, immoveable. "I'm not a toy, Drakon, not here for your amusement."

His hand snaked into her hair, twisting the dark length around his fist, holding her face up to his. "Good, because I'm not amused."

"No, you're just aroused," she answered coldly, furious

with herself for responding to him with such abandon. So typical. So pathetic. No wonder her family had locked her up.

He caught one of her hands and dragged it down his body and between their hips to cup his erection. "Yes," he drawled, amber gaze burning, "so I am."

She inhaled sharply, her fingers curving around him, clasping his thick shaft as if measuring the hard length, and it was a terrible seductive pleasure, touching him like this. She remembered how he felt inside her—hot, heavy—and how the satin heat of his body would stretch her, stroke her, hitting nerve endings she hadn't even known she had.

Curiosity and desire warred with her sense of self-preservation, before overriding her common sense.

Morgan palmed the length of him, slowly, firmly running her hand down his shaft and then, as if unable to stop herself, back up again to cup the thick, rounded head. She'd never thought a man's body was beautiful before she'd met Drakon, but she loved every muscle and shadow of his body, loved the lines and the planes and the way his cock hung heavy between his muscular legs. He was such a powerfully built man, and yet the skin on his shaft was so smooth and sensitive, like silk, and the contradiction between his great, hard body and that delicate skin fascinated her.

But then he fascinated her. No, it was more than that, more than fascination. It was an obsession. She needed him so much she found it virtually impossible to live without him.

"You want me," he said. "You want me to peel your trousers and knickers off and take you here, on these steps, don't you?"

Fire surged through her veins, fire and hunger and shame. Because yes, she did want him and her orgasms were the most intense when he pushed it to the edge, making every touch into something dangerous and erotic. "You do like to dominate," she answered breathlessly.

He tugged on her hair, and it hurt a little, just as he'd intended, making her nipples harden into tight, aching buds even as she stiffened against him, her body rippling with need.

"And you do like to be dominated," he rasped in her ear.

CHAPTER SIX

SHE SHOVED AWAY from him and this time he let her go and Morgan ran the rest of the way up the stairs, racing back to her room, his voice echoing in her head. *And you like to be dominated...*.

Morgan barely made it to her bed before her legs gave out, the mocking words making her absolutely heartsick, because he wasn't completely wrong. Part of her did like it. It was sexy...hot...exciting.

But she shouldn't like it. It wasn't politically correct. She couldn't imagine her mother approving. Not that she wanted to think about her mother and sex at the same time...or even about sex in general since she wasn't going to be having sex anytime soon and God help her, she wanted to.

She wanted to be ravished. Stripped. Tied up. Taken. Tasted. Devoured—

Oh, God, she was mad, she was. What sane woman wanted to be ravished? What kind of woman ached to be tied up and taken? Tasted?

What was wrong with her?

Before Drakon she'd never had these thoughts. She'd never imagined that sex could make one feel absolutely wild. She'd never dreamed that desire could be an uncontrollable fire that made one lose all perspective...as well as one's reason....

But desire was an inferno, and she felt absolutely consumed by need now. Lying facedown on her bed, her body ached with need. Her skin burned, her senses swam. Every muscle in her body felt taut and every nerve ending far too tight. She wanted relief, craved release, and the fact that she couldn't have it made the aching emptiness worse.

Morgan buried her face in a pillow and knotted her fists and screamed. And screamed some more.

She wanted him. She wanted him, wanted him, wanted him and he could give her what she wanted, too. He'd do it. He'd do anything she wanted and yet it was wrong. They weren't together, they hadn't been together in years, and she couldn't use him to scratch an itch...no matter how powerful the itch.

And yet, oh, God, her body ached and throbbed and she felt wild...hot and tense and so very raw.

Dammit. Damn him. Damn that kiss in the stairwell. Damn this terrible incredible unforgettable chemistry.

It wasn't right to want him this much still. Wasn't fair to still feel so much, either, especially when she knew how bad he was for her, how very destructive. She couldn't blame him entirely. The doctors said the problem was hers...that she didn't have proper boundaries. She didn't have a clear or strong sense of self and the only way she'd achieve a strong, mature sense of self was by leaving Drakon....

As if it were that easy...

Just leave him. Forget him. Forget he ever existed...

And now he was downstairs, so intense and real, so physical, so sensual, so fiercely beautiful.

Morgan beat the bed with her fist, maddened by the futility of her desire. Blood drummed in her veins, need coiled tightly, hotly in her belly, and her entire body ached with emptiness. How could emptiness throb and pulse? How could emptiness burn? But it did. And she felt wild and furious and frustrated beyond reason.

If only she could go to him, and beg for him to help her, beg him to give her release. Beg for pleasure.

She'd happily crawl for him, crawl to him, if it meant that he could tame the beast inside her…that voracious hunger that made her feel too wild, too frantic, too much.

Drakon stood just inside the doorway of Morgan's suite and watched her beat her fist against the bed, her dark hair gleaming, her tunic riding high on her thighs, the soft fabric clinging to the firm, rounded curves of her hips and butt.

She had a gorgeous butt, and it made him want to spank her, restrain her, knowing it'd arouse her, make things hotter, make her wet and anxious and hungry for him.

And then he'd make love to her.

With his mouth, his tongue, his teeth, his hands, his cock. He loved the softness of her skin and the scent of her, the way she blushed, the way her tongue traveled across the bow of her upper lip and the way she'd squirm beneath him, her slim body arching, her hips grinding up to meet his, her legs opening for him.

"Undress," he said, his voice pitched so low it sounded like a growl.

Morgan swiftly sat up, eyes enormous in her face, cheeks flushed.

"Do it," he said, folding his arms across his chest.

Her lips parted in silent protest and yet he knew she was tempted, seriously tempted, because she wanted the same thing he did—excitement, pleasure, release.

"And what?" she whispered, her tongue darting to her lower lip, moistening it.

He was already hard. Now he wanted to explode. "And let me look at you. I want to see you, my beautiful wife."

"I'm not your wife."

"Oh, you are my wife. And have been my wife and will be my wife until the day the divorce is granted. Then…you'll be someone else's woman, but until then, you are mine. And you know you are. That is why you came here to me, wanting my help. You knew I'd refuse you nothing."

He saw the flicker in her eyes, that recognition of truth. "Just as you know I've never refused you anything," she whispered, her voice unsteady.

No, she hadn't, he thought, his shaft growing even harder, making him hotter, remembering how she always responded to him.

He'd known plenty of women who liked hot sex, but he'd never been with anyone as passionate as Morgan. She wasn't comfortable with her passionate nature, though, and during their six months together she'd struggled with the concept of physical pleasure, and resisted giving in to her sensual side, viewing it as a weakness, or something shameful, instead of an intimacy that brought them closer together… binding, bonding, making them one. "But I've never forced you, Morgan—"

"Not forced, no, but you have pushed me, pushed me beyond what I was comfortable doing."

"Isn't that exciting, though? To try new things…explore new things…to know and then go outside your comfort zone?"

Another flicker of emotion passed over her lovely face. She had such fine, elegant features, as well as that famous Copeland reserve, a trait shared by her equally glamorous sisters. The reserve came from the way they'd been raised… from birth they'd been privileged, and had enjoyed a luxurious lifestyle of private schools, private jets, private islands. Their money attracted attention, and men, lots and lots of men, and by the time the four Copeland girls had become women, they knew they were special. Unique. They believed they deserved better.

Drakon had been drawn to Morgan's beauty, but also her reserve. He'd viewed it as a challenge to break through her cool, haughty exterior to discover the warm woman underneath.

And once he'd touched her, she'd been more than warm. She'd burned as if consumed by a fever and during their honeymoon, those four weeks here at Villa Angelica, he'd enjoyed discovering the depths of her passion and exploring her desires, her fears and her limits.

"But everything with you was outside my comfort zone," she said, trying to hide the quiver of her lower lip. "Everything was overwhelming."

She'd said this once before to him, during the last week of their honeymoon after an erotic afternoon on a private island, and he'd been startled that her memory of lovemaking on the pristine ivory beach had been so different from what he'd felt. Returning to his yacht, which had been anchored off the island while they picnicked on the beach, he had never felt closer to her, or more committed, and he'd been shocked when she accused him of taking advantage of her. Shocked and sickened.

He was Greek—a man of surprisingly simple tastes. He valued his family, his friends and his culture, which included good food, good drink and great sex. He wouldn't apologize for enjoying sex, either, or enjoying his wife's beautiful body. What did she expect him to do? Pretend he didn't like sex? Act as though he didn't find pleasure in her warmth and softness?

Back in Athens after the honeymoon, Drakon had tried to be the husband she wanted. He stopped reaching for her quite as often, and then when he did reach for her, he changed the way he touched her, holding back to keep from overwhelming her. He knew she didn't like it when he expressed hunger, or focused too much on her pleasure, and so instead of just being with her, and enjoying her, he practiced control and distance, hoping that a less passionate husband would be more to her liking.

Instead she'd left.

And just remembering how he'd turned himself inside

out trying to please her, trying to give her what she wanted, made him angry all over again now.

He'd hated second-guessing himself back then, hated not being able to please her, hated failing as a husband.

His gaze swept over her, slowly, critically, examining her as if he owned her, and he did…at least for a few more weeks.

"Undress," he said roughly, feeling raw and so very carnal, and liking it. Enjoying it. "I want to see my wife. It doesn't seem like too much to ask for, not after giving you seven million dollars."

One of her eyebrows lifted. "At least you didn't mention the four hundred million."

"That was to your father, not to you."

"I wonder what he had to do for four hundred million."

"You think I should have asked for some sexual favors, do you?"

"You like sex a lot."

"I liked it with you a lot." He suddenly reached down, palmed his erection through his trousers, and he saw her gaze settle on his shaft, measuring the length and size.

Dark pink color stormed her cheeks and she licked her lower lip, once and again, before finding her voice. "That's obscene," she whispered.

"You did it a moment ago."

"You made me."

"You liked it. But you'll tell me you didn't. You'll tell me sex is disgusting. You'll tell me I'm disgusting, but if I touched you now, my woman, you'd be dripping wet—"

"Disgusting."

"And I'd open you and lick you and taste you and make you come." His head cocked and he shoved his hands in his trouser pockets. "When is the last time you came? How long has it been since you had an orgasm? A day? A week? A month?"

"It's none of your business."

"I did it in the shower yesterday, before you arrived. Stroked myself as I thought about you, picturing your breasts and your pale thighs and how much I enjoy being between them."

"Is there any point to this, Drakon? Or do you just wish to humiliate me?"

"Humiliate you, how? By telling you how much I want you, even now, even after you walked out on me?"

"But you don't want me, you just want to have sex with me."

"That's right. You don't believe you're attached to your body, or that your body is part of you. Instead it's a separate entity, which makes me think of a headless chicken—"

"Don't be rude."

"Then stop jumping to conclusions. Just because I like your body, doesn't mean I don't appreciate the rest of you."

"Humph!"

His eyebrows shot up, his expression mocking. "Is that the best you can do?"

She crossed her arms over her chest, her chin jerking up. "I get nowhere arguing with you."

"Very wise. Much better to just dispense with the clothing and let me have what I want." He paused, and his gaze moved slowly, suggestively over her. "And what I know you want, too. Not that you'll admit it."

Her chin lifted another notch. "And what do I want?"

"Satisfying sex without pushing the limits too far."

Dark pink color stormed her cheeks. "Without pushing the limits at all."

The corners of his mouth curled. So she did want sex. Just nice-girl sex…sweet, safe missionary-position sex. His cock throbbed at the thought. He'd like some sweet, safe-missionary sex as well. "I'll see what I can do. But first, I'd like to see you. But I'm getting bored by all the discussion. Either we're going to do this, or we're not—"

"Your shirt first."

"Excuse me?"

"You want to do this? Then we'll do this. But you're not the boss and I'm not taking orders." Her tone was defiant and her eyes flashed and she'd never been angry before when they'd played these games. She'd been shy and nervous, but also eager to please. She wasn't eager to please now. "You don't get to have all the power anymore."

"No?"

"No. I'm not your servant or slave—"

"Which is good, since I don't make love with my servants, and I don't have slaves."

"The point is, you might be able to bark orders at Bronwyn, but not at me."

"I had no idea you were so hung up on Bronwyn," he drawled, liking this new feisty Morgan. She was a very different woman from the one he'd married and that intrigued him.

"I wasn't hung up on her. You were."

"Is that how it was?"

"Yes."

"So are we going to talk about Bronwyn, or are we going to have sweet, safe missionary-position sex?"

Her lips compressed primly. "You're horrible. You know that, don't you?"

"Horribly good, and horribly hard, and horribly impatient. Now, are we, or aren't we?" he asked, sauntering toward her, relaxed, easy, his arms loose at his sides. But it was a deceptive ease, and they both knew it as the temperature in the luxurious bedroom seemed to soar and the air sparked with heat and need, the tension between them thick and hot and electric.

Closing the gap between them, Drakon could feel Morgan tense, her hands squeezing in convulsive fists, even as her eyes widened and her lips parted with each quick shallow breath.

"You're trembling," he said, "but there's no need for that. I won't eat you. Not unless you want me to."

"Drakon." Her voice sounded strangled and her cheeks were crimson, making her blue eyes darken and shimmer like the sapphire sea beyond the window.

"I hope you'll want me to. I love how you taste, and how soft you are in my mouth…so sweet. But is that too risky for you? Pushing the limits too much?"

"You love to torment me."

"Yes, I do," he agreed, circling her slowly, enjoying just looking at her, and watching the color come and go in her exquisite porcelain complexion, and listening to her soft desperate gasps of air. "But this is nothing, Morgan. I haven't even gotten started." He stopped in front of her, gazed down at her, thinking she looked very young and very uncertain and very shy, much like his virgin bride. "Now tell me, what should I do to you first?"

Morgan's heart was pounding so fast she couldn't catch her breath, and she opened her mouth, lips parting, to gulp in shallow gasps of air. She felt as if she were balancing on the edge of a volcano while little voices inside her head demanded she throw herself in.

She needed to leave, to escape the villa, to summon the helicopter and fly far, far away. Remaining here with Drakon was stupid and destructive. She might as well fling herself into that volcano…the outcome would be the same.

And yet, wasn't she already there, in the fiery pit? Because molten lava seemed to be seeping through her veins, melting her bones and muscles into mindless puddles of want and need.

She actually felt sick with need right now. But could she do this…go through with this…knowing it would be just sex, not love? Knowing Drakon wanted her body but not her heart?

"Are you crying?" he asked, his voice dropping, deepening with concern, as his hands wrapped around her arms, holding her up.

She shook her head, unable to look him in the eye.

"What's wrong?" he asked.

She swallowed hard, tried to speak, but no sound would come out. Not when her throat ached and her heart was still thundering in her chest.

He reached up to smooth a dark tendril of hair back from her face. "Have I frightened you?" His deep voice was suddenly gentle, almost painfully tender.

Hot tears scalded the back of her eyes. She bit hard into her lower lip so that it wouldn't quiver.

"I would never hurt you, Morgan," he murmured, drawing her against him, holding her in his arms, holding her securely against his chest.

She closed her eyes as the heat of his body seeped into her hands, warming her. He felt good. Too good. It was so confusing. This was confusing.

She didn't push him away, and yet she couldn't relax, waiting for the moment he'd let her go. But she didn't want him to let her go. She wanted him closer. Wanted to press her face to his chest and breathe him in. She could smell a hint of his spicy fragrance and loved that fragrance—his own scent, formulated just for him—and what it did to his skin. He smelled like heaven. Delicious and warm and good and intoxicating. He smelled like everything she wanted. He smelled like home. He *was* home. He was everything to her, but wasn't that the problem? With him, she lost herself. With him, she lost her mind.

With a strangled cry, Morgan slid a hand up across his chest, to push him back, and just like before, once she touched him, she couldn't take her hand away. She stroked across the hard plane of muscle of his chest, learning again the shape of his body and how the dense smooth pectoral muscle curved and sloped beneath her palm. God, he was beautiful. And without his shirt, his skin would feel so good against hers. She loved the way his bare chest felt against her bare breasts, loved the friction and the heat and the delicious, addictive energy—

"Can't do this," she choked, shaking her head. "We can't, we can't."

"Ssshh," he murmured, cupping her face, his thumbs stroking lightly over her cheekbones, sweeping from the curve of the bone to her earlobes. "Nothing bad will happen—"

"Everything bad will happen," she protested, shivering with pleasure from the caress. She loved the way he touched her. He made her feel beautiful, inside and out, and she struggled to remember what bad things would happen if he touched her....

"You are so beautiful," he murmured, hands slipping from her face to tangle in her hair.

"And mad, Drakon, certifiably insane—"

"That's okay."

"Drakon, I'm serious!"

"I am, too." His head dipped lower and his lips brushed hers, lightly, slowly, and she shuddered, pressed closer, a stinging sensation behind her eyes. One kiss...could it be so bad? One kiss...surely she could be forgiven that?

His lips found hers again and the kiss was surprisingly gentle, the pressure of his mouth just enough to tease her, send shivers of desire racing up and down her spine. This was all so impossible. They couldn't do this, couldn't give in to this, it's all they had and while the chemistry was intense, chemistry wasn't enough. Sex wasn't enough. She needed more. She needed a relationship, love, intimacy, commitment, but right now, she also needed this.

She'd missed him so much. Missed his skin and his scent, his warmth and his strength, and her defenses caved as his hands framed her face, and he held her face to his, deepening the kiss, drinking her in.

She could feel him and smell him and taste him now and she was lost. Nothing felt better than this. Nothing felt better than him. He wasn't just her husband, he was home and happiness—

No. No, no, no. Couldn't think that way, couldn't lose sight of reality. He wasn't home or happiness. And he'd finally agreed to let her go. After five years of wanting out, and she *did* want out, she was free.

And yet when his tongue stroked the seam of her lips, she arched and gasped, opening her mouth to him. Drakon deepened the kiss, his tongue flicking the inside of her lip, making every little nerve dance. One of his hands slid from the back of her head, down over her shoulders to her waist before settling in the small of her spine, urging her closer, shaping her against his powerful body.

She shuddered with pleasure as his tongue filled her mouth and the fingers of his hand splayed wider on her back, making her lower belly throb, ache, just like her thighs ached.

Every thrust of his tongue shot another bright arc of sensation through her, sensation that surged to the tips of her breasts, tightening them into hard, sensitive peaks, and then deep into her belly and even deeper to her innermost place, and yet it wasn't enough, not even close. Morgan dug her nails into his shoulders, pressing her breasts to his chest, practically grinding herself against his hips to feel the ridge of his erection rub against her sensitive spot at the junction of her thighs and the heat of his palm against her lower back.

It was still so electric between them, still fierce and wild, and she felt overwhelmed by desire, overwhelmed by the memory of such dizzying, maddening pleasure and the knowledge that he was here, and there could be more. And right now, she wanted more. She literally ached for him and could feel her body soften and warm for him, her body also clearly remembering that nothing in the world felt better than him in her. Him with her.

And then his hand was slipping slowly across the curve of her hip, to cup the roundness of her butt, and she nearly popped out of her skin. "Drakon," she groaned against his mouth, feeling as if he were spreading fire through her, fire and such fierce, consuming need.

She trembled as he stroked the length of her, from her hip to her breast and down again. His hands were everywhere now, pinching a nipple, stroking the cleft of her buttocks, shaping her thighs. She wanted his hand between her thighs, wanted him to touch her, fill her, wanted him more than she'd wanted anything—

Wait.

Wait.

She struggled to focus, clear her head, which was impossible with Drakon's amazing hands on her body and his mouth taking hers, promising her endless pleasure.

She had to move back, away, had to, now.

But then his hands were up, under her tunic, his skin so warm against hers, and when he unhooked her bra to cup her breasts, his thumbs grazing her tight, swollen nipples, she gave up resisting, gave up thinking and gave in to him.

He stripped off her clothes while kissing her, his hands never leaving her body as the clothes fell away, giving her no time to panic or reconsider.

Once naked, he carried her to the bed, and set her on her back in the middle of the enormous bed. The room's windows and doors were open and the sunlight spilled across the floor, splashing on the walls while the heady sweet scent of wisteria filled the room.

Morgan watched Drakon's face as he moved over her, his hard, powerful body warm, his skin a burnished gold, his strong features taut with passion. But it was his eyes that once again captivated her, and the burning intensity of his gaze. When he looked at her he made her feel extraordinary…desirable…rare…impossibly valuable. She knew he didn't feel that way about her, not anymore, but with him stretched out over her, his skin covering her, warming her, it didn't seem to matter.

She lifted her face to his, and his mouth met hers in a blistering kiss that melted everything within her. There was nothing she wouldn't give him. And as he settled his weight between her thighs, his hips pressing down against hers, she shivered with pleasure.

He was resting his weight on his forearms, but she wanted more pressure, not less, and Morgan arched up, pressing her breasts to his bare chest, loving the friction of his nipples on hers even as she opened her thighs wider, letting him settle deeper into her.

"I want you," she whispered against his mouth, her arms circling his shoulders, her hands sliding into his thick hair, fingers curling into the crisp strands at his nape. He felt good and smelled good and in this moment, everything was right in the world…at least, everything was right in her world. "I want you in me. I need you in me."

"It's been a long time."

"Too long," she said, lifting her hips, grinding up against him, not wanting any more foreplay, not wanting anything but him, and his body meshed deeply with hers.

"Patience," he answered, kissing the corner of her mouth and the line of her jaw, smoothing her hair back from her face. "There's no need to rush—"

But there was. She didn't want to wait, had enough teasing and words and thinking, had enough of everything but him. And right now she just wanted him. She reached between them, caught his hard shaft and gripped it firmly, the way she knew he liked it, and rubbed his head up and down her, the warm, rigid shaft sliding across her damp opening, making him slick, and then bringing the silken head up to her sensitive nub, drawing moisture up over her clit.

She heard him groan deep in his throat, a hoarse, guttural sound of pleasure, and it gave her a perverse thrill, knowing she could make Drakon feel something so strong that he'd groan aloud.

His hands stroked the outsides of her thighs and then down the inside and she shifted her hips, positioning him at her wet, slick core. "Do you want me?" she whispered, her lips at his ear.

"Yes," he groaned, his voice so low that it rumbled through her. "Yes, always."

And then he took control, lowering his weight, forearms pressed to the bed, and kissed her, deeply, his tongue plunging into her mouth even as he entered her body, thrusting all the way until they were one, and for a nearly a minute he remained still, kissing her, filling her, until she felt him swell inside her, stretching her, throbbing inside her, making her throb, too. Her pulse raced and her body tingled and burned, her inner muscles clenching and rippling with exquisite sensation. He was big and hard and warm and she could come like this, with her body gripping him, holding him, and Drakon knew it, knew how just being inside her could shatter her.

"Not yet," she gasped, hands stroking over his broad shoulders and down the smooth, hard, warm planes of his back, savoring the curve and hollow of every thick, sinewy muscle. Men were so beautiful compared to women, and no man was more beautiful than Drakon. "Don't let me come, not yet. I want more. I want everything."

And maybe this was just the plain old missionary position, but it felt amazing, felt hot and fierce and intense and emotional and physical and everything that was good. Sex like this was mind-blowingly good, especially with Drakon taking his time, thrusting into her in long smooth strokes that hit all the right places, that made her feel all the right things. Morgan wished it could last forever, but she was already responding, the muscles inside her womb were coiling tighter and tighter, bringing her ever closer to that point of no return. Morgan's head spun with the exquisite sensation, the tension so consuming that it was difficult to know in that moment if it was pleasure or pain, and then with one more deep thrust, Drakon sent her over the edge and her senses exploded, her body rippling and shuddering beneath his.

Drakon came while she was still climaxing and he ground out her name as he buried himself deeply within her. She could feel him come, feel the heat and liquid of him surging within her, and it hit her—they hadn't used a condom. On their honeymoon they had never used protection. Drakon wanted children and she wanted to please him and so they had never used birth control, but this was different. They were divorcing. She'd soon be single. There was absolutely no way she could cope with getting pregnant now.

"What have we done?" she cried, struggling to push him off of her. "What did we do?"

Drakon shifted his weight and allowed her to roll away from him, even as a small muscle jumped in his jaw. "I think you know what we just did."

"We shouldn't have. It was wrong."

"Doesn't feel wrong to me," he said tersely, watching her slide to the edge of the bed and search for her tunic, or something to cover up with.

She grabbed Drakon's shirt, and slipped it over her arms into the sleeves and buttoned up the front. "Well, it was. We didn't use birth control, Drakon, and we shouldn't have even thought about sex without using a condom."

"But we never used a condom."

"Because we were newlyweds. We were hoping to have

children, we both wanted a big family, but it's different now. We're separated. Divorcing. A baby would be disastrous, absolutely the worst thing possible—"

"Actually, I can think of a few things worse than a baby," he interrupted, getting off the bed and reaching for his trousers. He stepped into one leg and then the other before zipping them closed. "Like famine. Disease. Pestilence. Or someone swindling billions of dollars—"

"Obviously I didn't mean that a baby was a tragedy," she retorted, crossing her arms over her chest to hide the fact that she was trembling. Just moments ago she'd been so relaxed, so happy, and now she felt absolutely shell-shocked. How was it possible to swing from bliss to hell in thirty seconds flat? But then, wasn't that how it had always been with them?

"No, I think you did," he countered. "It's always about you, and what's good for you—"

"That's not true."

"Absolutely true. You're so caught up in what you want and need that there is no room in this relationship for two people. There certainly was never room for me."

Her eyes widened. "You can't be serious, Drakon. You're the most controlling person I've ever met. You controlled everything in our marriage, including me—"

"Do I look like I'm in control?" he demanded tautly, dark color washing the strong, hard planes of his face.

He was breathing unsteadily, and her gaze swept over him, from his piercing gaze to the high color in his cheekbones to his firm full mouth, and she thought he looked incredible. Beautiful. Powerful. Her very own mythic Greek god. But that was the problem. He was too beautiful, too powerful. She had no perspective around him. Would throw herself in the path of danger just to be close to him.

Good God. How self-destructive was that?

Before she could speak, she heard the distinctive hum of a helicopter.

"Rowan," Drakon said, crossing to the balcony and stepping outside to watch the helicopter move across the sky. "He'll have news about your father."

"Then I'd better shower and dress."

CHAPTER SEVEN

MORGAN REFUSED TO think about what had just happened in her bed, unable to go there at all, and instead focused on taking a very fast shower before drying off and changing into a simple A-line dress in white linen with blue piping that Drakon had shipped over from the Athens house with the rest of the wardrobe.

In the steamy marble bathroom, she ran a brush through her long hair before drawing it back into a sleek ponytail and headed for her door, careful to keep her gaze averted from the bed's tousled sheets and duvet.

The maid would remake the bed while she was gone, and probably change the sheets, and Morgan was glad. She didn't want to remember or reflect on what had just changed there. It shouldn't have happened. It was a terrible mistake.

She took the stairs quickly, overwhelmed by emotion—worry and hope for her father, longing for Drakon, as well as regret. Now that they'd made love once, would he expect her to tumble back into bed later tonight?

And what if he didn't want to make love again? What if that was the last time? How would she feel?

In some ways that was the worst thought of all.

It wasn't the right way to end things. Couldn't be their last time. Their last time needed to be different. Needed more, not less. Needed more emotion, more time, more skin, more love...

Love.

She still loved Drakon, didn't she? Morgan's eyes stung, knowing she always would love him, too. Saying goodbye to him would rip her heart out. She only hoped it'd be less destructive than it had been the first time. Could only hope she'd remember the pain was just grief…that the pain would eventually, one day, subside.

But she wouldn't go there, either. Not yet. She was still here with him, still feeling so alive with him. Better to stay focused on the moment, and deal with the future when it came.

Reaching the bottom stair she discovered one of Drakon's staff was waiting for her. "Mrs. Xanthis, Mr. Xanthis is waiting for you in the terrace sunroom," the maid said.

Morgan thanked her and headed down the final flight of stairs to the lower level, the terrace level.

The sunroom ran the length of the villa and had formerly been a ballroom in the nineteenth century. The ballroom's original gilt ceiling, the six sets of double glass doors and the grand Venetian glass chandeliers remained, but the grand space was filled now with gorgeous rugs and comfortable furniture places and potted palms and miniature citrus trees. It was one of the lightest, brightest rooms in the villa and almost always smelled of citrus blossoms.

Entering the former ballroom, Morgan spotted Drakon and another man standing in the middle of the enormous room, talking in front of a grouping of couches and chairs.

They both turned and looked at her as she entered the room, but Morgan only had eyes for Drakon. Just looking at him made her insides flip, and her pulse leap.

She needed him, wanted him, loved him, far too much.

Her heart raced and her stomach hurt as she crossed the ballroom, her gaze drinking in Drakon, her footsteps muffled by the plush Persian rugs scattered across the marble floor.

He looked amazing…like Drakon, but not like Drakon

in that soft gray knit shirt that hugged his broad shoulders and lovingly molded to his muscular chest, outlining every hard, sinewy muscle with a pair of jeans. In America they called shirts like the one he was wearing Henleys. They'd been work shirts, worn by farmers and firemen and lumberjacks, not tycoons and millionaires and it boggled her mind that Drakon would wear such a casual shirt, although from the look of the fabric and the cut, it wasn't an inexpensive one—but it suited him.

He looked relaxed…and warm. So warm. So absolutely not cold, or controlled. And part of her suddenly wondered, if he had ever been cold, or if she'd just come to think of him that way as they grew apart in those last few months of their marriage?

Which led to another question—had he ever been that much in control, too? Or had she turned him into something he wasn't? Her imagination making him into an intimidating and controlling man because she felt so out of control?

God, she hoped not. But there was no time to mull over the past. She'd reached Drakon's side and felt another electric jolt as his gaze met hers and held. She couldn't look away from the warmth in his amber eyes. Part of him still burned and it made her want to burn with him. Madness, she told herself, don't go there, don't lose yourself, and yet the air hummed with heat and desire.

How could she not respond to him?

How could she not want to be close to him when he was so fiercely alive?

"It's going to be all right," he murmured, his deep voice pitched so low only she could hear.

Her lovely, lovely man that made her feel like the most beautiful woman in the entire world. Her lovely, lovely man that had pushed her to the brink, and beyond, and he still didn't know…still had no idea where she'd been that first year after leaving him, or what had happened to her trying to separate herself from him.

Part of her wanted to tell him, and yet another part didn't want to give him that knowledge, or power. Because he could break her. Absolutely destroy her. And she wasn't strong enough yet to rebuild herself again...not yet. Not on top of everything else that had happened to her father and her family with the Amery scandal.

"I promise you," he added.

She heard his fierce resolve and her heart turned over. This is how she'd fallen in love with him—his strength, his focus, his determination. That and the way he smiled at her... as if she were sunshine and oxygen all rolled into one. "Yes," she murmured, aware that once upon a time he'd been everything to her...her hope, her happiness, her future. She missed those days. Missed feeling as if she belonged somewhere with someone.

There was a flicker in his eyes, and then he made the introductions. "Morgan, this is Rowan Argyros, of Dunamas. Rowan, my wife, Morgan Copeland Xanthis."

Morgan forced her attention from Drakon to the stranger and her jaw nearly dropped. *This* was Rowan Argyros? *This* was one of the founders of Dunamas Maritime Intelligence?

Her brows tugged. She couldn't mask her surprise. Argyros wasn't at all what she'd expected.

She'd imagined Drakon's intelligence expert to look like one, and she'd pictured a man in his forties, maybe early fifties, who was stocky, balding, with a square jaw and pugilistic nose.

Instead Rowan Argyros looked like a model straight off some Parisian runway. He was gorgeous. Not her type at all, but her sister Logan would bed him in a heartbeat.

Tall and broad-shouldered, Argyros was muscular without any bulk. He was very tan, and his eyes were light, a pale gray or green, hard to know exactly in the diffused light of the ballroom. His dark brown hair was sun-streaked and he wore it straight and far too long for someone in his line of work. His jaw was strong, but not the thick bulldog jaw she'd come to associate with testosterone-driven males, but more angular...elegant, the kind of face that would photograph beautifully, although today that jaw was shadowed with a day-old beard.

"Mrs. Xanthis," Rowan said, extending a hand to her.

It bothered her that he hadn't even bothered to shave for their meeting, and she wondered how this could be the man who would free her father?

Rowan Argosy looked as if he'd spent his free time hanging out on obscenely big yachts off the coast of France, not planning daring, dangerous life-saving missions.

She shook his hand firmly and let it go quickly. "Mr. Argyros," she said crisply. "I would love to know what you know about my father. Drakon said you have information."

"I do," Rowan said, looking her straight in the eye, his voice hard, his expression as cool and unfriendly as hers.

Morgan's eyebrows lifted. Nice. She liked his frosty tone, and found his coldness and aloofness reassuring. She wouldn't have trusted him at all if he'd been warm and charming. Military types...intelligence types...they weren't the touchy-feely sort. "Is he alive?"

"He is. I have some film of him taken just this morning."

"How did you get it?"

"Does it matter?"

"No." And her legs felt like Jell-O and she took a step back, sitting down heavily in one of the chairs grouped behind them. Her heart was thudding so hard and fast she thought she might be sick and she drew great gulps of air, fighting waves of nausea and intense relief. Dad was alive. That was huge. "Thank God."

For a moment there was just silence as Morgan sat with the news, overwhelmed that her father was indeed alive. After a moment, when she could trust herself to speak, she looked up at Rowan. "And he's well? He's healthy?"

He hesitated. "We don't know that. We only have his location, and evidence that he is alive."

So Dad could be sick. He probably didn't have his heart medicine with him. It'd probably been left behind on his boat. "What happens now?" she asked.

"We get your father out, take him to wherever you want him to go."

"How does that happen, though?"

"We're going to have you call your contact, the one in Somalia you've been dealing with, and you're going to ask to speak to your father. You'll tell them you need proof that he's alive and well if they are to get the six million dollars."

"They won't let me speak to him. I tried that before."

"They will," Drakon interjected, arms folded across his chest, the shirt molded to his sculpted torso, "if they think you're ready to make a drop of six million."

She looked at him. "What if they call our bluff? Wouldn't we have to be prepared to make the drop?"

"Yes. And we will. We'll give them a date, a time, coordinates for the drop. We'll tell them who is making the drop, too."

"But we're not dropping any money, are we?" she asked, glancing from him to Rowan and back again.

"No," said Rowan. "We're preparing a team right now to move in and rescue your father. But speaking to your father gives us important information, as well as buys us a little more time to put our plan in place."

She nodded, processing this. "How long until you rescue him?"

"Soon. Seventy-two hours, or less."

She looked at Rowan, startled. "That is soon."

"Once we have our plan in place, it's better to strike fast." Rowan's phone made a low vibrating noise and he reached into his pocket and checked the number. "I need to take this call," he said, walking away.

Morgan exhaled as Rowan exited through the sunroom, into the stairwell that would take him back up to the main level of the villa.

"You okay?" Drakon asked, looking down on her, after Rowan disappeared.

"Things can go wrong," she said.

"Yes. And sometimes they do. But Dunamas has an impressive track record. Far more successes than failures. I wouldn't have enlisted their help if I didn't think they'd succeed."

She hesitated. "If Rowan's team didn't succeed...people could die."

"People *will* die even if they do succeed. They're planning a raid. The pirates are heavily armed. Dunamas's team will be heavily armed. It's not going to be a peaceful handover. It'll be explosive and violent, and yet the team they're sending are professionals. They're prepared to do whatever they have to do to get him out alive."

So some of them—or all of them—could end up dying for her father?

Nauseated all over again, Morgan moved from her chair, not wanting to think of the brave, battle-tested men, men the world viewed as heroic, risking their lives for her father, who wasn't a hero.

Stomach churning, she pushed open one of the sunroom's tall arched glass doors and stepped onto the terrace, into the sunshine. She drank in a breath of fresh air, and then another. Was she being selfish, trying to save her father? Should she not do this?

Panic and guilt buffeted her as she leaned against the terrace's creamy marble balustrade and squeezed her eyes closed.

Drakon had followed her outside. "What's wrong?"

She didn't answer immediately, trying to find the right words, but what were those words? How did one make a decision like this? "Am I doing the wrong thing?" she asked. "Am I wrong, trying to save him?"

"I can't answer that for you. He's your father. Your family."

"You know I tried everything before I came to you. I asked everyone for help. No one would help me."

"Who did you approach?"

"Who didn't I?" She laughed grimly and glanced out across the terraced gardens with the roses and hedges and the pool and the view of the sea beyond. "I went to London to see Branson, and then to Los Angeles to see Logan, and then to Tori in New York, and back to London, but none of them would contribute money toward Dad's ransom. They're all in tight financial straits, and they all have reasons they couldn't give, but I think they wouldn't contribute to the ransom because they're ashamed of Dad. I think they believe I'm wasting money trying to rescue him. Mom even said he's better off where he is…that people will find it easier to forgive us—his kids—if Dad doesn't come back."

"You mean, if the pirates kill him?" Drakon asked.

She nodded.

"Your mother is probably right," he said.

She shot him a swift glance before pushing away from the railing to pace the length of the terrace. For a long minute she just walked, trying to master her emotions. "Maybe," she said, "maybe Mom is right, but I don't care. I don't care what people think of me. I don't care if they like me. I care about what's right. And while what Dad did, just blindly giving Michael the money, wasn't right, it's also not right to leave him in Somalia. And maybe the others can write him off, but I can't."

She shivered, chilled, even though the sun was shining warmly overhead. "I can't forget how he taught me to swim and ride a bike and he went to every one of my volleyball games in high school. Dad was there for everything, big and small, and maybe he was a terrible investment advisor, but he was a wonderful father. I couldn't have asked for better—" Morgan broke off, covering her mouth to stifle a sob. She couldn't help it, but she missed him, and worried about him, and there was just no way she could turn her back on him now. No way at all.

"I think you have your answer," Drakon said quietly. "You have to do this. Have to help him. Right or wrong."

They both turned at the sound of a squeaky gate. Rowan was heading up toward them from the lower garden.

"And if anybody can get your father home, it's Argyros," Drakon said.

Morgan wrinkled her nose. "He looks like a drug smuggler."

The corner of Drakon's mouth lifted. "He isn't what one expects. That's what makes him so successful."

"As long as you trust him."

"I do."

On reaching their side, Rowan announced that his office was now ready for Morgan to try to phone her pirate contact in Somalia. "We have a special line set up that will allow us to record the conversation," he said. "And my team is standing by now, to listen in on the call."

"But I can only use my phone," she answered. "And my number. They know my number—"

"We know. And we can make it appear to look like your number. Today's technology lets us do just about anything."

In the villa's dark-paneled library they attempted the call but no one answered on the other end. Morgan left a message, letting her contact know that she had six million in cash, in used bills, and was ready to make the drop but she wanted to speak to her father first. "I need to know he's alive," she said, "and then you'll have the money."

She hung up, glanced at Rowan and Drakon. "And now what?"

"We wait for a call back," Rowan said.

They had a light lunch in the library while waiting, but there was no return call. Morgan wanted to phone again but Rowan said it wasn't a good idea. "We're playing a game," he explained. "It's their game, but we're going to outplay them. They just don't know it yet."

The afternoon dragged. Morgan hated waiting as it made her restless and anxious. She wanted to hear her father's voice, and she wanted to hear it sooner than later. After a couple hours, she couldn't sit still any longer and began to walk in circles. She saw Morgan and Drakon exchange glances.

"What?" she demanded. "Am I not allowed to move out of my chair?"

Drakon smiled faintly. "Come, let's go get some exercise and fresh air."

Stretching her legs did sound nice, but Morgan didn't want to miss the call. "What if the pirate calls back and I'm not here?"

"He'll leave a message," Drakon said.

"Won't he be angry?" she asked.

Rowan shrugged. "They want your money. They'll call back."

It was close to four when Morgan and Drakon left the house to walk down to the water, and the afternoon was still bright, and warm, but already the sun was sitting lower in the sky. Morgan took a deep breath, glad to have escaped the dark cool library and be back outside.

"Thank you for getting me out of there," she said to Drakon as they crossed the lawn, heading for the stone and cement staircase that hugged the cliff and took them down to the little dock, where they used to anchor the speedboat they used to explore the coast.

"You were looking a little pale in there," Drakon said, walking next to her. "But your father's going to be all right."

"If I was pale, it's because I was thinking about what we did earlier." Her fingers knotted into fists. "Or what we shouldn't have done." She glanced up at him as he opened the second wrought-iron gate, this one at the top of the stairs.

"Which was?" he asked innocently.

She shot him a disbelieving look and his golden brown eyes sparked, the corner of his sexy mouth tugging in a slow, wicked smile and just like that the air was suddenly charged, and Morgan shivered at the sudden snap and crackle of tension and the spike of awareness. God, it was electric between them. And dangerous.

"It can't happen again," she whispered, her gaze meeting his.

"No?" he murmured, reaching out to lift a soft tendril of hair back from her cheek, but then he couldn't let it go and he let the strand slide between his fingers, before curling it loosely around his finger and thumb.

Her breath caught in her throat and she stared up at him, heart pounding, mouth drying. She loved the way he touched her and he was making her weak in the knees now. "It confuses me."

"Confuses you, how?"

The heat between them was intense. Dizzying. So much awareness, so much desire, so impossible to satisfy. She swayed on her feet and he immediately stepped between her and the edge of the stairs, pressing her up against the wall. "I can't think around you," she whispered, feeling his dazzling energy before her, and the sun warmed rock at her back.

"Thinking is overrated," he murmured, moving in closer to her, brushing his lips across her forehead.

She closed her eyes, breathing in his light clean fragrance and savoring the teasing caress. "Is it?"

"Mmm-hmm."

"Does that mean you're not going to think, either?"

She felt the corners of his mouth curve against her brow. He was smiling. And God, didn't that turn her on?

She locked her knees, her inner thighs clenching, wanting him, needing. Damn him.

"One of us should probably keep our heads," he answered, his hands cupping her face, thumbs stroking her cheekbones. "Less frantic that way."

"And I suppose you think that should be you?" she breathed, trying to resist the pleasure of his hands pushing deep into her hair, his fingers wrapping around the strands, his knuckles grazing her scalp. He was so good at turning her on, making her feel, and he was making her feel now with a little tug, a touch, and just like that, desire rushed through her...hot, consuming, intense.

"Of course," he said, leaning in to her, his mouth lightly kissing down from her brow, over her cheekbone, to the soft swell of her lips.

"Why?"

"Because no one has ever loved you the way I loved you."

Her eyes flew open and she stared into his eyes. "Don't say that."

"It's true. You know how I feel about you. You know I can not refuse you anything."

"Not true. For five years you refused to grant me the divorce."

"Because I didn't want to lose you."

"Five years is a long time to wait for someone."

"I would have waited forever for you, Morgan."

Her heart was pounding again, even harder. "That doesn't make sense, Drakon. Nothing about this...us...makes sense."

"Who said love was supposed to make sense?"

She exhaled hard, in a quick, desperate rush, and she had to blink hard to clear her vision. "Did you *really* love me?"

"How can you doubt it?"

She frowned, thinking, trying to remember. Why had she doubted it? Why had she not felt loved? How did she get from besotted bride to runaway wife?

He reached out, tipped her chin up, so he could look deeper into her eyes. "Morgan, tell me. How could you doubt me?"

"Because after our honeymoon…after we left here…I didn't feel loved…." Her voice drifted off as she struggled to piece it together. How lost she'd felt in Athens, how confused waiting for him all day, needing him so much that when he walked through the door, she didn't know if she should run to him, or hide, ashamed for feeling so empty. "But then, after a while, I didn't feel anything anymore—" She broke off, bit down into her lip, piercing the skin. "No, that's not true. I did feel something. I felt crazy, Drakon. I felt crazy living with you."

"Don't say that."

"It's true."

He stepped away from her, turned and faced the sea, then rubbed his palm across the bristles on his jaw.

Morgan watched him just long enough to see the pain in his eyes. She'd hurt him. Again.

Hating herself, hating what they did to each other, she slipped past him and continued down the stairs to the water's edge.

She had to get out of here. And she had to get out of here soon.

CHAPTER EIGHT

HE SWORE SOFTLY, and shook his head.

God, that woman was frustrating. And to think he hadn't just fallen in love with her, but he'd married her.

Married her.

Long before his wedding day, Drakon had been warned by other men that getting married changed things. He'd been warned that wives—and marriage—were a lot of work. But Drakon hadn't been daunted. He didn't mind work. He'd succeeded because he'd always worked hard, put in long hours, never expecting life to be easy.

But marriage to Morgan hadn't started out difficult. It'd been amazing initially. She'd been amazing, and everything had been easy, since Morgan had been easiness herself…joyful, uncomplicated, undemanding. And then they moved into the new villa in Ekali, the affluent Athens neighborhood, and she'd changed…expressing worries, and then doubts, and then needs which came to sound like demands.

Be home from work early.

Don't work too late.

Why aren't you ever here?

And if he were honest, he had worked long hours, really long hours, and the more Morgan pressured him to come home, the more he wanted to be at the office, and he'd told himself he was working late to provide for her, working late to ensure she had everything she needed, when deep inside he knew he was just avoiding going home to her. It wasn't that he didn't love her…but he was suddenly so aware of how she now depended on him for everything. It overwhelmed him. How could he meet all those needs? How could he manage her, and his work, and his responsibilities?

While he grew more distant, she grew more emotional, her sunny smiles fading until they were gone, replaced by a woman who looked fragile and haunted, her eyes sad, her lovely face taut, her expression stricken.

It made him angry, this change in her. Made him angry that she couldn't be like his other women…happy to shop and visit salons and spas and just enjoy being spoiled, enjoy the prestige of being Drakon Xanthis's pampered wife. It was good enough for his other women. Why not for her?

Why did Morgan want more? More to the point, what did she want from *him?*

He'd never told her—or anyone—but in his mind, she'd become like his mother. Drakon loved his mother, he was a dutiful son, but he didn't want to be around her, and that's what happened with Morgan. Morgan made him feel inadequate and he dealt with it by avoiding her.

And then one day Morgan disappeared, abruptly returning to America, and he had exploded.

How could she have just walk away from him like that? How could she give up? How *dare* she give up? He hadn't been happy all those years ago, but he hadn't walked away from her. He hadn't felt the magic, either, but he wasn't a quitter—

And then it struck him. He had quit on her. Maybe he hadn't physically left, but he'd checked out emotionally.

And only now he could see that her needs hadn't been so overwhelming. She hadn't asked for that much. But the fact that she'd asked for anything—time, tenderness, reassurance—had triggered the worst in him, and he'd reacted like the boy he'd once been, retreating, hiding, rejecting.

He'd given her money but not affection.

He'd given her toys but not his heart.

He'd given her stuff…as long as she didn't engage him, want him, need him. Don't bother him because he couldn't, wouldn't, deal with anyone else's problems—he had plenty of his own.

Ah.

And there it was. The ugly, ugly truth.

Drakon Xanthis was a selfish, shallow, stunted man. A man that looked strong on the outside but was just an angry child on the inside. And that's when he knew, that he'd wronged Morgan…badly. Cruelly. He'd taken a twenty-two-year-old woman from her home and her country and dropped her into his white marble house and told her to be silent and to not feel and to not need. To not express emotion, to not reach out, to not cry, to not talk, to not be human.

My God.

He'd done to her what his mother had done to him. Be there, Drakon, but do not need. Be present, Drakon, but do not feel.…

Five years ago Drakon went in search of Morgan, seeking to right the wrongs, but she was gone. She'd vanished…completely disappeared…and his anger with himself grew. He'd loved Morgan and he'd treated her so badly. He'd taken the person who loved him, wanted him, the real him—the man, not the name, the bank account, the status—and crushed her.

He'd broken her.

He knew it. And all he'd wanted was to find her, apologize, fix everything. And he couldn't. Morgan was gone again. And Drakon was shattered. Until she came back, until he could make things right, he was a man in hell.

Now, from the top of the stairs, he watched Morgan step onto the platform down below, her brown hair gleaming in the sunlight, spilling down her back. His chest hurt, heavy and aching with suppressed emotion.

Morgan. His woman. His.

She stood on the platform, a hand shadowing her eyes as she looked out across the water. A wooden rowboat, the color of a robin's egg, was tethered to the platform and bobbed next to her. The blue rowboat, and dark sapphire sea, perfectly framed Morgan in her fitted white dress, which accented her slim curves.

She looked fresh and young standing on the platform, and when she slipped off her shoes and sat down on the pier's edge, pulling her crisp skirts high on her thigh so that she could put her bare feet in the water, he felt a fierce surge of emotion.

It had been his job to love her, cherish her and protect her. And he'd failed in all three counts.

Watching her, Drakon's chest grew tight. He'd vowed five years ago to make things right, and he hadn't made them right yet. Giving her a check and a divorce wasn't right. It was easy. Easier to let her go than to change, or struggle to save them. But he didn't want easy. He wanted Morgan. And she was worth fighting for, and she was worth changing for, and she was worth everything to him.

She was everything to him.

He'd known it the moment he'd lost her.

And now that she was here, he realized that he could not give up on her. Could not give up on them. Not because he needed to win her back, not because he needed to prove anything—for God's sake, he was Drakon Xanthis, and the world was his oyster—but because he loved *her*, Morgan Copeland.

And for the past five years, Morgan Copeland had tied him up in knots. But he was a smart man. He could figure out how to untie the knots. He could figure out how to reach her, how to make this—them—work.

It was a challenge, but he liked challenges. He'd never been afraid of tackling difficult situations. What was it that his father used to say? Problems were just opportunities in disguise?

Morgan being here was an opportunity. And Drakon would make the most of the opportunity.

"It was a mistake making love without protection," Drakon said quietly. "And I accept full responsibility should you get pregnant."

Morgan stiffened. She hadn't heard Drakon approach, but now she felt him there behind her, and her nape prickled, the hair on her arms lifted, and a shiver raced through her as she remembered how it felt being with him in her room, his skin on her skin, his mouth taking hers, his body giving her so much pleasure.

It had been so good. So intense and physical that she lost perspective. Forgot what was important. But then, hadn't that always been his effect on her?

"What does that mean?" she asked quietly, reaching up to pluck a fine strand of hair away from her eyelashes as she kept her gaze fixed on the watery horizon, where the sunlight shimmered in every direction. "That you will accept full responsibility if I get pregnant?"

"I'll assume full financial responsibility, for you and the child, and once the baby is born, I will assume full physical custody of the child—"

"What?" she choked, cutting him short as she turned to look at him where he was standing on the narrow stair landing behind her, leaning against the rock wall. "You'll take my baby?"

"Our baby," he calmly corrected, broad shoulders shifting, "and I am quite able to raise a child on my own, Morgan. I will get help, of course, but I'll be a good father—"

"You'd take the baby away from me?"

"If that would make you feel better—"

"It wouldn't."

"You said earlier that you didn't want to be a single mother."

"I don't. It wouldn't be right for the baby. But that doesn't mean you can have him or her."

He walked toward her. "But I'm ready to be a father, and you're not wanting to be a mother right now—"

"You can't say that. You don't know that. My God, Drakon! Where are you getting this from?"

"First of all, right now, as far as we know, there's no baby. And secondly, *should* you conceive, then of course I'd want to support my child—financially, emotionally, physically. I won't be an absentee father."

Her skin prickled as he stood above her. The man was pure electricity. The air practically pulsed with energy. "No, I don't want to be pregnant right now, it's not high on my to-do list at the moment, with my father being held hostage and my family in chaos, but if I was pregnant, I'd manage."

"That's not good enough. My child deserves better than that. If you are pregnant, we'll have to do the right thing for our child, which means raising him or her in a calm, stable home, without chaos."

"Then you'd be stuck with me, Drakon, because I'm not handing over my child."

"Our child."

"Which might not even exist."

"Which probably doesn't exist, because when we were newlyweds and having unprotected sex every day, twice a day, for months, you didn't get pregnant."

She bit into her lip, hating the panic rushing through here. This was just a conversation of hypotheticals. "Does that mean if I do conceive, you'd want the baby and me to live with you?"

"Yes."

It's not real, she reminded herself, don't freak out. "And we'd be divorced?"

"No."

"No?"

He shook his head. "Absolutely not. If you're pregnant, we'll stay together. If you're not, I'll have my attorney file the divorce papers. But as we won't know that for a couple more weeks, I won't have my attorney file until we know for certain."

"Awfully convenient," she muttered under her breath.

"Happily so," he answered, not rising to the bait. "This way there would be no stigma attached to the child. We're still legally married. The baby would be a result of our reconciliation."

"And if I'm not pregnant?"

"You'll be free—single—within a couple months."

Morgan didn't immediately speak. Instead she looked out across the water and listened to the waves break and felt the breeze catch and lift her hair. She might appear calm, but her thoughts were tangled and her emotions intense. "And should the unthinkable happen, should I conceive…we would all live together, as a family?"

"Yes."

She turned to look at him. "Where would we raise the baby?"

"Greece," he said firmly.

She made a rough sound, tucking a strand of hair behind her ear. "I'd prefer not to raise a child in Greece."

"Why not?"

"I don't like Greece."

"How can you not like Greece? It's beautiful and warm and so full of life."

"I found it excruciatingly isolating, and horribly boring—"

"There was no reason for you to be bored. You had money, a driver, you could have gone shopping. The salesclerks would have loved you. They would have waited on you hand and foot."

Battling her temper, Morgan drew her feet out of the water,

wrapped her arms around bent knees. "Not all women live to shop."

"Most women do."

"You can't generalize like that. It's not true." He started to protest and she overrode him. "Obviously one or more of your past girlfriends managed to convince you that retail therapy was the answer for everything, but I'm not one of them." She rose to her feet. "Shopping when I'm lonely just makes me feel worse...wandering alone from store to store looking for something to buy...how pathetic is that?"

"It would have been better than you sitting sulking at home."

Heat rushed through her, and her cheeks suddenly burned. "Sulking? Shopping? Why in God's name did you even marry shallow, materialistic me?"

"You were young. I thought you'd change."

"I can't believe you just said that! I can't believe you think you're so perfect...that you had no blame in our failed marriage."

"So what did I do wrong?" he asked.

"You didn't talk to me."

He laughed. "*That's* my mistake?"

Her eyes blazed. "Fine, laugh, but it's true. Our marriage ended because we didn't talk to each other. It ended because we both kept everything bottled inside and I think it's time we started talking, and saying those things that aren't comfortable, but true—"

"It's not going to change anything."

"No, but at least it'll clear the air. Perhaps give us better understanding of what happened...maybe help me understand you."

"Me?" he said incredulously. "What is there to understand about me?"

"Everything! I married one person and yet I ended up with another."

He drew back, shocked. "I didn't change. Morgan, it was you. When we married, you were strong and confident, and then before I knew what happened, you turned into an angry, silent woman who only responded when I touched her. So I touched you, as often as I could, as much as I could, trying to get you back."

"Words would have worked. Words and conversation."

"I don't trust words. Don't put much stock in conversation."

"Obviously, but would it have killed you to ask me about my day, or tell me about your day—" She broke off, averting her head, unable to look at him when her heart felt so bruised and tender. What a mistake it had been…falling in love… thinking it would work. "Let's just hope I'm not pregnant," she added hoarsely. "Because I don't want to go through life like this, trying to explain myself, trying to be accepted, only to be mocked by you."

Drakon shook his head, muttering something under his breath, something with quite a few syllables and from his inflection, sounded far from flattering.

"What did you just say?" she demanded.

"Doesn't matter."

"No, it does. I want to hear this. I want to hear everything you wouldn't tell me before."

"You gave up on us so quickly, Morgan. You didn't give yourself time to adjust to married life, nor did you try to make friends."

"Maybe I did give up too soon, but you could have tried to help me adjust to Athens. Instead you dropped me off at the house and expected me to keep myself busy until you returned every night."

"I had a job to do."

"You could have made more of an effort to help me adjust. You could have taken the time to show me around, or cut your day short now and then so we could take a walk, or visit a nearby beach, or even have people over."

Drakon looked bewildered. "Have people over? For what?"

"Have dinner, visit, socialize." She could see by his expression that he still didn't get it. "Surely, you're used to entertaining...having some friends over for a barbecue or a party."

"To my house?"

"Yes."

"Never have."

"Why not?"

"My family didn't. I never did. I don't have time, nor is it something I'd want to do. I work long days, and when I go home, I want to relax, rest, focus on what I need to do the next day."

"But while you were working twelve- and fourteen-hour days, Drakon, what was I supposed to do?"

"Read a book...take language courses...learn to cook?" He shrugged, sighed, running a hand through his cropped dark hair. "Eventually we would have had children. And then, of course, you had the house."

"The *house?*" Morgan suppressed a sudden urge to throw rocks at his head. "Did you actually just say I had the *house?*"

"Yes, the house. The one I had built for you."

"You did not build that marble mausoleum for me. You bought it for me——"

"No, I bought the lot, scrapped the old house that was there and built our home for you."

"I *hated* the villa."

"What?"

Her eyebrows lifted, her lips twisting. "Yes. I hated it. It's awful. It was too white and sterile, never mind cold, modern and boxy——"

"It's a ten-million-dollar architectural masterpiece, Morgan."

"Or merely an outrageously expensive ice cube tray!"

His eyes sparked. "You disappoint me."

"Yes, so I've gathered. You work twelve-hour days while I'm home learning Greek, and how to cook, and hopefully getting pregnant." She shuddered. "What a horrendous life that would have been. Thank God I escaped when I did!"

He reached out, his fingers wrapping around her bicep to haul her against him. "Do you know how many women would be thrilled to live in that house?"

"I have no idea, although I'm sure Bronwyn would love to be one." She flung her head back to look him in the eye. "How is she, by the way? Doing well?"

"She's fine."

"I bet she is."

"What does that mean?"

"What do you think it means, Drakon?"

"I think it means you're petty and irrational when it comes to Bron. She's never been anything but polite to you—"

"Give me a break!"

"—ordering you flowers, arranging for your birthday cake," he continued, as if she'd never interrupted.

Morgan shook his hand off her arm. "How nice of her to get me flowers from you and order birthday cake for me. It makes me feel so good to know that your vice president of Southeast Asia was able to do those little things to make my birthday special since you were too busy to do it yourself."

He tensed and his jaw popped. "That's not why I didn't do it."

"No? Then why didn't you do it?" She dragged in a breath of air, holding it a moment, fighting for control, not wanting to cry now. She would not cry while discussing Bronwyn. Would not lose it now when she needed to be strong. "Because I didn't want flowers picked out by the woman who is spending all day at the office with you. I didn't want a cake ordered by her, either. She's not my friend. She's not my family. She doesn't like me and is only trying to get closer to you."

"She was doing me a favor."

"Ah. I knew it. It was about you."

"What does that mean?"

"It means, that her favor to you, was not just unnecessary, but it actually hurt me."

"That's ridiculous."

And this was why she and Drakon weren't together. This was why she'd left him, and this was why they'd never be together.

Even though part of her would always love him, they couldn't be together, because outside the bedroom, they simply didn't work. There was no real understanding, no meeting of the minds. The only time they connected, the only time they made sense, was when they were having sex. But sex was just a part of a relationship, it couldn't be the relationship.

She looked up at him, her expression fierce. "Perhaps you will permit me to give you a little advice. Maybe I can do something for the future Mrs. Xanthis. Don't let Bronwyn, or any other woman, intrude so much in your personal life. The women you work with shouldn't be allowed to overshadow the woman you live with. And should you want to send your wife flowers, or a gift, do it yourself or don't do it at all."

His eyes glittered and he looked almost pale beneath his tan. "Anything else, Morgan?"

"Yes, actually. Next time you marry, ask your bride what kind of home she wants to live in. Or better yet, include her on the design process, or take her with you when you go house hunting. That way your poor wife might actually like her cage."

"Cage?" he choked out, expression furious.

She shrugged, shoulders twisting. "It's what it felt like," she said, slipping past him to climb the stone and cement stairs that led back up to the house. And then halfway up the staircase, she paused. "But I'm not your pet, Drakon, and I won't be kept!"

And then with her skirts in her hands, she raced on up, half hoping he'd follow and end this terrible fight the only way they knew how to end things—through sex.

Because right now she wanted him and needed him, not to make her come, but to make her feel safe. Sane. Only she didn't know how to ask him for comfort, and he didn't know how to give comfort. Just raw, carnal pleasure.

But even raw, carnal pleasure would be better than nothing right now, and as she continued up toward the house, she tried not to think how good it'd feel to have him push her back against the rock wall and capture her hands in his and hold her immobile all the while kissing her senseless, kissing her until she was wet and ready for him and he could take her here, in the sun, near the sea, with the tang of salt in her nose and the sweet heady fragrance of jasmine perfuming the air, and the taste of Drakon—her husband, and her heart—on her tongue.

CHAPTER NINE

THERE WAS NO call back from the pirates and Morgan spent the rest of the afternoon in her bedroom. She didn't have to stay in her room, but she thought it safer than wandering around the villa or the extensive grounds, where she might bump into Drakon.

In her room, Morgan tried napping and she actually fell asleep, but didn't sleep long, as her mother called, waking her. It was a brief, meaningless conversation about social events and it infuriated Morgan that her mother would even ask, much less expect, Morgan to drop everything to attend a charity fund-raiser with her.

"I'm in Italy working to bring Dad home," Morgan told her mother.

"No one is going to give you the money, Morgan." Her mother paused. "And if they do, they are fools."

After hanging up, Morgan tried to fall back asleep, but she couldn't, too unsettled from the call. So she took a long bath, trying to forget the things her mother said, remaining in the tub until the water turned cold and the skin on her fingers shriveled up.

Morgan was chilled by the time she got out of the bath, and she blew her hair dry and dressed carefully for dinner, trying to fill her time, trying to stay busy so she wouldn't go find Drakon.

She wanted Drakon. She missed him. Didn't want to be

at the villa with him and yet not with him. The last time she was here, on that delicious, luxurious honeymoon, they spent almost every moment together and it didn't seem right being at the villa and not seeing him.

But then, life didn't seem right without him in it.

But finally, thankfully, she'd managed to get through the afternoon and now it was almost dinner, and time for the nightly *aperitivo*.

Morgan was the first to the living room for the Italian *aperitivo*. The pre-dinner drink was a tradition at Villa Angelica, one she and Drakon had come to enjoy during their honeymoon.

In the living room, Morgan went to the antique table that had been set up as the bar with a selection of alcohol and juices, sodas, sparkling water and tonic water and other cocktail mixes. Morgan bypassed the mixes for the pitcher of Campari. Tonight it was Campari with pomegranate. Tomorrow night it might be Campari orange. The cocktail changed every night and Morgan enjoyed sampling the different variations.

She wandered now with her cocktail to the window to watch the sunset. It would be another stunning sunset and the sky was a fiery red orange at the moment and she sipped the cocktail, basking in the warm rays of the sun reaching through the glass.

This was like a dream, she thought, one of those dreams she had when she was at McLean Hospital, when she'd dream of Drakon every night, and in her dreams they were together still, and happy...so very, very happy....

Suddenly footsteps sounded in the stairwell and Morgan turned to watch Drakon descend the final flight of stairs and step into the grand entry. Her heart turned over in her chest as she watched him. He moved with such ease, and so much grace, that he made other men look clumsy. But then, he'd always had confidence, and a physicality that other men didn't have. She'd wondered if growing up on boats, working on cargo ships as if he were a deckhand instead of the owner's son, had given him that awareness and balance.

As he crossed the hall and joined her in the living room, the enormous Venetian chandelier bathed him in light and she sucked in a breath, struck all over again by his intensity and that strong, hard face with those intensely observant eyes.

He was looking at her now. She grew warm under his inspection, remembering how much she'd wanted to go to him earlier, how much she'd craved him all afternoon.

"Hello," she said, hoping he couldn't see her blush.

"Hello," he answered, the corner of his mouth quirking as if amused.

His smile did something to her and she felt a frisson of pleasure race through her. Flustered, Morgan lifted her drink to her lips, sipped her cocktail and studied Drakon covertly over the rim of her glass. He was wearing a crisp white dress shirt open at the collar and fine trousers and he looked like the Drakon she'd married—polished, elegant, handsome— but she'd learned something new about him during the last twenty-four hours. He wasn't as controlled as she'd imagined. If anything he was a man of passion.

And that was both good and bad. Good, because he met her intensity and answered her fierce need for touch and sensation. Bad, because soon he'd be out of her life again and she couldn't imagine ever feeling this way about any other man. Couldn't imagine ever wanting any other man.

"Were you able to get a nap?" he asked, turning away to pour himself a drink.

He, too, chose the Campari cocktail and for some reason that made her happy. "I did lie down," Morgan answered, her back now to the window so she could face Drakon, "but the moment I finally fell asleep, my phone rang. It was my mother."

"Calling to get news about your father?"

"No. She just wanted to know if I'd be home to attend a fund-raiser in Greenwich with her this weekend." Morgan shook her head incredulously. "A black-tie fund-raiser! Can you imagine?"

"You used to attend events like that all the time."

"Yes, when we were socially desirable, but we're not anymore. We're hated, loathed, but Mom doesn't get it. She's trying to carry on as if everything is the same, but nothing's the same. Only Mom refuses to face facts, refuses to accept that no one wants us at their balls or parties or fund-raisers anymore." Morgan tried to laugh but couldn't quite pull it off. "Dad's being held hostage in Somalia and Mom's trying to find a date for this Saturday's symphony gala. What a horrible family you married into, Drakon!"

His amber gaze suddenly locked with hers. "I didn't marry them. I married you."

"And I'm the craziest of them all!"

He said nothing for a long moment and then he smiled, a slow, wicked smile that put an equally wicked gleam in his eye. "Is that why sex was always so much fun?"

She blushed but was saved from answering by the sudden appearance of Rowan. "Your contact from Somalia just phoned," he said, entering the living room. "He left a message. They're not going to let you speak with your father. But since you have the money ready, they want to arrange the drop, and give you instructions on where you'll find your hostage."

Morgan's smile died on her lips and she glanced at Drakon, and then back at Rowan. "Did they really say it like that?"

Rowan nodded and Morgan paled and swallowed hard. "They make my father sound like a carcass," she whispered, sickened.

"We're not dealing with sensitive people," Rowan answered.

"But don't panic," Drakon added. "I'm sure he's still alive."

She drew a quick breath and lifted her chin. "I want him out of there."

"He will be," Drakon said.

Rowan nodded. "Soon.

It took them a while to move from the living room to the dining room for dinner, but once they got there, the dining room glowed with candlelight. The dining room's antique chandelier was filled with tapers, and the iron and glass sconces on the white walls reflected onto the ceiling making every surface gleam and dance with light. But the meal was definitely subdued. Morgan was both angry and heartsick and felt impossibly distracted. Rowan barely spoke and Drakon didn't say much more than Rowan. But every now and then Morgan looked up to find Drakon watching her, his expression shuttered and impossible to read.

Perhaps if she and Drakon had been alone, she would have asked him what he was thinking, but with Rowan present, Morgan left Drakon to his own thoughts, and she tried not to dwell on her father, or his conditions in Somalia.

As Drakon said, her father would be home soon. Rowan had agreed with him.

She had to focus on that, cling to that, not allow herself to slide into panic or doubt.

Finally the dinner dishes were being cleared away and coffee was served. But sitting in silence with coffee proved even more uncomfortable than eating in silence.

"I hate them," she choked out, unable to remain silent another moment. "I hate how they've taken him and are treating him like he's nothing...nobody...just an object to be bartered."

"It is horrendous," Drakon agreed quietly.

"But it's on the rise, isn't it?" She looked up at him as she added another half teaspoon of sugar to her coffee and gave it a brisk stir. "From what I read, attacks have doubled in the last few years."

Drakon's dark head inclined. "Last year there were more hostages taken than ever before."

"Nearly twelve hundred," Morgan murmured, having done a fair amount of research on her own, trying to understand what had happened to her father. "With many being held for nine months or more. Unthinkable. But it's real. It's happening."

"At least your father will be freed," Rowan said brusquely. "There are hundreds of hostages who haven't been ransomed…that will never be ransomed."

Morgan's insides twisted. She couldn't imagine being one of the unfortunate crew who were never freed. How terrible to sit day after day, week after week, month after month waiting for a ransom that might never come. "Because someone isn't willing to pay the ransom?" she asked.

"Or able to pay it. Not all shipping companies have insurance that will pay it, and most ordinary people can't come up with millions of dollars, not even to save a loved one," Drakon answered.

Morgan put her spoon down, her eyes burning, guilt eating at her because she was able to help her father. She was able to do something and yet she felt for those who couldn't. "Fortunately, I understand the counter-piracy measures put in place this past year seem to be helping. From what I read, piracy was down during the first quarter of the year—not enough of course to give cause for celebration, but enough to know that the experts might be on to something."

"That's true," Drakon agreed. "Right now there's a concerted international effort to check piracy, and it's helping, but it certainly hasn't stopped the pirates. It's just slowed them a little."

"How do you stop them?"

"Put a stable, strong, and effective government in place.

Change their economic structure. Take out the group who is arming the pirates, and profiting from the hostage ransoms." Rowan's lips curved, his expression hard. "But if that were easy, it would have been done already. And so we do the next best thing—increase maritime intelligence and continue international cooperation on monitoring the water off the Horn of Africa."

"Until I began researching piracy I didn't realize that until recently, few countries worked together…that for the most part, most countries just focused on their own pirated vessels," Morgan answered.

Rowan shrugged. "Typical nationalistic reaction."

"How so?"

"Every country has its own navy, military intelligence and sources, so it's not easy getting everyone on the same page. Governments are protective of their military and don't want to share resources," he answered her.

Morgan frowned. "But you're military?"

"Former, yes. Just as most of us in maritime intelligence have served in one arm of the navy or another."

"Were you in the Royal Navy?" she asked.

"I've actually served in both the U.S. Navy and the Royal Navy, but at different times and in different capacities."

Morgan glanced to Drakon and then back to Rowan. "How is that possible?"

"I have dual nationalities…I was born in Northern Ireland to an Irish mother, and an American Greek father, giving me both American and British citizenship."

"Irish, too," Drakon said.

"They let you have all those passports?" Morgan asked, rather amazed.

Rowan shrugged. "If you're good at what you do."

"And you are good, I take it?"

His lips curved but the smile didn't reach his eyes. "Have

to be. There's a lot at stake—" He broke off as the sound of high heels clicking briskly on hard tiles echoed in the hallway.

They were all listening to the footsteps and Morgan stiffened, her shoulders drawing back as unease rolled through her in a huge dark wave.

Bronwyn.

Morgan went hot and then cold. But no, it couldn't be. What would Bronwyn be doing here?

And yet no one else walked that way. No one else sounded so fiercely confident in high stiletto heels.

Then there she was, appearing in the dining room doorway as if she owned Villa Angelica, as tall and blonde and statuesque as ever, dressed tonight in a formfitting red jersey knit that clung to her curves, making the most of her voluptuous body. Bronwyn, a stunning blonde with brilliant blue eyes and a dark golden tan, knew how to make an entrance.

"Hope I haven't kept you waiting," she said, smiling, as her gaze swept the dining room, before lingering on Drakon.

Morgan's stomach hurt as she saw the way Bronwyn looked at Drakon. Drakon had always said that Bronwyn was just part of his management team, a valuable employee and nothing more, but from the possessive expression on Bronwyn's face, Morgan knew that Bronwyn was fiercely attached to Drakon.

"You haven't kept us waiting," Drakon answered, rising and gesturing to a chair at the table. "Join us. Have you eaten? Would you like coffee? Something sweet?"

Bronwyn flashed Drakon a grateful smile as she moved around the dining room table to take an empty chair. "A glass of wine would be perfect. You know what I like."

Morgan ground her teeth together as she glanced from Bronwyn to Drakon and then back to Bronwyn again. How could he have invited her here, now, when they were in the middle of a crisis? How could he possibly think it was appropriate?

Bronwyn sat down and crossed one leg over the other, then gave her head a small toss, sending her long, artfully layered blond hair spilling over her shoulders down to the tops of her high full breasts. "Drakon, next time, send the helicopter for me, not a driver. I was nauseous from Sorrento on. Such a grueling drive. So many hairpin curves."

Drakon didn't respond; too busy speaking to one of the kitchen staff, requesting Bronwyn's wine.

Bronwyn turned to Rowan. "Haven't seen you in a while. How are you?"

"Busy," he answered flatly, expression hard.

"But it must be nice to be in a business that is booming," she retorted.

"Not if there are people's lives at stake," Morgan said, unable to remain silent.

Bronwyn waved her hand in a careless gesture. "Most crews on hijacked ships aren't hurt. Most are eventually released when the ransom's paid."

"Most," Morgan said, hanging on to her temper by a thread. "But that's not all, and not a cause to celebrate."

Bronwyn smiled, her long lashes dropping over her eyes, but not before Morgan caught the glittering animosity in the blue depths. "Was I celebrating? I hope not. That would be most insensitive of me, considering your father is being held hostage as we speak."

For a moment Morgan couldn't breathe. The air caught in her throat and she balled her hands into fists. "We'll have him home soon, though," she answered, struggling to sound calm. "Drakon's brought in the best to secure his release."

Bronwyn flashed Rowan an amused glance. "The best, yes, as well as the most expensive. What will the job cost Drakon this time, Rowan? Seven million? Ten? More?"

"That's none of your business, Bronwyn," Drakon said gruffly.

The Australian turned wide blue eyes on him. "You assigned me the task of improving the corporation's bottom line, which includes cutting unnecessary spending—"

"And you know perfectly well that I will pay Dunamas Maritime Intelligence from my personal account, not the corporation, so enough." Drakon's tone was cool and firm, but not cold or firm enough for Morgan.

Why did he put up with Bronwyn? Why did he allow his vice president to speak to him the way he did? He wouldn't tolerate it from anyone else, Morgan was sure of that.

"Yes, boss," Bronwyn answered, rolling her eyes even as she glanced in Morgan's direction, the exasperation in Bronwyn's eyes replaced by bruising disdain.

Interesting, Morgan thought, air catching in her throat. *Bronwyn doesn't like me, either.*

Morgan had sensed it five years ago, and had mentioned her concern to Drakon, but Drakon had brushed Morgan off, telling her not to be petty, that Bronwyn was far too professional to have any ill will toward his new wife. Morgan had felt ashamed for being petty—if that's what how she was behaving—and properly chastised, tried not to object to Bronwyn's frequent intrusions into their personal life, but it was almost impossible. Bronwyn called constantly, appeared on their doorstep at strange moments, felt perfectly comfortable drawing Drakon out of the living room and off into his study for long, private business conversations.

Morgan hated it, and had come to resent Bronwyn, all the while feeling guilty for resenting someone that Drakon viewed as so indispensible to his work.

But now Morgan knew she'd been right to object to Bronwyn's intrusiveness. Because Bronwyn meant to be intrusive. Bronwyn wanted Drakon. She'd wanted him five years ago, and she still wanted him now.

Of course, Morgan had no proof, just her female intuition and that nagging gut instinct that told her something was wrong…the same gut instinct that was telling her now that Bronwyn was still a problem.

Abruptly Morgan stood, unable to remain one more moment in the same room with Bronwyn.

"It's late and I'm still jet-lagged," Morgan said, her voice sharper than usual. "If you'll excuse me, I think I'll head to bed."

CHAPTER TEN

THE NEXT MORNING Morgan had coffee brought to her in her room and she sat on her balcony, sipping her coffee, trying to figure out how she could avoid going downstairs today. She'd slept like hell, dreaming of Bronwyn, as well as Bronwyn and Drakon frolicking in the pool, and the ballroom, and everywhere else, and the last person Morgan wanted to see was the real Bronwyn, who Morgan knew was up and about, as she could hear her voice wafting up from one of the terraces below.

Morgan glared down into her coffee as Bronwyn's laugh spiraled up again. Why was Bronwyn here? What was Drakon thinking?

"More coffee? A pastry?" a deep, distinctive male voice coming from the bedroom behind her, asked.

Morgan glanced over her shoulder, to where Drakon lounged in the doorway, looking horribly handsome and very rested. "You should knock," she said tartly, hating him for bringing Bronwyn here, to the villa, when Morgan was here feeling overwhelmed and out of control.

"I did. You didn't answer."

"Then maybe you shouldn't have come in."

"I needed to speak with you."

"But it's not polite to barge in on ladies in the morning."

"Not even if I have an invitation for an outing?"

That did give her pause, and Morgan eyed him suspiciously, excited at the idea of escaping the villa for a few hours, before realizing that she needed to be here, available, in case the pirates tried to contact her. "How can we just leave right now in the middle of everything? What if the pirates want to talk to me? Or change their demands?"

"They're not going to change their demands. They're anticipating six million dollars being delivered any day now."

He was probably right, and yet she found it hard to contemplate doing something pleasurable when her father was still in such trouble. "I wish I knew if he had his heart medicine. I wish I knew he was okay…healthy…strong. Then I'd feel better about things. But I don't know, and the not knowing is really scary."

"It's always the scariest part." His broad shoulders shifted. "But worrying doesn't change his situation, it just makes you sick, and makes it more difficult for you to cope with stress. Which is why I'm taking you out for a couple hours. Fresh air and a change of scenery will give you some perspective."

"And we could be reached if something happens?"

"Absolutely."

She hesitated. "So who would be going?"

"Just you and me, if that's all right."

Her gaze slowly swept over his face with the high cheekbones, straight nose, firm, sensual mouth, before dropping to his body. God, she loved his body…his narrow hips, his long lean, muscular torso and those sinfully broad shoulders. She glanced back up into his face, noting his arched eyebrow and his amused expression. She blushed. "Yes, that's all right."

His warm golden brown eyes, framed by those long, dense black lashes, glinted. "I'm glad."

She looked at him for a long moment, wondering what Drakon had up his sleeve, and why he'd decided to be charming today. He was reminding her of the Drakon of their courtship, the Drakon of their honeymoon—mellow, amusing, easygoing, attentive. She liked this Drakon, very much, but why was he here now? And what did he want? "When do we leave?"

"When can you be ready?"

They took the helicopter towards Naples, flying above the stunning Italian coastline, where the blue sea butted against the green swell of land, before rising up into the hills and the slopes of Mount Vesuvius, the volcano that had erupted and wiped out Pompeii.

"So beautiful," Morgan murmured, her fingers pressed against the slick helicopter window, her gaze fixed on the landscape below. "And so deceptively serene."

"Because Vesuvius is still active?"

"Isn't it considered one of the world's deadliest volcanoes?"

"Unfortunately, yes. Its Plinian eruptions aren't a good fit for the three million people living at the base, as well as up and down the slopes."

"I'd be afraid to live there."

"Scientists believe they can predict an eruption before it happens, and they do have an emergency evacuation plan.

She shivered. "I understand ancient Pompeii was beautiful."

"The villas that were on the outskirts of town would rival the finest villas today."

"I'd love to see it."

"Good. Because we're on our way there now."

Morgan clasped his arm in delight. "Really?"

"Really."

A bubble of warmth formed in her chest, rising. "I'm so glad!"

Drakon glanced down at her hand where it rested on his arm. He'd hardened the moment she touched him, it was how he always responded to her.

He drew a breath and exhaled, trying to ease some of

the tightness in his gut. "I hope you'll enjoy today," he said, grateful he could sound controlled even when he didn't feel that way. "I'm hoping you will find something in Pompeii to inspire you and your next jewelry collection."

"I don't think there will be another—"

"Yes, there will be."

"I made terrible mistakes—"

"Everyone makes mistakes, but that doesn't mean you should give up. You have a gift. You're an artist. I believe in your vision."

She looked up into his eyes, fear and hope in the blue depths. "Do you really mean that?"

"Absolutely. You will have more collections, and you will succeed."

"How can you be so certain?"

"Because I've seen what you can do, and I know you. You're truly talented, Morgan. There's no one else like you."

Drakon's car was parked at a helipad outside Pompeii, waiting for them, and the driver whisked them to the ancient city to meet a private guide who was going to take them on a behind-the-scenes tour of the ruined city.

Morgan was glad she'd worn flat leather sandals since they walked from one end of the city to another, and she listened closely to everything the guide said, captivated by his stories of first century Pompeii, a thriving city of approximately ten thousand people. She was fascinated by the buried city and its restaurants and hotels and brothels, as well as the artwork revealed...frescoes and mosaics and sculptures.

"Pompeii is the most incredible place," she said as they made their way through the extraordinary villa, House of the Faun, and back into the sunlight. "But Pompeii also breaks my heart. It was such a beautiful city, and so full of life and people and passion—and then it was all wiped out. Gone in a matter of hours."

"Are you sorry I brought you today?"

She shook her head. "No. It's amazing. All of it. The houses, the streets, the restaurants, the statues and pots and artifacts. But it hurts, too. Life is so fragile, and unpredictable. There are no guarantees. Not for anyone."

"Your life changed overnight, didn't it?"

She looked at him, suddenly wary. "You mean, with the revelation of Michael's Ponzi scheme?"

Drakon nodded and Morgan bit down into her lip. "It did," she agreed softly. "I still find it hard to believe what's happened at home. Who would have thought a year ago…even three months ago…that my father would become one of the most hated men in America? That we'd lose everything… that so many others would lose everything, too, through his, and Michael's, actions?"

They'd come to a stop next to the cordoned-off fountain with its bronze statue of a dancing faun. This beautiful solitary faun was all that was left of this once glorious, elegant garden, and she held her breath a moment, pressing a fist to her chest, as if somehow she could control the pain, ease the tenderness.

"My father was horrified when he discovered that all his clients, all his investors, had lost their money. He found out on his way to a Valentine's Day soiree—another one of those black-tie balls my mother loves—when he got the text from Michael to say that it was over. That agents from the federal government had just left his house and there would be arrests made, and that Dad should flee, rather than be indicted." Her voice faded and she struggled to continue. "At first Dad didn't believe it. None of us could believe it. And then when the shock wore off, there was anger, and shame."

Morgan worked her lip between her teeth, tasting blood but thinking nothing of it, because everything hurt now, all the time. Pain was constant. Pain and that endless, overwhelming shame. "Dad wanted to kill himself. My brother talked him out of it, telling Dad that if he was innocent, then he owed it to his family, his friends and his clients to prove his innocence, and try to recoup as much of the lost investments as he could. But then Dad vanished, and Mom said Dad would have been better off killing himself. That by disappearing, Dad had left us in a worse situation. Maybe Mom was right. Maybe Dad should have died—"

"You don't really feel that way," Drakon said brusquely. "Or you wouldn't be trying so hard to help him now."

"I guess part of me keeps hoping that if he returns, he can fix this...salvage something. Branson, you know, is determined to see all the investors paid back—"

"That's impossible."

"I know, but Branson can't escape his name. Women can marry and take a new surname. But Branson's a man. He'll be one of those hated Copelands forever."

"Someday people will forget. There will be other news that will become more urgent and compelling. There will be disasters and tragedies that will eventually cover this scandal, burying it."

Just as the volcano had buried Pompeii.

Morgan's gaze drifted slowly across the columns and walls and the sunken garden, feeling the emptiness, hearing the silence. Everything was so still here, and yet once this villa had bustled with life, with the comings and goings of the family and its household servants and pets. And all that activity and laughter and anger, all the fears and needs and dreams, ended that August day, and for hundreds of years this city lay buried beneath layers of ash and soil, grass and the development of new towns. New construction. New lives. New dreams.

"Come," Drakon said, putting his hand on her bare arm, his touch light, but steadying. "Let's walk. This place is making you sad, and I didn't bring you here to be sad. I brought you here to inspire you."

"I am inspired, and moved. Gives one perspective...and

certainly a great deal for me to be thankful for." She flashed Drakon an unsteady smile, allowing him to steer her from the garden and back to the street. "Like life. And air. And sunlight."

"Good girl. Count your blessings. Because you have many, you know. You have your health, and your creativity, and your brother and your sisters—"

"And you," she said, catching his hand, giving it a quick squeeze. "You've been here for me, and have hired Rowan to help rescue Dad. I am so grateful—"

"Please don't thank me."

"Then let me at least apologize, because I am sorry, Drakon, I am so, so sorry for what my father did, and deeply ashamed, too."

"You didn't do it, love. You aren't responsible."

"But he's my father."

"And maybe he didn't know that Amery was just depositing all that money into his own account. Maybe he had no idea. Perhaps you're right. Perhaps we wait to judge and try him, until he is back, and he can answer the charges, answer everyone's questions?"

Her heart surged, a little rush of hope, and she turned quickly to face him. "Do you really think he could be innocent? Do you think—" And then she abruptly broke off when she saw Drakon's face.

He didn't think her father was innocent. He still despised her father. Drakon was merely trying to soften the blow for her. Make her disillusionment and pain more bearable.

Her eyes burned and she looked away. "You don't have to do that," she whispered. "There's no need to say things you don't mean just to make me feel better. I'd rather hear the truth from you."

"And I'd rather protect you, *agapi mou*."

Agapi mou. My love. Her chest squeezed, aching. "I remember when I really was your love."

"You will always be my love."

"But not the same way. It will never be the same."

"No, it won't be the same. It can't be."

He'd spoken gently, kindly, and for some reason that made it all even worse. "I hate what I did to us," she said. "Hate that I destroyed us."

"What did happen, Morgan? You were there one morning, and then gone that night. I just want to understand."

She hadn't planned on talking about what really happened, not here, not like this. "I wasn't prepared for life as a newly-wed," she said, stumbling a little over the words. "I…I had unrealistic expectations of our life in Greece."

"What did you think it would be like?"

"Our honeymoon."

"But you know I had to return to work."

"Yes, but I didn't know work for you meant twelve-hour days, every day." Her hands twisted anxiously. "And I understand now, that's just how you work, and I'm not criticizing you. But I didn't understand then, how it would be, and it didn't leave much time for me. I married you because I wanted to be with you, not because I wanted your money or a villa in Greece."

"Looking back, I know now I wasn't very flexible with my hours. I regret how much I worked."

"You loved your work."

"But I loved you more, Morgan."

She'd looked into his eyes as he said it and for a moment she was lost, his amber gaze that intense, searing heat of old, and her heart felt wrenched and she fought to hold back the tears.

She couldn't cry…couldn't cry…wouldn't cry….

"So where do we go now?" she murmured, holding back the tears by smiling hard, smiling to hide her pain and how much she'd missed Drakon, and how much she'd always love Drakon. "What's next on our tour?"

"Lunch," he said lightly, smiling back at her. "I've a restaurant in mind, it's on our way home in Sorrento."

They didn't actually eat in Sorrento, but at a restaurant just outside the city, on the way to Positano. The simple one-story restaurant was tucked high into the mountain, off the beaten path, with a beamed ceiling and breathtaking views of the coast.

Normally the restaurant just served dinner, but today they'd opened for them for lunch, and Morgan and Drakon had the place to themselves.

With the expansive windows open, and course after course of the most delicious seafood and pasta arriving at their table, Morgan felt the tension easing from between her shoulders. After finishing her coffee, she leaned back in her chair. "This was really lovely, Drakon. I feel almost optimistic again. Thank you."

"I've done very little, Morgan."

"You've done everything. You've brought in Rowan and his team, and while they work to free Dad, you're keeping me occupied and encouraging me to think about life, down the road. You've shown me incredible things today, and given me ideas for future designs, and best of all, peace of mind. You're my hero...my knight in shining armor."

"So much better than a husband."

"Husbands are overrated," she teased.

"Apparently so," he answered drily.

And then reality hit her, and the memory of what had happened to them. Her smile slowly, painfully faded. "I've cost you a pretty penny, haven't I? Four hundred million here, seven million there—"

"I don't think about the money when I look at you."

"What do you think about?"

"You."

She dipped her head, and while this is what she wanted

to hear, she did feel guilty. Love shouldn't be this expensive. Love shouldn't have cost Drakon so much. "I want to pay for Dunamas's services."

"They're expensive."

"But my father isn't your responsibility, and I can't allow you to keep picking up the tab, taking hits and losses, because you got tangled up with me."

"Tangled? Is that what they call wives and weddings these days?"

"Don't try to distract me. I'm serious about paying you back. It will take me some time. I'll pay in installments, but I'll pay interest, too. It's what the banks would do. And I may be one of those entitled Copelands, but I'm not entitled to your money, and I insist on making sure you are properly compensated—"

"You're ruining my lunch."

"You've finished eating, already."

"Then you're ruining my coffee."

"You've finished that, too." She held up a finger. "And before you think of anything else I'm ruining, please know I'm immensely grateful, which is why I'm trying to make things right, as well as make them fair."

"How is it fair for me to take what little money you earn over the next ten years? I'd be ashamed to take your money."

"And you don't think I'm ashamed that I had to come back to you, with my hand out, begging for assistance?"

Frowning, he pushed his empty cup. "We should go."

She reached across the table and caught his hand in hers. "Don't be angry, Drakon. Branson's not the only one who wants to put things right. If I could, I'd pay every one of my father's investors back—"

"You're not your father, Morgan. You're not responsible."

"I *feel* responsible."

"You'll make yourself sick, obsessing about this."

"And you don't obsess about what my father did to you?"

Drakon looked down at their hands, where their fingers were laced together. "Yes, I did lose a fortune," he said after a moment, his fingers tightening on hers. "But losing you five years ago was so much worse."

"No."

"Yes." He squeezed her fingers again. "There is always more money to be made, *gynaika mou*. But there is only one of you."

The driver stopped before the villa's great iron gates, waiting for them to open to give them access to the old estate's private drive and exquisite gardens. But Morgan wasn't ready to be back at the villa with Bronwyn and Rowan and the villa staff. After so many years of not being with Drakon, it was such a joy to have him to herself.

"We'll soon find out if Rowan's heard anything," Drakon said, glancing out the window as the four-story white marble villa came into view.

"Hopefully he has," she said, feeling guilty because for the past hour she hadn't thought of her father, not once. She'd been so happy just being with Drakon that she'd forgotten why she was here in Italy on the Amalfi Coast.

"And hopefully you had a good day," he added. "I'd thought perhaps you'd be inspired by Pompeii, but it can be overwhelming, too."

"I loved it. Every minute of it."

And it was true, she thought, as the car stopped in front of the villa's entrance and the driver stepped out to come around to open their door. But it wasn't just Pompeii she loved. She loved every minute of being with him today. This was what life was supposed to feel like. This is what she'd missed so much—his warmth, his strength, his friendship, his love.

His love.

She frowned, confused, suddenly caught between two worlds—the memories of a complicated past and the changing present. In this moment, the present, anything could happen. In this moment, everything was fluid and possible.

She and Drakon were possible. Life was possible. Love was possible.

She and Drakon could make different decisions, be different people, have a different future.

Could it be a future together?

"I enjoyed today, too," Drakon said.

"I hope we can do it again."

"Visit Pompeii?"

"Not necessarily Pompeii. But another outing...another adventure. It was fun."

Drakon suddenly leaned forward and swept the back of his hand over her cheek. "It was. And good to get away from here, and all this."

Her heart ached at the gentle touch. She'd forgotten how extraordinarily tender he could be. Over the years she'd focused on his control and his aloofness, in contrast to the wild heat of their lovemaking, and she'd turned him into someone he wasn't...someone cold and hard and unreachable. But that wasn't really Drakon. Yes, he could be aloof, and hard, and cold, but that wasn't often, and only when he was angry. And he wasn't always angry. In fact, he'd never been angry during their engagement or the first couple months of their marriage. It was only later, after they'd gone to Athens and gotten stuck in that terrible battle for control, a battle that had come to include Bronwyn, that they'd both become rigid and antagonistic.

She reached up, caught his hand, pressed it to her cheek. "Promise me we'll do this again soon. Please?"

"I promise," he said, holding her gaze as the driver opened the door to the back of the car.

Drakon stepped out and Morgan was just about to follow when heavy footsteps crunched the gravel drive and Rowan appeared at their side.

"Where have you been?" Rowan demanded. "I've been trying to reach you for the past hour."

"My mobile didn't ring," Drakon answered.

"I called," Rowan said. "Repeatedly." He turned to look at Morgan, his expression apologetic. "Your father was moved from his village today and we don't know where he is at the moment. But my office is gathering intelligence now that should help us understand what happened, why and where he's being held now."

CHAPTER ELEVEN

MORGAN PACED THE living room, unable to stop moving, unable to be still.

How could her father have vanished? Where had he been taken? And why? Had he gotten sick? Had he died? What were his captors reason for moving him?

She reached the end of the living room, turned and started back again. She'd traveled this path for ten minutes now but there was no way she could sit, not when fear bubbled up in her, consuming her.

Drakon was at the opposite end of the living room, watching her, keeping her company. "Where did they take him, Drakon?" she said, stopping midstep. "Why did they move him?"

She'd asked him the same questions already, several times, as a matter of fact, but he answered just as patiently now. "As Rowan explained, high-profile hostages are often moved from one location to another to stymie rescue attempts."

"Do you think they knew we were planning something?"

"I doubt it. Rowan doesn't think so, either, but we don't know for sure. Fortunately, his office is diligently gathering intelligence now and we should know more soon. Believe me, your father is at the top of Dunamas's priority list."

"He's right," Bronwyn said, entering the living room with a brisk step, her deceptively simple knit dress, the color of ripe plums, making the most of her lush shape. "Dunamas is pulling all their sources and resources from other tasks to gather information on your father, leaving dozens of ships, countless sailors and hundreds of millions of dollars of cargo vulnerable to attack."

"That's not necessary, Bron," Drakon said, rebuking her.

"But it's true." She leaned on the back of a wing chair, her blond hair smooth and sleek and falling forward in an elegant golden shimmer. The expression in her blue eyes was mocking and she shot Drakon a challenging glance. "I know you don't like to discuss business in front of your wife, but shouldn't she know the truth? That Dunamas is dropping everything, and everyone, because Morgan Copeland's criminal father has changed village locations?"

Morgan flinched at Bronwyn's words. "Is that true? Has Dunamas pulled all its surveillance and protection from its other clients?"

"No," Drakon said flatly. "It's not true. While Dunamas has made your father a priority, it continues its surveillance and protective services for each ship, and every customer, it's been hired to protect."

"But at tremendous personal expense," Bronwyn retorted.

"That's none of your business," he answered, giving her a look that would have crushed Morgan, but Bronwyn wasn't crushed.

"Funny how different you are when she's around." Bronwyn's blue gaze met his and held.

Drakon's jaw thickened. "I'm exactly the same."

"No. You're not. Normally Drakon Xanthis rules his shipping empire with a cool head, a critical eye and shrewd sense…always fiscally conservative, and cautious when it comes to expenses and investments." Bronwyn's lips pursed. "But the moment Morgan Copeland enters the picture, smart, insightful, strategic Drakon Xanthis loses his head. Suddenly money is no object, and common sense is thrown out the window—"

"Bronwyn," he growled.

The Australian jerked her chin up, her expression a curious mixture of anger and pain. "You're just a fool for love, aren't you?"

Drakon looked away, his jaw tight, his amber gaze strangely bleak. Morgan glanced from Drakon to Bronwyn and back again, feeling the tension humming in the room, but this wasn't the sparky, sexy kind of tension that zinged between her and Drakon, but something altogether different. This tension was dark and heavy and overwhelming....

It felt like death...loss...

Why? What had happened between them? And what bound Drakon to Bronwyn, a woman Morgan disliked so very intensely.

But then on her own accord, Bronwyn walked out, pausing in the doorway to look at Drakon. "Don't be putty in her hands," she said. "You know what happens to putty."

The pressure in Morgan's chest should have eased after Bronwyn left. There should have been a subtle shift in mood, an easing of the tension, some kind of relief.

But Morgan felt no relief, and from Drakon's taut features, she knew there would be no relief.

Whatever it was that Bronwyn had just said to Drakon—and Morgan had heard her, but hadn't understood the significance, only felt the biting sarcasm—it'd hit the mark. Drakon had paled and was now ashen, his strong jaw clenched so tightly the skin along the bone had gone white.

"What just happened?" Morgan asked, her voice cracking.

Drakon didn't answer. He didn't even look at her.

She flushed as silence stretched and it became evident that he wasn't going to answer her, either.

"What was she saying, Drakon?" Morgan whispered, hating the way shame crept through her, shame and fear and that terrible green-eyed monster called jealousy, because she was jealous of Bronwyn, jealous that Bronwyn could have such a powerful effect on Drakon.

But once again Morgan's question was met with stony silence. And the silence hurt. Not merely because he wasn't talking to her, but because Bronwyn had done this to him—to *them*—again.

Again.

Morgan's hands fisted at her sides. What was Bronwyn's power? Because she certainly had something...some strange and rather frightening influence over Drakon....

Something had to have happened between Drakon and Bronwyn. Something big...

Something private and powerful...

Morgan's head pounded as she left the living room. She needed space and quiet, and headed downstairs to the sunroom, and then outside to the broad terrace beyond. But the terrace still felt too confining and Morgan kept walking, down more stairs, to the lower garden, through manicured boxwood and fanciful hedges to the old rose garden and the herb garden and then to the miniature orchard with its peekaboo views of the sea.

She walked the narrow stone path through the orchard before reaching the twisting path that followed the cliff, the path dotted with marble benches. Morgan finally sat down in one of these cool marble benches facing the sea, and drew a slow breath, trying to process everything, from her father's disappearance, to Drakon and Bronwyn's peculiar relationship, to her own relationship with Drakon. There was a lot to sort through.

She sat on the bench, just breathing in the heady, fragrant scent of wisteria and the blossoms from the citrus trees in the small orchard, when she heard someone talking.

It was Rowan approaching on the path, talking on the phone, speaking English to someone, his tone clipped, nononsense, and his low brusque voice was such a contrast to his appearance. He looked like sex, but talked like a soldier. And suddenly the warrior king from the film *Spartacus* came to mind.

Rowan spotted her and ended his call.

"Any news about my father?" she asked him as he stopped before her bench.

"Not yet. But don't panic."

"I'm trying not to."

"Good girl."

The sun had dropped significantly and the colors in the sky were deepening, the light blue turning to rose gold.

"It's going to be another beautiful sunset," she said. "I love the sky here, the red and orange sunsets."

"You do know its pollution, ash and smoke just scattering away the shorter-wavelength part of the light spectrum."

Morgan made a face. "That's so not romantic."

He shrugged. "As Logan will tell you, I'm not a romantic guy."

Shocked, Morgan turned all the way to look at him. "You know my sister?"

"Drakon didn't tell you?"

"No."

"Thought he had."

"How do you know her?"

"I live in L.A. Malibu."

Which made sense as Logan lived in Los Angeles, too. "How well do you know her?"

He hesitated, just a fraction too long, and Morgan realized that he *knew* her, knew her, as in the Biblical knowing. "You guys...dated?"

"Not dated, plural. One date. Met at a celebrity fund-raiser."

"What fund-raiser?" she asked, finding it impossible to imagine Rowan Argyros at a charity event.

"It's inconsequential."

But from his tone, she knew it wasn't, and Morgan fought the sudden urge to smile. There was much more to the Rowan-Logan story than what he was telling her, and Morgan eyed him with new interest, as well as appreciation, because Logan might be her fraternal twin, but Logan and Morgan were polar opposites. Morgan was quieter and shyer, and Logan was extremely confident and extroverted, as well as assertive., especially when it came to men. Morgan had married Drakon, her first love, while Logan didn't believe in love.

"How did you two get along?" she asked now, lips still twitching, amused by the idea of Logan and Rowan together. They were both so strong—it would have been an interesting date…an explosive date.

"Fine."

"I doubt that."

Rowan looked at her from beneath a cocked brow, smiling, clearly amused. "Why do you say that?"

"Because I know Logan. She's my sister. And I've met you."

"Whatever happened—or didn't happen—is between your sister and me, but I will say she talked about you that night we were together. Told me…things…about you, and your past, not knowing I was connected to Drakon."

"Did you tell her you knew Drakon?"

"No."

"Well, there you go."

He stared down at her, expression troubled. He looked as if he wanted to say something but wasn't going to.

Morgan sighed. "What is it? What's on your mind?"

"Have you told Drakon about the year following your separation? Does he know what happened?"

Morgan eyed him warily. "About what?"

"About you being…ill."

She opened her mouth, and then closed it, shaking her head instead.

"Maybe you should. Maybe it's time."

Morgan turned back to the sea, where the horizon was now a dramatic parfait of pink and orange and red, with streaks of luscious violet. So beautiful it couldn't be real. "I don't think it'd change anything…if he knew."

"I think it would change a great deal. Maybe not for you, but for him."

She shot Rowan a cynical glance, feeling impossibly raw. "How so?"

"You weren't the only one who had a hard year after you left. Drakon's world fell apart, too."

Drakon was in his room, just stepping out of the shower when he heard a knock at his door. He dried off quickly, wrapped the towel around his hips and headed to the bedroom door. Opening it, he discovered Morgan in the hall.

"You okay?" she asked, looking up at him, a shadow of concern in her eyes.

He nodded. "I was just going to dress and come find you."

"Do you mind if I come in?"

He opened the door wider, and then once she was inside, he closed the door behind him.

"You look nice," she said, her voice low and husky.

"Almost naked?"

Color swept her cheeks. "I always liked you naked. You have an amazing body."

He folded his arms across his chest and stared at her. "I can't believe you came here to compliment my body."

"No…no. But it kind of…relates…to what I was going to say."

He rocked back on his hips, trying not to feel anything, even though he was already feeling too much of everything.

But wasn't that always the way it was when it came to Morgan? He felt so much. He loved her so much.

"Can I kiss you?" she blurted breathlessly.

He frowned, caught off guard.

"Just a kiss, for courage," she said, clasping her hands, nervously. "Because I don't know how to tell you this, and I'm not sure what you'll say, but I probably should tell you. 'Cause I don't think anyone did tell you—"

He drew her to him, then, silenced her stream of words with a kiss. His kiss was fierce, and she kissed him back with desperation, with the heat and hunger that had always been there between them.

He let the kiss go on, too, drawing her close to his body, cupping the back of her head with one hand while the other slid to the small of her back and urged her even closer to his hips. Just like that he was hard and hot and eager to be inside her body, wanting to fill her, needing to lose himself in her, needing to silence the voices in his head…voices of guilt and anger, failure and shame….

But then Morgan ended the kiss and lifting her head she looked up into his eyes, her blue eyes wet, her black lashes matted. "I'm not right in the head." Her voice quavered. She tried to smile even as tears shimmered in her eyes. "I'm crazy."

"You're not crazy."

She nodded, and her lower lip quivered. "That's why you couldn't find me after I left you. I had a nervous breakdown. My family had me hospitalized."

Drakon flinched and stepped backward. "Why are you saying this?"

"It's what happened. I left you and I fell apart. I couldn't stop crying, and I couldn't eat, and I couldn't sleep, and everybody said it was this or that, but I just missed you. I wanted you."

"So why didn't you come back?"

"They wouldn't let me."

Drakon's gut churned, and his hands clenched involuntarily at his side. "*Who* wouldn't let you?"

"The doctors. The hospital. My family. They made me stay there at McLean. It's a…mental…hospital."

"I know what McLean is." Drakon looked at her in barely masked horror. "I don't understand, Morgan. You were there…why?"

"Because I was crazy."

"You *weren't* crazy!"

"They said I was." She walked away from him, moving around his room, which had been their room on their honeymoon. She touched an end table, and the foot of the bed, and then the chaise in the corner before she turned to look at him. "And I did feel crazy…but I kept thinking if I could just get to you, I'd feel better."

"So why didn't you come home to me?"

"I couldn't." She struggled to smile, but failed. "I couldn't get to you, couldn't call you or write to you. They wouldn't let me do anything until I calmed down and did all the therapy and the counseling sessions—"

"What do you mean, they wouldn't let you out? Didn't you check yourself in?"

She shook her head, and sat down on the chaise, smoothing her skirt over her knees. "No. My parents did. My mother did. My dad approved, but it was Mother who insisted. She said you would never want me back the way I was." Morgan looked up at him, eyes bright, above the pallor of her cheeks. "So I went through the treatment, but it didn't help. It didn't work. They wanted me to say I could live without you, and I couldn't."

"Why not?"

Her slim shoulders lifted and fell. "Because I couldn't."

"So why did you leave me in the first place?"

"I started falling apart in Ekali. I was fine when we first

got there, but after the first month, something happened to me. I began to cry when you were at work and I tried to hide it from you when you came home, but you must have known, because you changed, too. You became colder and distant, and maybe it wasn't you…maybe it was all me… because I needed too much from you, and God knows, my needs weren't healthy—"

"And who told you that you needs weren't healthy?" he growled, trying desperately hard to hang on to his temper. "Your parents?"

"And the doctors. And the therapists."

"Christ," he muttered under his breath, dragging a hand through his hair. "That's not true, you know," he said, looking at her. "You were young and isolated and lonely and I wasn't there for you. I know that now. I know I wasn't fair to you. I worked ridiculous hours, and expected you to be able to entertain yourself, and I owe you an apology. Actually, I owe you many, many apologies."

She managed a small, tight smile. "It's hard to remember… hard to go back…because what we had was good, so good, and then it all became so bad…." She sighed and rubbed her head. "I wish we could go back, and do it all again, and make different decisions this time."

"There's no going back, though, only going forward."

Morgan nodded. "I know, and I'm trying. And seeing Pompeii with you today made me realize that we have to go forward. We have to have hope and courage and build new lives."

He came to her, crouched before her, his hands on either side of her knees, his gaze searching hers. "I know I failed you—"

"No more than I failed you, Drakon."

"But you didn't fail me. You were perfect…you were warm and real and hopeful and sensitive."

"So why did you pull away? Why shut me out…because it felt like you did—"

"I did. I definitely shut you out, and you weren't imagining that I pulled away, because I did that, too."

"Why?"

He hesitated a moment and then drew a breath. "Because I loved you so much, and yet I was overwhelmed by feelings of inadequacy…I couldn't make you happy, I couldn't meet your needs, I couldn't be who or what you wanted, so I…pushed you away."

Her eyes searched his. "It wasn't my imagination?"

"No."

"I wasn't crazy when I left you then?"

"No."

She made a soft, hoarse sound. "So I just went crazy when I left you."

"You were never crazy, Morgan."

She smiled, sadly. "But I was. Leaving you tore me apart. I felt my heart break when I left you. Everyone kept telling me I was developing this disorder or that disorder but they didn't understand…I just needed you. I just wanted you. And they wouldn't let me have you." Tears filled her eyes. "No one believed that I could love you that deeply…but why was it wrong to love you so much? Why did it make me bad… and mad…to miss you that much?"

"They were wrong, Morgan. And I was wrong. And I know you weren't insane, because I felt the same way, too. And I couldn't get to you, either. I couldn't find you, and all I wanted was to find you and apologize, and fix things, and change things, so that we could be happy. I knew we could be happy. I just needed you home."

She reached up to knock away a tear before it could fall. "But I didn't come back."

"No. But I wouldn't give up on you, or us. I still can't give up on us." He reached out to wipe her cheek dry with his thumb. "Tell me, my love, that I haven't waited in vain. Tell me there's a place in your life for me. Give me hope, Morgan."

She just looked at him, deep into his eyes, for a long moment before leaning forward and kissing him. "Yes," she whispered against his mouth. "Yes, there's a place in my life for you. There will always be a place in my life for you. I need you, Drakon. Can't live without you, Drakon."

His mouth covered hers, and he kissed her deeply, but it wasn't enough for her. Morgan needed more, craved more, and she wrapped her arms around his neck, and opened her knees so he could move between them, his big body pressed against hers. Still kissing her, he pressed her back onto the chaise, his towel falling off as he stretched out over her, his hand sliding up her rib cage to cup her breast.

Morgan hissed a breath as his fingers rubbed her nipple, making the sensitive peak pucker and tighten. His other hand was moving down her torso, tugging up the hem of her dress, finding her bare inner thigh, his touch sending lightning forks of sensation zinging through her body, making her body heat and her core melt. She wanted him, wanted him so much, and she sucked on his tongue, desperate for him to strip her and feel his warm, bare skin on hers.

And then his phone rang on the bedside table, chiming with a unique ringtone that Morgan had never heard before.

He lifted his head, listened, frowning. "Damn."

"What?"

He shook his head and rolled away from her, leaving the chaise to pick up his phone from the table near the bed. "Damn," he muttered, reading the message. "She needs to talk to me before she returns to Athens."

Morgan didn't even need to ask who "she" was, knowing perfectly well it was Bronwyn. "Now?"

"She's leaving soon. Tonight."

"Surely she can wait a half hour?"

He didn't answer immediately, simply rolled away, his towel falling off in the process. "I won't be long."

"You really have to go now?"

"I'll be back in less than fifteen minutes."

Morgan watched him walk, without a stitch of clothing, to the closet. Dressed, Drakon Xanthis was a handsome, sophisticated man. Naked, he was absolutely beautiful.

He was beautiful now, and her mouth dried, her heart hurting as he disappeared into the closet, his body tan, skin gleaming, his muscles taut. Honed. He had those big shoulders and broad chest and lean flat abs and long strong legs, and between those legs hung his thick shaft, impressive even now, when he wasn't erect.

As the closet light came on, Morgan felt a surge of jealousy, hating that Drakon and his beautiful, hard, honed body was leaving her to go meet Bronwyn.

When he emerged a few minutes later, buckling the belt on his trousers, buttoning his shirt and tucking it into the waistband, Morgan felt almost sick.

Suddenly she felt like the young bride she'd been five years ago…uncertain, insecure, overwhelmed by her new life as Drakon Xanthis's American bride.

Drakon must have seen her fear because his brow furrowed as he gazed down at her. "There's no need to be threatened by Bronwyn. She works for me, but you're my wife."

But she'd been his wife before, and it hadn't helped her feel secure, or close to him. And while she'd been home alone for twelve, fourteen, sometimes sixteen hours a day, he'd been at the office with Bronwyn. Even if there was nothing sexual between him and Bronwyn, by virtue of being his trusted right hand, Bronwyn still got to spend time with Drakon…time Morgan would love to have. Not because Morgan couldn't be alone and needed Drakon to prop her up, but because she loved Drakon and enjoyed his company more than anyone else.

"I just don't want to feel as if I have to fight Bronwyn for you anymore," she said quietly, calmly, grateful that her voice could sound so steady when her heart was racing so fast.

"But you don't have to fight Bron for me. You never have."

And while this conversation was brutal, it was also necessary and long overdue. They should have talked about Bronwyn years ago. Morgan should have told Drakon how uncomfortable she was around her when they first married, but she hadn't, too afraid of displeasing him. And so the wound had festered, and her fear grew, until their entire relationship had become stunted and toxic.

"You love me?" she whispered.

"How can you doubt it?"

She bit down into her lip, holding back her fears, and her need to be reassured, knowing that her fears were irrational. Drakon wouldn't be here, helping her, if he didn't want to be. Drakon wouldn't have brought in Rowan to rescue her father if he didn't care about her. It was time she stopped panicking and stopped allowing her insecurities to get the upper hand. Drakon loved her. Drakon had always loved her. But he wasn't a woman…he was a man, a Greek man that had been raised to conceal vulnerabilities and avoid emotion. "I don't doubt it," she whispered. "I know you love me. Without question."

"There is no competition between you and Bron," he said roughly, his handsome, chiseled features hard.

She nodded, wanting to believe it, needing to believe it, but as he'd told her once, actions spoke louder than words. If he stayed at his office night after night until ten, making decisions, talking with Bronwyn, how was Morgan supposed to feel?

She felt a twinge of panic at the idea of returning to that life, but she had to be strong and confident. She believed in Drakon, and she had to believe that Drakon would do what was right for her…for them.

"Promise me you're not threatened by her," he said, stalking closer to her, forcing her to tilt her head back to meet his eyes.

"Promise me you won't be upset if I have to work long days, and late into the night, with her," he added.

Morgan's mouth opened, closed. She wanted to tell him she'd be fine, and she would try to be fine with it, but she couldn't promise him she'd be perfectly comfortable. She didn't know any woman who'd be perfectly comfortable with her husband being alone with a gorgeous woman night after night…day after day. Working in such close proximity created an intimacy that could lead to other things…and Morgan was sure Bronwyn did have feelings for Drakon. In fact, Morgan was sure Bronwyn was the problem here, not Drakon, but how could she tell him that?

She couldn't. But she also couldn't lie. And so with her heart racing, she swallowed convulsively. "I'm here for the long haul, Drakon. I'm here to stay. I'm playing for keeps."

His amber gaze drilled into her. "Playing for keeps," he repeated softly.

She licked her dry lips. "Yes."

"Is that a threat or a promise?"

"It's whatever you want it to be."

He laughed once, the mocking sound such a contrast to the sudden fire in his eyes. And then he was gone, walking out, leaving the door wide open behind him.

CHAPTER TWELVE

HE WASN'T GONE just a few minutes. He was gone a long time, over an hour, and Morgan returned to her room, wondering if she should dress for dinner, or if dinner would even be served tonight as it was growing late, well past the time they normally gathered in the living room for *aperitivos*.

Morgan eventually did change and go downstairs. Rowan was in the living room, having a drink.

"Can I pour you something?" he offered as she entered the candle lit living room.

"The Campari," she said, even as she tried to listen to the house, trying to hear where Drakon and Bronwyn might be.

Rowan filled her glass, handed her the cocktail. "They're outside," he said. "Or they were."

She sipped the cocktail. Campari and orange. It was tart and sweet at the same time. "Why do you say, 'were'?"

"A car arrived a half hour ago, and it just pulled away a few minutes ago." Rowan turned, nodded at the hall. "And here he is. Drakon Xanthis in the flesh." Rowan raised his glass. "I've a few calls to make. I'll have more privacy elsewhere. Cheers." And then Rowan walked out, leaving Drakon and Morgan alone.

Drakon walked past Morgan without saying a word, going to the bar where he made himself a drink. Morgan watched him, wondering what had happened between him and Bronwyn.

Drakon carried his drink to the window, where he sipped it and stared out at the dark sky.

"She's gone," he said at last. "Back to Athens."

Morgan looked at his rigid back, and the set of his shoulders. "Did something happen?" she asked quietly.

"I let her go."

"What?"

"I let her go. Fired her. Terminated her employment. Whatever you want to call it."

"Why?"

"I watched her here, how she behaved around you, and I didn't like it. She has worked for me for a long time—eight years—and she was good at what she did, but I won't have any woman snubbing you, not anymore. I won't look the other way, especially if it's my employee, or a friend of mine. It's not acceptable, and you shouldn't have to endure slights and snubs...not from anyone."

Morgan heard what he was saying and appreciated everything he was saying, but there was something else happening here. Drakon was upset...angry...but Morgan didn't understand who he was upset with—Bronwyn, himself, or Morgan.

"You didn't have to fire her because of me," Morgan said, choosing her words carefully. "I meant it when I said, I was sticking around. I'm not going to let anyone scare me away. I'm not twenty-two anymore. I'm twenty-seven and I know a lot more about the world now, and a lot more about myself."

He sipped his cocktail. "I agree you've changed, but I've also changed, and Bronwyn has, too. There was a time I needed her—and she saved me, I owe her a lot, if not everything—but that was four years ago, and things are different and it's time for her to move on. It'll be better for her."

Morgan's inside flipped nervously. "How did she save you?"

He took another long drink from his crystal tumbler and then looked over his shoulder at Morgan. "If it weren't for her, I wouldn't have a company. I wouldn't have this villa. I wouldn't have anything."

"I don't understand."

"I know you don't." He sighed, shrugged, took another quick drink before continuing. "I would prefer you didn't know, and I'd promised Bron years ago I wouldn't tell you, she didn't want me to tell you. She said you wouldn't like it… you wouldn't respect me…but that's a risk I'll have to take."

Morgan sat down in one of the chairs. "Please tell me."

He walked the length of the room, and it was a long room, before dropping into a chair not far from hers. "A number of years ago, I made a mistake. Normally it wouldn't be an issue, but with the situation being what it was, the mistake was serious. It nearly bankrupted me."

He closed his eyes, shook his head, then opened them again and looked at her. "I was close to losing everything. And I mean everything. The company. The ships. The contracts. Our offices. Our homes. The cars, planes, yachts… everything…" His voice faded and for a moment there was just silence, a heavy, suffocating silence that blanketed the room. "And the worst of it was, I didn't care."

Drakon was still looking at her, but he didn't seem to see her. He seemed to be seeing something else, his expression tortured. "I didn't care," he repeated lowly, strangely detached.

Morgan had never heard him talk this way, or sound this way, and her heart thumped uncomfortably and she wasn't sure if she wanted to hear more, but there was no way she would stop him from talking.

After a long, uneasy moment Drakon continued. "I wasn't able to make good decisions during this time, and I didn't do what I should have done to protect my company, my future, or my employees. I was willing to lose it all. But Bronwyn refused to just stand there, a witness, as my company and life imploded."

"So she took over," he continued. "She stepped into my empty shoes and vacant office and became me...became president and CEO and no one knew it was Bronwyn Harper forging my signature, shifting funds, slashing spending, liquidating assets." Drakon's gaze met Morgan's. "Not all of her decisions were the right ones. Some of her actions had negative consequences, but if she hadn't stepped in when she did, there would be nothing here today."

It was hard for Morgan to hear Drakon speak of Bronwyn so reverently, because Morgan wished she'd been the one who had been there for Drakon when he needed someone. "I'm glad she helped you," Morgan said huskily. "Glad she was able to help you, because I couldn't have, even if I'd wanted to."

He looked at her, amber gaze piercing. "So yes, she helped me, but she was never more than a valuable employee. She was never your rival. I never once wanted her. I have only wanted you."

"Then why fire her? If she was such a help, and you feel so grateful—"

"She wanted more than what we had." His mouth curved but the smile didn't reach his eyes. "She made it clear she wanted more, that she was in love with me, but I didn't feel that way about her. I loved you, and only you, and Bronwyn knew that."

"But she stuck around all these years...she stuck around because she had to hope she had a chance."

He shrugged. "Maybe. Probably. But she didn't. If I couldn't have you, there wouldn't have been anyone else for me. It was you or nobody."

Morgan exhaled slowly, her head spinning. "She must be heartbroken right now."

"She'll be fine. She's strong. She's smart. She'll have a better life now, away from me." Drakon drew Morgan into his arms and pressed a kiss to her temple, and then another to her cheekbone. "It's you I'm worried about."

"You don't need to worry about me."

"Rowan hasn't found your father yet."

"But he hasn't given up."

"No. And Rowan won't, not until we find your father. There is no one better than Rowan and Dunamas. They will continue looking for your father, until he is found."

"What if it takes weeks…months…years?"

"Doesn't matter. I promise you, we will never forget him, and never give up."

CHAPTER THIRTEEN

THEY ATE DINNER, just the two of them, as Rowan was no-where to be found, and then skipping coffee and dessert, they headed upstairs to Drakon's room, where they made love, soundlessly, wordlessly, so quiet in the dark silent night.

Their lovemaking wasn't fierce and hot, or carnal and raw, but slow, careful, tender, so tender that Morgan wept after she climaxed because she'd never felt this way with Drakon before, had never made love with him like this before, their bodies so close, so connected, they'd felt like one.

Afterward, they lay side by side, his body wrapped around hers, his muscular arm holding her close to him, and still they said nothing, because there were no words, at least not the right ones. So much had happened since they'd met. So much love and yet so much loss. So much anger and pain and heartbreak...

But words right now wouldn't help, words would just get in the way, so they didn't talk, but instead lay close, filled with emotion, intense emotion that surged and ached and trembled and twisted.

Lying there in the dark, wrapped in Drakon's warmth and listening to him breathe, Morgan knew these things—she still loved him, deeply, passionately.

She also knew she wouldn't leave him. Not ever again.

But for them to have a future, they would have to talk

more, and they'd need patience, forgiveness, courage and strength.

She knew she was willing to fight for Drakon and her marriage, but there were still things she didn't understand about Drakon, things she didn't understand about the past.

And when, a half hour later, he kissed her shoulder but eased away to climb from the bed, she was filled with unease.

Turning over, she watched as he stepped into his cotton pajama pants, settling the drawstring waist low on his hips, leaving that magnificent torso bare. She watched him walk to the French door and push open the curtains. Propping an arm against the glass, he stared out at the sea, which rippled silver with moonlight.

She sat up and wrapped an arm around her knees, pressing the covers closer to her legs. "I've been thinking about what you said earlier, and how you feel so grateful to Bronwyn for saving your company…and saving you…when you made a mistake and nearly lost everything. But I know you. You don't make mistakes. What mistake did you make, that could have possibly cost you your company?"

He said nothing right away and Morgan was afraid he wouldn't speak, but then he shrugged. "I was distracted. Wasn't focused on work. And suddenly there was no money. No money to pay anybody, no money for taxes, no money at all."

"How could there be no money? Where did it go?"

Again, another long, excruciating silence. "Bad investments."

Ice filled her veins and she flashed to her father, and Michael Amery. No…he wouldn't…not a second time. She held her breath, even as her heart began to race. "You said…bad investments….plural." Morgan swallowed around the lump of panic forming in her throat. "Did you mean, investments, plural, or was there just that one horrible, huge loss to my father?"

He was silent so long that bile rose up in her throat, and she knew, she knew, there was more. She knew something else had happened, something he'd never told her. "Drakon, *agapo mou,* please, please tell me."

Drakon shifted his weight, muscles ripping across his shoulders and down his back, and then he turned toward her, the moonlight glancing briefly over his features until he'd turned his back to the window, with the light behind him, shadowing his face again. "Your father came to me asking for help after you'd left me."

Pain shot through her. Tears filled her eyes. "You gave him more money."

Drakon's lips compressed. "He was your father. He needed help."

"How much did he ask for?"

"A billion."

"Oh, my God." She pressed her hand to her mouth. "Drakon, no. You didn't…"

"What was I to do, Morgan? He was in trouble. I was his son-in-law, and I loved you. Family is family—"

"But I'd left you!"

"But I hadn't left you."

She ground her teeth together, tears blinding her, her stomach churning in bitter protest. "I can't believe this."

He laughed hollowly. "When your father came to me, telling me he was in trouble…that he had investors who needed their money back, but he didn't have the liquidity to give them their money…I thought it was my chance to win you back. But I didn't have that kind of money sitting in an account, no one has money like that, so I took loans from banks, as well as other resources, to come up with the money for your father."

"And you didn't get me back, did you?" she whispered.

For a minute there was just silence, and an almost unbearable pain, and then Drakon shook his head. "No. I gave him the money but Daniel refused to tell me where you were. Said that you'd contact me when you were ready."

"And I couldn't contact you, not at McLean." She blinked to clear her eyes. "And then what happened?"

"The economy started crashing. My creditors and lenders began to call their loans. But there was no money to give them. There was nothing I could do but file for bankruptcy, and fold. And I was fine with that, because without you, I didn't care."

"You're breaking my heart," Morgan whispered.

"I was pathetic. Bron said you'd find me pathetic—"

"Pathetic? How could I find you, who sacrificed everything for me, pathetic?" She rose up on her knees. "You were a hero. You loved me. You fought for me. You were willing to sacrifice everything for me."

He turned and looked at her, his face still shadowed but she felt his intensity. "I don't want to live without you, Morgan. I don't like life without you. And maybe that's weak—"

"Not weak," she said, leaving the bed to go to him, wrap her arms around his waist. She held him tightly, chilled by what he had told her, as well as chilled by the reality of her parents taking her to McLean and leaving her there when they knew Drakon wanted her, when they knew Drakon loved her. She didn't understand their motivations, but then, their lives were about money and appearances and Morgan knew she'd embarrassed them by coming home from Greece, heartbroken and hysterical.

He slid a hand down her back, shaping her to him. "I don't think you understand how much I loved you," he said roughly. "How much I will always love you." His voice cracked, turned hoarse. "There is no one else for me, but you. You aren't just my wife. You are my world."

"And you are mine."

"Why did you leave then?"

"I was honestly falling apart."

"Why?"

"I loved you so much, it scared me. I'd never felt for anyone what I felt for you…but the feelings were so intense, it made me feel out of control. And then when we made love… that started to do something to my head. Played games with me, made me afraid."

"Afraid? Why? How?"

"I had so little experience when I met you, and you had so much, and in bed you're…hot. Erotic. Demanding. You make everything hot and erotic, too."

"I demanded too much of you?"

"There were times I felt overwhelmed."

"Thus, your disgust."

"You never disgusted me. I shouldn't have said that. It wasn't true. I was just angry and hurt, and trying desperately hard to keep you at arm's length since I find you impossible to resist."

He stepped away from her and went to flip the light switch, turning on the small wall sconces so the room glowed with soft yellow light. "Maybe I didn't disgust you, but I must have scared you at times for you to even say such a thing."

"I never minded it being…hot…when you were relaxed with me, and spent a lot of time with me, but once we returned to Athens, I didn't see you often and then we weren't talking and it didn't feel the same. It didn't feel as warm and safe. It felt more dangerous."

"But you always came."

"Because you've got great technique." She managed an unsteady smile. "But I'd rather not come, and just be close to you, feel close to you, than have erotic sex and have you feel like a stranger."

He sat down on the side of the bed. "Come here." He smiled crookedly. "Please."

Morgan walked to him, heart thumping, and feeling painfully shy. "Yes?"

He drew her down onto the bed next to him, and kissed her, once and again, before lifting his head to look down into her eyes. "I love how sensual you are. I love your passionate nature. But I never want you to be uncomfortable with me again…in bed, or out of bed. I love you too much to hurt you or scare you or to push you away. But you have to tell me when something is too much. You have to tell me when I'm being distant or when you feel nervous or lonely or afraid."

"You want me to talk to you," she said.

"Yes. I want you to talk to me."

"That means you have to talk to me, too."

He smiled even more crookedly. "I know."

"Okay."

"But I don't want you bored…especially in bed."

"My God, Morgan, I could never be bored in bed with you."

"No?"

"No! When we're together it's not about sex…its about me showing you how much you mean to me. How much I cherish you. How much I worship you. When I touch you, Morgan, I'm telling you that nothing is more important to me than you, and that I love you with all of my heart, and all of my soul."

"Really?"

"Really." His gaze searched hers. "All I have wanted for these past five years is to have you come home. I want you home. Morgan, please come home with me—"

"Yes." She reached up, cupped his cheek, drawing his face toward hers. She kissed him, deeply, and a shiver raced through her as his tongue met hers, teasing her. "Yes. I'm staying with you, going home with you, back to Athens."

"Even though you hate that white ice cube tray?" he asked, turning his mouth into her hand and kissing her palm.

Another delicious shiver ran through her and she smiled.

"But would you mind if I added a few colorful rugs? A few paintings…some throw pillows?"

"Maybe what we really need is a new house for a fresh start—"

"No."

"Yes. I don't like the house, either."

"What?"

He laughed softly. "I hate it. It's awful. I never liked it. Not while they were building it, and not even when we moved in, but I thought you did like it, so I never told you."

"I think we have a slight communication problem," she said drily.

"You think?" he teased, pressing her backward onto the bed, and then stretching out over her, his long hard body covering hers.

"We need to work on it."

"Mmm," he agreed, kissing her throat and pushing the covers down to bare her breasts. "We're going to have to start talking more," he said, alternately kissing and licking the slope of her breast.

She sighed and arched as he latched onto one of her tight, pebbled nipples. "Okay," she gasped, desire coiling in her belly.

"Do you like this?" he asked, as he stroked down her flat belly.

"Um, yes."

"And this?" he asked, his fingers slipping between her legs.

She gasped as he caressed her most sensitive spot. "Yes. And I'm glad we're talking…but do we have to do it now?"

She felt his silent laughter as his teeth scraped her nipple. "No," he answered. "I'd much rather just concentrate on you, and making you come."

"Good."

She gasped again as his fingers slipped down, where she

was slick and wet, and then caressed up over the nub again. "Drakon?"

"Yes, *gynaika mou?*"

"Make love to me. And love me. Forever."

He shifted, bracing his weight on his arms and looked down into her eyes for an endless moment. "Always. Always, and forever, until I die."

EPILOGUE

"WILL YOU DO it, Logan? Cover for me for a few days so Drakon and I can have a brief getaway?" Morgan asked, speaking calmly into the phone, trying to sound relaxed, even though she was frustrated with Logan for dodging her calls for the past week. "You'd just be a point person for a few days, if there are any communication issues, but I doubt there will be."

"I can't drop everything and take over Dad's search just so you and Drakon can have a second honeymoon," Logan said, her voice sharp on the speakerphone. "Some of us have jobs, Morgan. Some of us must work as we don't have wealthy husbands to take care of us."

"Would you like a wealthy husband, Logan?" Drakon said, unable to remain silent in his seat across from Morgan's on his private jet. They were still on the ground, hadn't closed the doors, because Morgan had refused to take off until Logan promised she'd help. "You know it can be arranged."

"No, thank you, Drakon. I am quite capable of taking care of myself," Logan retorted crisply.

Drakon smiled. "You might actually enjoy a strong Greek husband…almost as much as he'd enjoy managing you."

"Not going to happen," Logan snapped. "But if it will help me get off this call, then yes, Morgan, I will be your contact person should something happen while you and Drakon are doing whatever you and Drakon do."

Drakon arched a brow at Morgan, and Morgan shook her

head at him, blushing. "I seriously doubt anything will happen, though. We're only going to be gone a few days...just for a long weekend—"

"I got it. You're just gone a few days. Dunamas is doing all the intelligence work and orchestrating the rescue. They'll call me if they can't reach you should there be developments." Logan paused. "Did I forget anything?"

Morgan grimaced. "No. That's pretty much it."

"Good. Now go...scram. Enjoy your trip. And try to have fun. Dad's going to be okay." Logan's voice suddenly softened. "I'll make sure he is, I promise."

Morgan hung up and looked at Drakon, who had just signaled to his flight crew that they were ready to take off. "Why am I worrying so much?"

His amber gaze met hers. "Because you deliberately withheld information from her, knowing she'd never agree to help us if she thought she'd have to deal with Rowan."

Morgan chewed on her lip. "Let's just hope she doesn't have to deal with him. Otherwise there's going to be hell to pay."

"Rowan said the exact same thing."

* * * * *

FORGIVEN BUT
NOT FORGOTTEN?

ABBY GREEN

This is especially for Crispin Green,
Polly Green, Barney Green and Katie Green.
I'm so proud to be your half-sister and one
of the 'Greens in Cornwall'.

Irish author **Abby Green** threw in a very glamorous career in film and TV—which really consisted of a lot of standing in the rain outside actors' trailers—to pursue her love of romance. After she'd bombarded Mills & Boon with manuscripts they kindly accepted one and an author was born. She lives in Dublin, Ireland, and loves any excuse for distraction. Visit www.abby-green.com or e-mail abbygreenauthor@gmail.com

PROLOGUE

SIENA DEPIERO HELD her older sister's hand tightly as they left their *palazzo*. Even though she was twelve and Serena was fourteen they still instinctively sought each other for support. Their father was in an even more mercurial mood than usual today. Their car was waiting by the kerb, a uniformed driver standing by the open door. Siena knew that her father's bodyguards were nearby.

Just feet away from the car a tall young man with dark hair seemed to spring from nowhere, stopping their father in his tracks. He was gesticulating and calling their father *Papà*. Siena and Serena had come to a halt too, with burly guards standing between them and this confrontation.

Siena looked around the bodyguards. She could instantly see the resemblance of this young man to their father. He had the same shaped face and deep-set eyes. But how could he be related? Suddenly there was a dull crunching sound and the young man was sprawled on the ground, looking up with shock on his face, blood running from his nose. Their father had hit him.

Siena gripped Serena's hand tight in shock at the sudden violence. Their father turned back and gestured angrily for them to follow him. The path was so narrow that they had to step over the young man's legs. Siena was too scared to look at him—he was so wild and feral.

They were ushered into the back of the car and Siena heard their father issue terse instructions to his men. Just then she heard the young man roar, 'I'm Rocco, your son—you bastard!'

When their father got into the car and it pulled away, Siena couldn't stop herself from looking behind them. She saw their father's men dragging the young man out of sight. She felt sick. Serena was looking stonily ahead but her hand gripped Siena's.

Their father caught Siena by the ear painfully and jerked her head round. Siena clamped her mouth shut. She knew better than to make a sound.

He forced her to look at him. 'What do you think you are doing?'

'Nothing, Papà.'

His mouth was a thin line of anger. 'Good, because you know what happens if you anger me.'

Serena's grip on Siena's hand was so tight she nearly cried out. Quickly Siena said, 'Yes, Papà.'

After a long, tense moment their father let her go and faced the front again. Siena knew very well what happened when she angered him. He would punish her sister Serena. It was never her. Always her sister. Because that was what amused him.

Siena didn't look at her sister, but they kept their hands tightly gripped together for the rest of the journey.

CHAPTER ONE

ANDREAS XENAKIS DIDN'T like the strength of the thrill of triumph that moved through him. It signified that this moment held more importance for him than he'd care to admit. Bitterly, he had to concede that perhaps it did. After all, practically within touching distance now was the woman who had all but cried *rape* for her own amusement, to protect her untarnished image in her father's eyes. She'd merited him a savage beating, losing his job, being blacklisted from every hotel in Europe and having to start over again on the other side of the world. Far away from anyone he'd known or who had known him.

She was still exquisite. More so. Andreas had found himself imagining that she couldn't possibly be as stunning as she'd been since he'd seen her five years ago. But she was. She was a woman now, not a teenager.

Her hair was so blonde it shone almost white under the soft lighting of a hundred chandeliers. It was pulled up into a high bun. She held herself with the same effortlessly regal bearing he'd first noticed in that glittering ballroom in Paris. His mouth compressed. She was a thoroughbred in the midst of lesser beings. He could see how women near her instinctively shut her out, as if sensing competition.

His eyes moved over the curve of her cheek and jaw. The patrician line of her nose more than hinted at the blue-blooded heritage of her Italian ancestry, diluted only in part by her half-

English mother who had been related to royalty. Her skin was still pale and looked soft: as soft as a rose petal. Andreas's belly clenched hard to recall just how soft it *had* felt under his fingers.

He'd touched her reverently, as if she were an ethereal goddess, and he'd felt as if he was marking her, staining her purity with his touch. His hands were fists by his sides now as he thought of how she'd urged him on with breathy, sexy entreaties in his ear: *'Please...I want you to touch me, Andreas.'* Only to turn on him almost in the same breath and accuse him of attacking her...

She turned then, to face towards him, and that low, simmering anger was eclipsed when blood rushed to his head and to his groin, making him simultaneously dizzy and hard.

He couldn't escape the impact of those huge, glittering bright blue eyes ringed with long dark lashes. But it was her mouth which drew his gaze and kept it. Sinfully lush and pink. Just waiting to be kissed...crushed under his. Andreas had to consciously will down the intense desire. He was fast being reduced to the instincts of an animal, and he hated her for having this effect on him. Still. *For ever*, mocked the small voice in his head.

No. Andreas rejected it fiercely. Not for ever. Just until he'd had her. Until they'd finished what she'd started when she'd upended his life so cruelly and comprehensively. Because she'd been curious and bored. Because she'd had the power. Because he'd been nothing.

Resolve firmed in Andreas's gut. He was far from nothing any more, and thanks to a cruel twist of circumstances Siena DePiero was reduced to lower than he'd ever been, rendering her exposed and vulnerable—to him.

Her blonde head dipped out of view momentarily and Andreas's insides contracted with something indefinable that went beyond where he wanted to investigate. He didn't like the fact that he was uncomfortably aware of other men's interest, of their gazes after her, covetous and even lascivious. It made him feel possessive and that was not welcome.

She'd had the gall to play with him once. Andreas desired her. That was all. His eyes caught sight of her bright blonde head again and he watched and waited as she drew ever closer to him in the crowd.

Siena DePiero was in the act of navigating through the crowd with a heavy tray, trying not to upend the contents over someone's feet, when a broad chest at her eye level stopped her from moving forward.

She looked up and had the impression of a very tall man, broad all the way through to his shoulders. A pristine tuxedo with a white bow-tie marked him out as slightly different. As Siena's mouth opened to say *excuse me* her gaze reached his face and her heart stopped.

He was no stranger.

Andreas Xenakis. Here.

The recognition was instantaneous. The knowledge was cataclysmic. It was as if mere minutes had passed since she'd last seen him, yet it had been five years. He looked bigger, darker, leaner.

She could instantly read the unmistakable light of cold hatred in his eyes and her insides contracted painfully. Of all the people to meet in this situation… No one would get more mileage out of it than Andreas Xenakis. And could she even blame him? a small voice mocked.

'Well, well, well.'

His voice was painfully familiar, immediately twisting her insides into a knot of tension.

'Fancy meeting you here.'

Siena could feel his eyes rake her up and down, taking in her server's uniform of white shirt, black tie and black trousers. The effect he had on her now was as devastating as it had been five years before. It was as if she had been plugged into an electrical socket and the current was running through her blood, making it hum, as disturbing and disconcerting as she remembered—especially in light of what had happened.

Her insides contracted even more painfully.

Dark slashing brows framed his incredible navy blue eyes. High cheekbones drew the eye down to a strong jaw. And his mouth…that beautiful sensuous mouth…was all at once sexy and mocking. He lifted one brow, clearly waiting for a response.

Struggling to retain some sense of composure, when she felt like a tiny boat being lashed on high seas, Siena managed to find her voice and said coolly, 'Mr Xenakis. How nice to see you again.'

His arched brow went higher and he let out a curt laugh. His voice wasn't so heavily accented any more. It had more of a mid-Atlantic twang. 'Even now you can make it sound as if you're greeting me at your own dinner party—not serving drinks to people you once woudn't deign to look in the eye.'

Siena flinched minutely. She didn't have to be psychic to recognise that the man who stood before her now was a much harder and more ruthless creature than the man she'd met in Paris. Xenakis's meteoric rise to become one of the world's most prominent hoteliers at the ridiculously young age of thirty had been well documented in the press.

'I'm flattered you remember me,' he drawled, 'After all we've met only once—as memorable as that meeting was.'

He mocked her. Siena felt like pointing out pedantically that it had actually been twice. After all, she'd seen him again the morning after that catastrophic night. But *that* memory was far too much to handle right now.

'Yes.' She glanced away for a minute, uncomfortable under that dark gaze. 'Of course I remember you.'

Suddenly it was too much. The tray of glasses started to wobble alarmingly in Siena's hands as the full magnitude of seeing him again hit her. Surprising her, Andreas took it competently out of her white-knuckled grasp and put it down on a nearby table before she could object.

Just then they were interrupted by Siena's boss, who was shooting none too subtle daggers at Siena while smiling obsequiously at Andreas.

'Mr Xenakis, is everything all right here? If my staff have been in any way remiss—'

'No.' His voice was abrupt, cold. He truly was Lord of all he surveyed now. Exuding power and confidence and that tangible sexual charisma.

Feeling a little dizzy, Siena tuned back in to Xenakis's voice, being directed to her boss.

'Everything is fine. I am acquainted with Miss—'

Siena cut in urgently before Xenakis could say her hated name, 'Mr Xenakis, like I said, it was nice to see you again. If you'll excuse me, though, I really should get back to work.'

Siena picked up the heavy tray again and, without looking at Andreas Xenakis or her boss, fled on very shaky legs.

Andreas followed the progress of the bright blonde head, inordinately annoyed with this small rotund man for interrupting them. He was saying now, in a toadying voice, 'I'm so sorry about that, Mr Xenakis. Our staff have the strictest instructions not to make conversation with any of the guests, but Miss Mancini is new—'

Andreas bit out coldly, '*I* spoke to *her*, actually.' Then he realised something and looked at the man, 'You say her name is Mancini?'

'Yes,' her boss said absently, and then he smiled even more slimily, saying *sotto voce* to Andreas, 'Of course her looks are a bonus—she could be a model, if you ask me. I don't know what she's doing waitressing, but I can't complain. I've never had so many requests for her phone number.'

Andreas desisted from informing the man that she was waitressing because she was *persona non grata* in polite society across Europe. He pushed aside the fact of her name-change and felt something like rage building inside him. He fixed the manager with a look that would have felled many. 'I presume you do not give out her number, of course?'

The man immediately went puce and blustered, 'Well, I... Well, of course not, Mr Xenakis. I don't know what kind of a service you think I'm running here, but I can assure you—'

'Don't worry,' Andreas sliced in cuttingly. 'I *will* be assured once I've checked out your company thoroughly.'

With that he turned and walked in the direction he'd last seen Siena moving. He had something much more urgent to take his attention now: making sure Siena DePiero didn't disappear into thin air.

A couple of hours later Siena was walking quickly through the moonlit streets around Mayfair. She still hadn't fully processed that she'd seen Andreas Xenakis, here in London, where she'd come to hide and move on with her life. To her everlasting relief she hadn't bumped into him again, but she'd been horribly aware of his tall form and had endeavoured to make sure she stayed on the far side of the room at all times.

Now, as she walked and felt the blisters on her heels, she cursed herself for letting Andreas get to her like that. Yes, they had history. She winced inwardly. It wasn't a pretty history. She didn't want to be reminded of the blazing look of anger and betrayal on his face when she'd stood beside her father five years ago, holding her dress up over her chest, and agreed shakily: '*Yes, he attacked me, Papa. I couldn't stop him...*'

Andreas had cut in angrily, his Greek accent thick. 'That's a downright lie. She was begging me—'

Her father had held up an imperious hand and cut Andreas off. He'd turned to face Siena and she'd looked up at him, terrified of his power to inflict punishment if he chose to believe Andreas.

He'd said quietly, 'He's lying, isn't he? You would *never* let a man like this touch you, would you? Because you know you're infinitely better than him.'

Struggling to hide her disgust and hatred, Siena had given the only answer she could. She'd nodded and felt sick. 'Yes, he's lying. I would never allow someone like him to touch me.'

Thinking of the unpalatable past made Siena feel trembly and light-headed. She didn't want to contemplate the very uncomfortable fact that he still had such a profound effect on her.

Once again, though, she marvelled at how far removed he was from the man who had once presided over servers in a hotel. In all honesty she was surprised he'd recognised her at all from his lofty position. She knew how easy it was to see only the hand that served you, not the person. Siena recalled her father's blistering anger when he'd berated her once for aiding a waiter who'd dropped a tray at one of his legendary parties. He'd hauled her into his offce and gripped her arm painfully.

'Don't you know who we are? You step over people like him. You do *not* stop to help them.'

Siena had bitten back the angry retort on her lips. *Just like you stepped over your own illegitimate son in the street? Our own brother?* That audacious comment alone would have merited her sister a severe beating. That was his preferred twisted form of torture—if Siena provoked him, Serena would be punished.

Siena saw the bus stop in the distance and breathed a sigh of relief. Tomorrow she would have forgotten all about bad memories and running into Andreas Xenakis. Her insides lurched, mocking her assertion. For one second earlier, when she'd first seen Andreas, she'd imagined she was dreaming.

She'd never forgotten what she had done to that man by falsely accusing him. More often than she cared to admit she remembered that night and how, with just a look and a touch, he'd made her lose any sense of rationality and sanity. On some level, when she'd read about his stellar success in the newspapers, she'd been relieved; to see him flourishing far better than she would have ever expected assuaged some tiny part of the guilt she felt.

Resolutely Siena pushed down her incendiary thoughts. Familiar nagging anxiety took their place. She wondered now, as she approached the bus stop, if the two jobs she had would be enough to help her sister. But she knew with a leaden feeling that nothing short of a miracle could do that.

Siena had just arrived under the shelter of the bus stop when she noticed a sleek silver sports car pulling up alongside where she stood. Even before the electric window lowered on the passenger side Siena's heart-rate had increased.

The starkly handsome features of Andreas Xenakis looked out and Siena backed away instinctively. His presence was evidence that he wasn't about to let her off so easily. He wanted to torture her and make the most out of her changed circumstances. In a second he'd jumped out of the car and was lightly holding her elbow.

'Please.' He smiled urbanely, as if stopping to pick up women at bus stops resplendent in a tuxedo was entirely normal for him. 'Let me give you a lift.'

Siena was so tense she felt as if she might crack in two. Very aware of her ill-fitting thin denim jacket in the biting early spring breeze, and the fatigue that made her bones ache, she bit out, 'I'm fine, thank you. The bus will be along shortly.'

Andreas shook his head. He had that same incredulous expression that he'd worn when she'd spoken to him before. 'Are your co-workers aware you could probably have conversed with every foreign guest in that room in their own tongue?'

Hurt at this back-handed compliment, and his all too banal but accurate assessment of her misery Siena pulled her arm free. She acted instinctively, wanting to say something to prick his pride and hopefully push him away. 'I said I'm fine, thank you very much. I'm sure you have better things to do than follow me around like some besotted puppy dog.'

His eyes flashed dangerously at that, and Siena hated herself for those words. They reminded her of the poison that had dropped from her lips that night in Paris. They were the kind of words Andreas would expect her to say. But they weren't having the desired effect at all. She should have realised that he wasn't like other men—she remembered the way he'd stood up to her father with such innate pride. One of the very few people who hadn't cowered.

He merely looked even more dangerous now, and grabbed her arm again. 'Let's go, Signorina DePiero. The bus is coming and I'm blocking the lane.'

Siena looked past Andreas and saw the double-decker bus bearing down. A sharp blast of the horn made her flinch. She could see the others waiting at the bus stop shooting them dirty looks because their journey home was being held up.

Siena looked at Andreas and he said ominously, 'Don't test me, Siena. I'll leave the car there if I have to.'

Another blast of the horn had someone saying with irritation, 'Oh, just take the lift, will you? We want to get home.'

For a second Siena felt nothing but excoriating isolation. And then Andreas had led her to the car and was handing her into the low seat before shutting the door. He slid smoothly into the other side.

'Do up your belt,' he instructed curtly, before adding acidly, 'Or are you used to having even *that* done for you?'

His words cut through the fog of shock clouding her brain

and she fumbled to secure the belt with hands that were all fingers and thumbs.

She retaliated in a sharp voice. 'Don't be ridiculous.'

Andreas expertly negotiated the car into the stream of traffic. It was so smooth it felt as if they were gliding above the ground. It had been long months since Siena had been in such luxurious confines, and the soft leather seat moulded around her body, cupping it in a way that was almost sensual. Her hands curled into fists on her lap against the sensation and her jaw was taut.

She unclenched it. 'Stop the car and let me out, please. I can make my own way home. I got in purely to stop you causing a scene.'

'I've spent six months looking for you, Siena, so I'm not about to let you go that easily.'

Six months ago her father had disappeared, leaving his entire fortune in tatters, and leaving Siena and Serena to stand among the ashes and take the opprobrium that had come their way in their father's cowardly absence. Siena looked at Andreas with horror on her face and something much more ambiguous in her belly. Tonight *hadn't* been an awful coincidence?

Shakily she said, 'You've been looking for me?'

His mouth tightened and he confirmed it. 'Since the news of your father's disappearance and the collapse of your fortune.'

He glanced at her and she held herself tightly, wanting to shiver at the thought of his determination to find her again. To punish her? *Why else?* a small voice crowed.

Softly, lethally, he said, 'We have unfinished business, wouldn't you agree?'

Panic constricted Siena's throat. She wasn't ready for a reckoning with this man. 'No, I wouldn't. Now, why don't you just stop the car and let me out?'

Andreas ignored her entreaty and drawled easily, 'Your address, Siena...or we'll spend the night driving around London.'

Siena's jaw clenched again. She saw the way his long-fingered hand rested on the steering wheel. For all of his nonchalance she suddenly had the impression that he was actually far more intractable than her father had ever been. He'd certainly proved that he had a ruthless nose when it came to business.

Siena had on more than one occasion closeted herself in her father's study to follow Andreas's progress online. She'd read about him shutting down ailing hotels with impunity, his refusing to comment on rumours that he didn't care about putting hundreds out of work just to increase his own growing portfolio. In the same searches she'd seen acres of newsprint devoted to his love-life, which appeared to be hectic and peopled with only the most beautiful women in the world. Siena didn't like to admit how she'd noticed that they were all lustrous brunettes or redheads. Evidently blondes weren't his type any more.

Suspecting now that he would indeed drive around all night if she didn't tell him, Siena finally rapped out her address.

'See? That wasn't so hard, was it?'

Siena scowled and looked right ahead.

There was silence for a few minutes, thickening the tension, and then he said, 'So, where did you get Mancini from?'

Siena looked at him. 'How did you know?' Then she remembered and breathed out shakily. 'My boss must have mentioned it.'

'Well?' he asked, as if he had all the time in the world to wait for an answer.

Tightly, Siena eventually replied, 'It was my maternal grandmother's maiden name. I didn't want to risk anyone recognising me.'

'No,' the man beside her responded dryly, 'I can imagine why not.'

Anger at his insouciance, and the ease with which he'd just turned up to humiliate her, made Siena snap, 'You really shouldn't have followed me, you know.'

He replied all too easily. 'Look on it as a concerned friend merely wishing to see how you're doing.'

Siena snorted scathingly but her heart was thumping, '*Friend?* Somehow I doubt you've ever put yourself in that category where I'm concerned.' It was more likely to be a definite foe.

Andreas Xenakis shot her a look then, and Siena recoiled back in her seat. It was so…so carnal and censorious.

He growled softly, 'You're right. We were closer to lovers. And friends don't, after all, cry rape when it suits them to save face.'

Siena blanched. 'I *never* used that word.'

Andreas's jaw clenched hard. 'As good as. You accused me of attacking you when we both know that only seconds before your father arrived you were begging me to—'

'Stop!' cried Siena, her breathing becoming agitated.

She could remember all too well how it had felt to have Andreas Xenakis pressing her down into the chaise longue, the way she'd strained up towards him, aching for him to put his hands on her *everywhere*. And when he'd moved his hand up between her stockinged legs she'd parted them…tacitly telling him of her intense desire.

'Why?' Andreas drawled. 'You can't handle the truth? I thought you were made of sterner stuff, DePiero. You forget you showed your true colours that night.'

Siena turned her head and looked stonily out of the window. The truth was that she had no excuse for her reprehensible behaviour that night. She *had* begged Andreas to make love to her. She *had* kissed him back ardently. When he'd pulled her dress down to expose one breast she'd sighed with exquisite pleasure and he'd kissed her there.

The car pulled up to a set of traffic lights at that moment, and the urge to escape was sudden and instinctive. Siena went to open her door to jump out, but with lightning-fast accuracy Andreas's arm restrained her with a strength that was awesome. Long fingers wrapped around her slender arm, and the bunched muscle of his arm against her soft belly was a far more effective restraint than if he'd locked the doors. Her skin tightened over her bones, drawing in and becoming sensitised. Her breasts felt heavy and tight, her nipples stiffening against the material of her bra.

The car moved off again and Siena pushed his arm off her with all her strength. That brief touch was enough to hurtle her back in time all over again and she struggled to contain herself. The fact that he was so determined to toy with her like this was utterly humiliating.

He pulled up outside a discreetly elegant period apartment building on a wide quiet street. He'd hopped out of the car and was at her open door, holding out an expectant hand, before she knew what was happening.

Siena shrank back and looked up at him. 'This isn't where I live.' *It's a million miles from where I live,* she thought.

'I'm aware of that. However, it is where *I* live, and as we were passing I thought we'd stop so we can catch up on old times over a coffee.'

Siena held back a snort of derision and crossed her arms, looking straight ahead with a stony expression. 'I am not getting out of this car, Xenakis. Take me home.'

Andreas's voice was merely amused. 'First I couldn't get you into it and now I can't get you out of it. They say women are mercurial…'

Before she knew it Andreas had bent down to her level and reached in to undo her seat belt. Siena flapped at his hands in a panic until he stilled them with his. His face was very close to hers and Siena could feel her hair unravelling. She was breathing harshly. His scent teased her nostrils, exactly as she remembered it. Not changed. Oaky and musky and very male.

A voice came from behind Andreas. 'Mr Xenakis? Do you want me to park the car?'

Without taking his eyes off Siena's, Andreas answered, 'Yes, please, Tom. I'll be taking Ms DePiero home shortly, so keep it nearby.'

'Aye-aye, sir,' came the jaunty response.

Siena struggled for a few seconds against Andreas's superior strength and will. She saw the boy waiting behind him. Innate good manners and the fear of causing a scene that had been drummed into her since babyhood made her bite out with reluctance, 'Fine. One coffee.'

Andreas stood up, and this time Siena had no choice but to put her hand in his and let him help her out of the low-slung vehicle. To her chagrin he kept a tight hold of her hand as he tossed his keys to the boy and led her into the building, where a concierge held the door open in readiness.

Once in the hushed confines of the lift Siena tried to pull her hand back, but Andreas was lifting it to inspect it. He opened out her palm and his touch made some kind of dangerous lethargy roll through her, but she winced when she followed his gaze. Her palm sported red chafed skin, calluses. Proof of her very new working life.

He turned it over and Siena winced even more to see him inspecting her bitten nails—the resurgence of a bad habit she'd had for a short time in her teens, which had been quickly overcome when her father had meted out a suitable punishment on Serena, her sister.

Her hands were a far cry from the soft lily-white manicured specimens they'd used to be. Exerting more effort this time, and knowing that she'd just been cured of her nail-biting habit once again, she finally pulled free of Andreas's grip and said mulishly, 'Don't touch me.'

With a rough quality to his voice that resonated inside her, Andreas asked, 'How did they get like this from waitresssing?'

Siena fought against the pull of something that felt very vulnerable. 'I'm not just waitressing. I'm working as a cleaner in a hotel by day too.'

Andreas tipped up her chin and inspected her face, touched under her eyes where she knew she sported dark shadows. That vulnerability was blooming inside her, and for a second Siena thought she might burst into tears. To counteract it—and the ease with which this man seemed to be able to push her buttons—she said waspishly, 'Feeling sorry for the poor little rich girl, Andreas?'

At that moment the lift bell pinged and the doors opened silently. Siena and Andreas were locked in some kind of silent combat. Andreas's eyes went dark, their blue depths becoming distinctly icy as he took his fingers away from her face and smiled.

'Not for a second, Siena DePiero. You forget that I've seen you in action. A piranha would be more vulnerable than you.'

Siena couldn't believe the dart of hurt that lanced her at his words, and was almost glad when he turned. With his hand on her elbow, he led her out of the lift and into a luxuriously carpeted corridor decked out in smoky grey colours with soft lamps burning on a couple of tables.

The one door indicated that Andreas had no neighbours to disturb him, and Siena guessed this must be the penthouse apartment in the building. The lift doors closed behind them and then Andreas was opening the door and standing aside to allow Siena to precede him into his apartment. Only his assurance to the car park valet that he would be taking her home shortly gave Siena the confidence to go forward.

She rounded on him as he closed the door and blurted out belatedly, 'Don't call me DePiero. My name is Mancini now.'

After a long second Andreas inclined his head and drawled, with a hint of dark humour, 'I'll call you whatever you like…'

Stifling a sound of irritation, Siena backed away and turned around again, facing into the main drawing room. Her eyes widened. She'd grown up in the lap of luxury, but the sheer understated level of elegance in Andreas's apartment took her breath away. She'd been used to seeing nothing but *palazzos* laden down with antiques and heavy paintings, everything gold-plated, carpets so old and musty that dust motes danced in the air when you moved…but this was clean and sleek.

Siena only became aware that she had advanced into the drawing room and was looking around with unabashed curiosity when she saw Andreas standing watching her with his hands in his pockets. The sheer magnificence of the man in his tuxedo shocked her anew and she flushed, wrapping her arms around herself in an unconscious gesture of defence.

Andreas shook his head and smiled wryly before walking towards a sideboard which held several bottles of drink and glasses. He said now, with his back to Siena, 'You really know how to turn it on, don't you?'

Siena tensed. 'Turn what on?'

He turned around, a bottle of something in his hand, eyes gleaming in the soft light. 'It must be automatic after years of acting the part of innocent virginal heiress…'

When Siena was stubbornly silent, because he had no idea how close to the truth he skated, Andreas gestured half impatiently and clarified, 'That air of vulnerability, and looking as though butter wouldn't melt in your mouth.'

Hating herself for being so transparent, and hating him for misjudging her so comprehensively while knowing she couldn't very well blame him for his judgement, Siena schooled her expression. She carefully uncrossed her arms and shrugged one shoulder negligently. 'What can I say? You have me all figured out, Mr Xenakis.'

He poured a dark liquid into two glasses and came over, holding one out. 'I know I offered you a coffee, but try this. It's a very fine port. And you didn't have a problem using my name when we first met. Mr Xenakis is so...*formal*. Please, call me Andreas.'

Siena took the glass he offered, suddenly glad of something to hold onto—anything to will down the memory of how she had used his name before, *'Andreas, please kiss me...'*

He gestured to the comfortable-looking couch and chairs arranged around a low coffee table which held huge books of photographs that looked well thumbed. 'Please, take a seat, Siena. Make yourself comfortable.'

Siena was torn for a moment between wanting to demand he take her home and curling up in the nearest chair so she could sleep for a week.

A little perturbed by how weak she suddenly felt, she went and sat down in the nearest chair. Andreas sat on the couch to her left, his long legs stretched out and disturbingly close to her feet, which she pulled primly close to her chair.

He smiled and it was dangerous.

'Still afraid you might catch some social disease from me, Siena?'

CHAPTER TWO

'DON'T BE SILLY,' Siena replied quickly, humiliated when she thought of what had happened, of the vile untruths she'd uttered and all to protect her sister.

When she thought of how innocently she'd wanted him that night in Paris and how it had all gone so horribly wrong she felt nauseous. This man hated her. It vibrated on the air between them and Siena had the very futile sense that even if she tried to defend herself and tell him what her reasons had been for acting so cruelly he'd laugh until he cried. He looked so impervious now. Remote.

Andreas sat forward, the small glass cradled between long fingers. 'Tell me, why did you leave Italy?'

Siena welcomed this diversion away from dangerous feelings and looked at him incredulously, wondering how he could even ask that question. She hated the familiar burn of humiliation that rose up inside her when she thought of the odious charges that had been levelled at her father after his business had imploded in on itself, revealing that he'd been juggling massive debts for years and that everything they possessed, including his precious family *palazzo* in Florence, was owned by the banks.

Her mouth twisted. 'As you can imagine, the price on myself and my sister's heads fell dramatically when it became apparent that we'd lost our fortune. I'm sure I don't need to tell you that we became *personae non grata* overnight.'

Andreas's eyes narrowed. 'No. It would be untruthful of me not to admit that I knew your father had been soliciting prostitutes for years, and about the evidence of his involvement in drugs and political corruption. But proof that he'd been trafficking women all over Europe for sex must have been the killer blow for two penniless heiresses. No one wants to be seen to be associating with a scandal of that level.'

The shame Siena felt nearly strangled her. Her father had solicited prostitutes while married to their mother because it had excited him. He'd fathered a son with one of those women. She'd thought she'd hated her father before...but she'd hated him even more when he'd disappeared into thin air to avoid the numerous charges levelled against him. To this day no one knew where he was, and Siena never wanted to see him again.

The thought of all those poor defenceless and vulnerable women being sold into a life of torture and degradation... Even now bile rose in her throat, because it had also been proved that her father had been more than just involved in a peripheral sense. He'd been an active participant.

Andreas must have seen something in her expression and he said quietly. 'Your father's sins are not your sins.'

Siena was taken aback at this assertion. She looked at him, unable to read his face. 'Perhaps not, but people don't want to believe that.'

'Did the press in Italy gave you a hard time?' He answered her disbelieving look with a shrug. 'I was travelling in South America for work when the full extent of your father's scandal hit. By the time I got back to Europe your father had disappeared and a new scandal was unfolding. I missed most of it.'

Siena thought of the relentless days of headlines like: *Heiresses no more. Who will marry the poor little rich girls now?* And: *Serena DePiero caught in flagrante just days after dis-*

graced father's disappearance! That had been the moment
Siena had known she had to get herself and Serena out of Italy.
Her sister had been spiralling dangerously out of control, and
she'd been barely clinging onto sanity after everything they'd
known had been ripped asunder.

Siena hadn't expected any quarter from the press—she'd
seen how they delighted in savaging the once lofty and untouchable of society—and thanks to her father's extreme hubris the DePieros had had it coming. Nevertheless she voiced
an understatement in a flat voice. 'Yes, you could say they
gave us a hard time.'

Andreas was surprised at the lack of emotion in Siena's
voice. The lack of reproach or injury. He could well imagine
the field-day the press had had at seeing two blonde and blue-
eyed princesses reduced to nothing.

Once again he had to marvel at her sheer natural beauty.
She wore not a scrap of make-up but her skin glowed like a
pearl. In this world of artifice and excess she really was a rare
jewel. Even in the plain shirt and tie, that threadbare denim
jacket, he could see the tantalising curves of her body. Fuller
now that she was a woman, not a teenager.

Desire was hot and immediate, tightening his body. A fit of
pique went through Andreas when he realised that he'd sub-
consciously avoided blonde women in the last five years, seeking out the complete opposite and telling himself that she'd
burned his taste for blondes. But she hadn't. He just hadn't
wanted any blonde except *her.*

Women didn't usually reduce him to such immediate carnal reaction, no matter how desirable or beautiful. And yet
she had from the very first moment he'd laid eyes on her...

Andreas looked at her now with fresh resolve filling his
belly and lifted his glass. 'To whatever the future might bring.'

Siena had a very scary suspicion that the future Andreas
was envisaging had something to do with *her.* Very deliber-

ately she ignored his toast and drained her glass, put it down on the nearby table. The alcohol blazed its way down her throat.

Andreas looked merely amused and chided softly, 'A 1977 port should be savoured a little more delicately than that, but each to their own.'

He downed his too. Siena blanched. She could just imagine how much it had cost. Her father had thought of himself as an expert in fine wines so she'd learnt something by proxy.

Thinking of her father made her think of her sister, and that made her stand up jerkily, only vaguely aware of the stunning view of London on the other side of the huge windows. 'I really do need to get home. I have an early start in the morning.'

Andreas rose too, as fluidly as a panther, rippling sinew and muscle very evident despite the severe cut of his suit. As if it barely contained him. Siena would have taken a step back, but the chair was behind her.

She sensed a spiking of electricity in the air and there was a pregnant pause just before he said innocuously, 'Very well.'

He went to a discreet phone on the sideboard and picked it up, saying to someone, 'I'm coming back down. Please have my car brought round. Thank you.'

He extended his arm to allow her to precede him from the room, and to Siena's utter chagrin her overwhelming feeling wasn't one of relief. She was a little confused. She'd expected…*more*. More of a fight? And yet he was happy to let her go so easily. Something bitter pierced her. Perhaps he'd just wanted to amuse himself by seeing the disgraced heiress up close and he was already bored.

So why did she feel so desolate all of a sudden?

Andreas stepped into the lift behind Siena and pressed the button. He might be giving her the illusion of letting her go, but that was not his intention in the slightest. Seeing her again had merely solidified his desire to have her in his bed. Finally.

Acquiescent and *his*. That disdain she did so well would have no place in the relationship they would have. She was in no position to argue or resist him, and the thought of seeing her come undone was heady in the extreme.

His car was waiting by the kerb and a young security guard jumped out, giving the keys to Andreas, who held the passenger door open for Siena to get in.

Siena stood stiffly by the open door and looked at Andreas without meeting his eye. She was still trembling at the way his hand had rested lightly on the small of her back the whole way down in the elevator. And also at the speed with which he now appeared to want to get rid of her.

'If you can point me in the direction of the nearest tube I'll make my own way home.'

Andreas's voice was like steel. 'It's almost eleven-thirty at night. There is no way you're taking the tube alone. Get into the car, Siena, or I will put you in myself. Don't think I won't.'

Siena looked at him properly and saw how stern he seemed. She felt a shiver of something go through her—recognition of how huge and broad he was against the night sky. And yet she wasn't scared of him. Not as she'd been of her father. She somehow knew instinctively that Andreas would never lash out like that. Violence towards women was born of weakness and fear. Andreas didn't have that in him. And it surprised her to admit that she trusted this gut feeling so much.

Knowing that if she walked off now he'd just follow her again, Siena gave in and slid into the car, its luxurious confines once again surrounding her like a cocoon. Until Andreas got in beside her and the atmosphere turned from relaxing to electric.

As they pulled away from the kerb Andreas asked easily, 'Did your sister come to London with you?'

Instantly Siena tensed. She answered carefully, 'No... She went to...to the south of France to stay with friends of hers.'

Andreas glanced at Siena, who was looking stonily ahead.

He had to concede that she'd never taken after her more obvious sister by appearing in the gossip columns. Siena clearly preferred to clean toilets rather than to be seen in polite society again and be exposed to ridicule or censure.

He had to admit to a grudging and surprising respect that Siena was doing the sort of work she would have taken completely for granted her whole life. Perhaps now that their father was gone Siena saw no need to be responsible for the precious family name and was happy to wash her hands of her infamous sister, who had been well known as a party girl.

In truth, Andreas didn't really care about Serena. The sister he was concerned about was sitting right beside him, her legs looking very long as she angled them well away from him. He allowed himself a small predatory smile to think of a time when they would be wrapped around his hips as he finally exorcised this demon from his blood for good.

He hadn't elaborated on the fact that he had been actively looking for her for six months. In fact he'd been thinking about her ever since Paris. However, it had only been six months ago, when he'd finally had the luxury of time after establishing himself, that he'd begun to focus on such a personal pursuit. Siena DePiero had always been in his sights...

To Siena's relief Andreas seemed to be done with questioning her, and they drove in silence through the empty London streets. Rain started to spatter gently on the windscreen. For the first time since she'd left Italy Siena felt a pang of homesickness and it surprised her. She'd left Italy never wanting to see it again.

She'd spent many a night looking out of her window dreaming of another life—one without constrictions and pain and tension and always the unbearable pressure to act a certain way. She'd dreamed of a life full of love and affection. The only affection she'd really known had come from her sister—her poor, damaged sister. Their mother had died when they were both small girls. Siena had only the vaguest memories of a fragrant blonde woman who'd used to come into their room at night dressed in glittering finery.

She realised that they were close to her street already, and she directed Andreas into the labyrinth of smaller streets that led to her home. He pulled to a stop and looked out incredulously at the bleak, lonesome apartment block standing on wasteground.

'You're living *here?*'

Defensively Siena said, 'It's near the tube and the bus.'

Andreas was shaking his head in disbelief. He undid his seat belt and got out. Siena noticed that he'd taken an umbrella from somewhere and was holding it up now, as he came to her door and opened it.

She got out and the wind whipped around her, tugging her hair out of its bun completely. Feeling flustered, she said, 'Look, thanks for the lift…'

She moved to walk around Andreas and go into the flats, but stopped when Andreas kept pace beside her. She looked at him. 'Where do you think you're going?'

He was grim. 'I'm walking you to your apartment. You are *not* going in there alone.'

A new sense of pride stiffened Siena's backbone. 'I've been living here alone for months now and I've been fine. I can assure you that—'

Andreas wasn't listening. He'd taken her elbow in his hand and was guiding her across the litter-strewn ground. Irritation raced up Siena's spine. This was exactly what her father had used to do.

Once inside the main door, which hung haphazardly on broken hinges, and under the unforgiving flourescent lights, Siena pulled free, 'This is fine.'

Andreas was folding down the umbrella, though, and then he spotted a sullen youth lurking in a corner. He called the boy over and handed him a folded note and the umbrella. 'Keep an eye on the car for me?' he said.

The boy looked at the money and went white, then looked back to Andreas and nodded his head vigorously.

He took the umbrella before speeding off to stand guard.

Siena didn't like how the tiny gesture of Andreas giving him the umbrella made her feel soft inside. Churlishly she said, 'It'll be up on blocks by the time you leave.'

'O, ye of little faith,' Andreas murmured, and hit the elevator button.

Siena watched as he grew impatient when the lift didn't materialise straight away, and stood back to point at the stained concrete stairs. 'It's a cliché, I know, but the lift isn't working—and I'm all the way up on the fourteenth floor.' She couldn't quite keep the satisfaction out of her voice.

The light of determination was a definite glint in Andreas's eye as he said, 'Lead the way.'

Siena was huffing and puffing by floor ten, and very aware of Andreas right behind her. When they finally reached the door to her flat she turned to face him. She felt hot, and the hair on the back of her neck felt damp with perspiration. Her heart was hammering.

'Thank you. This is me.'

Andreas barely had a hair out of place, and not so much as a hint of the effort of climbing up fourteen sets of hard concrete stairs. Although somewhere along the way he had tugged his bow-tie loose, and the top button of his shirt was open, revealing the top of his olive-skinned chest and some springy dark hair.

Siena's belly clenched hard. She could remember impatiently undoing his shirt buttons that night in Paris, ripping his tie open...

Andreas was looking around the bare corridor. Someone

was shouting in a nearby flat and then something smashed against a door, making Siena flinch.

Andreas cursed and took the keys out of her numb fingers. 'Let's get you inside.'

He was doing it again. Taking command, all but pushing her through the door into a bare and forlorn-looking space filled with stained carpet. Siena had done her best to get rid of the stains, with little success. She only hoped that they weren't what she thought they were…

Siena put on her one small lamp and regretted it as soon as she did so, because it sent out a far too seductive pink and warm glow. Feeling thoroughly threatened now, she put out her hand for her keys and snapped, 'You've seen me safely in—now, please leave.'

Looking supremely at ease, Andreas just shut the door behind him and said softly, 'This must be hard for you…'

Siena went very still and her hand dropped to her side. He had no idea…how *easy* this had been for her. To leave behind the tainted trappings of suffocating wealth and excess had been a relief. But that was something no one would ever understand. She'd certainly never be explaining it to *this* man, who had grabbed onto success and wealth with both hands and was thoroughly enjoying it. And could she begrudge him that? Even if his methods were dubious? Of course not. She had given up that right five years before.

She put her hand out again for her keys. 'I have to be up early for work.'

Andreas didn't move. He just looked at her, those dark, unreadable eyes roving over her face and over her hair, which was tumbled around her shoulders now, making Siena want to drag it back, tie it up.

Feeling desperate, she said, *'Please.'*

'But what if you didn't have to get up early?'

Siena blinked at Andreas, not understanding him. She

shook her head. 'What do you mean? I start work at six-thirty a.m. It takes me an hour to get there…'

Andreas's face was so starkly beautiful in the dim light that she could feel herself being hypnotised. Much as she had been when she'd stood in front of him in that hotel boutique shop, in that dress. She'd taken it off after that night and thrown it in the bin, unable to look at it and not feel sickened.

He said now in a silky tone, 'What I mean is that you have a choice, Siena… I'd like to offer you an alternative.'

It took a second…but then his words sank in along with the very explicit look in his eyes. Since she'd been in England other men had posed much the same question—like the man who had come back to get something from his hotel room and found her making his bed. Except what he'd been offering had been stated in much cruder terms.

Shame and something much hotter curled through her belly, making self-disgust rise. She took a sidestep back and injected as much icy disdain as she could into her voice. 'If you're suggesting what I think you're suggesting then clearly you refuse to believe that I want you to leave me alone.'

Andreas took a step closer and panic spiked in Siena, making her take another step back. She felt out of her depth and unbelievably vulnerable. All of the familiar surroundings of her old life were gone. The part she'd played had been as good as scripted. Now she was utterly defenceless, and the one man in the world who hated her guts was propositioning her. And she hated that it didn't disgust her the way it should.

He reached out to trail a finger down one cheek, across her jawbone and down to where the pulse beat hectically under her skin at her throat. 'Even now you affect disgust, but your body betrays you. What happened in Paris…you were as involved as I was—as hot and eager as anything I've ever seen. And yet you didn't hesitate to shift the blame to me to keep yourself pure in your father's bigoted eyes. God forbid the untouchable heiress had been rolling around on a chair with a mere hotel employee.'

Siena slapped his hand away and stepped back, hating how breathy she sounded. 'Get out of here now, Xenakis. Rehashing the past is of no use.'

The anger Andreas had been keeping in check spilled over into his voice. 'You can't bring yourself to offer up even the most grudging of apologies, can you? Even now, when you don't have a cent to your name or a reputation to safeguard.'

Shame gripped Siena—and guilt. Ineffectually she said, 'I…am…sorry.'

Derision laced Andreas's voice as he sneered, 'Spare me the insincere apology when it's all but dragged from you.'

His face was suddenly etched with self-disgust, and he half turned from Siena, raking his hair with a hand. She had a vivid memory of seeing him the following morning, shocked at his black eye and swollen jaw. Evidence of her father's men's dirty work. She'd tried to apologise then, but hadn't been able to speak over his very justified wrath.

Contrition and a stark desire to assure him that she *was* truly sorry made her reach out impulsively to touch his sleeve. She dropped her hand hurriedly when he looked at her suspiciously. She gulped under his almost black gaze and said truthfully, 'I never intended to…to lie about what happened. Or that you should lose your job.'

Andreas smiled, but it was harsh. 'No, possibly you didn't. You would have had your fun with me on the chaise longue of that boutique and then you would have gone on your way, with another notch on your busy bedpost. You forget that I know exactly what you girls were like: avaricous, bored and voracious. But you hadn't counted on Papà finding you *in flagrante delicto,* and you made sure that he would not suspect his precious daughter had such base desires. It was much easier to accuse a poor Greek hotel employee.'

Siena blanched. That was exactly what she had done. But not for *her* survival, for her sister's. That was something she could never imagine explaining to this intractable, vengeful man. Especially not when Serena was still so vulnerable. And not when Siena was still reeling with the effect he had on *her*.

Andreas slashed his hand through the air and said curtly, 'You're right, though. Rehashing the past is of no use.'

Those dark blue eyes narrowed on Siena again, with a renewed gleam of something that looked suspiciously like determination.

'Are you really telling me you're so proud that you relish living like this?' His voice became cajoling. 'Don't you miss sleeping until lunchtime and having nothing to worry about other than what time you've scheduled your beauty appointments or which dress you'll wear that evening?' He continued relentlessly. 'Are you really expecting me to believe that you wouldn't have all that back if you could? That you wouldn't seize the opportunity to walk amongst your peers again?'

Siena felt sick. The thought of allowing this man to get any closer, where he could possibly discover the vulnerability hidden deep inside her, made her break out in a cold sweat. He thought she had the wherewithal to handle him, that it would be second nature, when she didn't have the first clue about handling a man like him.

She pushed aside the fact that her apology had been as futile as she'd believed it would be and tossed her head in her most haughty fashion, eyes flashing. 'I would prefer to clean your toilets rather than do as you're suggesting. Perhaps you think that because I'm desperate I'll say yes to becoming your mistress. Is that it, Xenakis?'

Andreas smiled and bared his teeth. 'I thought I told you to call me Andreas—and, yes, I think you'll agree because you miss your life of luxury. But, more than that, because despite everything you want me…'

Siena went cold. She did want him, but he had no clue who she really was, or why she'd had to betray him so awfully. He had no idea about the tender beating inner heart of her that had very fragile hopes and dreams for a life far from the one she knew. He only saw a spoilt ruined heiress and a way to humiliate her. Because she'd rejected him. He had no idea who she'd had to protect, and that *that* was why she'd let him be accused in the worst way possible. She'd had no choice.

She knew now that, if given a chance, this man would take her and humiliate her for his own pleasure. For revenge.

In her most cutting voice Siena said, 'Contrary to your over-inflated view of your own levels of attraction, I *do not* want you. I may well be in a desperate situation *Mr Xenakis,* but I still have my pride and I wouldn't become your mistress for your sick amusement if you were the last man on this earth.'

Andreas looked at the woman standing just a few feet away from him and felt like clapping. Her clothes were crumpled and stained, her hair was tumbled around her face and shoulders in messy golden abandon, but she could have been a queen berating a lowly subject. And he wanted her with a hunger bordering on the very word she'd used herself: *desperation.*

He growled, 'I'm not in the habit of propositioning women who don't want me, Siena.'

She backed away at that, and reiterated with not a little desperation, 'I *don't* want you.'

'Liar.'

She saw the danger in Andreas's eyes. He advanced on her and she backed away, panic constricting her vocal cords, stopping her from saying anything. Panic at the awful, traitorous way her body was already getting hot, tingling with anticipation. If he kissed her now… Her mind blanked at the thought.

'Once again you're just too proud to admit you want me, Siena DePiero, and I'm going to prove how much you want me right now.'

It was insulting how easily Andreas was able to gather her into his arms and pull her close. From somewhere deep inside Siena dredged up the fight she needed. This man was far too dangerous to her. When he pulled her even closer and his head started to descend Siena acted on a visceral reflex to protect herself. She stiffened in his arms and lifted a hand to try and block his mouth from touching her. He obviously misread her intention and caught her wrist with lightning-fast reflexes. The strength of his grip made her gasp.

'Oh, no, you don't.'

Siena protested, 'But I wasn't—'

'No?' Andreas's mouth was hard.

He didn't believe her. Siena had never hit anyone in her life, and she felt sick at the thought that he could believe her capable of such violence.

'I wouldn't have hit you…' she whispered, willing him to believe her, staring directly into fathomless deep blue eyes.

Andreas's expression was stern. 'And you won't ever get the chance.' The threat in his voice was a very sensual one.

He kept her close with one arm secure around her waist and let her wrist go to bring his other hand up to cup her jaw with surprising gentleness, considering what he'd believed her about to do. And then, before she could make another move, Andreas angled his head down and his mouth closed over hers.

Shock rendered Siena helpless against the sensual attack Andreas administered. His mouth moved over hers with a confidence that was heady, eliciting an immediate response from Siena that she wasn't even aware of giving.

He was the only man who'd kissed her like this and she'd gone up in flames the first time. Nothing had changed. Heat pooled in her lower belly and spread slowly outwards, incinerating everything in its path. Her breasts tightened and felt heavy, achy. His arms around her were like a steel cage, but it was one she was pathetically loath to escape.

Siena was drowning in the scent of musky male, dimly aware of Andreas's hand moving down her jaw, caressing, and his fingers undoing the tie at the throat of her shirt, opening the top buttons.

His tongue teased her lips, making her strain to get closer, to allow him access so that he could stroke his tongue along hers. This was the headiest of illicit pleasures...

Unbeknownst to Siena, her hands had unfurled from the fists they'd been against Andreas's chest and were now spread out wide. She was up on tiptoe, as if to get closer to him. Andreas's hand cupped the back of her head, fingers tangled in long, silky blonde strands of hair. His other hand gripped her hip, kneading the flesh, making Siena move against him.

It was only when she felt air touch the exposed flesh of her neck and throat that Siena came to her senses and pulled back. She looked up, completely dazed, into dark blue eyes. Heavy-lidded and explicitly sexual.

Slowly realisation came over her like a chill wind, making all that heady sensuality wither away. One touch and she'd become a slave to her senses. Unable to rationalise anything.

Siena used her hands to push back violently, almost falling over in the process.

A million and one things were clamouring in her head, but worst of all was that she'd spectacularly—in neon lights and with fireworks—humiliated herself. She winced when she recalled her haughty tones—'*I don't want you.*' And what had she just been doing? Proving herself a liar *again*.

She grasped at her open shirt and couldn't look Andreas in the eye. 'I'd like you to leave now.' Her voice sounded rusty and raw to her ears.

CHAPTER THREE

ANDREAS LOOKED AT Siena, holding onto her open shirt, looking almost shell-shocked, pale as the moonlight outside. His chest felt tight. This reaction was not something he'd expected. And then he realised: acting was second nature to this woman. It was in her blood—that made *his* blood boil. To have been duped again, even for a nanosecond…

His voice was harsh. 'There's no one here to cry wolf to now, Siena. You have to take responsibility for your actions.'

He started forward and suddenly her head came up. Her blue eyes were once again sparkling like jewels, her chin determined. Andreas stopped, his body still throbbing with heat. But he forced it back. Something hardened inside him. To think that for a second that he'd seen some kind of vulnerability…? Ludicrous.

He forced himself to be civilised when he felt anything but. 'You still want me, Siena, and you can deny it all you want but it's a lie. I am not leaving here without you tonight. You'll pay for what you did: *in my bed.*'

Siena opened her mouth and shut it again, shock pouring into her body. He sounded so utterly determined. As if he was prepared to carry her bodily from this place. Siena's mind skittered away from that all too disturbing scenario to think of his other assertion. How could she deny she wanted him after that little display of complete lack of control? His words terrified her, though—his easy assumption that she would just *go with him*. Just as her father had always expected her to do his bidding.

She'd tasted personal freedom for the first time since their father had disappeared and it terrified her to think of someone dictating her every move again.

Siena dropped her hand from her open top buttons and lifted her chin. 'You seriously think that I'll just walk out of here with you? How unbelievably arrogant *are* you?'

Andreas's eyes darkened ominously. 'I paid a high price for your petulant need to save face with your father that night, Siena. I was sacked and blacklisted from every hotel in Europe overnight, and I had the very unsavoury rumour of my having forced myself on a woman dogging my heels. My fledgling career was ruined. I had to go to America to start again.'

Siena couldn't bear to feel that shame again and she lashed out. 'So—what? I pay you now by becoming your mistress?'

Andreas smiled and it was feral. 'That and more, Siena De-Piero. You pay me by admitting to yourself *and me* just how much you want me.'

She looked at this man in the soft light of her grotty flat. He was standing like a maurauding pirate, legs firmly planted wide apart. Chest broad and powerful. Strip away the civilised veneer of the tuxedo and this man was a pure urban animal of the most potent kind.

He's been looking for you for six months. He's not just going to walk away... The realisation sent tendrils of panic mixed with something much more humiliatingly exciting through Siena's blood. The confines of the tiny flat seemed to draw in around them even more.

She emitted a curt laugh to hide her trepidation. 'So—what? You'd lock me into your penthouse apartment and take me out like a toy of some kind for your pleasure only?' She'd been aiming to sound scathing but her voice betrayed her, sounding almost as if she was considering this.

Andreas's eyes gleamed in the dim light and he smiled. 'I can't deny that that image does have its appeal, but, no, I'd have no problem being seen with you in public. *I* don't have an issue with public opinion—unlike some people.'

Andreas was looking at her coolly, clearly waiting for her to say something.

'And what then?' she asked, feeling a little hysterical at being in this situation, discussing this with Andreas Xenakis. 'You just drop me back here at the side of the road when you're done?'

Andreas's mouth firmed. 'I take care of all my...lovers.' He shrugged negligently. 'They're usually self-sufficient, but with your range of language skills alone I don't doubt that with a little help you could find a decent job...certainly something better than menial labour.'

Siena laughed. The hysteria was taking over. Controlling herself with an effort, she looked at Andreas. 'This truly is a turn-up for the books, isn't it? *You* offering to help *me* find a job...'

Siena's cutting voice was hiding one of her deepest vulnerabilities: the fact that she had no qualification beyond her exclusive education. Yes, she had numerous languages and could speak them fluently. Yes, she knew how to host a dinner party for fifty people and more. Yes, she knew how to arrange flowers and how to behave in front of royalty and diplomats, how to conduct conversation ranging from world politics to the history of art... But when it came to the real world—real life—she knew nothing. Had no skills or qualifications. She'd been destined for a life of social politics. And Andreas knew that.

She prayed he wouldn't touch her again and moved around him on wobbly legs to open the front door. There were no more disturbing sounds coming from her neighbours. She looked back into the room with relief, to see that Andreas had followed her. But the relief was short-lived when he gently but firmly pushed the door shut again.

Sounding eminently reasonable, Andreas said, 'I'm offering you an opportunity, Siena, a chance to move upwards and make a life for yourself again.'

Siena crossed her arms against this threat. He wasn't moving. She forced herself to look up at him. Her mouth twisted and she spoke her fears. 'We both know it's not an *offer,* Andreas. You haven't spent six months searching for me to just walk away.'

He smiled again and agreed equably, 'No, I haven't. It really wouldn't be such a chore, Siena... I'd see to it that you enjoyed yourself. You'd want for nothing.'

'For as long as your interest lasts?'

His face immediately became more stark and Siena knew she'd hit a nerve. She was intrigued despite herself. 'That's all I'm offering, Siena. A finite amount of time as my lover until we're both ready to move on. I have no desire for anything more permanent—certainly not with you.'

Siena barely registered his insult. She was fighting against his dark pull and she opened the door again—only to have Andreas reach out lazily and shut it. She wanted to stamp her feet and glared at him.

'Look, Xenakis—'

'No!'

His voice stopped the breath in her throat. He looked fierce and magnificent in the gloom. He came closer and her heart thudded painfully.

'*You* look. This is only going to end one way: by you agreeing to come with me now. If you want a further demonstration of how susceptible you are to me then by all means I'm happy to provide it here and now, but—' He cut himself off and looked around the room with clear disgust, then back to Siena. 'I personally would prefer to make love to you for the first time in more…luxurious surroundings.'

The thought and, worse, the knowledge that he could take her here if he so wanted made Siena move further away. She felt as if a noose was tightening around her neck.

Andreas watched as Siena distanced herself and curbed the almost animalistic urge he had to put her over his shoulder and carry her bodily out of this pathetic, stinking place. His blood was boiling with lust and determination. As soon as his mouth had touched hers he'd known with a visceral certainty that he would *not* be leaving her behind in this place. He didn't like to admit that a part of him couldn't bear to think of her in these surroundings. It was like dropping a perfect diamond into the filthiest of stagnant ponds.

Trying to curb the impatience he felt, Andreas pointed out, 'You don't have anyone to turn to, Siena. If you're hoping for some blue-blooded knight to ride up on a white horse and forgive you the sins of your father it's not going to happen. Don't forget—I *know* your sins.'

Siena turned to face Andreas again, hugging her arms even tighter around herself, unaware of how huge her eyes looked in her face.

His words had cut her far deeper than she wanted him to see. He was right. She didn't have anyone to turn to. She and Serena did have an older half-brother, but she had little doubt that after the treatment he'd received at the hands of their father, not to mention the way Siena and her sister had ignored him so blatantly when they'd seen him in the street the day he'd confronted their father, he would not relish her getting in touch out of the blue. He had become a billionaire financier against all the odds and must despise her just as he must despise their father, for humiliating him like a dog in the street.

Her sister was in no position to be of any support and never really had been, despite being the older by two years. And that brought Siena back to the stark realisation that *she* might have no one to turn to, but Serena was expecting to turn to Siena when she needed her. And she needed her now. Dismay filled her. How could she have forgotten even for a moment about Serena?

The hectic pulse of her blood mocked her. The reason was standing just feet away from her. Siena could feel the fight draining from her weary body. A sense of inevitability washed over her. It had been no coincidence that Andreas had met her tonight. He'd *searched* for her. And he would not rest now he knew where she was. She had nowhere else to go. Nowhere to hide. No resources.

As if he sensed the direction her thoughts were taking, Siena could see Andreas's eyes flash triumphantly in the gloom.

Suddenly, as if she'd been injected with a dose of adrenalin, her brain became clear. Thinking of her sister focused her thoughts. *If* she was going to walk out of this apartment with this man she had to make sure that the one person who needed *her* was going to benefit.

The thought of telling Andreas about her sister, appealing to his humanity, was anathema. If anything, this evening had proved just how far Andreas was willing to go to seek his revenge. If she told him about Serena he might very well use her against Siena in some way, exactly as her father had. Siena shivered at the very thought. No way could she ever let that happen again.

She knew, though, that the very audacious plan forming in her head would ensure Andreas's hatred of her for ever.

Andreas's blood hummed with anticipation as he watched the woman who stood just feet away, her chin still lifted defiantly, even though they both knew she was about to give in.

She would be *his*. Her little act of pride had just been an exercise in proving to Andreas that he was still the last man she'd choose on earth, even if there was enough heat between them to melt an iceberg. And even if she *was* desperate.

His mouth tightened into a line. If anything it just proved that he was right: Siena wanted out of her challenging circumstances and back into the world she knew so well.

All *he* cared about was sating this burning desire inside him. Witnessing Siena DePiero swallow her pride and her denial of their mutual attraction would be a delicious revenge, and the very least he deserved after suffering so acutely at her hands.

'Well, Siena? What's it to be?'

Siena hated the smug tone of arrogance in Andreas's voice. She couldn't believe she was even contemplating what she was about to do, but assured herself she could do this. She had to.

In a way it should be easy—she'd merely be reverting to the type she'd played well for as long as she could remember: that of a privileged heiress with nothing more on her mind than the dress she'd wear to the next charity function. No one except for Serena had ever known of her deep hatred of that vacuous world where people routinely stabbed one another in the back to get ahead. Where emotions were so calcified that no reaction was genuine.

Before she could lose her nerve altogether, Siena blurted out, 'I will come with you—right now if you wish.' She saw Andreas's slow smile of triumph curling his mouth and said quickly, before he thought he was about to have everything his way, 'But I have terms for this…if we're to embark on…' Words failed her. She simply could not articulate what he wanted and expected. What she'd agreed to in her head.

He arched a dark brow. 'This affair? Becoming lovers? Companions?'

Siena flushed. The word *companions,* even though he'd

meant it sarcastically, struck her somewhere very deep and secret. They would never be companions.

Feeling agitated, she moved behind her one rickety chair, putting her hands on its back as if it could provide support. She nodded once, jerkily. 'Yes. I have terms.'

Andreas folded his arms across his chest. He looked almost amused, and Siena welcomed this as it made the fire grow in her belly. He only wanted her for one thing, and she was only exploiting him for his desire.

Baldly she declared, 'I want money.' And then she winced inwardly. She'd been brought up to be the ultimate society diplomat, yet here with this man she regressed to someone barely able to string a sentence together. She was too raw around him. She couldn't call up that fake polite veneer if her life depended on it.

As Andreas registered Siena's words something dark solidified in his gut. He should have expected this. A woman like Siena DePiero would never come for free. She would expect him to pay handsomely for the privilege of bedding her. As much as he'd paid for touching her in the first place.

Disgust evident in his voice, he said coolly, 'I've never paid for a woman in my life and I'm not about to start now.'

Siena went as pale as parchment and Andreas had to curb the urge to sneer. *How* could she look so vulnerable when she was effectively standing there asking for payment to be his mistress?

Two spots of colour bloomed then in her cheeks and bizarrely he felt comforted. He could see her struggling with whatever she wanted to say. Finally she got out, 'Those are my terms. I want a sum of money or else I'm not going anywhere—and if you come near me I'll scream the place down.'

His lip curled. 'Just like your neighbours? I didn't see anyone rush to *their* aid.'

Siena flushed more. It made Andreas bite out, 'Just how much money are we talking about?'

He saw Siena swallow and she licked her lips for a second, effortlessly drawing Andreas's eye to those lush pink swells and making that heat in his body intensify. Damn her, but he wanted her—possibly even at a price.

Siena felt sick. But she was too far gone to stop now. She saw the disgust etched in the lines of his starkly handsome face. He would despise her for this, but if he could despise her and still want her that was fine with her.

She named her price. The exact amount of money she would need to ensure Serena's care for a year. If she was going to do this then she had to make it worthwhile. Six months wouldn't be enough to ensure Serena's long-term recovery. A year in therapy and rehabilitation would.

Andreas whistled softly at the amount and Siena saw how his eyes became even icier. He came close again and she fought not to back away, her eyes glued to his. In a bizarre way, now that she'd said it, she found a weight lifting off her shoulders.

'You value yourself very highly.'

Siena burned. Shame came rushing back. Nevertheless, she tossed her head and said defiantly, 'What if I do?'

Andreas looked her up and down and walked around her. Siena could feel his eyes roving over her body.

He said from behind her, 'For that kind of money I think it would be within my rights to sample the goods again before making a decision, don't you? After all, that's just good business sense.'

Siena whirled around indignantly even as heat suffused every particle of her skin, but words got lodged in her throat. She would be the worst kind of hypocrite if she were to lambast him.

She could see that Andreas was livid, with dark colour slashing his cheeks. Before she could stop him he was snaking a hand around her neck and pulling her towards him. She had to go with it or fall off balance completely.

He ground out with disgust, 'I don't pay women for sex. I never have and I never will. It's heinous and disgusting and demoralising. Especially when you want it as much as I do...'

And with that his mouth was on hers and he was obliterating any sense of reality—again. Siena's thoughts were lost in a blaze of heat. Her hands were on Andreas's chest and he'd gathered her closer by curling his arm around her back, arching her into him, where she could feel the burgeoning evidence of his arousal against her belly.

His mouth was forcing hers open, and once that happened she didn't have a chance. His tongue found and tangled with hers, stroking along it, demanding a response. Siena mewled deep in her throat, almost pitifully. Andreas was possessing her with sensual mastery and, far from being disgusted, she found that her arms itched to climb higher, to curl around Andreas's neck, and her tongue was dancing just as hotly as his.

His hand left her waist and travelled up along her ribs. Siena was aware of an intense spiking of anticipation in her blood as her breasts seemed to swell in response, nipples peaking painfully, waiting for his touch.

But Andreas didn't cup her breast as she was suddenly longing for him to do. He stopped just short and pulled his head back. She opened her eyes with an effort, to see his, hot and molten, searing her alive, damning her for her audacity and stubborn denial of their attraction. Her breath was coming in rapid bursts and a million and one things were vying for supremacy in her brain, all of them urging her to pull away—fast. But she couldn't move.

Roughly he said, with disgust lacing his voice again, 'Much as I hate to admit it, I think that perhaps you might just be worth paying an astronomical amount of money to bed.'

He was the one to pull away, leaving Siena feeling adrift and wobbly.

He ran a hand through his hair and looked at her, his mouth taut with condemnation. 'You've learnt your lessons well, De-Piero…in the beds of however many countless lovers you've entertained. Were they the ones to teach you that intoxicating mix of innocence and artless sensuality designed to inflame a man?'

Siena looked at Andreas, stunned at his words. He had no idea. He couldn't tell her gauche responses were all too *real*. And she vowed then that he never would know—however she had to do it.

She fought to find some veneer of composure and said, as cynically as she could, considering she was shaking inwardly like a leaf, 'What else did you expect? A disgraced virgin heiress? This is the twenty-first century—surely you know better than most that virgins are as mythical as the knight on a white horse you just spoke of?'

Andreas stalked away from her, tension emanating from his body in waves. In that moment he hated her, and he hated himself, because he knew he didn't have the strength to just walk away and leave her here. To show her nothing but disdain. If he did he knew she would torment him in dreams for ever. He'd spent five years haunted by her. He had to have her—had to have this closure once and for all. And he despised himself for his weakness.

He looked at Siena and to his chagrin all of his previous thoughts were blasted to smithereens and rendered to dust. Her hair was tousled from his hands, her cheeks were rosy and her lips full and pouting, pink from his kisses. Her chest still rose and fell with uneven breaths and those glorious blue eyes flashed defiantly.

Andreas had the very strong urge to take her right here in his scummy flat—to turn that expression of defiance into something much more acquiescent. And he would if he thought that once would be enough. But he knew with a preternatural prickling of awareness that it wouldn't be enough. He hardened his resolve. She would *not* reduce him to such baseness.

Siena was slowly regaining control of herself. His words rang in her head: *'I don't pay women for sex. I never have and I never will. It's heinous and disgusting and demoralizing.'* The pity of it was she agreed with every word he'd said, and had to admit to respecting him for it.

She finally dragged her almost stupefied gaze from his and walked on very shaky legs back to the door, about to open it—because surely he would be leaving now, for good? Once again Siena didn't like the hollow feeling that thought brought with it.

Before she could open the door, Andreas said ominously, 'What do you think you're doing?'

Siena looked at him, the breath catching in her throat for a moment. 'But you just said you wouldn't pay…'

Andreas's face was like stone, his eyes so dark they looked navy. 'Yes, I did, and I meant it.'

Siena struggled to understand. 'So, what…?'

Andreas crossed his arms. 'There are other means of payment that aren't so…' his lip curled '…obvious.'

Something very betraying kicked in Siena's gut at the thought that he wasn't leaving her. 'What do you mean?'

'Gifts…' He smiled cynically. 'After all, how many women and men have benefited from the largesse of their lovers for aeons? You can do what you like with them when our relationship is over, and if that means converting them into the money you want so badly then you're welcome to do it.'

Suspicious now, and feeling supremely naive because she'd never been in this situation before, she said, 'Gifts…what kind of gifts?'

Andreas's jaw tightened. 'The expensive kind. Jewels. Like the ones you were wearing that night.'

Siena flushed to recall the priceless diamond earrings and necklace her father had presented her with on the evening of that exclusive debutante ball in Paris. They'd belonged to her mother, but had been seized by the authorities along with everything else she had owned.

Siena found herself feeling almost a sense of sick relief that he wouldn't just be handing her a sum of money. The thought of receiving jewellery made what she'd just asked for a little more palatable, despite the fresh shame heaped on top of old shame. Siena comforted herself with the thought that Andreas must have presented plenty of his lovers with tokens of his affection.

'Fine,' she said shakily, barely believing she was agreeing to this. 'I'll accept gifts in lieu of payment.'

Andreas smiled. 'Of course you will.'

Siena had a vision of walking out of here with him and fresh panic galvanised her to ask, a little belatedly, 'What.. what will you expect of me?' She held her breath.

Andreas's smile faded. He suddenly looked harsh, forbidding. Not like a man who wanted her in his bed so badly that he'd sought her out and was prepared to pay her in kind for it.

'Considering the price you've put on yourself…I will expect you to be a very willing, affectionate and inventive lover. I'm a very sexual man, Siena, and I pride myself on satisfying my lovers, so I expect the same in return. Especially from you.'

Siena struggled to hold down a hysterical giggle. *Inventive lover?* He'd be lucky if she managed not to betray her innocence, and she could imagine now with a lancing feeling of pain just how unwelcome *that* knowledge would be. It might even be enough to turn him off altogether. As tempted as Siena was to suddenly blurt out that intimate truth, she thought of her sister and clamped her mouth shut. No going back. Only forward to accept the consequences of her actions, which she'd set in motion five years before.

Not wanting to think of how his assertion that he was 'a very sexual man' had impacted her deep inside, Siena asked rather shakily, 'How long will you want me for?'

Andreas came close to Siena, where she stood near the door, and touched her jaw with his finger, making her shiver with helpless sensation. His eyes travelled up and down her body with dark intent and then rose back to hers.

With almost insulting insouciance he said, 'I think about a week should satisfy my desire for retribution and for you.'

Siena flinched minutely. There was a wealth of insult in his assumption that a week would be enough, and Siena hated that it felt like an insult when it should feel like a reprieve. Anyone could handle anything for a week. Even this.

'A week, then.' Siena assured herself that seven days was a blip in the ocean of her life. She could do it.

Andreas smiled, but it didn't reach those dark eyes. 'I'm already looking forward to this time next week, when the past truly will be in the past. For ever.'

Siena's sense of vulnerability increased. 'The feeling is mutual, believe me.'

After a tense moment Andreas dropped his hand, stepped back and said, 'Get your stuff packed, Siena, and don't leave anything behind.'

'But I'll be coming back here...'

Andreas's mouth thinned as he took in the meagre furnishings with a disdainful glance. 'You won't be returning here. *Ever.*'

Siena opened her mouth to protest and then stopped. Of course he thought she wouldn't be coming back here if she was going to turn his gifts into cash. Andreas didn't know that in a week's time she'd be as broke as she currently was, and she didn't want his razor-sharp brain to pick that up.

Faintly she assured herself that she'd worry about it when the time came and went into the tiny bedroom and pulled out her case. Only a few hours ago she'd had nothing more on her mind than how to get through the evening without keeling over from exhaustion and the constant niggling worry about how she would be able to look after Serena, because they didn't have enough money to continue paying for her psychiatric care.

But now her life had been turned upside down and she had a very unexpected and unwitting benefactor for Serena.

The next week stretched ahead like a term of penal servitude. But, treacherously, Siena felt a shiver of anticipation run through her. Would Andreas expect her to sleep with him tonight? The thought made her heart leap into her throat and her mouth went dry. She wasn't ready—not in a million years.

The thought of all that intense masculinity focused on her was overwhelming when she was so inexperienced. Siena felt numb as she started to pull the paltry collection of clothes from the rail. She didn't even have a wardrobe. She could almost laugh when she thought of the palatial bedroom she'd had all her life, with its medieval four-poster bed. It would have encompassed this entire flat about twice over...

A huge shadow darkened her bedroom door and Andreas rapped out with clear impatience, 'Actually, you can leave everything here. Unless there's something of sentimental value. I'll be supplying you with a new wardrobe.'

Siena just looked at Andreas. She saw an austerely handsome man, eager to get out of this hole of a place and take her with him so that he could mould her into what he wanted. He was so sure of himself now—a Titan of industry, used to having what he wanted when he wanted.

Siena didn't doubt that most of the women in Andreas's life were only too happy to comply with his demands, and she had to quash the dart of something dark at the thought of those women. Dismay gripped her. It wasn't jealousy. It couldn't be jealousy. She hated this man for what he was doing and what he'd become—he was welcome to his hordes of satisfied lovers.

Self-derision that she could allow this to happen to her and the knowledge that she had no choice because this was her only hope to help Serena made Siena's spine straighten. Tersely she bit out, 'Give me five minutes.'

CHAPTER FOUR

'WHAT WILL HAPPEN to my flat?'

Siena was trying not to notice Andreas's big hands on the steering wheel of his car, the way he handled it with such lazy confidence. Of course his car hadn't been on blocks when they'd gone outside. The young kid had been watching it like a hawk and had stared at Andreas as if he was a god.

Siena didn't know how to drive. Her father hadn't deemed it necessary. Why would she need to drive if she was going to be chauffeur-driven everywhere?

Sounding crisp, Andreas replied, 'I'll have my assistant settle up with your landlord. She can also inform your employers that you won't be coming back.'

Siena's hands tightened in her lap. In a way it was karma. She'd lost him his job and now he was losing her hers. Just like that. With a mere click of his fingers, Andreas was changing her life and ripping her very new independence out from under her feet. If she only had herself to worry about she wouldn't be here now, she assured herself inwardly, and hated the tiny seed of doubt that even then she could have held out against Andreas's will, or the guilt she felt.

She wondered what Andreas would have done if he'd known that she couldn't care less for his fortune? That his money wasn't for her at all? But she was forgetting that this man didn't care. Just as the younger man from five years ago hadn't cared. He'd only wanted her because it had been a coup to seduce one of the untouchable debutantes; their supposed virtue had been more prized and guarded than a priceless heirloom in a museum.

Except that virtue had been a myth. Siena had known all too well just how *touchable* the vast majority of her fellow debs had been. They'd looked innocent and pure, but had been anything but. She could recall with vivid clarity, how one of the girls—a princess from a small but insanely wealthy European principality—had boasted about seducing the porter who had brought her bags up to her room while her mother had slept in a drug-fuelled haze in the next room. She'd threatened the man with losing his job if he told anyone.

Siena's mouth hadn't dropped open—but only because her own sister had told her far more hair-raising stories than that, and had inevitably been a main participant when she'd been a debutante.

That evening she'd managed to escape from her father and had tried to find Andreas, to explain why she'd lied, hating herself for the awful falsehood. She'd explored an area reserved for staff only, and had come to an abrupt halt outside a half-open door when she'd heard a newly familiar voice saying heatedly, 'If I'd known how poisonous she was I'd never have touched her.'

A voice had pointed out coldly, 'You've done it now, Xenakis. You shouldn't have touched her in any case. Do you really think you would ever have had a chance with someone like her? She'll be married within a couple of years to one of those pale-faced pretty boys in that ballroom, or to some old relic of medieval Italian royalty.'

Andreas had said bitterly, 'I only kissed her because she was looking at me as if I was her last supper—'

The other voice came again, harder now. 'Don't be such a fool Xenakis. She seduced you because like every other spoilt

brat in there she was bored—and you were game. Do you seriously think she hasn't already got a string of lovers to her
name? Those girls are not the innocents they seem. They're
hardened and experienced.'

Siena had barely been breathing by then, her back all but
flattened to the wall by the door. She'd heard Andreas emit
an expletive and then she'd heard footsteps and fled, unable to
countenance offering up an apology after that character assas-
sination—after hearing his words, *'I only kissed her because
she was looking at me as if I was her last supper.'*

The following morning Siena had woken early and felt
stifled in her opulent bedroom. She'd dressed in jeans and
a loose sweatshirt and had sneaked out through the lobby at
dawn, with a baseball cap on her head in case she saw anyone
she knew. She'd craved air and space—time to think about
what had happened.

That searing conversation she'd overheard had been rever-
berating in her head and she had run smack into a stone wall.
Except it hadn't been a wall. It had been Andreas, standing
beside a motorbike, in the act of putting on a helmet. Siena's
baseball cap had fallen off, and she'd felt her long hair tumble
around her shoulders, but shock had kept her rigid. In the cold
light of day, in a black leather jacket and jeans, he'd looked
dark and menacing. But she'd been captivated by his black
eye and swollen jaw.

Startled recognition had turned to blistering anger. 'Don't
look so shocked, sweetheart. Don't you recognise the work
of your father's men? Don't you know they did this to avenge
your honour?'

Siena had felt nauseous, and had realised why his voice
had sounded so thick the previous evening. She should have
known. Hadn't her father done the same thing, and worse, to
her half-brother—his own son?

'I—' she'd started, but Andreas had cut her off with a slash of his hand through the air.

'I don't want to hear it. As much as I hate you right now, I hate myself more for being stupid enough to get caught. You know I've lost my job? I'll be lucky to get work cleaning toilets in a camping site after this…'

He'd burnt her up and down with a scathing look.

'I'd love to say that what we shared was worth it, but the only thing that would have made it remotely worth it is if you'd stopped acting the innocent and let me take you up against the wall of that dressing room as I wanted to. *Then* your father might not have caught us in the act.'

The crudeness of his words—the very confirmation that all the time she'd been quivering and shivering with burgeoning need, half scared to death, he'd assumed she was putting on some sort of an act and had wanted to take her standing up against the wall—had frozen Siena inside. Not to mention the excoriating knowledge that he'd merely made the most of an opportunity, and she'd all but thrown herself at him like some kind of sex-crazed groupie.

He'd taken her chin in his fingers, holding her tight enough to hurt, and he'd said, 'As the French say, *au revoir,* Siena De-Piero. Because some day our paths will cross again. You can be sure of that.'

He'd let her go, looked at her and uttered an expletive. With that he'd put on his helmet, swung his leg over the powerful bike and with a roar of the throttle had left her standing there, staring after him as if she'd been turned to stone.

The streets of London at night made Siena's memories fade. But the tangible anger she'd felt from Andreas that day would never fade.

'We're here.'

Siena looked to see that they were indeed pulling up outside

Andreas's apartment. Butterflies erupted in her belly. It felt as if aeons had passed since she'd been there already that evening.

The same young man who had parked the car earlier appeared to open her door. Siena was relieved, not wanting to touch Andreas. He was waiting as she emerged from the car with her one case in his hand. She couldn't stop him putting a hand to her back as he guided her into the apartment block. Futile anger burned down low inside her at being so vulnerable to this man…

Andreas was very aware of Siena's pale and tightly drawn features as they stood in the lift. He held her pathetically small case in his hand and had to quash the dart of something that felt ridiculously like pity at the knowledge that this was all she possessed now, when she had been one of the most privileged women in Europe. He reminded himself that this woman was one of the most invulnerable on the planet. She'd contrived every single moment of that evening in Paris, and when it had come to it she'd saved her own pretty neck.

Back in that grotty flat, when she'd asked how long this would last, Andreas had been about to say a month until he'd stopped himself. He'd never spent longer than a week with a lover, finding that he invariably needed his space or grew bored. So to find himself automatically assuming he'd need a *month* was unprecedented. He wanted Siena with a hunger that bordered uncomfortably on the obsessional, but there was no way she was going to turn out to be any different from his other lovers.

But, a snide inner voice pointed out, this was already different, because he was bringing her back to his apartment without even thinking about it. He'd never lived with a lover before. He'd always instinctively avoided that cloying intimacy. It made him feel claustrophobic. Andreas cursed himself now and wondered why he hadn't automatically decided to put Siena in a suite in a hotel, rather than bring her to his place. He didn't want to investigate his adverse gut reaction to that idea, when it was exactly what he *should* be doing.

Andreas hated that she was already making him question his motives and impulses. It made him think of dark, tragic memories and feelings of suffocation.

Before Andreas had left his home town at the age of seventeen he'd had a best friend who had been planning on leaving with Andreas. They were going to make something of themselves—*make a difference.* But that final summer his friend had fallen for a local girl and had become a slave to his emotions, telling Andreas he no longer wanted to travel or achieve anything special. He just wanted to settle down. Andreas had been incapable of changing his mind, and he'd watched his smart, ambitious friend throw away his hopes and dreams.

When his friend had found his girlfriend in bed with someone else he'd been so distraught that he'd killed himself. Andreas had been deeply affected by this awful violence. By the way someone could lose themselves so completely and invest so much in another person. *For love.* When that love hadn't even been reciprocated.

Andreas's own father had achieved a scholarship to a university in Athens—the first in his family to do so. But before he could go he'd met and fallen in love with Andreas's mother. She'd become pregnant and his father had decided to stay and get married, giving up his chance to study medicine.

Andreas had always been aware of his father's missed chance at another life. And after witnessing his friend's descent into horrific tragedy he'd been more determined than ever to leave. He had vowed never to let himself be sidetracked by *feelings.*

And he hadn't… Until he'd had far too close a brush with disaster in Paris, when he'd lost himself for a moment with a blonde seductress who had blown hot and then colder than the Arctic. She'd been a necessary wake-up call. A startling reminder of what was important. Not to get side-tracked.

Andreas reassured himself that this time things were different. When the lift stopped and the doors opened a rush of anticipaton and pleasure seized him, washing aside all his doubts. Siena DePiero was here and that was all he needed to know. Having her anywhere but close to him was not an option.

He'd been waiting for this moment for a long time—ever since that night, when he'd felt a kind of helpless anger and a sense of betrayal that he never wanted to feel again. Ever since that following morning, when she'd emerged from the hotel like a manifestation of his fantasies, her hair tumbled around her shoulders, backlit against the Paris dawn light. He'd wanted her then—fiercely. Even after what she'd done. It had taken all of his strength to get on his motorcycle and leave her behind.

'This is your room.'

Andreas was standing back to let Siena go into a vast bedroom. She'd just been given a tour of the jaw-dropping apartment. Silently she went in, relieved to hear Andreas say: *'your room'*. It was stunning, decked out in sumptuous but understated dark blues and complementary greys. A king-sized bed dominated the room, and Siena could see a glimpse of a white-tiled *en suite* bathroom and an entrance to another room.

Exploring, she found herself walking through a large dressing alcove to a separate lounge area, with a sofa, chairs, desk and a TV. Effectively she had her own suite.

She turned around to see Andreas leaning with his shoulder against the entrance to the dressing room, his hands in his pockets giving him a rakish air.

'This is...lovely,' she said stiffly, knowing that *lovely* was woefully inadequate in the face of this opulence. She was stunned again at Andreas's world now, and stunned anew to see him in his open-shirted tuxedo and realise that only hours before Andreas Xenakis had still been firmly in her shameful guilt-ridden past, not her tumultuous present.

But he was going to find you sooner or later, an inner voice reminded her.

'I'll arrange for a stylist and a beautician to come tomorrow, to attend to whatever you need.'

To make her beautiful for *him.*

Siena felt light-headed all of a sudden and swayed ever so slightly.

Immediately Andreas was standing straight, alert. 'What is it? Are you hungry?'

Siena beat back the waves of weakness, determined not to show Andreas any vulnerability. She shook her head. 'No. It's nothing. I'm just tired. I'd like to go to bed now.'

Andreas just looked at her for a long moment and then as if deciding something, he stepped back and said, 'By all means, Siena. You're my guest now and you know where everything is. Help yourself to anything you want.'

He backed away, and just before he got to her bedroom door he said softly, 'You should sleep while you can, Siena. You'll need it.'

Siena fought back a fresh wave of light-headedness at hearing him say that and watched as he walked out of the room, closing the bedroom door behind him. Sudden weariness nearly felled her. Her head hurt after everything that had happened. She couldn't take any more in.

Finding her small suitcase, she extracted what she needed and dressed for bed. She couldn't block out the way her weak body rejoiced to sink into expensive bedclothes, and gratefully slipped into what felt like a coma.

Andreas knew he was in the grip of a dream but he couldn't seem to pull himself out of it. He was back in that glittering ballroom in Paris. He could feel the ambition rising up within him to *own* such a place one day. It would be a remarkable achievement for a boy from a small town outside Athens with only the most basic qualifications to his name.

And then, like a camera zooming in for a close-up, all he could see was *her* face. Pure and beautiful. Haughty and cold. Perfect. The white-gold of her hair was in a complicated chignon. Jewels sparkled brilliantly at her neck and ears. Her profile was as regal as any queen. The only thing marring the picture was the blood-red stain of wine that was blooming outwards from her chest and up over her cleavage.

The dream faded and shifted, and now they were in that boutique, surrounded by mannequins in beautiful dresses and sparkling jewels behind locked displays. She was laughing, girlishly and innocently, huge blue eyes sparkling with mischief as she pointed to one of the mannequins and said imperiously, 'I want *that* one!'

Andreas bowed down in a parody of a manservant and she laughed even more, watching as he clambered into the window display to tussle with the mannequin and take off the dress. She was in fits of giggles now, watching him wrestle the stunning dress off the dummy before finally handing it to her with a flourish of triumph.

She curtseyed and said, with a flicker of those black lashes, 'Why, thank you, kind sir.' And then she vanished into the dressing room, pulling velvet folds of material behind her.

There was a fizzing sensation in his blood. Andreas felt buoyant when only minutes ago, surveying the crowd in the ballroom, he'd felt cynical...

And then she was there, in front of him again, and Andreas was falling into eyes so blue it hurt to look at them. And then the hurt became a real pain, and he looked down stupidly, to see a knife sticking out of his belly and blood everywhere.

He looked up and she was smiling cruelly. 'No, I did not ask you to touch me. I would never let someone like you touch me.'

His friend who had died, Spiro, was behind Siena, laughing at him. 'You thought you could remain immune?'

And then Andreas was falling down and down and down...

Andreas woke with a start, clammy with sweat, his heart pounding. He looked down and put a hand to his belly, fully anticipating seeing a knife and blood. But of course there was none. It was a dream. A nightmare.

He'd had that dream for months after he'd left France but not for a long time. He remembered. *Siena.* She was here, in his apartment. His heart speeded up again and he got out of bed, pulling on a pair of boxers. He assured himself that it was just her presence that had precipitated the dream again.

But it had left its cold hand across the back of his neck. He went into the darkened drawing room and poured himself some whisky, downing it in one. He slowly felt himself come back to centre, but was unable to shake the memory of that evening.

Andreas had been duty manager, overseeing the exclusive annual debutante ball, making sure it went without a hitch. He'd viewed all those beautiful spoilt young women with a very jaundiced eye, having heard all sorts of stories about their debauched ways.

Still, he'd barely believed them. They'd all looked so *innocent.* And none more so than the most beautiful of them all: Siena DePiero. He'd noticed that she was always slightly apart from the others, as if not part of their club. And the way her father kept her close at all times. He'd read her aloofness as haughtiness. And then he'd seen the moment when her dinner partner had accidentally spilled red wine all over her pristine white dress. Andreas had clicked into damage limitation mode and smoothly offered to take her to the boutique for a fresh dress.

Her father had been clearly reluctant to let her out of his sight but had had no choice. He wouldn't let his daughter be presented at the ball in a stained gown. And so Andreas had found himself escorting the cool beauty to the boutique, and had been very surprised when she'd confided huskily, 'Please excuse my father's rudeness. He hates any sort of adverse attention.'

Andreas had looked at her, taken aback by this politeness when he'd expected her to ignore him. Shock had cut through his cynicism because she'd looked nervous and blushed under his regard. To his complete embarrassment he'd found his body reacting to her...this very young woman, even though he'd known she wasn't that young. Her eighteenth birthday was the following day, and her father had already organised a brunch party with some of the other debutantes to celebrate.

He'd said something to put her at ease and she'd smiled. He'd almost tripped over his feet. By the time they'd reached the boutique his body had been an inferno of need. Siena had been chattering—albeit hesitantly and charmingly.

In the empty shop the sexual tension between them had mounted, instantaneous and strong enough to make Andreas reel. He'd had lovers by then—quite a few—and thought he knew women. But he'd never felt like that before. As if a thunderbolt had connected directly with his insides.

Her artless sensuality and apparent shyness had been at such odds with her cool and haughty beauty. With the reputation that had preceded her. That preceded all the debs every year.

She'd grimaced after a few minutes and looked around the shop, before glancing at a dress on a mannequin in the window. It was fussy-looking, but not far removed from what she wore.

'That's the one my father will approve of.'

She'd sounded so resigned and disappointed that Andreas had inexplicably wanted to see her smile again. He'd hammed it up, extricating the dummy from the dress. And he'd made her laugh.

Then she'd disappeared into the dressing room and Andreas had found every muscle in his body locked tight as he thought of her in a state of undress, fantasising about hauling back the curtain, pulling down his trousers, wrapping her legs around his hips and taking her there and then, against the wall…

And then she'd emerged and his blood had left his brain completely. She'd turned around and showed him a bare back, asking with a shy look over her shoulder, 'Can you do me up?'

To this day Andreas wasn't sure how he'd done it without pulling that dress down and off completely. But he hadn't. She'd turned round and some of her hair had been coming loose. He'd reached out and tucked one golden strand behind her ear and she'd blurted out, 'What's your name?'

Andreas had looked at her and said, 'Andreas Xenakis.'

She'd repeated his name and it had sounded impossibly sexy with her slight Italian accent. 'Andreas.'

And then all Andreas could remember was *heat* and *need*. His mouth had been on hers and she'd been clinging to him, moaning softly, sighing into his mouth, her tongue making a shy foray against his, making him so hard…

Andreas's mind snapped back to the present. He was holding his glass so tightly in his hand he had to relax for fear of shattering it. He grimaced at his body's rampant response just at the memory of what had happened and willed himself to cool down.

He looked out at the millionaire's view of London he could afford now. A far cry from his roots and from painful memories of lives wasted. His mouth twisted. *Wasted because of love.* But, strangely, his usual sense of satisfaction deserted him. Because a new desire for satisfaction had superseded it. For a satisfaction that would only come from taking Siena into his bed and sating himself with her.

He'd never forgotten the way she'd changed in an instant that night—from a she-witch, writhing underneath him, begging him to touch her and kiss her all over, to pushing him off as if his touch burnt her. The way she'd sprung up, holding her dress against her, looking at him accusingly. He'd only realised then that there was someone else in the room. Her father. Looking at him with those cold eyes, as if he were a piece of scum.

The dream and the memory made Andreas shiver. Because it reminded him of how duped he'd been that night. How, despite his better instincts, he'd let himself believe that Siena had really been that giggling, shy, artlessly sexy girl. And, worst of all, how she'd made him want to believe that girl existed.

He should have known better. He of all people. As soon as he'd started working in the city of Athens his looks had attracted a certain kind of sexually mature and confident woman. Inevitably wealthy. They'd offered him money, or promotion, and had laughed at his proud refusal to get help via their beds. One had mocked him. 'Oh, Andreas, one day that hubris will get you into trouble. You'll fall for a pretty girl who pretends not to be as cold and hard as the rest of us.'

And he had. He'd fallen hard. In front of Siena and her father that night. In all honesty Andreas hadn't truly become so cynical yet that he'd believed someone as young as Siena could be so malicious and calculating. But he'd watched her transform from shy sex kitten to a cold bitch. Colder than any of those other women he'd known. And just like that he'd grown his cynical outer skin and his heart had hardened in his chest.

Since then he'd surrounded himself with the kind of women who populated the world he now inhabited. The kind who were sexually experienced and worldly-wise. He had no time for women who played games or who pretended they were something they weren't. And he would never, *ever,* believe in the myth of sweet innocence again.

A flare of panic in his gut propelled Andreas out of the drawing room, setting down his glass as he did so. He went to Siena's bedroom door and opened it silently. It took a second for his eyes to adjust to the dimmer light, and when it did and he saw the shape on the bed his heart slowed. Relief made a mockery of all of his assurances that he was in control but he pushed it aside.

For a second he'd thought it part of the dream. That she wasn't really here. That he was still looking for her.

He found himself standing by her bed and looking down. She was on her back, hair spread out around her head, breathing softly, dressed only in a T-shirt. Her breasts were two firm swells that had the blood rushing to Andreas's groin *again*.

Triumph was heady. She was here. She would be his.

Andreas knew that if her father's business hadn't imploded the way it had he would have been equally determined to get to her, but it would have been much harder to get close.

In the dim light he could see dark shadows under her eyes and he frowned. She looked tired and he felt his chest constrict. Just then she moved slightly, making him tense. As she settled she snored softly. Andreas found his mouth tipping up at this most incongruous sound from one so perfect.

Then he remembered the way she'd asked for money and the smile faded. He had to remember who she was, how she had fooled him so easily into thinking she was something she was not. He'd already learnt his lesson and he wasn't about to repeat his mistake.

The following evening Siena was standing at the window of the main living area in Andreas's palatial apartment. She turned her back on the evocative dusky view of London's skyline and sighed. She couldn't be more removed from the hovel of a flat she'd been living in. But as much as she'd hated it, on

some perverse level she'd loved it because it had been sym-
bolic of her freedom.

And now once again she was incarcerated in a gilded
prison. Andreas had already gone to work when she'd woken
up that morning, and she'd been relieved not to have to deal
with him when she still felt dizzy with how fast things had
moved. He'd left a curt note, informing her that it was his
housekeeper's day off but she must help herself to whatever
she wanted, and that a stylist and a beautician would be arriving later that morning.

Sure enough, a couple of hours later two scarily efficient-
looking women had arrived, and within hours Siena had been
waxed, buffed and polished. She now had a dressing room
full of clothes, ranging from casual right up to *haute couture.* Not to mention cosmetics, accessories and lingerie so
delicate and decadent it made her blush. And shoes—a whole
wall of shoes alone.

The sheer extravangance had stunned Siena. Her father had
been extremely tight with his money, so while she and Serena
had always been decked out in the most exclusive designs it
had been to perpetuate an image—nothing more.

Andreas had called a short while before and informed her
that there should be some beef in the fridge. He'd instructed
her to put it in the oven so they could eat it when he returned
to the apartment. Siena had just spent a fruitless half-hour
trying to figure out which furturistic-looking steel appliance
was the oven, to no avail.

She went back into the kitchen now, to try again, and started
to go hot with embarrassment at her pathetic failing when she
still couldn't figure it out. Her father had forbidden Siena and
her sister ever to go near the kitchen of the *palazzo,* considering it a sign of a lack of class should either of his daughters
ever know its ins and outs.

Before Siena had a chance to explore further she heard the

apartment door open and close and distinctive strong foot-falls. She tensed and knew Andreas had to be in the door-way, looking at her. She turned around slowly and fought to hide her reaction to seeing him in the flesh again, dressed in a dark suit. His sheer good looks and charisma reached out to grab her by the throat. She could feel her body respond-ing, as if it had been plugged into an energy source coming directly from him to her.

Siena retreated into attack to disguise her discomfiture. She lifted her chin and crossed her arms. 'I didn't put the beef in the oven because I refuse to be your housekeeper.'

Andreas regarded her from the doorway. Siena noticed that his jaw was darkly stubbled in the soft light. He was so in-tensely masculine and her blood jumped in response.

'Well, then,' he said with deceptive lightness as he came further into the room, his hair gleaming under the lights, 'I hope you had a decent lunch today. Because I refuse to be your chef just because you can't be bothered to take something out of the fridge and put it in the oven.'

At that moment Siena felt an absurd rush of self-pity. She was actually starving, because she'd only had a sandwich ear-lier, but she clamped her mouth shut because she knew she was acting abominably. And if she had no intention of telling him why then she had no one to blame but herself. She would spend all day tomorrow working out where the blasted oven was and how to work it even if it killed her.

Lying through her teeth, and trying desperately not to look at the succulent lump of meat he was taking out of the fridge, Siena said loftily, 'I'm not hungry anyway. In fact I'm quite tired. It's been a long day. I'm going to go to my room, if you have no objections.'

Andreas looked up from his ministrations and said easily, 'Oh, I object all right. I think you could do with being forced to watch me eat after your pettish spoilt behaviour, but the expression on your face might put me off my food.'

He went on coolly. 'As it happens I have some work to continue here this evening...so feel free to entertain yourself. You don't have to confine yourself to your room Siena, like some kind of martyr.'

She turned and walked out, not liking the way Andreas was dealing with preparing himself dinner so dextrously. It caused something to flutter deep inside her. She didn't like these little signs that Andreas couldn't be boxed away so neatly.

She was about to go towards her room when she found herself seeking out the more informal sitting area that Andreas had shown her the previous evening. She forced herself to relax in front of the TV, even though she really wanted to escape to her room and avoid any more contact with Andreas.

A short time later Andreas gave up any attempt to work. It was impossible when he knew that Siena was somewhere nearby. He shook his head again at her spoilt behaviour. He didn't know why it had surprised him, but it *had*. It was as if some stubborn part of him was still clinging onto the false image of that sweet girl in Paris, before she'd morphed into the spoilt heiress.

He got up and put his cleared dinner plate in the dishwasher in the kitchen, noticing as he did that nothing else had been touched. His mouth flattened into a hard line at this further evidence of Siena's stubborness. She was too proud for her own good. He walked back out and stopped when he heard the faint sound of canned laughter. He followed the sound and found Siena curled up on the couch, fast asleep. Her lashes cast long dark shadows on her cheeks.

Absently Andreas found the remote and switched the TV show off. Siena stirred but didn't wake. He'd been blocking out how it had felt to see her in his kitchen when he'd come home earlier. Dressed in softly worn jeans and a T-shirt. Hair in a ponytail. Bare feet. He wasn't sure what he'd expected but it hadn't been that. He wasn't used to women dressing down, but told himself that she was obviously making a petty point, refusing to make an effort for him.

He knew Siena had seen the beautician, and inevitably his mind wandered to the parts of her body that would be sleek, smooth. He hadn't noticed any discernible physical difference but then, he reminded himself cynically, it was hard to improve on perfection. And even as she was now, asleep on a couch in jeans and a T-shirt, she *was* perfection.

Andreas saw her hands now and bent down. They looked softer already, and he could see that her bitten nails had been cleaned up, but they had been filed very short. He felt that constriction in his chest again at noticing that.

And then suddenly she was awake, looking up at him with those huge startling blue eyes. For a moment something crackled between them, alive and powerful. And then he saw Siena register where she was and with whom. The way she grew tense and her eyes became wary. He straightened up.

Siena struggled to a sitting position, more than discomfited to find Andreas watching her so coolly while she slept. 'What time is it?' Her voice felt scratchy.

He flicked a glance at his watch. 'After midnight.'

Siena stood up and only realised then how close she was to Andreas, and how tall he was when she was in bare feet. 'I should go to bed.'

'Yes,' he observed. 'You seem to be extremely tired. It must have been all that pampering and choosing dresses today.'

Siena was about to protest at the unfairness of his attack, and inform him of just how hard she had been working, but the words died in her throat. He was too close all of a sudden, those dark navy eyes looking at her and reminding her of another time when they'd stood so close and she'd breathed, *'Andreas...'*

She moved back suddenly, but forgot about the couch behind her and felt herself falling back. With the reflexes of a panther Andreas reached out and circled her waist with his hands, hauling her against him.

The breath whooshed out of Siena's mouth. Her hands were on his chest and he felt hot to the touch even through his shirt. 'What...' Her mouth went dry at the thought that he might kiss her. 'What are you doing?'

'What I'm doing, Siena, is...' He stopped and the moment stretched between them.

Siena fancied she could hear both their hearts beating in unison. In that moment she wanted him with a sudden fierce longing deep in her abdomen. She was mesmerised by his mouth. She wanted him to kiss her. And that knowledge burned inside her...

'...letting you go to bed.'

CHAPTER FIVE

ANDREAS HAD PUT Siena away from him before she'd realised what he was doing and instantly she felt foolish. She blushed and he raised a brow.

'That really is some skill—to be able to blush at will. But you forget that it's wasted on me, Siena. I'm a sure thing. You don't have to pretend with me.'

Siena's betraying flush increased—with anger now. 'That's good to know. I won't waste my energy, then.'

She whirled around to leave but was caught when Andreas reached out to take her hand. Electricity shot up her arm. She looked back warily.

'Actually, I have something for you. Come with me.'

Curious, Siena followed Andreas into his huge dimly lit study. It was a beautiful room, very masculine, with floor-to-ceiling shelves that heaved with books. He had the latest high-spec computers and printers.

He'd gone to a picture in the corner and pulled it out from the wall to reveal that it hid a safe. He entered the combination and pulled out a long velvet box. He came over and opened it, so that Siena could see that it was a stunningly simple yet obviously very expensive diamond bracelet.

Her heart thumped once, hard, and she felt a little sick. Andreas was taking it out and reaching for her wrist so that he could put it on. He said coolly, 'You've been here for one night already. I don't see why I can't reward you.'

Feeling very prickly, and not liking the way the cool platinum and stones sat against her pale wrist, winking brilliantly, Siena said acerbically, 'You don't have to reward me as if I'm a child, Andreas.'

He dropped her wrist and looked at her, his eyes turning dark. 'I know you're not a child, Siena. I'm rewarding you because you asked me to. Tomorrow evening we are going to a charity function in town…tonight will be the last night you sleep alone.'

Trepidation and fear were immediate. The thought of being seen and recognised, having people point and whisper about the disgraced DePieros… But Siena wouldn't let Andreas see how much it terrified her, or let him see how even more terrifying she found the thought that this time tomorrow night she would be in his bed…

Siena backed away. 'I can't wait.'

She'd almost got to the door when Andreas called her name again. She took a deep breath and turned around.

'I've arranged for one of London's top jewellers to come to the apartment tomorrow morning.' His jaw tightened. 'You can choose a selection of jewels to your hard little heart's content.'

Siena said nothing. She suddenly looked starkly pale and whirled around, walking quickly out of the room. Andreas watched her go and had to relax his hands because they'd clenched to fists. Once again he wasn't sure what kind of reaction he'd expected, but it hadn't been that.

He had to take a deep breath, and he wondered why he wasn't following his base instincts and taking her here and now. Either on the couch earlier, or here in his office. Or following her to her bedroom. She was here. She was his. She was making him pay for it. But he wouldn't do it now. Because she made him feel a little wild and out of control.

She reminded him far too easily of the raw, ambitious young man he'd once been. Desperate to be a part of the world she'd so easily inhabited because he'd believed that if he was, then he'd truly be as far away from stagnating in his home town as he could possibly be. But he'd changed since then. Being forced into exile had made him appreciate his home and where he came from. It had given him a more balanced view.

He might not want to be a part of his family's cosy, settled world, but he respected it and their choices. A tiny voice mocked him, reminding him that sometimes when he went back now he found himself feeling a pang when he saw the interaction between his sisters and their husbands and children. It even made him feel slightly threatened—as if, if he stayed too long, everything he'd worked for would disappear and he'd become that young man again, with nothing to his name.

He would not let Siena bring back those memories or reduce him to such baseness. She'd done it once before, before he'd even realised what was happening, and she'd torn his world apart.

No, he would be urbane and civilised—all the things he'd become since he'd stood before her in Paris and been made to feel utterly helpless, at the mercy of the huge emotions seething inside his gut. She didn't have that power over him any more and she never would.

Back in her room, Siena struggled to get the diamond bracelet off but refused to go and ask Andreas for help. She was far too volatile when in close proximity to him. Finally it sprang free and Siena put it down with a kind of fascinated horror. He'd given her a diamond bracelet—just like that. Tomorrow he'd be giving her a lot more. And tomorrow night…

Siena sank back down onto the end of the bed and crossed her arms over her belly.

She wanted to hate Andreas for this…but she had no real

reason to hate him. So he'd used her five years ago, when she'd all but thrown herself at him…? What young red-blooded man wouldn't have done the same? It wasn't his fault it had meant nothing to him. She was the one who had imbued the situation with a silly fantasy that something special had happened between them. Had he deserved to lose his job and be beaten up over it? *No.*

She shivered when she thought of that young beaten man, getting on his bike to ride away that dawn morning, and the man he'd become now. For a second that morning, despite his anger, Siena had had a fantasy of getting on the back of that bike with him and fleeing into the dawning light. If she hadn't had to think of her sister she might well have done it.

Siena knew very well that if Andreas hadn't stopped kissing her the other night in her flat he would have had her there and then, realised that she was woefully inexperienced, and most likely walked away without a backward glance, having satisfied his curiosity and his desire for revenge. Treacherously, that thought didn't fill her with the kind of relief it ought to.

What happened to her when he touched her was scary. It was as if he short-circuited her ability to think rationally. When she'd woken on the couch earlier and found him staring at her she'd reacted viscerally: her blood humming and her body coming alive. There hadn't been a moment's hesitation in that acceptance. And then she'd realised where she was and why and reality had come tumbling back…

Andreas's restraint towards her told her that he was in far more control of this situation than she was. The thought of going out in public…the thought of Andreas making love to her… Siena would have to call on that well-worn icy public persona—the one her father had so approved of because it made her seem untouchable and aloof. Desirable. Unattainable.

She clenched her hands to fists. The only problem was,

she was all too attainable. The minute Andreas touched her *aloof* and *icy* went out of the window to be replaced with heat and insanity.

Much to Siena's relief, when she woke and went exploring in the morning there was no sign of Andreas initially—but her skin prickled with that preternatural awareness that told her he was somewhere in the apartment. She figured he might be in his study, and made sure to avoid going near it.

To her added relief there was an array of breakfast things left out in the kitchen, but she didn't like the way her belly swooped at the thought that he'd done this for her. She poured herself some coffee, which was still hot, and took a croissant with some preserves over to the table and sat down.

'Nice of you to join the land of the living. I was beginning to think I might need a bucket of cold water to wake you.'

Siena looked up and nearly choked on her croissant. She hadn't even heard him coming in, and to see him dressed in jeans and a dark polo shirt moulded to his impressive chest was sending tendrils of sensation through every vein in her body.

She swallowed with difficulty, but before she could say anything Andreas was looking at his watch and saying, with not a little acerbity, 'Well, it *is* ten a.m., I expect this is relatively early for you?'

Siena fought down a wave of hurt as she thought of how hard she'd been working for the last few months. Usually by now she'd have done half a day's work. But of course he was referring to her previous life. In fact she'd always been an early riser, up before anyone else. What she wasn't used to, however, was the current exhaustion she was feeling, thanks to the unaccustomed hard work. And that made her angry at herself for being so weak.

She kept all of this hidden and said to Andreas sweetly,

'Well, I'd hate to disappoint you. Tomorrow I can make it midday, if you like?'

He prowled closer, after helping himself to more coffee, and said, 'I'd like it very much if we were in bed together till one o'clock.'

It took a monumental effort not to react to his provocative statement. He was so *audacious*. He sat down at the table, long legs stretched out, far too close to Siena's. She fought the urge to move her own legs.

'Yes, well, I can't imagine you neglecting your business to that level.' After all, she knew well how her father had consistently relegated his children to the periphery, only to be trotted out for social situations.

She looked away from that far too provocatively close rangy body and concentrated on eating the croissant.

'Don't worry,' Andreas commented drily, 'my business is doing just fine.'

Siena flashed back, 'At the expense of all those poor people who are losing their jobs just because of your insatiable ambition.'

Andreas's eyes narrowed on her and Siena cursed herself. Now she'd exposed herself as having followed his progress.

'So you read the papers? I would have thought that you should know better than to believe everything you read in print. And since when have you been concerned with the *poor people?*'

There was ice in his tone, but also something more ambiguous that sounded like injured pride, and Siena felt momentarily confused. A sliver of doubt pierced her. Weren't those stories true?

Andreas uncoiled his tall length, and stood up, going to the sink, where he washed out his cup—a small domestic gesture that surprised Siena.

He turned and said, 'The jeweller will be here shortly.'

He'd walked out before Siena could respond, and she watched his broad back and tall body disappear, radiating tension. She felt wrong-footed. As if she should apologise!

Siena took her things to the sink, where she washed up perfunctorily and thought churlishly that at least she could figure out the taps. Just as she was turning to leave an older lady walked in, smiling brightly. 'Morning, dear! You must be Ms DePiero. I'm Mrs Bright, the housekeeper.'

Siena smiled awkwardly and said, 'Please call me Siena...'

As accomplished as she was in social situations, Siena was an innately shy person and came forward faltering slightly. The older woman met her halfway and took her hand in a warm handshake, smiling broadly. Siena liked her immediately and smiled back.

Siena wisely took the opportunity to ask Mrs Bright about the kitchen, and liked the woman even more when her eyes rolled up to heaven and she said in a broad Scots accent, 'I thought I'd need a degree in rocket science to figure it all out, but it's actually very simple once you know.'

When Siena explained about the previous evening Mrs Bright said conspiratorially, 'Don't worry, pet. I couldn't work out which one was the oven either at first.'

Unbeknown to the two women, who were now bent down by the oven, Andreas had come back to the doorway. He listened for a moment and then said abruptly, 'The jeweller is here, Siena.'

The two women turned around and he could see the dull flush climbing up Siena's neck. He flashed back to the previous evening, when he'd found her looking so defiant in the kitchen, refusing to put the meat in the oven.

She said thank you to the housekeeper and walked over to him. Andreas caught her arm just as she was about to pass and said, *sotto voce,* 'You didn't know where the oven was. Why didn't you just tell me?'

He could see Siena's throat work, saw that flush climb higher, and felt curiously unsteady on his feet.

Eventually she bit out, avoiding his eye, 'I thought you'd find it funny.'

Andreas didn't find it funny in the least. He said, 'You could have told me, Siena. I'm not an ogre.'

Siena was trembling by the time they got to the drawing room, where Andreas had directed her. Two small men were waiting for them, with lots of cases and boxes around them and an array of jewels laid out on a table before them. Siena noticed a security guard in the corner of the room. She felt sick.

Later that evening Siena was waiting for Andreas. He'd gone to his office that morning after the jewellery show-and-tell, and she'd been left with a small ransom's worth of jewellery. A special safe had been installed in Andreas's office just for her use.

She still felt jittery. Andreas had insisted that to fully appreciate whether or not the jewellery was suitable Siena should get changed into an evening gown. He'd led her, protesting, into her dressing room and picked out a long black strapless dress.

'Put this on.'

Siena had hissed, 'I will not. Don't be so ridiculous. I'll know perfectly well what will suit me and what won't.'

'Well, seeing as I'm paying for the privilege of your company this week, I'd like to see you try out the jewellery in more suitable garb than jeans and a T-shirt—which, by the way, I expect to be in the bin by the end of today.'

'You're just doing this to humiliate me.' Siena had crossed her arms mulishly and glared at Andreas, who had looked back, supremely relaxed.

'Put the dress on, Siena, and put your hair up. Or I'll do it for you. I'll give you five minutes.'

With that chilling command he'd turned and walked out of

the room. Siena had fumed and resolved to do no such thing. But then an image of Andreas, striding back into her room and bodily divesting her of her jeans and T-shirt, had made her go hot. He wouldn't, she'd assured herself. But a small voice had sniggered in her head. *Of course he would.*

Gritting her teeth and repeating her mantra—*one week, one week*—Siena folded her jeans and T-shirt into her small suitcase, with no intention of following his autocratic command to throw them away, and slipped on the dress. It was simple in the way that only the best designer dresses could be, and beautifully made. Gathered under her bust in an Empire line, it flowed in soft silken and chiffon folds to the floor.

The bodice part of it clung to her breasts, making them seem fuller, and was cut in such a way as to enhance her cleavage. Siena had felt naked. Her father would never have allowed her to wear something so revealing…so sensual.

She'd pulled her hair back into a ponytail and returned to the salon barefoot. When the two jewellers had stood up on her return Siena had barely noticed, only aware of the dark blue, heavy-lidded gaze that had travelled down her body with a look so incendiary she'd almost stumbled.

Andreas had taken her hand and pulled her in beside him on a small two-seater couch, his muscular thigh far too close to hers through the flimsy covering of her dress. His arm had moved around her, his fingers grazing the bare skin of her shoulder, drawing small circles, making her breath quicken and awareness pierce her deep inside.

She'd cursed him and tried to move away—only to have him clamp his hand to her waist, pulling her even more firmly against him, so that her breasts had been crushed to his side and she'd been acutely aware of how hard his chest felt. The way his big hand curled possessively around her, fingers grazing her belly.

The jewellery itself had been a blur of glittering golds and diamonds, pearls, sapphires and emeralds. Andreas had picked things out and taken Siena's wrist to slip jewelled bracelets on, before adding them to a growing pile. When he'd put neck-laces around her neck his hands had trailed softly across her bare shoulders, his fingers lightly touching her collarbone. Si-ena's face had flamed. It had felt like such an intimate touch.

She had tried to hold herself as rigidly as possible, aghast at how much it was affecting her to be subjected to what were relatively chaste touches. They'd been under the beady eyes of the jewellers, but Siena had had to remind herself they were being observed.

Losing count of the mounting pile of jewellery, Siena had been ready to scream by the time Andreas had tried a simple platinum and diamond necklace and matching bracelet on her and said, 'Wear this dress and these jewels tonight.'

She had bitten back a retort—a knee-jerk reaction to being dictated to. Her new-found sense of independence had surged forth, but then she'd reminded herself that he'd bought her. Therefore he could have her any which way he wanted. She'd had a very disturbing image of herself, naked, splayed across Andreas's bed, dressed in nothing but all these jewels.

When Andreas had finally declared himself satisfied the other men had started to gather up the remaining jewellery. But Siena had spotted something out of the corner of her eye. A flash of something delicate and golden. Before she could stop herself she'd reached out to touch the necklace, hidden in folds of velvet.

As she'd lifted it out it had become clear that it didn't have the same glittering *wow* factor of the other gems, but it was exquisite: a simple golden chain with a wrought-gold bird-cage detail. The tiny filigree door was open and further up the chain was a bird flying, suspended. Siena's belly had clenched. Something about the bird flying out of its cage had resonated deeply within her.

The senior jeweller had cleared his throat uneasily. 'That's actually not meant to be part of the display we brought today. It was included by accident. It's by a Greek jeweler...'

'Angel Parnassus.' Siena had said, half absently. She knew the famous delicately crafted designs of the renowned jeweler and had always admired them.

'Yes...' the man had confirmed.

'We'll take that too,' Siena had heard Andreas say brusquely.

She'd started to protest, hating that Andreas had witnessed her momentary distraction and vulnerability. She'd looked at him and his eyes had been hard.

'It's a fraction of the price of the earrings you'll wear tonight. Have it if you like it so much, Siena.'

Siena hadn't wanted anything for *herself*, but she'd had no chance to speak. Andreas had already been standing up, shaking hands with the two men, seeing them out, leaving her with the necklace clutched in her hand.

Siena heard a noise now and tensed, her attention brought back to the present. Andreas had arrived a short while before, knocking on her door to check that she was nearly ready. When she'd swallowed the frog in her throat and assured him that she was, he'd disappeared—presumably to get ready himself. Siena was waiting in the drawing room, feeling ridiculously nervous at the thought of the evening ahead. This was a situation she'd never experienced before.

She was wearing the black dress, as decreed by Andreas. But when it had come to the jewels Siena had had a moment of rebellion. Instead of the diamond necklace and bracelet he'd wanted her to wear she'd picked out a bold diamond and sapphire necklace, with a matching cuff bracelet.

Somehow the brashness of the necklace felt like some kind of armour. But then Siena heard a familiar footfall behind her and any illusion of armour went out of the window.

* * *

When Siena turned to face Andreas he felt as if someone had just punched him in the belly. For a second he couldn't breathe. He'd dreamed of her so often like this…as he remembered her… Stunningly beautiful, elegantly aloof. Untouchable in a way that made him ache to touch her.

Her hair was drawn back and up into a high bun, effortlessly simple and yet the epitome of classic grace. Her make-up was understated, perfect. Nothing so brash as red lipstick. She didn't need it. The drama came from her cool blonde perfection.

His eyes narrowed on her necklace and a spurt of something hot went through him. 'You have defied me.'

Siena's chin hitched up minutely. 'You may have all but bought me for a week, but that does not mean I can't exercise some free will.'

Andreas inclined his head and tamped down on the hotness inside him. 'Indeed. That necklace is equally…beautiful.'

He had to admit that it set off her rather understated appearance with just the right amount of *élan*. The thick collar piece was studded with tiny diamonds and it curled around her neck and throat in a sinuous line down to where an enormous sapphire pendant hung against the creamy pale skin of her upper chest. The dark blue of the precious stone inevitably made the lighter blue of her eyes pop out.

Andreas pushed down the niggling vague doubts he'd had all day, ever since he'd overheard the conversation between her and Mrs Bright in the kitchen, when he'd learned that Siena had preferred to appear like a spoilt brat rather than reveal she didn't know where the oven was.

And then her reaction to the jewellery hadn't been the unmitigated greed and glee he'd expected to see. Siena had barely looked at the impressive array of jewellery, and the one thing that had caught her eye had been a simple gold pendant. Exqui-site, yes, but not in the same league as the other jewels at all.

Andreas put such disturbing thoughts out of his head now. She hadn't shown much interest in the jewellery because she would be converting it all into cold hard cash within days. How could he forget that?

More importantly, by tonight all that cool, untouchable beauty would have come undone. She would be bucking against him and begging for release. She would no longer look so pristine. She would be as naked and sated as he in-tended to be. Flushed and marked by his passion.

His blood surged. He put out his hand. 'Come. It's time to go.'

A couple of hours later, after a sumptuous sit-down dinner, Siena was standing at Andreas's side and it felt as if her skin was slowly going on fire. Since he'd taken her hand in his in the apartment to lead her out he hadn't stopped touching her. Even if it was just a hand at the small of her back to guide her into the ultra-luxe Grand Wolfe Hotel, where the charity din-ner banquet was taking place.

For someone who generally shied away from physical con-tact, because she'd never really experienced it growing up, Siena was dismayed at how much her body seemed to gravi-tate towards Andreas's touch. She wished pettily that she could break out in a rash, allergic to his touch.

'Drink?'

She looked at Andreas to see him holding out a glass of champagne. Siena shook her head. After a couple of glasses of wine with dinner, and an aperitif of Prosecco when they'd arrived, her head was feeling woozy enough. Andreas merely shrugged and put the glass back on a passing waiter's tray.

'Uncomfortable?'

Siena looked at Andreas again. For a second she thought

he meant in her dress or shoes, but then she saw the gleam in his eye and thought to herself, *Bastard.* She schooled her expression. 'I'm perfectly comfortable, thank you, considering the level of public interest in seeing who your new mistress is, and the realisation that she is one of the disgraced DePieros.'

Siena knew Andreas had to be aware of the way people had been looking and pointing all evening. The way a hush would fall when she came close, only to spark a flurry of whispers as they passed.

'Don't tell me it's actually *affecting* you? The debutante who so coldly excised a momentary mistake from her life?'

Andreas's voice was mocking and Siena held herself stiffly. She hadn't known just how much it would affect her to be in public again, exposed to people's excoriating judgement, but could she blame them? Even now as she caught someone's eye they looked away hurriedly.

Her voice was cool. 'Why would I deny you your moment of public retribution? No doubt this is highly entertaining for you.'

She turned and looked up into his face properly, making his hand which had been resting on the small of her back fall away. It was a tiny pathetic triumph.

'Perhaps,' she said, 'you should consider taking me to Rome to get the full effect of people's censure? After all, here in London I'm relatively unknown.'

Andreas's eyes flashed and he effortlessly put his arm around her and pulled her tight in against him, making Siena gasp softly. His body was so lean and hard. Like a wall of muscled steel. And against her belly she could feel the potent stirring of his body. Inside she went hot.

'I think it's time we danced.'

Before she could even remember what they'd been talking about Andreas was pulling Siena in his wake onto the dance floor, where other couples were already dancing in the seductively dim light. A very smooth jazz band were playing, but Siena hardly even registered the music as Andreas swung her round and into his arms, holding her close.

Siena tried to pull back in his embrace but it was impossible. His arm was a steel band high across her back and her hand was held high in his, against his chest. Dark blue eyes glittered down into hers and reminded her of the deep blue of the sapphire pendant that swung against her chest, the thought leaving a tart taste in her mouth. But even that couldn't impinge when she was this close to Andreas, breathing his evocative masculine scent deep.

Feeling his body harden even more against hers was rendering her completely defenceless. How could she remain immune to this level of sensual attack? This was his punishment, his revenge, right here on this dance floor. Making her mute with aching need and a burning desire which seemed to writhe within her like a coiled snake. Everything else fell away, and she was suddenly terrified that she wouldn't be able to contain this feeling. It was as if they were enclosed in a bubble, completely separate from everyone around them, even though Siena was dimly aware that Andreas was steering them expertly around the floor.

She'd danced with plenty of men since that debutante ball in Paris, usually propelled into their arms reluctantly by her father, but no dance had ever felt this raw or carnal. Andreas's hand on her back rested against bare skin and she could feel his fingers stroking rhythmically, making her legs weaken and the secret apex between them grow hot and wet.

This went far beyond what she'd felt that evening in Paris, when this same man had aroused her with just a look and a sexy smile. She'd been too young then to truly be able to handle everything he'd aroused within her. Now she knew he'd unleashed a completely alien part of her—a part of her that felt wild and needy, aching for something she'd never known before. She'd always found it so easy to be detached, contained, until she'd met him. And all that was rushing back now.

At that moment Andreas stopped, and Siena realised that the music had also stopped. The air crackled between them and Siena knew with a fatalistic feeling in her belly that this was it.

Eyes locked with hers, Andreas said huskily, 'It's time to go.'

Keeping her hand in his, Andreas swiftly negotiated their way off the dance floor. Siena felt as if she couldn't really breathe. Her skin prickled and felt hot. Her belly was tight. Somehow, magically, someone appeared to hand Siena her wrap, and she took it with both hands, pathetically grateful that Andreas wasn't touching her for just a second.

But then her hand was in his again and he was leading her out into the cool spring air. His car was already waiting by the kerb, its back door held open by a hotel doorman.

Once they were in the car it pulled away smoothly from the glittering hotel.

Andreas said curtly to his driver, 'Tom, some privacy, please.'

Instantly Siena saw the silent glide of the black partition cutting them off from the driver. She looked at Andreas and his eyes glowed in the dim light. He looked feral, wild, and her heart beat wildly in her chest.

'Come here,' he instructed throatily.

CHAPTER SIX

PANIC GRIPPED SIENA. She wasn't ready for this. Threadily she answered, 'No.'

Andreas arched a brow. His voice was deceptively mild. 'No?'

Siena shook her head, and then words were tumbling out. 'Look, you can't just expect that I'm going to—'

But her words were stopped mid-flow when Andreas reached across almost lazily and took her by the waist. He slid her along the seat until their thighs were touching. His hands felt huge around her and her eyes were locked with his. The air around them felt heavy and dense, thick with something Siena didn't really understand.

But when Andreas raised his hands up her body, brushing against the curves of her breasts, and slanted his mouth across hers Siena understood what it was. It was desire, and suddenly she was alive with it. Humming all over. It thickened her blood, forcing it through veins and arteries, pooling low in her pelvis, between her legs.

Her hands had been up, almost in a gesture of self-defence, but now Siena found herself putting them on Andreas's chest, to balance herself when he tugged her forward so that she half lay across him. She couldn't concentrate, couldn't think beyond the hot slide of his mouth against hers, and her mouth opened of its own volition under his.

Their tongues touched and Siena's hands curled into his shirt, bunching it unconsciously, seeking something to hold onto when she felt as if she were falling down and down.

One of Andreas's hands went down to her back and pulled her into him, making her arch against him. She was dimly aware that his other hand had moved up, was undoing her hair so that it fell around her shoulders, sensitising nerve-ends that were already tingling.

The kiss grew hotter. Andreas's tongue stabbed deep. His hand was tangled in her hair now, and he pulled back gently so that he could claim even more access. Siena couldn't hear anything through the blood roaring in her head and ears. When Andreas's mouth left hers she heard a low moan and only seconds later realized it was coming from her.

By then his mouth was trailing hot kisses across her jaw and he was pulling her head back even more, to press his mouth against her throat and down to where she could feel her pulse beat against his tongue.

Siena had the barest sensation of her dress feeling looser before she realised that Andreas had pulled the zip down at the back. He lifted his head and leant back for a moment. Siena tried to force some air into her lungs, but they seized again when she felt him pull down the bodice of her dress to reveal one naked breast.

They were in a cocoon. Siena wasn't even aware of the city streets and lights as they glided through London. They could have been transported to another planet. She was only aware of herself as some very primal feminine being, and of Andreas as her masculine counterpart.

She saw Andreas's head dip down, felt his hot breath feather over an almost painfully tight nipple before his mouth closed around it. Siena sank back against the seat, every bone in her body melting at the exquisite tugging sensation that seemed to connect directly to where a pulse throbbed between her legs.

As if reading her mind, Andreas moved his hand under her dress and up her legs, pushing them apart. She was helpless to resist as he expertly pulled down the bodice of her dress completely and bared her other breast, to which he administered the same torture.

Everything was coalescing within Siena, building to some elusive crescendo of tension. Her hips were rolling and one of her hands was in Andreas's hair, fingers tangling in silken strands as she held him to her breast. Her other hand was clenched tight, and an ache of gigantic proportions was growing between her thighs.

Andreas's long fingers had found her panties and he was tugging them down over her hips. Siena was mindless, wanting Andreas to alleviate this exquisite tension inside her. Her hips lifted and he slid the black lace down her legs, over her feet in their vertiginous heels and off completely.

And then Andreas's mouth left her breast and he straightened up. It took a second for Siena to register that he was just looking at her. Her breasts were bared and throbbing slightly, wet from his mouth and heaving with her laboured breath. Her dress was hiked up almost to her waist and her legs were parted. She saw her flimsy lace panties dangle from his fingers, and then he put them in the pocket of his jacket.

Siena's tongue felt thick. 'What are you doing?'

It was only then that she realised how pristine Andreas looked in his jacket and tie, barely a hair out of place. Far too belatedly she scrabbled with numb hands to pull her dress up over her breasts and down over her thighs.

'I'm making sure there's no delay once we get inside.'

Inside. It was only then that Siena became aware that they were outside his apartment building and the young valet was approaching the door of the car. Siena felt Andreas push her forward slightly, the brush of his fingers against her back as he pulled her zip up. Then he was handing her her wrap and the door was opened.

By the time she was out in the cool air she was incandescent with rage—not only at Andreas, but at herself for being so weak. When Andreas touched her back to guide her into the building she jerked away from him. She all but ran to the door and yanked it open before he could open it for her, making straight for the lift, punching the button with unnecessary force. Andreas was a tall dark presence beside her which she ignored.

When they stepped into the lift Siena moved to one corner and resolutely looked forward. To her absolute horror she could feel heat prickling at the backs of her eyes and her throat tightening. She willed down the emotion which had sprung up with every fibre of her being and swept out of the lift when the doors opened.

When Andreas joined her and opened the apartment door he had barely shut it behind him when she rounded on him, hands curled into fists.

'How *dare* you?'

Andreas looked so cool and composed and Siena was completely undone. Her hair was around her shoulders and she'd never felt more vulnerable.

'How dare I what, Siena? Kiss you?' His mouth twisted. 'How could I *not* have kissed you? Don't you know by now that I have a fatal attraction to your unique brand of remote aloofness?'

Siena could have laughed out loud. She'd never felt less remote or aloof. Right then she hated Andreas with a passion that scared her with its intensity.

She couldn't stop the words tumbling out. 'I hate you.'

'Be careful, Siena,' he mocked, 'Love is just the other side of hate, and we wouldn't want you falling for me, now, would we?'

Siena spluttered. '*Fall* for you? I couldn't think of anything less likely to happen.' Her words fell into a hole inside her and echoed painfully.

Siena lifted her chin, determined to get off that disturbing topic and claw back some control. 'I am not going to be ritually humiliated by you, whenever and wherever it takes your fancy.'

Andreas prowled closer and drew Siena's lace panties from his pocket, holding them up. Siena died a small death.

'It takes two to tango, Siena, and you were with me every second of the way back there. To be honest I hadn't expected you to be a back seat of the car kind of woman.'

Siena lifted her hand to grab her underwear but Andreas snatched them back out of her reach and then deposited the lacy scrap of material back into his pocket. Without realising he'd even moved, Siena found herself with her back against the main door of the apartment, her wrist held high in Andreas's hand, above her head. He was pressing against her and she could feel herself responding to that tall muscular length all over again. The heated insanity of what had happened came back in lurid Technicolor.

'Let me go,' Siena gritted out, desperately afraid of how susceptible she was.

He shook his head and his eyes glowed like dark jewels. 'Never. You're mine now, Siena, until I say so.'

And then he bent his head and his mouth found hers, and when she tried to turn her head away he only brought his free hand to her head and held her there, captive, as he kissed and stroked her weak resistance away with his clever tongue.

Siena was so full of turbulent emotions and sensations that it was almost a relief to give in to the sheer physicality of the moment. Here, with Andreas kissing her like this, she couldn't think. And she didn't want to.

When he finally released her hand she found herself, not pushing him away but clutching his shoulders, before finding that her hand was sneaking underneath his jacket, to push it off.

Their mouths were fused together, tongues a tangle of heated lust, and when Andreas removed his hands so that he could shrug off his jacket Siena sought and found his bow-tie, undoing it so that she could open the top button of his shirt.

In some very dim place she told herself that she had a desire to see him as undone as she felt, but in truth she just had a growing need to see him naked.

Siena felt her zip being pulled down again, and it was almost a relief to have her breasts freed. Andreas's mouth and tongue was a potent memory. She wanted to feel him again. Her hands took his head, guiding him away from her mouth and down…

Only minutes after she'd stood in front of him, vowing she hated him, Andreas's mouth was on her breast and Siena was once again reduced to some writhing wanton. But her mind skittered weakly away from that anomaly.

Siena felt feverish. Her legs were weak. But she couldn't move. Andreas had straightened and was opening his shirt, ripping it off, and Siena's eyes grew huge and round as she took in his olive-skinned magnificence. Not an ounce of fat. All lean muscle. Flat brown nipples enticed her to lean forward and touch with her tongue, exploring his salty taste.

Andreas groaned softly and slid his hand into her hair. After a minute of her mouth torturing him with some pseudo-innocent touch she must have learned somewhere Andreas dragged her head back. Her mouth was open, she was panting slightly, and her eyes were wide and slumberous, pupils dilated. His erection thickened and with an impatient hand he undid his belt and zip, pulling down his trousers and his briefs with them. He had to have Siena *now*. He couldn't even move from this spot. He was aware that he was about to take her exactly as he'd fantasised five years ago, standing up, like some kind of feral animal. But he didn't care.

All he could see was that white-blonde hair tumbled over bare shoulders, her full round breasts, flushed and moist from his touch and his mouth. All he could think about was how her nipples had felt against his tongue—tight and puckered—the way she'd moaned when he touched her there.

Feeling ruthless, Andreas kicked away his clothes. He was naked now, and Siena's eyes grew bigger as she looked down his body, making him throb with a need to be inside her, thrusting up into the tight core of her body, seeking his release. Finally.

Cursing softly, having a flash of clarity at the last moment, Andreas reached down and pulled protection from his jacket, fumbling in a way he hadn't in a long time as he ripped it open and stroked the rubber along his length.

The scent of Siena's arousal hit him like a ton of bricks and, unable to stop himself, he fell to his knees before her, pulling her dress down all the way until it pooled at her feet in a tangle of chiffon and lace. Now she wore only her shoes, and Andreas removed them, hearing her husky, hesitant-sounding entreaty.

'Andreas...'

He ignored it.

His need was too strong to resist.

She was more than he could have ever imagined in his fantasies. Long slender limbs, pale all over. A triangle of blonde curls between her legs. Andreas knelt there and parted her thighs. He could feel her resistance but said gutturally, 'Let me taste you.'

After a second when her legs trembled so lightly he might have imagined it her resistance faltered and Andreas bared her to him, his mouth and tongue seeking and finding her essence, revelling in her sweetly musky smell and taste.

Her hand was in his hair, gripping tightly enough to be

painful, but it only fired him up even more. He could feel his erection strain against its rubber confinement between his legs and knew he couldn't wait. There would be more time to savour her later. But now he had to have her. He had to be buried so deep inside her that he would forget his own name.

Andreas surged up and just managed to catch Siena before she collapsed. He wrapped his arms around her, feeling her back arch into him, her breasts crushed against his chest.

'Wrap your legs around my waist,' he instructed roughly.

Siena put her arms around his neck, and then her legs were wrapped around his waist. Andreas hitched her up and rested her back against the door, so that it would take some of her weight, even though she felt as light as a feather.

Holding her with one arm, he reached down between them and ran his finger along her cleft. *She was so wet.* It nearly undid him there and then. He spread his legs and positioned himself, taking himself in his hand and guiding the head of his erection to those moist folds of flesh.

Andreas forced himself to curb the desire to thrust so far and so deep he'd find instant release. He was more than that. He wouldn't let her do this to him. He found her mouth and braced himself, before thrusting up and into the giving wet clasp of her body.

He felt her open-mouthed gasp of surprise before he registered that he'd felt an impediment to his movement. Sweat broke out on his brow. He drew away and looked at Siena, every nerve and muscle protesting at this interruption.

'What...?'

Siena was pale, and the unmistakable light of shock shone in her eyes. Stripped bare of that hazy pleasure he'd seen a moment ago. He flexed his buttocks and saw her wince as he moved a bit deeper. Her arms tightened around his neck. Andreas felt something cold prickle at his neck. It couldn't be possible... The information simply wouldn't compute...

He spoke out loud. 'You can't be…'

Siena was biting her lip now, and Andreas saw the sheen of moisture in her eyes. It was as if a two-ton lorry had crashed into his chest. He started to withdraw, but as he did he saw that moisture fade and a light of determination come into those glorious eyes.

She tightened her legs around his waist. 'No.' Her voice sounded raw. 'Don't stop.'

It hurt to breathe, but Andreas managed to get out, 'I'll hurt you…if we move—'

'No.' Siena's legs tightened even more. 'We do this. Here. Now. Just the way you said you wanted to five years ago…'

Andreas's brain felt as if it would explode. He was caught between heaven and hell. Siena's musky scent was all around him, her body clasped him, but not in the way he knew it could. He cried out for release.

And there was something so…*determined* about her. The fact that she was still a virgin was too much to process right now.

Andreas gave in. 'Try to relax your muscles…it'll be easier…'

He could see how she concentrated and he felt her body allowing him to go deeper. He all but groaned out loud at the exquisite sensation. She was so tight around him, almost painfully tight.

Moving her slightly, he bent his head and drew one taut nipple into his mouth, rolling it, sucking it back to life. He could feel what it did to Siena when her body relaxed even more, and with an exploratory move Andreas thrust a little higher. She hitched in a breath but he could sense that it wasn't a breath of pain. It was a breath of awareness.

When he lifted his head to look at her again she was not pale any more. She was flushed, biting her lip again. Slowly he withdrew from her body and then thrust back in, going even deeper this time.

Her hips twitched against his. She was breathing heavily now, saying almost against her will, 'I feel so full...'

'I know...just let me...trust me...it'll ease.'

Andreas was surprised he could string a sentence together. His world was reduced to this moment, this woman, this inexorable slide of his body in and out of hers. His passage was becoming easier and sweeter with every second. Siena's head fell back against the door and he could see her eyes closing.

Andreas put his hand to her chin and tugged it down. 'Look at me...Siena.'

She opened her eyes and they were feverish. With a feeling of triumph Andreas felt the ripples of her body around his as the onset of her orgasm approached. Ruthlessly he held his own desperate need for release at bay and pushed her higher and higher, seeing how her eyes widened, her cheeks flushed deep red. Her lips were engorged with blood. Her breasts were flushed, nipples like tight berries.

Somewhere in his head a voice crowed, *She's undone.* But it barely broke through Andreas's single-minded need to drive her over the edge. And when she fell it was spectacular. Her eyes grew even wider. She stopped breathing. Her whole body grew as taut as a string on a bow and then he saw the moment she fell and felt her body clench so tightly around his in waves of spasms that he was helpless except to allow his own release to finally break free.

He could do nothing but close his eyes and bury his head in her breast. Their laboured breathing sounded harsh in the silence of the foyer. His body pulsed within hers minutely. He felt her grip around his neck grow slack as if she couldn't hold on any more.

Eventually Andreas found some strength from somewhere and straightened. Siena was avoiding his eyes now, and she winced slightly as he pulled free and helped her to stand. Their clothes were strewn around them in chaotic abandon, but she still wore the necklace and bracelet.

Andreas had a sudden visceral need to take the jewellery off Siena. It was a reminder that wasn't welcome now. He undid the clasp of the necklace, letting it fall heavily into his hand, and then the bracelet. They clinked together with a hollow sound.

The sound of the jewellery knocking together seemed to resonate deep within Siena. Avoiding looking at Andreas, she bent down to pick up her dress, holding it against her like a very ineffectual shield. Resounding in her head with crystal clarity was the fact that she'd just lost her virginity to this man while standing up, against the door of his apartment.

She could remember the moment when she'd thought he was about to pull away, perhaps to take her into the bedroom. There'd been a look in his eyes that had threatened to shatter something inside her. And then the memory of that dawn morning in Paris, when Andreas had admitted that he'd wanted to take her up against the wall of the dressing room had rushed back.

Siena had seized on it and fought against the pull to make this easier…to be taken to surroundings more conducive for making love for the first time. Because this was not about romance.

She didn't want to think of the deeply disturbing emotion which had surged the moment he'd joined their bodies. That had made her feel weak and tender.

'*Theos,* Siena…' Andreas rasped. 'You were a virgin. Why didn't you tell me?'

She looked at Andreas and paled when she saw the look on his face, relieved to see that he'd pulled on his trousers. She couldn't handle him naked. Desperate to convince him it meant nothing, so that she could consider what it *did* mean in a private space on her own, she shrugged. 'It's no big deal. I was a virgin and now I'm not.'

Andreas's mouth twisted. 'So your father really was going to offer you up to a crusty blue-blooded relic like some virginal sacrifice?'

Siena's chest tightened. That was exactly what he'd planned. 'Yes,' she whispered, her bravado slipping. 'Something like that.'

Andreas cursed and Siena tried to avoid looking at his bare chest. It reminded her of how it had felt, crushed against her breasts.

'You should have told me, Siena...' he grated. 'If I'd even suspected you were innocent I'd have gone slower...been more gentle.'

'I'm fine,' Siena muttered, picking up her shoes, still avoiding looking at Andreas.

The air around them smelled of something unfamiliar but heady. *Sex.* Siena was too overwhelmed even to acknowledge that after the initial pain it had transcended anything she might have imagined.

She saw Andreas's bare feet come into her line of vision and gulped. As his finger tipped up her chin her eyes moved up and took in the fact that his top button was open, revealing that tantalising line of hair which led down— Her gaze landed on his face.

She felt the urge to strike first and said, 'Don't look so shocked just because I was a virgin, Andreas.'

He was angry, eyes blazing now. 'If I'd known I would never have taken you like that...'

'Why?' she taunted. 'It's exactly how you wanted to take me before—I didn't want to deny you the chance to fulfil your fantasy.'

Siena heard the words but wasn't really sure where on earth

the nerve to say them was coming from. She saw Andreas's face turn expressionless, shuttered. He took his hand away and stepped back, making Siena feel bereft.

'You should have a bath. You're likely to be sore.'

Siena was a lot more intimidated by this cool specimen than the anger Andreas had just displayed. The idea that he might have cared enough about her innocence to make it a more pleasurable experience was…

Before she could say anything else that might betray her, Siena fled.

Andreas watched Siena retreat and cursed silently. He'd expected that after making love to her, *finally,* he would be feeling a whole lot more sated and at peace. It was laughable. He'd never felt less sated and at peace. He wanted her again— *now.* Wanted to taste that lush, mutinous mouth, to make her eyes widen with desire again. Wanted to watch her tumble over the edge and feel her body clamp around his with those spasms of orgasm.

Andreas ran a hand through his hair impatiently and then bent to pick up the rest of his own clothes. Under the stinging hot needles of his shower a few minutes later he cursed again, volubly. He certainly hadn't intended on mauling Siena in the back of his car, but by the time they'd been pulling up outside his apartment and he'd realised what he was doing he'd had her panties in his hand, ready to take her there and then in the back seat.

From some distant area of his brain he'd managed to find something to mutter to make it sound as if he'd fully intended divesting her of her underwear so that they could continue where they left off as soon as as they were in a private space. Outside the car, though, she'd all but spat at him—and could he blame her? He'd never been so unrestrained with a woman.

He should have remembered that evening in Paris. Remembered how she was capable of making him lose all sense of civility. But when they'd danced in that hotel… Andreas had been sorely tempted to drag her into the lobby, demand a suite and take her upstairs right there. It was little wonder he'd been unable to resist touching her in the back of the car… she'd been melting into him like his hottest fantasy and he'd been lost.

Andreas switched off his shower with a curt flick of his wrist. *Siena had been a virgin.* He looked at himself in the mirror and saw how fiercely his eyes glittered.

It was the one thing he had not expected in a million years. A lot of his bitterness about what had happened in Paris had centered around the belief that Siena had knowingly seduced him because she was bored…and experienced. But she'd been a virgin. And what virgin got hot and heavy with a hotel duty manager? He knew damn well that if they hadn't been interrupted he would have discovered her innocence that night.

He recalled her pale face when she'd bumped into him the following morning. The way she'd looked when he'd told her how he should have taken her up against the wall of the dressing room. He'd said that because he'd felt like such a fool. Because he'd felt exposed, betrayed. Because he'd believed she was experienced, like all those other scarily worldly-wise debutantes.

The irony of it was Siena had been the real deal. Probably the only one there. And how in hell had she stayed a virgin till now? Andreas wanted to smash something with his fist.

He heard a faint noise from outside his bathroom and hitched a towel around his waist before going out. Siena was standing in the centre of the room, in a voluminous towelling robe, hair damp, and his body reacted instantaneously.

His recent unwelcome revelations made Andreas say curtly, 'Yes?'

He saw how Siena tensed and it only made him want to snarl more—but not at her. At himself.

'I just want you to know that it didn't mean anything…the

fact that you were my…first. And you're right, I should have told you. But I thought…'

Andreas saw her falter and bite her lip for a second. She looked almost unbelievably vulnerable. Then she went on, 'I thought you wouldn't notice, I didn't realise it would be so… obvious.'

Siena wanted the ground to swallow her whole and she looked down.

For a long moment nothing happened, and then Andreas conceded, 'It might not have been obvious to some men… but I knew.'

Siena flushed. She could imagine the kind of man her father would have wanted her to marry—some old lecher from the Italian Middle Ages—and just how that scenario might have played out.

She stubbed her toe against the luxurious carpet of his bedroom. 'Yes, well, I just wanted to assure you that it doesn't change anything.'

Siena looked up warily, very aware of Andreas's naked chest and long powerful legs. The excuse for a towel that barely covered his intense masculinity. Unbelievably, Siena could feel herself clench inwardly at the thought of how he'd surged up and into her…how it had felt when he'd slid in and out, taking her higher and higher.

Too late she realised her mistake in coming here like this and turned to leave, but quick as a flash Andreas inserted himself between her and the door.

'Where do you think you're going?'

Siena gulped. 'To my room. To bed.'

Andreas smiled and it was wicked. 'There's a perfectly good bed here.'

Siena blanched. As responsive as her body was proving to be, she didn't in all honesty think she could take a repeat so soon. She'd stung when she'd lowered herself into the bath and she ached all over.

Reading her mind, Andreas said, 'Don't worry, I think it's too soon—but there are other ways of achieving the same result.'

He took Siena by the hand and led her unresisting—much to her disgust—to the bed. He sat down and pulled her between his legs. His towel parted and when Siena looked down she could see the dark thatch of hair and his body stirring and hardening.

Andreas was undoing her robe and then pulling it open. Siena felt absurdly shy and tried to stop him, but he was too strong. It was off her shoulders, falling down her arms to the ground, and she was naked.

Andreas's gaze was fixed on her breasts and Siena could feel them grow, the tips hardening, tingling. She wanted to groan. How could she be so affected when he just looked at her?

With his hands clamped around her waist, Andreas brought her even closer and lavished her breasts with attention, licking and suckling until Siena wanted to cry out. The first time round it had all been happening so fast she hadn't had a chance to draw breath, drowning in sensations before she could really register them.

Now Andreas was conducting a slow, sensual torture, and Siena found it almost overwhelming. With a smooth move he caught her just as her legs threatened to buckle and laid her on the bed. He whipped aside his towel so that he was naked.

Siena said brokenly, 'I thought you said—'

He put a finger to her mouth and said, 'Shh, I did.'

Siena felt something scary erupt in her chest, because in that moment she realised that she trusted Andreas. He wouldn't hurt her, or push her further than she could go. But now his mouth was on hers and his hands were moulding and cupping her breasts and Siena gave up any coherent thought.

By the time his hand reached between her legs and sought where she felt so hot and wet Siena's hips were rolling impatiently. She wanted Andreas to take her again, soreness be damned. But he wouldn't.

Almost crying with frustration, she felt him move down her body and replace that hand with his mouth. He'd touched her like this before, but now it felt much more intimate. Siena was aware of how wanton she must look—legs stretched apart, hands clutching at Andreas's head, breathing fast, heart thumping painfully.

Andreas found her sensitised clitoris and flicked it with his tongue, while thrusting two fingers into her clasping body. *This* was what Siena wanted and needed. Her back arched and her hips all but lifted off the bed as she became some primal being, focused solely on Andreas's mouth and fingers as they made that tension within her coil so tight that she shouted out as he finally tipped her over the edge.

Siena seemed to float for a long time on a blissful haze of sated lethargy before she opened her eyes and realised that Andreas was lowering her into her own bed and pulling the covers over her. He'd carried her here, after pleasuring her senseless.

Siena quickly clamped her eyes shut again, not wanting to see the expression on his face and not liking how ambiguous her feelings were about his putting her back in her own bed. Eventually she heard his footfall and the sound of her door clicking shut. Her eyes opened again, seeing nothing for a moment in the darkened gloom.

Her whole body tingled and hummed with pleasure…and yet Andreas hadn't sought his own release. Siena turned over and looked unseeingly into the dark. She had no frame of reference for this kind of a relationship, but she hadn't expected Andreas to be a selfless lover.

Her head felt tangled and jumbled. She'd somehow naïvely expected that a physical relationship with Andreas would be something she could ultimately rise above, remain immune to, even if she fell apart slightly. She felt anything but immune now. She felt as if she'd been turned inside out and reconfigured and—terrifyingly—she wasn't sure if she even knew who she was any more.

CHAPTER SEVEN

THE FOLLOWING DAY, Siena was in one of Andreas's chauffeur-driven cars, being transported to a private airfield. She'd found a cheerful Mrs Bright in the kitchen that morning, and she had directed Siena's attention to a note left for her by Andreas.

Siena had been inordinately relieved not to have to face him again so soon. She'd read the note.

> I have a meeting in Paris tomorrow morning. We will spend tonight there and go to the opera this evening. Pack accordingly and be ready to leave at three p.m.
> Andreas

Siena could see that they were approaching the airfield now, and felt nervous at the thought of confronting Andreas again after he'd explored her body with such thorough intimacy and then deposited her back in her bed like an unwelcome visitor.

They swept in through wide gates and Siena could see a small Lear jet and a sleek silver sports car nearby. Andreas was taking out a small case and suit bag. Her belly swooped. He looked so tall and handsome. Intimidatingly so. Especially now that she knew the barely leashed power of the body underneath that suit.

The car stopped and Siena saw Andreas register it and straighten up. He looked intense, serious, and her nervous flutters increased. She had no experience of how to handle this situation. She smoothed her hand down her dress, feeling vulnerable now when she thought of how she'd chosen it over more casual clothes, how carefully she'd chosen a dress for the evening, along with the ubiquitous jewelry Andreas would expect her to wear. Because, after all, an inner voice reminded her, she'd demanded it.

Andreas watched Siena emerge from the back of the car and was glad he wore sunglasses which would hide the flare of lust in his eyes. She was wearing a champagne-coloured silk shirt dress, cinched in around her waist with a wide gold belt. The buttons were open, giving just enough of a hint of cleavage, and her hair was tumbled around her shoulders in golden abandon.

Her legs were long and bare, flat gold gladiator-style sandals on her feet. She looked effortlessly *un*-put-together in the way that only women wearing the best clothes could. The knowledge made him reel again: she was here and she was his. More irrevocably his than he'd ever imagined. But even now, much to his chagrin, he couldn't seem to drum up that sense of triumph. It was more of a restless need. As if he'd never get enough of her. It made him very nervous.

Andreas wanted to rip open the buttons of that dress and take her right there, standing against the car. *Like you took her against the door of your apartment last night?* Shame washed through him as he recalled the heated insanity of that coupling. The fact of her innocence. And the fact that while he'd managed to restrain himself from making love to her again before she was ready he'd had to touch her again.

Andreas cursed. This woman had made him useless for the whole day. He'd lost his train of thought in meetings and his assistant Becky had looked at him strangely when he'd left his office. He didn't need her to tell him that his usual cool, organised self had deserted him.

Before he could dwell on the disturbing side-effects of having Siena in his life and in his bed, Andreas strode forward and let an attendant take his things before taking Siena's bag in his hand.

And then, because once he came close to her and her scent hit his nostrils he was unable not to, he wrapped his other hand around her neck and pulled her close, settling a hot, swift kiss to her mouth. When he felt momentary hesitation give way to melting, his body hardened.

He drew back and without saying a word took her hand and led her up into the plane.

By the time they'd landed in Paris and were driving into the city centre Siena was feeling even more on edge. Andreas had largely ignored her for the flight, apart from one brief conversation. She wondered if this was what he did: ignored his lovers once he'd taken them to bed?

She'd been completely unprepared for that swift but incendiary kiss by the plane. It had unsettled her for the entire journey, making her nerve-ends tingle. Andreas had appeared unaffected, though, concentrating on his laptop with a frown between his brows and conducting a lengthy business discussion in Spanish. Siena could understand Spanish, as it had been one of her languages at finishing school, and she'd been surprised to hear him discussing the fate of hotel workers in a small hotel he'd just acquired in Mexico.

He'd said, 'That area is challenged enough as it is. I won't have those people struggling to find new jobs when I'm going to need their experience when the new hotel opens. I want you to offer them retainers, or help find them alternative employment until the work on the new hotel is finished.'

He clearly hadn't liked whatever the person on the other end of the phone had said, and had replied curtly, 'Well, that's why you work for me, Lucas, and not the other way around.'

Andreas had caught her looking at him as he'd terminated the conversation, and had raised a brow. She'd flushed and said, 'I'm the first to admit that I don't know much about business, but surely that isn't exactly good financial sense?'

Andreas had settled back in his seat, a small smile curving that sensual mouth. 'You agree with my field manager? And why not? You're right. It's not good financial sense. But the fact is that this small town in Mexico is where my benefactor and mentor came from. When I moved to New York I worked in a hotel for Ruben Carro. He liked me, saw that I had potential, and essentially groomed me to take over from him.

'He had no family or heirs, and unbeknown to me had an inoperable brain tumour. I think he felt an affinity with me, arriving from Europe, penniless. He'd come from Mexico as an impoverished worker. Both his parents were killed trying to get across the border. When he died he left everything to me with the proviso that I continue his name and that I do something to help improve his home town. He left a substantial part of his fortune to be used to that end. Buying this hotel is just the first step. There are further plans to develop the infrastructure and employment opportunities.'

Siena had felt a little shaky hearing all of this. She'd heard of the legendary billionaire hotelier Carro. 'That's a very ambitious project.'

Andreas had smiled. 'I'm a very ambitious man.'

'That's why your hotel chain is known as Xenakis-Carro? After him?'

An unmistakable look of pride had crossed Andreas's face. He'd nodded. 'I'm proud to be associated with his name. He was a good man and he offered me the opportunity of a lifetime. It's the least I can do to continue his legacy.'

Andreas had turned away then, back to his work, and the knowledge had sat heavily in Siena's belly. Clearly the newspaper reports about his business ethics had been wrong, and yet Andreas hadn't cared enough to defend himself when she'd slung that slur his way.

Siena's focus came back to the present now, as the familiar lines of the Champs-Elysées unfolded before them. Dusk was settling over the iconic city and Siena felt tense. She'd always loved Paris. Until the debutante ball. Until that evening. Since then, coming back here had been fraught with painful reminders of her own naïvety and what she'd done. And never more so than now, when she shared a car with the very man who was at the centre of those memories and emotions.

He was looking out of his window and seemed remote. Was he remembering too? Hating her even more? Siena shivered slightly. They were drawing around to the front of the huge glittering façade of a hotel, and Siena only realised where they were when they came to a smooth halt.

She looked at Andreas, who was regarding her coolly from the other side of the car. 'Is this some kind of a sick joke? Returning to the scene of the crime?'

Andreas's mouth tightened, and then he answered far too equably, 'Not at all, Siena. I don't play games like that. We've come here merely because it's impractical to go to another hotel when I own this one.'

Shock hit Siena and she looked out again at the stunning façade of the world-famous Paris hotel where the debutante ball was still held every year. She was aware of Andreas getting out of his side of the car and then he was opening her door. She looked up at him and suddenly, despite her shock, her breath got stuck in her throat and she saw only him, silhouetted against the dusk. He had never looked more gorgeous, or more dark and threatening with his stern visage. Images of the previous night slammed into her. She felt hot deep down inside her, where secret muscles clenched.

He put out a hand and said imperiously, 'Come.'

Siena fought the childish urge to cross her arms and say

stubbornly *no*. But eventually she put her hand into Andreas's and stepped out. He kept a tight hold of it as they walked into the hotel with much bowing and scraping from the staff.

Siena was surprised to see that the hotel had undergone a very beautiful overhaul since she'd seen it last. Gone was the rather over-fussy atmosphere. It felt lighter, younger, yet still oozed elegance and timeless wealth. This, Siena guessed, must be one of the reasons Andreas had become so successful in such a dizzyingly small amount of time.

Andreas was talking briefly to someone who looked like a manager, and then he was walking forward again without even a glance back to Siena. His hand was still tight around hers. A lift set apart from the others was waiting with open doors.

They stepped in and an attendant greeted them politely before pressing the one button. Siena was beginning to feel claustrophobic in the familiar surroundings, and tried to pull her hand free of Andreas's. He turned to look at her and only gripped hers tighter. This silent battle of wills went on behind the attendant, who was looking resolutely forward, avoiding eye contact.

After what seemed like aeons the lift came to a halt and the doors opened. Andreas said *merci* to the attendant and then they were stepping straight into what could only be described as a shining palace of golds and creams, with acres of soft cream carpet, parquet floors with faded oriental rugs, and floor-to-ceiling French doors and windows. Outside the Place de la Concorde was spectacularly lit up like a golden beacon.

Siena forgot herself for a moment, and only came back into the room when she realised that Andreas had finally let her hand go and was striding into the main drawing room, shucking off his suit jacket and dropping it into a nearby chair.

Everything that had brought her here to this moment—the fact that she had slept with this man and so blithely given him her innocence, his cool demeanour since she'd seen him again today—all combined now to make her feel very prickly and unsure of herself.

He had his back to her, hands on his hips, and she remarked caustically, 'So, you bought the hotel where you were once a lowly assistant manager because this is where you've always had the fantasy of bedding the debutante who got you sacked—is that it?'

Slowly Andreas turned around and Siena steeled herself. His hand came up to his slim silver-grey tie and long fingers undid it. He opened the top buttons of his shirt and just looked at her with a burning intensity before saying quietly, 'You regard yourself very highly if you think I did all that just so I might one day get you into bed seven floors above where you once teased me because you were a spoilt little socialite who got bored between her main course and dessert.'

Siena flushed at his rebuke. She knew what she'd said was grossly unfair, but if Andreas came too close she might shatter completely. Once again the knowledge that he wouldn't welcome the truth of that night washed through her with a sense of futility. Even if he did choose to believe her it would mercilessly expose her and her sister to his far too cynical judgement.

He crossed the space between them and Siena's breath caught in her throat. His eyes were narrowed on her. Instinctively Siena took a step back, panic and something much more treacherously exciting rising from her gut.

'Oh, no.' Andreas shook his head and reached for her with strong hands, wrapping them around her waist. 'We have some time before going to the opera and I know exactly how to spend it.'

Breath was a strangled bird in Siena's throat as Andreas blocked out everything behind him and bent his head, slanting that wicked hot mouth over hers. As predictable as the inclement English weather her body fizzed and simmered. Blood rushed to every nerve-point and to all parts of her body, engorging them, making them tight and sensitive.

It felt as if he was devouring her, sucking her under to some dark wicked place where all she wanted was to feel his mouth on hers. Siena wrapped her arms around Andreas's neck and her whole body strained to get closer to his. His tongue was rough and demanding, making Siena mewl a little when he took his mouth away to trail kisses over her jaw and down further.

Siena's spiteful little barb about his motives for buying the hotel had lodged in Andreas's gut, driving him to seek out physicality rather than think about it. But when he had to lift his head to draw in an unsteady breath and Siena's eyes stared up into his he couldn't escape...

He'd claimed otherwise, but he had to admit that once he'd known this hotel was up for grabs he'd had to have it—with a viscerality that went beyond mere business. But when he'd returned here, conquering owner, it hadn't felt as satisfying as he'd thought it would. It had felt somehow empty, hollow.

Andreas tried to force the unwelcome thoughts out of his head. He saw Siena's slightly swollen lips and flushed cheeks, felt her breasts rise and fall against his chest with her breath. Something caught his eye and he looked down to see that the only piece of jewellery she wore was the simple gold birdcage necklace. For some reason it made him unaccountably nervous. As if there was some hidden message he wasn't getting. He wasn't sure he wanted to get it.

He touched the necklace with a finger. 'I hope you've brought something more substantial than this to wear?'

Siena flushed and avoided his eyes. 'Of course.'

Her voice sounded husky, and just like that it pushed Andreas over the brink of control. With a smooth, effortless move he lifted Siena into his arms and strode to the master bedroom. She gave a little squeal and her arms tightened around him.

'This time—' he was grim '—we'll make it to the bedroom.'

When Siena woke a couple of hours later it was to feel fingers running up and down her bare back, along the indentations of her spine. It was delicious, and yet she felt as if she would never be able to open her eyes again. She frowned and made some incoherent mumble, distantly aware of pleasurable aches and sensations in her body, a faint tingling.

'Come on...we don't have much time to get ready.'

Siena's eyes snapped open when she heard that deep dark voice. Andreas was sitting on the edge of the bed in nothing but a small towel, smelling clean and fresh, his hair damp. He'd just had a shower. Siena was instantly awake.

He stood up, and she couldn't help but watch his sheer leonine grace as he unselfconsciously dropped the towel and went to the wardrobe to look for clothes. Siena averted her eyes. She still felt shellshocked by what had just happened. The way Andreas had stripped her bare, laid her on the bed and proceeded to explore her entire body with a thoroughness that had had her gasping, pleading and begging. Like some wanton stranger.

When he'd finally surged between her legs it had been all she could do not to explode right then, and Andreas had been a master of torture, bringing her close to the brink but never over...until she had been crying genuine tears of frustration. She could still feel them now, slightly sticky on her face. She hated that feeling of being a slave to his touch.

Humiliation washed through her and she cursed her relative innocence, not liking the thought of other, more proficient lovers who undoubtedly drove *him* over the edge.

After all, hadn't he specified that he expected her to be an inventive lover? Except when he touched her any semblance of thought went out of the window and she could only feel.

Realising that she was still lying there, naked and mooning, Siena sat up and took advantage of Andreas disappearing into the bathroom to jump out and pull on her dress again, covering up. She noticed that one or two buttons were missing and blushed when she thought of Andreas's big hands, fumbling until he'd become irritated and yanked it open. A small glow of pleasure infused her. Perhaps he wasn't as insouciant as she thought?

Andreas reappeared, and Siena avoided looking at him buttoning his shirt and scooted into the bathroom, closing the door behind her. She rested with her back against it for a moment, breathing in his provocative scent, then closed her eyes and tried to convince herself that she could get through this week and emerge at the other end unscathed and intact.

Andreas heard the shower running and imagined the water running in rivulets over Siena's breasts and body. Arousal was instant and Andreas cursed, gave up trying to close a cufflink as if that was the problem.

He closed his eyes, but all he saw was how Siena had looked lying face down in the bed moments before, naked, arms stretched out, the curve of her breast visible. That stunning face looked somehow very innocent and young in repose, her mouth a soft moue.

Making love to her this time had had none of the madness of last night, but a different kind of insanity. Sliding into her body had felt disturbing—as if he was touching a part of himself that was buried deep. He'd never lost himself so much while making love to a woman that he literally became some kind of primal animal, able only to obey his body's commands.

He'd expected that after making love to her he'd feel a steady beat of triumph. After all, this was exactly what he'd envisaged. Siena, naked and undone on his bed. Underneath him, begging for release.

She'd cried just now, when they'd made love. Sobbed for him to let her go, to stop torturing her. And he didn't like how her tears had affected him, making him feel guilty.

He'd been punishing her as much as himself, and when she'd finally tipped over the edge the strength of her orgasm had almost been too much for him to handle. He'd worn protection, but Andreas wouldn't have been surprised if the strength of his release had rendered it impotent.

In truth he hadn't expected sex to be this good with Siena. He'd expected her to be cool, distanced. Too concerned with how she looked to let herself be really sensual. Slightly uptight. And yet she was blowing his mind.

He heard the shower stop and suddenly felt a very uncustomary spurt of panic. He couldn't guarantee that if she walked out of that bathroom right now he wouldn't be able *not* to take her again and to hell with the opera.

Only one woman had ever entranced him so much that he'd deviated from his plans. And the fact that he'd willingly invited her back into his life was not a welcome reminder of his weakness.

Fear of keeping her father waiting had instilled within Siena an ability to get ready in record time, so she wasn't surprised when she saw Andreas's look of shock when she walked into the main salon a short time later.

The way his eyes widened sent a shaft of something hot to her belly. The dress was, after all, exquisite. It was one-shouldered, a swathe of dusky pink layers of chiffon, shot through with gold. It hugged her chest and waist and then fell to the floor. She'd pulled her hair up and wore a pair of large teardrop pink diamond earrings.

Feeling absurdly nervous, Siena asked, 'Will I do?'

Andreas smiled, but it looked harsh in the soft lighting of the palatial room. 'You know you'll do, Siena. I'm sure you don't need compliments from me.'

Siena flushed. She hadn't been searching for a compliment. Andreas looked more than stunning in a black tuxedo with a classic black bow-tie. His hair gleamed, still slightly damp, and his eyes looked like dark jewels.

He flicked a glance at his watch and then moved towards her.

'We should go or we'll miss the first half.'

Those nerves assailed her again when Andreas took her elbow in his hand, and Siena asked, 'Which opera is it?'

Andreas was opening the main door and he glanced at her. 'It's *La Bohème*.'

Siena couldn't stop the spontaneous rush of pleasure. 'That's my favourite opera.'

Dryly Andreas remarked as they got into the private lift, 'Mine too. Perhaps we have something in common after all.'

The rush of pleasure died. No doubt Andreas was alluding to the disparity in their upbringings. She didn't know much about his early life, but she knew it had been relatively humble.

Curious in a way she hadn't been before, Siena found herself asking when they were in the back of his car, 'Do you come from a big family?'

Andreas looked at her, but his face was in shadow. She could sense him tense at the question and wondered why.

Eventually he answered, 'I have five younger sisters and my parents.'

Siena felt her curiosity increase on hearing this. 'I didn't realise you came from such a big family. Are you close?'

She could make out his jaw tightening. More reluctance. Clearly he didn't want to talk about it. Siena confided nervously, 'It was just me and Serena. I always wondered what it would be like—' She broke off because she'd been about to say: *to have an older brother.* But of course she did have an older brother.

Andreas, as if seizing the opportunity to deflect attention, asked, 'What *what* would be like?'

Siena swallowed. 'Just…what it would have been like to have other siblings.'

Andreas arched a brow. 'More sisters for your father to parade like ice princesses?' Before Siena could react to that Andreas was saying curtly, 'My family is not up for discussion. We come from worlds apart, Siena, that's all you need to know.'

It was like a slap in the face. Siena sat back into the shadows and looked out of the window. That tiny glimpse into Andreas's life had intrigued her, but she berated herself now for showing an interest, and hated that her imagination was seizing on what it would have been like to grow up in a large family. How being an only son might have impacted Andreas, fed his ambition to succeed.

She didn't care, she told herself ruthlessly, as they pulled up outside the opera. A long line of beautifully dressed people were walking in ahead of them. Andreas came around to her door and held out his hand imperiously. Siena longed to be able to defy him but she thought of her only family: Serena, in a psychiatric unit in England, depending on her. She put her hand into Andreas's.

Three nights later Siena was standing in Andreas's London apartment, waiting for him to emerge from his room where he'd gone to get changed. She was already dressed and ready as Andreas had been delayed with work.

Since that evening in Paris things had cooled noticeably between them. Not, she had to admit, that they'd ever really been *warm.* Andreas had barely said another two words to her that night, and when they'd returned from the opera he'd told her he had to do some work and had disappeared into an office in the suite.

When she'd woken the next morning the bed beside her had been untouched, so Andreas must have slept somewhere else. Siena hadn't liked the feeling of insecurity that had gripped her as she'd waited for Andreas to finish his meetings that morning so they could return to London.

However, when they'd returned to London that evening Andreas had led her straight to his bed and made love to her with such intensity that she hadn't been able to move a muscle. Siena didn't like to think of how willingly she'd gone into his arms, or the sense of relief she'd felt. Was she so weak and pathetic after a lifetime of bullying by her father that she welcomed this treatment? She seized on the fact that soon she would be independent again, and that she'd gone into this arrangement very willingly for an end which justified the means.

The following day Andreas had exhibited the same cool, emotional distance, confirming for Siena that this was how it would be unless they were in bed. On one level she'd welcomed it. She didn't need Andreas to charm her, to pretend to something their relationship would never be.

On both evenings they'd gone out to functions. Last night had been a huge benefit for a charity that provided money for children injured in war-torn countries to be brought to Europe or the USA for medical treatment. It covered all their costs, including rehabilitation.

Siena had had tears in her eyes when a beautiful young Afghan woman had stood up to tell her story. She'd been shot because she'd spoken out about education as a teenager and this charity had transported her to America, where she'd received pioneering surgery and not only survived but thrived. She now worked for the UN.

It was only when the head of the charity had introduced the charity's patron and invited him up to speak that Siena had realised it was Andreas. She'd sat there, stunned, listening to him speak passionately about not letting the children of conflict suffer. She'd felt absurdly hurt that he hadn't told her of his involvement.

When he'd come back to the table, Siena had pushed down the hurt. 'What made you want to get involved in something like this?'

His stern expression had reminded Siena that she was straying off the path of being his mute and supplicant mistress, and in that moment she'd wanted to stand up and walk out. Only thinking of Serena had kept her where she was.

Eventually he'd said, 'A child in Mexico was caught in the crossfire between drug gangs. Ruben arranged for him to be brought to New York for treatment…unfortunately the child died, despite the doctors' best efforts. I have eight nieces and nephews and they take their safety and security completely for granted—which is their right. This child from Mexico… It opened my eyes. After he died I knew I wanted to do more…'

Siena had realised then that she could not cling onto any prejudice she'd had about the kind of man Andreas was now she'd met him again. He was not power-hungry and greedy. Or amoral.

Ignoring his silent instruction not to pursue this topic, Siena had asked, 'Do you want children?'

Andreas had looked at her and smiled mockingly, making Siena instantly regret her reckless question. She'd realised then that she'd asked it in a bid to pierce that cool control, because the last time they'd shared any meaningful dialogue it had been about his family.

'Why, Siena? Are you offering to be the mother of my children? So that you can bring them up to follow in your footsteps and tease men before letting them fall to the ground so hard that their whole world shatters? Maybe if we had a daughter we could call her Estella, after that great Dickensian heroine who beguiled and bewitched poor hapless Pip with her beauty only to crush him like a fly…'

She had been so shocked at this softly delivered attack that she'd put down her napkin and stood up, saying quietly, 'You're no Pip, Andreas, and you don't remember correctly. Estella was the victim.'

Siena had walked blindly to the bathroom and shut herself inside. She hadn't been able to stop the hot prickle of tears from overflowing. She'd been stunned at how hurt she felt, and at the mixture of guilt and shame that churned in her gut along with the awful image Andreas had just put in her head.

He could never know how cruel his words were. Her deepest, most fervent dream was some day to be part of the kind of family unit she'd never known.

She'd used to look out of her bedroom window in Florence to a park on the other side of the tiny *piazza* outside their *palazzo*. There she would see mothers and fathers and children. She'd seen love and affection and laughter and she'd ached with a physical pain to know what that would be like. To love and be loved. To have children and give them all the security and affection she'd never known… She'd never even realised until Andreas had uttered those words how badly she still wanted it.

When she'd felt composed enough to return Andreas had been waiting impatiently and they'd left. He'd looked at her in the dark shadows of the back of his car and Siena had instinctively recoiled, unable to bear the thought of him touching her when she felt so raw.

He'd said roughly, 'You say Estella was the victim? From where I'm sitting she looks remarkably robust.'

He'd reached for her then, and Siena had resisted with all the strength in her body, hating him with every fibre of her being. But with remorseless skill Andreas had slowly ground down her defences and her anger until desire burned hotter than anything else…

By the time they'd made it to the apartment she'd forgotten all about her hurt and had been thinking only about Andreas providing her with the release he could give her, like someone pathetically addicted to an illegal substance.

'We should go or we'll be late.'

Andrea's terse voice made Siena jump slightly. She'd been caught up in the memory. She turned around and wondered if she'd ever get used to the little shock of awe when she saw him in a tuxedo. Thinking of the previous evening and what had happened made Siena look down, hiding her gaze. She picked up her wrap and bag and for the first time could appreciate the armour of her shimmering black designer dress. The heavy weight of a diamond necklace at her throat, the earrings in her ears and the bracelet on her wrist would keep her anchored tonight. She couldn't afford to lose herself for a second. Or let him goad her.

If Andreas had a hint of her vulnerability he'd annihilate her.

CHAPTER EIGHT

ANDREAS WAS DRIVING them to the function in his sports car. It served the purpose of occupying his hands and his mind, so that he wasn't in danger of ravishing Siena in the confined space of the back of his chauffeur-driven car. He would not debase himself again by proving that he could not last a few minutes without touching her. He didn't want to think of the amount of times he'd almost made love to her in the back of that car.

It made him think of the other night and how he'd still had to touch her even when she'd detonated a small internal bomb with her question about whether or not he wanted children. He didn't want to remember how she'd looked when he'd likened her to Estella from *Great Expectations* not once, but twice. It had worked, though. He'd welcomed the anger sparking in her eyes. Far easier to deal with that than the look in her eyes when she'd asked her question so inoccuously.

Lovers had asked Andreas before if he wanted children, and in every case Andreas had looked at them coolly and mentally ended the affair with little or no regret. Siena had asked and he had felt a primal surge of something very proprietorial. Something very disturbing that *wasn't* an immediate and categoric rejection of what should be anathema to him. In that moment he'd felt exposed and reminded of his humiliation in Paris. Had Siena seen something he'd been unaware of?

Something that had told her it was okay to ask that question because one week would not be enough for him? Because inevitably he couldn't help but want more?

Andreas had felt like Pip then, from that great book. Chasing after an ever unattainable beauty. Forever destined to fall short. And so he'd lashed out. Had watched her pale and told himself she was acting.

He needed to maintain the distance he'd instigated in Paris. Too much had made him uneasy there and since: Siena's insight into why he'd bought that hotel, the hunger for her which only seemed to be growing stronger, not weaker, and the way she'd asked him about his family...making him remember what he'd worked so hard to avoid.

So much of Andreas's youthful rejection of his family had been brought into sharp focus after his humiliating rejection at her hands. He'd gone abroad with little or no warning, and he knew it had confused and upset his parents. They'd never really understood his hunger to succeed, how he'd had an irrational fear of not making it out of that small town—especially after Spiro had died.

Andreas reminded himself that this wasn't a relationship like any other. With other lovers Andreas made an effort, small-talked, was witty and charming. With Siena it was about settling a score, sating the fever in his blood, exorcising the demons. He conveniently blocked out the fact that he appeared to be no closer to his goal than he had been a few days ago...

A couple of hours later Siena was feeling pain in the balls of her feet from the high heels. She wondered what Andreas would say if he knew that, contrary to his opinion of her, she'd give her right arm never to go to one of these functions again. Just then a tall, very good-looking man with dark hair approached Andreas and the two men greeted each other warmly. Siena found herself transfixed by Andreas's wide smile. She'd seen it so rarely since they'd met again, and never directed at *her*.

He was introducing the stranger. 'This is Rafaele Falcone, of Falcone Industries. He's recently moved to London to extend his domination of the motor industry.'

Siena recognised the name of the iconic Italian car company and put her hand out. She smiled at the other man, who matched Andreas in height and build. He truly was sinfully gorgeous, with astonishing green eyes, and Siena had a fleeting moment of wishing he would have some effect on her which might prove that Andreas didn't dominate her every sense. But when their hands touched there was nothing—despite the fact that Rafaele held her hand for a split second longer than was necessary, with a smile that made Siena feel like apologising because its effect was wasted on her.

'If you find things getting dull with Xenakis, do give me a call.'

He was handing her a card, flirting outrageously, and Siena found herself smiling at his chutzpah with genuine amusement. She was reaching for the card out of politeness when it disappeared into Andreas's fingers. His arm had come around her waist and brought her to his side in a way that had her looking at him, bemused. He'd never claimed her like this in public before.

Rafaele Falcone was putting up his hands in a gesture of mock defeat and backing away. 'We'll talk soon, Xenakis, I'll be interested to hear how that deal goes, and I have a new car being launched next month that I think you'll like...'

His gaze encompassed Siena and she flushed, suddenly not liking the way he was all but telling her of his interest if she were not with Andreas. She wasn't really used to this kind of casual interplay. Her father had always been so protective.

When he'd turned and walked away Andreas let Siena go and turned to her. He was livid, and Siena took a step back.

'Don't even *think* about it.'

Siena was genuinely confused. 'Think about what?'

Andreas jerked his head in the direction of his departing friend. 'Falcone is off-limits.'

Rage filled Siena, and she knew it was coming from a dangerous place—more from Andreas's dogged coolness in the past few days than what he'd just said. His possessiveness made her feel something altogether much more disturbing.

'How dare you? When we're done I can do what I like, and I intend to. If I think that includes having a rampant affair with Rafaele Falcone then I'll be sure to give him a call.'

For a second Andreas looked so feral that Siena felt fear snake down her spine. He looked capable of violence.

'You're mine, Siena,' he growled. 'No one else's.'

She lashed back. 'One week, Xenakis. I'm yours for one week. You're the one who put a time limit on it.' Realisation hit her then, along with something very hollow. 'And that one week is up in two days—or have you come to enjoy my company so much that you'd forgotten? Perhaps you want more?'

Siena wasn't sure what was goading her when she said waspishly, 'If you're so concerned with keeping me out of other men's beds it's going to cost you a lot more than a few baubles.'

'So this is how you're funding yourself after our father's spectacular crash and burn? I shouldn't be surprised.'

It took long seconds before Siena realised that it wasn't Andreas who had spoken in his deep voice. It was another voice—one that rang the faintest of bells. She tore her eyes from Andreas and looked to her left. She felt the blood drain from her face.

Rocco DeMarco. Her brother.

Siena barely heard Andreas acknowledge him tersely, 'DeMarco.'

Her brother's dark brown eyes left Siena momentarily to

flick to Andreas, and he inclined his head slightly. 'Xenakis. I see that my little half-sister Siena has found a benefactor to keep her in the style to which she's accustomed.'

His resemblance to their father stunned her anew, as it had all those years before, and Siena wanted to weep with the ill-timing of this meeting. It was effortlessly confirming his worst opinion of her.

Faintly she said, 'You recognise me.' It wasn't a question.

Those dark eyes went back to her. His mouth curled. 'I followed the demise of our father in the press with great interest. You and your sister were featured prominently, but it would appear you've landed on your feet.'

Feeling weak, Siena said, 'This…it's not what it seems.'

Disgust was evident in Rocco's expression, ice in his eyes, and Siena felt an ache in her heart. He was her flesh and blood.

'Did you really think I would ever forget you? After you and Serena stepped over me like a piece of trash in the street? And as for our father… Tell me—have you heard from him?'

Siena shook her head, feeling sick. How could she explain here and now to this man that she hated her father as much as he did?

Just then a petite and very pretty red-haired woman joined Rocco, slipping her hand into his arm. The change in her brother was instantaneous as he drew her close and looked down at her, warmth and love shining from his eyes. When he looked back at Siena the ice returned and she shivered.

'This is my wife—Gracie. Gracie, I'd like you to meet Siena. My youngest half-sister.'

Siena watched the woman tense and a wary expression came into her kind hazel eyes. Clearly she understood the significance of this meeting. She held out a hand, though, and Siena forced herself to shake it, feeling sick. She only noticed then the other woman's very pregnant belly, and something sharp and poignant lanced her at the realisation that she might have a nephew or niece already.

Rocco looked at Andreas and said with deceptive lightness, 'I presume from your expression that Siena hasn't told you about our familial connection? Or about when I confronted our father and he knocked me to the ground as if I was nothing more than a dog in the street?'

'Rocco...'

Siena heard his wife speak reprovingly, but his face remained ice-cold.

Siena found herself appealing to the other woman instinctively, saying, 'I was only twelve. Things really weren't as they seemed.'

The compassion in his wife's eyes was too much for Siena. She pulled free of Andreas, whose expression she did not want to see, and all but ran from the room. The emotion blooming inside her was too much. Here was incontrovertible proof that she and Serena were on their own. She'd known very well that she couldn't go to their brother, but it was another thing to see it for certain, no matter how kind his wife looked.

She'd always harboured a secret fantasy that one day she might go to Rocco and explain about their lives. That truly they weren't all that different in the end...they had a common nemesis: *their father.*

Her throat burned as she tried to suppress the emotion, expecting Andreas's presence at any moment. He wouldn't stand for her running out like that. Not when she had a duty to fulfil by his side. Perhaps he'd be so disgusted by what he'd just learned that he'd be happy to see the back of her?

She heard his voice, cold behind her in the quiet part of the lobby she'd escaped to.

'Why didn't you tell me Rocco DeMarco was your half-brother?'

Siena didn't turn around, struggling to compose herself. 'It wasn't relevant.'

Andreas snorted indelicately. 'Not relevant? He's one of the most powerful financiers in the world.'

Siena turned then and looked up at Andreas, steeling herself for his expression. It was exactly as she'd feared: a mixture of disgust and confusion. Siena retreated into attack to hide her raw emotions. She shrugged minutely. 'As you can see he hates my guts, and my sister's. Why should I bother myself with my father's bastard son—born to a common prostitute?'

Siena's insides were lacerated at her words. It was the opposite of what she believed. After that day when he'd confronted their father Siena had used to dream of him returning in the dead of night to take her and Serena away with him. But there was no way she would reveal that to Andreas.

'Why, indeed?' Andreas said now, and looked at her strangely. And then he started walking away, towards the entrance.

Siena faltered for a moment and went after him, having to hurry to keep up. When it was clear he was asking for his car, she asked a little breathlessly, 'Don't you want to go back inside?'

Andreas glanced at her and said curtly, 'Rocco DeMarco and his wife are friends of mine. I won't have them feeling the need to leave just because you're with me. I told them we'd leave.'

Pain, sharp and intense, gripped Siena as the car pulled up beside them and the valet jumped out, handing Andreas the keys. Solicitous as ever, even when he despised her, he saw Siena into the car and walked around the bonnet. Siena had the bleakest sense of foreboding that this was it. And after a silent journey back to the apartment Andreas confirmed it.

Barely looking at her, he was in the act of removing his jacket and taking off his cufflinks when he said, 'I'll arrange for a security guard to take you to the jewellers in the morning. There you'll be able to get your money.'

Siena stood stock-still. The stark finality of his words seemed to drop somewhere between them and shatter on the floor.

Faintly, pathetically, she said, 'But...there's two days left.'

Andreas speared her with a cold look. 'Five days is enough for me.' His mouth twisted. 'Don't worry. I won't dock you any *payment*.'

His words seem to bounce off her. She was numb. Just like that he'd lifted her up and now he was dropping her from a height. And yet...what else had she expected?

Siena felt sick when she had to admit that on some very deep and secret level she'd imagined that Andreas might not despise her so utterly—but when had they ever had a chance to go beyond that?

He'd stonewalled any attempts she'd made to talk about personal things, or even non-personal things, and yet this evening she could remember a betraying flare of hope at seeing him so possessive when another man flirted with her.

But that had been purely male posturing. No doubt he'd be quite happy to see her in anyone else's arms when *he* was done with her. Which was now, Siena realised a little dazedly.

She hated herself for not feeling more relieved, and she felt humiliated. Because she had to acknowledge that, despite telling herself she was with Andreas for this week purely to help her sister, she knew it was a lie. She would have wanted Andreas no matter what. For herself. Because he'd always been her dark fantasy. He would only ever have wanted her in revenge, so she'd had to have him like this or not at all.

Using Serena had been a buffer—a device for fooling herself that she was somehow in control...

Siena felt cold inside. The only good thing that could come out of this now was the help she could give her sister. She would take this man's largesse and damn herself in his eyes for ever. She'd do it with a willing heart because she had no right ever to have imagined anything else.

Siena forced herself to move, to say something. 'Goodnight, then.' It couldn't be more apparent that Andreas would not touch her now if his life depended on it.

She was walking away when she heard him say, 'It's goodbye, Siena. I'll be gone in the morning. I leave for New York to work.'

Siena turned and a wave of emotion surged upwards. She couldn't stop the words tumbling out in spite of her best intentions to stay cool. 'I *am* sorry, Andreas. Really sorry for what happened…it wasn't my intention…'

And then, before she could say anything more, she fled.

Andreas looked at the empty space Siena had left behind, along with the most fragile scent, and wanted to storm after her, to whirl her around and demand to know what she'd meant by *'it wasn't my intention'*. He wanted to put her over his shoulder and take her to his bed one more time.

But it would not be enough, he realised. It would never be enough. His body burned with need. Even after that distasteful scene with her half-brother and the knowledge of what he'd been through.

Andreas had had no idea of their connection. But as Rocco had spoken he'd felt the man's pain and had all too well been able to imagine the scenario—the two precious blue-eyed heiresses stepping over their prone brother.

It had brought back all of his own anger and rage, far too easily forgotten in the heat of passion or when Siena looked at him with those huge blue eyes. He too had suffered at those hands.

Until she'd reminded him that a week was almost up he had forgotten. And that had sent shockwaves through his system—along with a knee-jerk impulse to negate it, to tell her he'd let her go when he was ready.

But he'd caught himself in time. He'd forgotten and she'd remembered, because *she* was counting each day and evaluating how much she'd take from him.

She'd made him jealous. He thought of the red haze of rage that had settled over his vision on seeing his friend Rafaele Falcone flirt with Siena. And how she'd smiled at him so guilelessly, as she'd once smiled at him... That was when the scales had finally fallen from Andreas's eyes, and he'd realised how in danger he was of becoming a slave to his desire for this woman—how, far from being exorcised, she was gaining a stronger hold over him.

Andreas castigated himself. He should never have looked for her. It had been a huge mistake. Tomorrow she would be gone and he *would* move on.

A month later, London.

Andreas stepped into his apartment, bone-weary. He'd extended his trip to New York, not liking to investigate why he'd wanted to avoid coming back to London too soon. Silence descended around him, telling him he was alone. He ignored the hollow sensation and put down his bag.

He walked into the main salon and a vision hit him right between the eyes of Siena as she'd turned to face him that last evening in her black dress. So perfect. So beautiful. Andreas cursed and quickly walked out again.

He went to the kitchen, but that only brought him back to the moment when he'd heard Mrs Bright clucking and explaining to Siena about the oven. Or how Siena had looked sitting in jeans and a T-shirt, eating a croissant with her fingers.

Telling himself he was being ridiculous, he went to her room and opened the door, almost steeling himself for her scent. It lingered only faintly, but it was enough to have heat building low in his pelvis. He cursed her ghostly presence again. He was about to walk out when he spotted something out of the corner of his eye and walked towards the dressing area.

He couldn't be certain, but it looked as if every single piece of clothing he'd bought her was still there, neatly hung up or folded away. The long pink chiffon gown. The black dress she'd worn that first night, which had ended up on the floor of the foyer as he'd taken her up against the front door with all the finesse of a rutting bull... Andreas flushed.

The clothes would have been worth a fortune, if she had felt inclined to sell them, but they were here. Something very alien gripped Andreas and he strode out and into his study. Already he could see the safe door open and all of the jewellery gone.

He didn't like his momentary suspicion that perhaps she'd left the jewellery too. Some last second attack of conscience, because... *Why?* he mocked himself. *Because she'd come to feel something for you?*

Andreas pushed aside the rogue thought, not liking how it made him break out in a cold sweat. He sat down and picked up his phone. He had to know for sure.

'Yes, Mr Xenakis. She came that morning, as you'd arranged, and handed back every item of jewellery. We exchanged it all for a very fair price. She was a pleasant young lady.'

Andreas did not want to get into a conversation about how Siena DePiero could turn on the charm when it suited her, and he was about to put the phone down when the man on the other end said, 'Actually...there was one item she wanted to keep. Ah... Let me see...'

He was clearly looking at some list, and Andreas bit down on his impatience. He really didn't want to hear about which emerald bracelet Siena had—

'Ah, yes. Here it is.'

The man interrupted his train of thought.

'She wanted to keep the gold birdcage necklace by Angel Parnassus, and she was very insistent that she pay for it out of her own money. Everything else was cashed.'

Andreas muttered his thanks and put the phone down. As soon as Siena had singled out that understated necklace it had made him nervous, and he didn't like to be reminded of that now—of that elusive sensation that he'd missed something.

With a curse, Andreas stood up and went to his room to change for the reception of a wedding that he was invited to that evening in one of his London hotels.

His brief interlude with Siena DePiero was over, and he didn't really care why she had wanted to hang onto some relatively inexpensive piece of gold. Nor did he want to dwell on the fact that she was out there, somewhere in the city, living off his money and undoubtedly seducing the next billionaire stupid enough to fall under her spell.

A sudden vivid image of her with Rafaele Falcone made Andreas feel as if something had just punched him in the gut, and he had to breathe deeply to ease the sensation.

Curse her to hell. He was done with her for good, and soon the bad taste left in his mouth would fade. If she was with Rafaele Falcone he was welcome to her.

Siena turned away from another group of wedding guests who had barely looked at her as they'd helped themselves to some of the *hors d'oeuvres* she was offering from a silver tray. She welcomed the anonymity. She'd had this job for two weeks now, and she knew how lucky she was to have found another job so easily.

Every penny that had come from the sale of the jewellery from Andreas had gone straight to cover Serena's fees. She'd spent an emotional afternoon with her sister, assuring her that she would be okay, and in that moment Siena had had no regrets about what she had done.

It was when she lay in bed at night, in a similarly dingy apartment to her last one, or took the bone-rattling bus journey to work every day that she felt acute regret for deceiving Andreas all over again. She'd never forget the way he'd looked at her that last evening, or the painful reunion with her brother. Something she hadn't yet divulged to Serena.

Siena was making a beeline towards another group of guests in their finery when one of the men turned slightly to speak to a man at his side. Siena stopped in her tracks just feet away. Her belly plummeted. It couldn't be. The universe couldn't be so cruel.

But apparently the universe *could* be that cruel. Andreas Xenakis glanced momentarily in her direction and Siena saw the shock of recognition cross his features.

She immediately turned on the spot and walked quickly away, assuring herself a little hysterically that he wouldn't have recognised her. He would thhink he was mistaken because he would have assumed she'd be on a yacht, sunning herself in the Mediterranean, spending the money she'd received.

But even as she thought that she knew it was too good to be true. A heavy hand fell on her shoulder and she was whirled around so fast that the tray flew out of her hands, landing upside down on the plush and very expensive carpet nearby.

Siena immediately jerked free and bent down to pick up the tray and limit the damage, terrified her stern boss might have seen. Andreas bent down too, and Siena hissed at him, hating the way her heart was threatening to jump free of her chest, 'Please just leave me alone. I can't afford to lose this job.'

'And why,' he asked with deceptive mildness, 'would that be, when only weeks ago you cashed in a small fortune? No one could have run through it that quickly.'

Siena finished putting the last of the ruined canapés on the tray and lifted it up again. She looked at Andreas and hated how shaky she felt. 'Just pretend you haven't seen me. *Please.* If I'd had any idea you'd be a guest here…'

'Mr Xenakis, is everything all right?'

'No, it's not all right,' Andreas snapped at Siena's boss, who blanched.

Siena went hot with embarrassment. People were looking at them now, interested in whatever it was that had taken Andreas Xenakis's attention. The sense of déjà-vu as Siena remembered how she'd first seen him again was not welcome.

Andreas took the tray out of Siena's hand and before she knew what was happening handed it to her boss, taking her hand. 'I'm sorry, but you'll have to do without her. She's resigning from her job.'

Siena gasped, 'No, I'm not! How dare you?' But her words were lost as Andreas all but dragged her through the throng of merry wedding guests. She tried to free herself but Andreas's grip was too tight.

He stopped suddenly and she almost careened into his back—only to hear him say to the tall dashing groom and his stunning bride, 'So sorry…something has come up. I wish you all the best.'

And then he was moving again.

Her face puce with mortification, Siena was forced to follow. When they were finally in the clear, in a relatively empty corridor, Siena broke free and stopped in her tracks. She was shaking with adrenalin and shock.

'How *dare* you just lose me my job like that?'

Andreas rounded on her, eyes blazing. Siena couldn't fail to react to his sheer masculine magnificence. His jaw was slightly stubbled and an insidious image slipped into her mind of him waking in bed with some new lover who had distracted him enough to persuade him back into bed. Something she'd never done. She'd never woken in his arms.

'Lose you your job?' he practically shouted. 'Why the hell are you working as a waitress again when you walked away with a small fortune in your pocket just a month ago?'

Siena opened her mouth and shut it again. What could she say? That she liked back-breaking work and being on her feet for eight hours solid at a stretch? Of course she didn't.

She just needed Andreas gone so that she could get on with trying to forget about him and all the tangled emotions he was responsible for. She folded her arms. 'It's none of your business.'

Andreas folded his arms too, as immovable as a large, intimidating statue. Siena knew with a flicker of trepidation that she'd never make him budge.

'You owe me an explanation, Siena.'

Siena shook her head, panic surging. 'No, I don't owe you anything.'

Andreas looked stern. 'Oh, yes, you do—and especially after this stunt.'

He reached for her hand again and started leading her down the corridor, away from the high society wedding. A sense of inevitability washed through Siena. She knew she hadn't a hope of resisting Andreas when he was like this.

To her dismay she realised that they were in one of his hotels when he went to the reception desk and she heard him demand the key for the Presidential Suite. Then they were in the lift and ascending to the top floor. He still had hold of her hand, and Siena didn't like the way her body was already reacting to his touch—her blood pooling hotly in her belly and fizzing through her veins.

When Andreas opened the door to an opulent-looking suite he led her in and only let her go when they were safely inside. Siena walked into the reception room. The lights of the Houses of Parliament shone from across the river in the gathering dusk.

She felt self-conscious in her uniform, which consisted of a black knee-length skirt, a white shirt and black bow-tie. Her hair was pulled back into a ponytail, face scrubbed free of make-up, and the only jewellery she wore was the gold bird-cage necklace she'd kept. It seemed to burn into her skin like a brand now, even though she'd actually used the last of her own money to pay for it.

She heard the sound of Andreas pouring himself a drink and turned around to find him handing her a small tumbler of Baileys. She was surprised that he'd remembered her favourite drink and took it in both hands, avoiding his eye.

'Sit down, Siena, before you fall down.' His tone was admonitory.

Siena looked around and saw a chair sitting at right angles to the couch. She sat down and took a tiny fortifying sip of her drink, feeling the smooth, creamy liquid slide down her throat.

Andreas went and stood with his back to her at the window and Siena regarded that broad back warily, her eyes dropping to his buttocks. Instantly she had a flashback to how it had felt to have him between her legs, thrusting so deep—

He turned around abruptly and she flushed.

'So, is it that you have some masochistic penchant for menial labour after a life of excess? Or perhaps you've acted completely out of character, had a fit of conscience and handed all the money over to a worthy charity? I want to know what you've done with my money, Siena. After all, it's not an inconsiderable sum…'

Siena saw the narrow-eyed gaze focused on her and sensed his insouciance was a very thin veneer hiding simmering anger. Futility threatened to overwhelm her. She could try to lie—*again*—make up some excuse. But she did owe this man an explanation. A lot more than an explanation. She owed him his money back.

Carefully she put down her drink. Her mind was whirling

with what she was contemplating. Could she just...*tell* him? Appeal to his sense of compassion? After all, hadn't she seen it in action?

Knowing that her sister was finally safe and would be looked after for the forseeable future, and telling herself that she didn't have to divulge *everything,* Siena tried to glean some encouragement from Andreas's expressionless face.

She looked down at her hands in her lap for a long moment, and just before the silence stretched to breaking point said quietly, 'The money was for my sister, not me.'

Silence met her words, and she looked up to see Andreas was genuinely confused. 'You said she was in the South of France with friends...'

Siena could see when understanding dawned, but it was the wrong kind of understanding, and she winced when he spoke.

'*She* needed the money? To fund her debauched lifestyle? *That's* why you were willing to prostitute yourself?'

His crude words drove Siena up out of the chair. She realised somewhat belatedly that she would never have got away with such a flimsy explanation. Her whole body was taut, quivering.

'No. It's not like that.' Siena bit her lip and took a terrifying leap of faith. 'Serena was never in the South of France. She's here. In England. She came with me when we left Italy. I lied.'

Andreas's mouth twisted, 'I know your proficiency for lies, Siena. Tell me something I don't know.'

Siena winced again, but she knew she deserved it. Unable to bear being under Andreas's scrutiny like this, she moved jerkily over to the other window and crossed her arms, staring out at the view as if it would magically transport her out of this room.

'My sister...is ill. She's had mental health issues for years. They probably started not long after our mother died, I was three and Serena was five. She had always been a difficult child…I remember tantrums and our father locking her in her room. Her illness manifested itself as bouts of severe depression in her early teens, along with more manic periods when she would go out and go crazy. It got so bad that she had psychotic episodes and hallucinations. She tried to take her own life during one of those times…not to mention developing a drink and drug addiction.'

Siena heard nothing from Andreas, and was too scared to look at him, so she continued, 'Our father was disgusted at this frailty and refused to deal with it. It was only after her suicide attempt that she was diagnosed with severe bipolar disorder. Our father wouldn't allow her to take medication for fear that it would leak to the press…' Siena's voice grew bitter. 'Despite her party girl reputation she was still a valuable heiress—albeit slightly less valuable than me.'

Siena closed her eyes briefly, praying for strength in the face of Andreas's scorn, and turned to face him. His face was still expressionless.

'Go on,' he said coolly.

'When our father disappeared Serena went through a manic phase. It was impossible to control her. Physically she's stronger than me, and her drinking was out of control. All I could do was wait until the inevitable fall and then persuade her to come to England. She knew she needed help. She wanted help. I found a good psychiatric clinic and she was accepted. I had some money left over from our mother's inheritance that hadn't been seized by the authorities and that paid for our move, and for Serena for the first few months of her treatment. It's complicated, because she has to be treated for her addictions first.'

Siena looked away, embarrassed by her own miscalculation. 'I thought that with my wages I could continue to pay for her upkeep, but I hadn't really factored in the weekly cost. When I met you…again…there was only enough money left for a few weeks. She's at a delicate stage in her treatment. If she'd had to leave now because we couldn't afford it, the doctors warned me that it could be catastrophic.'

Siena braced herself for Andreas's reaction, remembering all too well their father's archaic views on mental illness.

Desperate to try and defend her sister, Siena looked back, eyes blazing. 'She's not just some vacuous socialite. It *is* a disease. If you could have seen her…the pain and anguish… and there was nothing I could do…'

To Siena's chagrin, hot tears prickled and she quickly blinked them back. 'She's my sister, and I'll do anything to try and help her. She's all I have left in the world.'

'What about your half-brother?' Andreas asked quietly.

Siena still couldn't make out his expression and her heart constricted when she thought of Rocco.

'I knew I could never go to him. You saw yourself what his reaction was. I expected it. I remember that day he spoke of. It's etched into my memory.' Quietly she said, 'I didn't mean what I said about him…afterwards. I was angry and felt vulnerable. The day we saw him confront our father, if Serena or I had so much as looked in his direction we would have been punished mercilessly. You have no idea what our father was capable of.'

'Why don't you tell me?'

Siena felt as if she was in some kind of a dreamlike state. Andreas was asking these innocuous questions that cut to the very heart of her, making her talk about things that she'd talked about with no one. *Ever.* Not even Serena.

Her legs suddenly felt weak and she went back to the couch and sat down. She looked up at Andreas and said starkly, 'He was a sadist. He took pleasure from other people's pain. But especially Serena, because she had always been so wilful and difficult to control. She became his punching bag because he knew that I was the one he could depend on to perform, to be good.'

Siena took a shaky breath and glanced at her pale hands. 'I learnt what would happen from an early age if I wasn't good. He caught me painting over one of the *palazzo* murals one day…a painter had left some paints behind. He told me to follow him and sent for Serena. He brought us into his study and told Serena to hold out her hand. He took a bamboo stick out of his cupboard and whipped her until she was bleeding. Then he told me that if I ever misbehaved again this was what would happen: Serena would be punished.'

Siena looked at Andreas. She felt cold inside. 'Serena didn't blame me. Not then. *Never.* It was as if in spite of her own turmoil she knew that what he was doing was just as damaging to me.'

Andreas's voice was impossibly grim, sending a shiver down Siena's spine. 'How old were you when this happened?'

'Five.'

For long seconds there was silence. Siena fancied she could see something in Andreas's eyes. His jaw twitched, and then he said, 'I want you to tell me what happened in Paris that night.'

Siena had known it would come to this. She owed Andreas this much. An explanation. Finally. Not that it could change the past or absolve her of her sins.

She fought to remain impassive, not to appear as if this was shredding her insides to bits. 'That evening in Paris… when my father caught us…I panicked. I had not premeditated what happened. I was overwhelmed at the strength of the attraction between us. I'd noticed you all evening. I'd never felt anything like it before…'

Siena looked back at her hands. 'I know you might not believe that…especially after I tried to make you believe I was more experienced than I was…' She was afraid of what she'd see if she looked at him so she kept her gaze down. 'When my father appeared I knew instantly what I had done—how bad it was. Serena was going through a rough patch. She was at home in Florence, being supervised by a doctor, but only because I had begged our father not to leave her alone…I was terrified of what he would do if he thought that what we'd been doing had been…mutual.'

Siena felt movement and then Andreas was sitting down beside her. His fingers were on her chin and he was forcing her to look at him. Her belly somersaulted at the look in his eyes. It was burning.

'You're telling me that you *didn't* set out to seduce me? That it *wasn't* just boredom? And that you only denounced me out of fear of what your father would do?'

Siena swallowed. Shame filled her belly. She whispered, 'Yes. I was a coward. I chose to protect my own sister over you… But I had no idea how far my father would go.'

Andreas let her chin go and stood up, his whole body vibrating with tension—or anger. Siena couldn't make out which.

And then he exploded, '*Theos,* Siena. You wilfully ruined my life just because you were too scared to stand up to your *father?*'

Siena stood up. It was as if a lead weight was making her belly plummet. She should have expected this, but still her head swam and her stomach churned. 'I'm sorry, Andreas… so sorry. I went looking for you that night to try and explain…'

Suddenly Siena's powers of speech failed her. All she could see was Andreas's eyes, burning into her, scorching her. With a soft cry she felt the world fall away, and only heard the faintest of guttural curses before everything went black.

CHAPTER NINE

ANDREAS STOOD WATCHING Siena's sleeping form on the bed. He'd only just managed to catch her before she crumpled to the floor, and he cursed himself for lashing out. Emotions had roiled in his gut. He'd been so angry—incandescent—to learn the truth of what had happened. *If it was the truth.*

A small part of him wanted to insist that she was lying— making it up, thinking on her feet—but he'd seen the ashy pallor of her face. The way her eyes had looked inward, not even seeing him. No one could have faked that.

The magnitude of what this meant, how it changed things, was impossible to take in. *If it was the truth.*

Andreas threw off his jacket and dropped it to a nearby chair, where he sat down and pulled at his bow-tie. He'd taken off Siena's shoes and covered her with a blanket. From here he could see that perfect profile, the shape of her body, and he felt the inevitable beat of desire. It had surged into his blood as soon as he'd seen her again, as if it had merely lain dormant.

His fists clenched. The thing was, could he believe her? Andreas's mind went back to that cataclysmic evening, and when he thought about it now, without the haze of anger and rage, he could remember that Siena had been icy, yes, but there had been something else in her eyes. Terror?

Her father had had a tight grip on her arm. Too tight. He'd

forgotten that detail. And her father had fed her the words: *'You would never kiss someone like him, would you?'*

Andreas felt disgust. She'd been a day away from eighteen. Innocent. Naïve. Terrified of her father. And not for herself, for her vulnerable sister.

Questions piled on top of questions.

Andreas frowned as another wisp of a memory returned. He'd been called to his boss's office after DePiero's henchmen had laid into him, and had had to explain what had happened.

Andreas had been so angry at his own pathetic naïvety when he should have known better that he'd lashed out. Tried to make it seem, at least to himself, as if he might have had some control over the situation. At one point they'd heard a noise outside and Andreas had gone to the door, which had been ajar. He'd looked out and thought he was seeing things when a flash of ballgown disappeared around a corner.

Had that been Siena? Looking for him? Andreas frowned deeper, trying to remember what he'd said, and it came back in all its brutal clarity: *'I'd never have touched her if I'd known she was so poisonous...'*

He could laugh now. As if he'd had a choice! As if he'd have been able to stop himself from touching her! She'd enthralled him then and she enthralled him today. He was incapable of not touching her if she was within feet of him.

Uneasiness prickled over Andreas's skin. Without the anger and rage he'd clung onto for so long he felt stripped bare and made raw by all these revelations. And yet one thing was immutable: now that Siena was back in his life he was not about to let her go again easily.

When Siena woke she was completely disorientated. She had no idea who or where she was. And then details started emerging. She was in a huge bed and what looked like a misty dawn light was coming through the open curtains. She could see only sky.

She looked around and saw a palatial room, rococo de-sign. She frowned. How did she know it was rococo? She was covered in a soft blanket and her head felt sore. Siena raised it and winced when her hair tugged. She pulled it free of the band, loosening it.

She pulled back the blanket and saw she was in a white shirt and black skirt. It all came rushing back. The reception. *Seeing Andreas*. Him pulling her out, bringing her here. All her words tumbling out. She'd told him…*everything*. He'd been angry. And she'd fainted. Siena was disgusted with herself.

Siena put a hand over her eyes, as if that could stop the painful recollections. Slowly she sat up and pushed the blanket aside, stumbled on jelly legs to the bathroom. When she saw herself in the mirror she made a face. She looked wan and washed out, her hair all over the place. She felt sticky in her uniform. She saw the shower and longed to feel clean again, so she stripped off and turned on the powerful spray, stepped under the teeming water.

Andreas. She shivered. After washing herself thoroughly Siena stepped out and dried herself off. It was time to face Andreas in the cold light of day.

When Siena emerged into the main reception room of the sumptuous suite she still wasn't prepared to see Andreas sit-ting at a table, drinking coffee and eating some breakfast. She'd dressed in her shirt and skirt, leaving off the bow-tie and shoes. She was barefoot and felt self-conscious now—which was ridiculous when this man knew every inch of her body in intimate detail.

Andreas lowered his paper and stood up. A chivalrous ges-ture that caught at Siena somewhere vulnerable. She moved forward, her heart thumping against her breastbone. 'I'm sorry.' Her voice was husky. 'I don't know what came over me... Thank you for letting me sleep.'

Andreas pulled out a chair at right angles to his and said coolly, 'Sit down and have something to eat. You've lost weight.'

Siena came forward and avoided his eye. She *had* lost weight. She'd hadn't had much money for food. Sensing his gaze, Siena looked at Andreas and it was intense.

Tightly he said, 'I'm sorry for lashing out at you like that last night... It was just...a lot to take in.'

Siena's heart contracted. 'I know. I'm sorry.'

'I checked out what you told me about Serena.' He sounded defensive. 'I would have been a fool not to after everything...'

The brief warmth that had invaded Siena cooled. 'Of course.'

Siena felt fear trickle down her spine even as hurt lanced her. He hadn't trusted her. 'What are you going to do?'

Andreas's mouth tightened. 'Nothing. Your sister deserves all the care she can get after a lifetime of being subjected to that kind of treatment.'

Siena felt momentarily dizzy. 'Thank you,' she said, and then she blurted out, 'I'll pay you back...the money. If you could let me set up a payment plan...?'

Andreas looked at her incredulously. 'On the kind of wages you've been earning? You'd be paying me out of your pension.'

Siena flushed and straightened her back, clinging to the small amount of pride she had left. 'I'll find another job. There are grants for people on minimum wage, training schemes...'

Andreas was grim. He poured her some coffee and pushed a plate of bread towards her. 'You don't need to pay me back. If you'd told me in the first place what you needed the money for I would have helped you.'

Now Siena was the one to look at him incredulously, and she remarked bitterly, 'Forgive me if I don't believe you. You hate my guts. You wanted revenge. If I had told you that my feckless sister was in a clinic to sort out her addictions and mental health issues you would have sneered in my face.' Siena looked down. 'I was afraid you might try to use her to get back at me—after all, that's what my father always did.'

Siena missed the way Andreas winced slightly.

He said heavily, 'My best friend committed suicide years ago, and I witnessed the devastation it wrought. I don't underestimate mental health illness for a second. I might not have been initially inclined to help, but if you had explained to me—'

Siena looked up, unsettled by this nugget from his past. 'What? Explained the tawdry reality of our lives? The sadistic bullying of our father?'

Andreas's eyes narrowed on her. 'Why did Serena not leave once she could?'

Siena swallowed, 'She didn't leave because of me. She wouldn't leave me behind. And then…once I got older…she was too dependent on our father's money to fuel her drink and drugs addiction. When she *could* have left she didn't want to. As perverse as that sounds.'

Andreas was grim. 'And so as long as she stayed you were stuck too?'

Siena nodded.

Andreas put down his napkin. 'Now that I know…everything…I will take care of Serena's bills. You don't have to pay me back.'

Siena's heart lurched. 'But I do. You don't owe me—*us*—anything.' The line of her mouth was bitter. 'I owe you so much. More than I can ever repay. If it wasn't for me you would never have been sacked or had to leave Europe.'

To Siena's dismay she could feel tears threaten, but she forced herself to look at Andreas. 'You don't know how much I wanted to go back in time, to undo what happened.'

Andreas's eyes grew darker and he leaned forward. 'That's wishful thinking. If we had that moment over again nothing could have kept us from touching each other. It was inevitable.'

Siena's heart beat faster. Her belly swooped. 'What are you saying?'

'What I'm saying is that the chemistry between us was too powerful to ignore. Then and now.'

Stupidly Siena repeated, *'Now?'*

Andreas nodded and stood up. He came around the table and took Siena's hands, pulling her up out of her chair. He was suddenly very close, very tall. Siena could feel his heat reach out and envelop her, and a wave of intense longing came over her, setting her whole body alight. She'd not even admitted to herself how much she'd missed him in the past month, how she'd ached for him at night.

'We're not done, Siena.'

Andreas put his hand to the back of her neck, fingers tangling in her hair, and urged her closer. And then his mouth was on hers, hot and urgent. She could feel him hardening against her belly and she groaned. She couldn't deny this either—not when every cell in her body was rejoicing.

She lifted her arms and fisted her hands in Andreas's hair, bolder than she'd been before, arching herself into him. The knowledge resounded in her head. He knew everything but he still wanted her. She'd believed his desire had died a death the night he'd let her go. A fierce exultation made her blood surge, and her heart soared when he pulled back and looked at her for an incendiary moment. She felt him picking her up and quickly covering the distance back to the bedroom.

As he was lying her on the bed Andreas was already opening the buttons of her shirt, and Siena's hands were mirroring his. She almost wept when her fingers were too clumsy. Andreas took her hands away and ripped it open, buttons popping everywhere.

An urgency that Siena hadn't experienced before infused the air around them. Her shirt was open and Andreas pulled the cups of her bra down so that her breasts spilled free. He bent his head to pay homage to the puckered peaks, making Siena cry out at the exquisite sensation.

Siena barely noticed that Andreas was arching her into him so that he could undo her skirt at the back, but then his mouth was gone and he was lying her down again so that he could pull her skirt over her hips and thighs and off.

It was hard to breathe. Especially when she saw his hands go to his belt and he made quick work of taking off his trousers and boxers. And then he was naked. And aroused. Siena's heart-rate increased when she saw the telltale moisture bead at the tip of his erection, and a gush of heat made her even wetter between her legs.

Andreas came down on the bed beside her, the rising sun outside making his body gleam. With deft hands her shirt and bra followed her clothes and his to the floor and soon they were both naked.

A surge of something scarily tender gripped Siena. She raised a hand and touched Andreas's jaw, relishing the stubble prickling against her palm.

He took her hand and brought it down, curling her fingers around him. Her eyes widened when she felt the solid strength of him, how he twitched and seemed to swell even more. Her hand moved up and down in an instinctive rhythm and Siena watched Andreas's cheeks flush with blood, his eyes grow even darker.

Stretching up, she pressed her mouth to his, open, her tongue seeking and finding his, sucking it deep. Her breasts were full and tight, and Andreas's hand moved down her body until he pushed between her legs, making them fall apart. His fingers found the moist evidence of her arousal and stroked with a rhythm that made her curve into him, pull her mouth from his so she could suck in oxygen.

And then his fingers thrust into her, and Siena's body spasmed with pre-orgasmic pleasure.

Andreas's voice was guttural, rough. 'You're so ready for me. I want you *now*. I've missed you.'

'I've missed you.' Siena's heart stopped for a long second and she searched Andreas's face. He looked as if he was in a fever. She slammed down on the momentary joy his words had provoked. He was talking in the heat of the moment, that was all.

Her whole body seemed to be poised on the brink. She felt Andreas take her hand from him and heard the ripping of foil, and then he was back, the blunt head of his erection pressing against her body, teasing.

Siena opened her legs wider, bit her lip and arched upwards, forcing Andreas to impale her. The pleasure was like nothing she'd experienced yet with this man. It was more intense than anything before.

Andreas slid deep into her body before pulling out again, and then moved back in. Siena's head went back and she looked up at him, her chest feeling so full that she could only gasp when he slid so deep that it felt as if he touched her heart…and in that moment the knowledge burst into Siena's consciousness.

She loved this man. She loved him as she'd never loved another being—not even her sister.

But she couldn't fully absorb it. Andreas was wresting away her ability to think as his powerful body surged, robbing her of breath and speech.

The intense dance between their bodies became all she could focus on. She was willing herself not to tip over the edge too soon, revelling in Andreas's power and control. But then it became too much. She couldn't hang on. Not when she wrapped her legs around Andreas's hips and their chests were crushed together. And not when he bent his head and found one taut peak, sucked it deep.

Siena cried out as emotion soared and realisation struck her: she'd thought she'd never experience this again.

Her body tightened on that delicious plateau just a second before she fell and fell, her body clenching tight around Andreas's shaft, urging him on until he too fell and their bodies were just a sweaty tangle of limbs on the tousled covers of the bed.

When Siena woke again she was disorientated once more, but this time because Andreas was in bed with her, his head resting on one hand as he looked at her. She blushed, and he smiled, and her heart palpitated. So much had happened in the space of twenty-four hours.

His smile faded. 'I want you to come home with me.'

Those words caused a lurch in Siena's chest. 'Home? To your apartment?'

Andreas nodded, and then said with familiar intractability, 'I'm not going to take no for an answer. You're coming with me, Siena.'

She looked at him for a long moment. His jaw was more stubbled now. He had that look she recognized. Slightly stern. Determined.

Feeling claustrophobic under his dark blue gaze, Siena looked away and saw the bathroom robe at the end of the bed, where she'd thrown it earlier. Moving before she could lose her nerve, she sat up and reached for it, pulling it around her and awkwardly feeding her arms into the sleeves. She got out of the bed to stand apart from him, belting the robe tightly and trying not to think of how dishevelled she felt. *How deliciously sated.*

'Andreas...' she began, not really knowing what to say.

He lay back against the pillows, arms behind his head, broad chest swelling with the movement, and Siena was hopelessly distracted for a moment.

With an effort she tore her avid gaze away and looked back to his eyes, narrowed on her. She started again. 'Andreas.'

He arched a brow.

'Things are...different now. I owe you a huge sum of money.' Siena blushed. 'I didn't feel comfortable taking the jewellery, or cashing it in, but I felt as if taking care of Serena was more important than my guilty conscience.'

She steeled herself, but it was hard when Andreas was like a lounging pasha in the bed.

'But now I won't feel comfortable unless you let me come to some agreement. I can't. It's not right. Not with everything else that has happened. I'd prefer to let you have your money back and try to take care of Serena myself than let you pay.'

Andreas sat up. 'That is not an option. Not now that I know what her situation is. You *will* let me pay, Siena.'

Siena wrung her hands and all but wailed. 'But can't you see? I'll be beholden to you for ever. I can't have that. My father was a tyrant...he owned us.' She saw a dangerous look on Andreas's face but rushed on. 'I'm not saying you're the same...but I couldn't bear to go back into that kind of...obligation.'

Andreas rested his arms on his knees, still managing to look intimidating despite his being naked under the sheets.

'You weren't so conflicted when you walked away with a fortune in jewellery.'

Siena's face grew hotter. 'I didn't think I'd ever see you again. I only took it because I thought I was making the best choice—that the end justified the means.' She hitched her chin. 'You were only too happy to let me walk away. And it's not as if you got nothing in return.'

His eyes flashed, but he said silkily, 'That's true. After all

I got the precious DePiero innocence. But now I want you to come back to me.'

'Come back to me.' Siena felt weak. Questions reverberated in her head: *For how long? Why? Is it just about the sex?*

A voice answered her. *Of course it was just about the sex.*

'I—' Siena began, but Andreas cut in harshly.

'We both know I can have you flat on your back moaning with need in seconds—don't think I won't prove to you that you can't just walk away from this.'

Andreas didn't like the feeling of panic that gripped him when her eyes grew wide. He had nothing to hold Siena now. Not really. Only a complete lowlife would make her pay him back for her sister's treatment.

So quietly that he almost didn't hear her, Siena said, 'If I come back to you I want things to be different.'

Andreas went still, not liking the way his blood surged. She looked serious, and heart-stoppingly beautiful with her hair feathered over her shoulders.

'I want to find a job—a better job if I can—and start paying you back.' Andreas opened his mouth but Siena held up a hand, stopping him. 'That's non-negotiable. I have some skills...I can type and file. I used to act as my father's secretary when his PA was off or on leave, and I worked sometimes at a local school, helping the special needs assistants. I'm hoping that will count for something.'

'Also, I don't want any more jewellery.' She shuddered slightly. 'I don't want to see another piece of jewellery as long as I live.'

'Anything else?' Andreas prompted, seeing her biting her lip and feeling the rush of need make him harden again.

'As soon as this...chemistry...whatever it is...is over it ends. Because it won't last for ever, will it? It can't...'

There was a tinge of desperation to her voice that reso-

nated in Andreas and he held out a hand. 'It's not over yet…
Come here, Siena.'

She stood stubbornly apart. 'Do you agree? To what I've
said?'

'Yes,' Andreas growled, his need making his voice sound
harsh. 'Now come here.'

Six weeks later.

''Night, Siena. See you on Monday. Have a good weekend.'

Siena smiled. ''Night, Lucy. I hope your little girl feels
better soon.'

The other woman left and the door swung shut behind her.
Siena looked around and stretched. She was the only one left
in the typing pool. She was due to receive her very first pay-
check next week, and it was almost embarrassing how excited
she was about it.

Sometimes she couldn't fathom how lucky she was: Serena was safe and secure, and receiving the best treatment,
and Siena was fulfilling a lifelong ambition to be independent. Well, she qualified, as independent as she could be with
a dominant alpha male lover who resented everything that took
her away from him. Even though, as she'd pointed out heatedly, he didn't count *his* work in that equation…

She got up and went to the rack to get her coat. She looked
out of the window. A spurt of desire heated her insides when
she saw a familiar silver sports car and Andreas standing beside it, phone to his ear.

She hadn't seen him in two days as he'd been in New York
on business.

She'd been working here for almost a month now, but he
insisted on picking her up every day, or having his driver do it.

He'd grumbled in bed the other morning at dawn, 'I want

you to come with me. *Why* do you insist on working when you don't have to?'

Siena had rolled her eyes. It was a familiar argument, but she stuck to her guns, not wanting to lay out in bald language that one day, when Andreas stopped desiring her, she'd be on her own again.

He was the one who had patiently helped her put together a CV which flagrantly glossed over the fact that she had no *bona fide* qualifications. He'd pulled her close on his lap and they'd sat in his study in front of his computer. 'Anyway, it doesn't matter," he'd said. "You'll walk into the office and they'll all be drooling too hard to even notice what's on your CV…'

Siena had punched him playfully, hating the see-saw emotions that still gripped her in his presence. It was different this time. *He* was different. Not more open, exactly—he always kept a piece of himself back—but she was seeing a side to him now that made her fall for him a little more each day. He was lighter, made her laugh.

It reminded her painfully of what it had been like the evening they'd met in Paris, before the world had crashed down around them. She resolutely pushed aside the painful knowledge that for him it had just been an opportunity…

When she'd got the job, after two rounds of interviews, Andreas had surprised her by cooking a traditional Greek dinner and producing a bottle of champagne with a flourish.

Siena could see him now, looking at the door of her building with barely disguised impatience, and hurriedly put on her coat and got her bag. As she went downstairs she reflected that Andreas still hadn't ever really opened up to her about his personal life. After mentioning his family the last time, and the way he'd shut down, she didn't like to bring it up.

After all, she thought a little bleakly, what was the point? It wasn't as if she was ever likely to become a more permanent fixture in Andreas's life.

When she got outside the breath stuck in her throat at the narrow-eyed, heavy-lidded look he gave her. She wasn't unaware of the interest of women passing by, and a fierce surge of possessiveness gripped her. A primal reaction of a woman to her mate.

He put his phone in his pocket and caught her to him, slanting his mouth across hers in a kiss that was not designed for public consumption. Siena didn't care, though. Two days felt like two months, and she arched her body into his and fisted her hands in his hair.

When he pulled away he chuckled and said, 'Miss me, then?'

Siena blushed. She was so *raw* around him. She affected an airy look and said, 'Not at all. How long were you gone anyway?'

The ease that had built up between them in the past few weeks made Siena feel dizzy sometimes. It was so different from how it had been before.

Andreas scowled. 'You'll pay for that. *Later.*'

He stepped back and opened the car door, letting Siena get in. She took a deep breath, watching him walk around the car with that powerful, leonine grace, and her belly somersaulted.

When he got in she felt unaccountably shy. 'My boss came and told me today that I might be getting a promotion—moving up to work with someone as a personal secretary within another month.'

Andreas looked at her and put a large hand on her leg, under her skirt, inched it up. 'I can offer you a promotion if you want—to my bed.'

Siena rolled her eyes and stopped Andreas's hand with her own—mostly because she was embarrassed by how turned on she already was.

'I'm already in your bed. You know I'm not going to give up my job...'

Andreas rolled his eyes and put his hand back on the wheel. 'At least they won't be demanding your attention over the weekend. You're mine for the next forty-eight hours, DePiero.'

Siena noticed then that they weren't taking the turn for where he lived in Mayfair and asked idly, 'Where are we going?'

Andreas glanced at her and looked a little sheepish.

Instantly Siena's eyes narrowed. 'Andreas Xenakis, what are you up to?'

He sighed. 'We're going to Athens for the weekend.' As if he could see her start to protest he held up a hand and said, 'I promise you'll be back at your desk by nine on Monday morning.'

'But I don't have anything with me—do you have to go to a function?'

Andreas nodded. 'It's a charity ball. I instructed my secretary to go to the apartment and pack some clothes, get your passport.'

At times like this it still stunned Siena how much power Andreas had.

They hadn't been to many functions in the last few weeks, but then Andreas said, with an edge to his voice, 'My youngest sister has just had a new baby. I promised my parents we'd call for lunch on Sunday before going home.'

Siena tamped down the flutters in her belly when he said 'we'. 'Oh?' she said, in a carefully neutral voice. 'That sounds nice.'

She avoided Andreas's eyes, not wanting him to remember how he'd reacted when she'd asked him about his family before. Not wanting to remind him of *before* at all.

The following evening, in the ballroom of the hotel where they were staying, Andreas looked at Siena weaving through the crowd as she came back from the ladies' room. The ache that seemed to have set up residence in his gut intensified. She was wearing the black dress she'd worn on their first night out—except this time her face wasn't a mask of faint hauteur and she wore only the gold birdcage necklace.

It was so obvious now that she'd put on a monumental act when she'd been with him for that week. Uncomfortably he had to concede the many signs had given her away, if he'd cared to investigate them at the time. Her antipathy for the jewellery, her visible reluctance at being on the social scene, which he'd put down to embarrassment but which he now knew went deeper. *Her innocence.* Both physically and actually.

When Andreas thought of her father, he wanted to throttle the man.

And even though her brother was a billionaire she hadn't attempted to go to him for a hand-out.

Siena's make-up was as subtle as ever, and yet she outshone every woman in the room. She *glowed*. She saw him in the crowd and she smiled—a small, private smile. Andreas wanted to smile back—he could feel the warmth rising up within him, something deeper than mere lust and desire—but something held him back. That ache inside him was unyielding.

He saw Siena's smile falter slightly and fade. Her eyes dropped and Andreas felt inexplicably as if he was losing something. Someone waving caught his eye and he looked over to see a familiar face with relief. He welcomed the distraction from thinking too much about the way Siena made him feel.

When she arrived by his side, however, he couldn't stop himself from snaking an arm around her, relishing her proximity. *His.* It beat like a tattoo in his blood.

Belying his turbulent emotions, he said, 'How would you like to meet the designer of your necklace? She's the wife of a friend of mine and they're just across the room.'

Siena's hand flew to the gold chain and she looked up, eyes

wide and bright. 'Really? Angel Parnassus is here? I'd *love* to meet her!'

As Andreas led Siena by the hand through the crowd he pushed down the way her simple joy at meeting a mere jewellery designer made something inside him weaken. Things might have changed but the essentials were the same. Siena was with him only until he could let her go…and that day would come. *Soon*.

CHAPTER TEN

ANDREAS HAD ORGANISED a helicopter to take them from Athens on Sunday to a small landing pad near his parents' town. Siena couldn't stop the flutters of apprehension in her belly, and wasn't unaware of Andreas's almost tangible tension.

A four-wheel drive vehicle was waiting for them at the landing pad and soon they were driving out and ascending what looked like a mountain.

Curiously, Siena asked, 'How often do you come home?'

Andreas's profile was remote. 'Not often enough for my mother.'

Siena smiled but Andreas didn't. She couldn't understand his reluctance to come home. If she'd come from a family like his she didn't think she'd ever have left…

She could see a town now, colourful and perched precariously on a hill above them. 'Is that it?'

'Yes,' Andreas answered.

When they drove in Siena looked around with interest. It looked modestly prosperous—wide clean streets, people walking around browsing market stalls and colourful shops. They looked friendly and happy. Siena could see a lot of construction work going on and had an instinct that Andreas was involved, for all his apparent reluctance to come home.

They drove up through winding streets until they emerged

into a beautifully picturesque square with a medieval church and very old trees.

Andreas came to a stop and Siena opened her seat belt, saying, 'This is beautiful.'

'You can see all the way to Athens on a clear day.'

'I can believe that,' Siena breathed, taking in the stunning view.

Andreas got out and she followed suit, and suddenly from around the corner came a screaming gaggle of children. They swarmed all over Andreas, and Siena's heart twisted at seeing him lift a little one high in the air with a huge smile on his face.

She intuited that he might not like coming home, for whatever reason, but he loved his family.

He put the child down and the other children disappeared as quickly as they'd arrived. He held out his hand for her and smiled wryly. 'Some of my nieces and nephews. They'll have heard the helicopter.'

Siena took his hand. She'd followed his lead, dressing down in smart jeans and a soft dusky pink silk top with a light grey cardigan. Flat shoes made her feel even smaller next to Andreas, fragile, and it wasn't altogether welcome.

As they approached a very modest-looking stone house, with trailing flowers around the windows and door, there were shouts and laughter coming from inside and a baby's wail. Siena unconsciously gripped Andreas's hand, making him look at her.

'Okay?'

She smiled and gulped. 'Yes. Fine.' But she wasn't. Because she'd suddenly realised that if Andreas's family were as idyllic as she feared they might be it would break her open.

But it was too late to turn back. A small, rotund grey-haired woman had come bustling out and was drawing Andreas down to kiss him loudly on the cheeks. When he straightened she had tears in her eyes and was saying, 'My boy...my boy...'

Then Andreas drew Siena forward and introduced her in Greek, of which Siena could only understand a little. His mother looked her up and down and then took her by the arms in a surprisingly strong grip. She nodded once, as if Siena had passed some test, and drew her into her huge soft bosom, kissing her soundly.

Siena felt inexplicably shy and blushed profusely, not used to this amount of touching from a stranger. But Andreas's mother had her hand in hers and was leading her into a lovely bright house, very simple.

There seemed to be a bewildering amount of people and Siena tried to remember all of Andreas's sisters' names: Arachne, who had the new baby, which slept peacefully in a corner; Martha, Eleni, Phebe and Ianthe. They were all dark and very pretty, with flashing eyes and big smiles.

Andreas brought Siena over to meet his father, whom she could see was quite bowed with arthritis, but it was easy to see where Andreas's tall good looks had come from. The man was innately proud, his face marked with the strong lines of his forebears.

Lunch was a somewhat chaotic affair, with children running in and out and everyone talking over everyone else. But the love and affection was palpable. Andreas had one of his nephews curled up trustingly in his lap, and Siena's womb clenched as she saw how at ease he was with the children.

And then Siena recalled his cruel words when she had asked him if he wanted children.

When Arachne, his youngest sister, approached Siena after lunch with the new baby Siena froze with panic. Being faced with this brought up all her deepest longings and fears. For how could she ever be a mother when she had no idea what it felt like to *have* a mother?

But Arachne wouldn't take no for an answer and she handed the baby into Siena's arms, showing her how to hold her.

Andreas had seen Siena's look of horror when Arachne approached her with the baby and had got up, incensed at the thought that she was rejecting his family, but his mother stopped him.

'Wait. Let her be,' she said.

It was only then that Andreas watched and saw Siena's look of horror replaced by one of intense awe and wonder. He realised it hadn't been horror. It had been panic. He could remember his own panic when he'd held a baby for the first time. He realised that Siena had never held a baby before.

Before he could stop himself he was walking over to sit beside her.

She glanced at him and smiled tremulously. 'She's so perfect and tiny. I'm afraid I'll hurt her.'

'You won't,' Andreas said through the tightness in his throat. To see the baby at Siena's breast, Siena's hair falling down over her cheek, her little finger clutched in a tiny chubby hand… Andreas dreaded the inevitable rise of claustrophobia but it didn't come. Something else came in its place—a welling of emotion that he couldn't understand and which wasn't the habitual grief for his dead best friend that he usually felt in this place. This felt new. Far more fragile. Tender. *Dangerous.*

When the baby mewled Siena tensed and whispered, 'What did I do?'

Weakly, Andreas used it as an excuse to break up that disturbing image, gently taking his niece and putting her over his shoulder, patting her back like a professional. Siena's worried face made emotion swell.

'Nothing,' he said gruffly. 'She's probably just hungry again.'

His sister came and took the baby out of Andreas's hands. Andreas watched as Siena stared after Arachne and the baby with an almost wistful look on her face. That galvanised him into moving up onto his feet and he caught her by the hand. She looked at him.

'We should leave if we're to get back to Athens and make our flight slot this evening.'

Just then Andreas's mother came up. She was saying something but she was speaking too fast for Siena to understand. When she was finished Siena asked, 'What did she say?'

Andreas looked at Siena with an unreadable expression. 'She asked if we'd stay for the night...'

Siena couldn't help the silly fluttering of something, but then Andreas reminded her, 'You have to be back for work in the morning.'

Siena's stomach fell. *Work.* 'Oh, yes...'

Andreas's eyes glinted. 'You don't want to miss that, do you?'

Siena looked at him and saw the challenge. He would stay if she relented over her work. She met it head-on and took her hand out of his. 'No, I don't.' Even though she found herself wishing that they *could* stay here longer. Not that she would admit it to Andreas.

Andreas's family bade them a friendly farewell, with Andreas suffering under copious kisses and hugs from his sisters and nieces and nephews. And then his mother came and pulled Siena close again, hugging her tight. When she put her away from her his mother tucked some wayward hair behind her ear in an effortless yet profoundly simple maternal gesture.

She looked at Siena with the kindest dark eyes, and Siena felt as if she could see all the way through to her deepest heart's desires and pain. A ball of emotion was spreading inside Siena and for a panicky second she wanted to burst into tears and bury her head in this woman's chest, to seek a kind of comfort she'd only dreamt existed.

But then Andreas was there and the moment was defused. And soon they were back in the Jeep, and in the helicopter, and by the time they'd got to the plane Siena felt as if she was under control again.

'What did you think?'

Siena turned to look at Andreas, where he was sprawled across the other side of the aisle on the small private jet. She'd been avoiding looking at him because she still felt a little raw. How could she begin to explain to this man that seeing his family had been like a dream of hers manifested? All that love and affection in one place...

'I liked them very much.'

'Still,' Andreas said, with something Siena couldn't decipher in his voice, 'it's not really your scene is it? The rustic nature of a backwater like that and a big, sprawling messy family?'

Siena felt nothing for a second, as if protecting herself, and then hurt bloomed—sharp and wounding. After everything he now knew about her Siena couldn't believe that he still had her very much placed in a box.

It seemed as if not much had really changed at all, in spite of the last few weeks. She wanted to berate him, ask him what his issues over going home were, but she was feeling too fragile. Clearly she still had to play a part.

Feeling very brittle, Siena forced a short sharp laugh. 'As you said yourself, we're from worlds apart.'

And she turned her head and looked out of the window, blinking back the hot prickle of tears, feeling like a fool.

Andreas pushed down the uncomfortable awareness that Siena was upset. Bringing her to see his family had been a mistake. He should have gone on his own. Maybe then he wouldn't have seen them in another light, and not in the usual suffocating way he usually did. Maybe then he wouldn't have noticed his father with one of his nieces on his knee, telling her a story. Wouldn't have had to wonder for the first time in his life what the anatomy of his family would have looked like if his father hadn't stayed to support his wife and children.

There were plenty of marriages in that town that were fragmented because the men had had to go to Athens to work, leaving their family behind. But his father had chosen to stay, and as a result they'd all had a very secure and stable upbringing.

Andreas didn't like to acknowledge that seeing Siena in that milieu hadn't been as alien as he'd thought it would be. She'd charmed them all with that effortless grace, and he could recognise now her genuine warmth.

Andreas glanced at Siena but her face was turned away, her hair spilling over her shoulders and touching the curve of her breast. She was not the woman he'd believed her to be. Not in the slightest.

Andreas looked out of the window beside him blindly, as if she might turn her head and see something he struggled to contain. He thought of how quickly she'd dismissed meeting his family and clung to that like a drowning man to a raft. Of course she'd *liked* his family, but she would never be a part of that world in an indelible way.

Andreas assured himself that the very ambiguous emotions she'd evoked when he'd seen her cradle his baby niece had merely been a natural response to his realisation that one day he too would have to settle down and produce an heir. For the first time it wasn't an image that sent a wave of rejection through his body.

But it wouldn't be with Siena DePiero. Never her.

In bed that night, Siena and Andreas came together in a way that Siena could only lament at. This heat was inevitable between them, and it was good at hiding the fact that there was little else. She wished she could be stronger, but she felt as if time was running out and so she seized Andreas between her legs with a fierce grip, urging him on so that when the explosion came it was more intense than it had ever been.

When he was spooning her afterwards, and she was in a half-asleep haze, Siena opened her eyes. What she'd said earlier about Andreas's family hadn't been truthful, and she was sick of lying to him.

She turned so that she was on her back, looking into Andreas's face. He opened slumberous eyes and that heat sizzled between them again. *Already.* Siena ignored it valiantly and put her hand on Andreas's when it started exploring up across her belly.

'No... I wanted to say something to you...'

Siena felt the tension come into Andreas's big body. He removed his hand from her.

She took a deep breath. 'Earlier, when you said that your home town and meeting your family probably wasn't really my scene, I agreed with you... Well, I shouldn't have. Because it's not true. It's more my scene than you could ever know, Andreas. That's the problem. I dreamed my whole life of a family like yours. I longed to know what it would be like to grow up surrounded with love and affection...'

Siena couldn't read Andreas's expression in the dim light but she could imagine she wouldn't like it.

'When your mother hugged me earlier...she really hugged me. I've never felt that before, and it was amazing. I'm glad you took me. It was a privilege to meet them.'

There was a long moment of silence and then Andreas said in a tight voice, 'You should sleep. You have to be up early.'

When Siena's breaths had evened out and he knew she was alseep Andreas carefully took his arms from around her, noting as he did so that not one night since she'd come back had they slept apart. He got out of bed and pulled on a pair of loose sweats and walked out of the bedroom.

He went into the drawing room and spent a long time looking out of the window. Until he could see the faintest smudge of dawn light in the sky. The knowledge resounded inside him that he couldn't keep fighting it.

Then he went into his study and opened his safe and took out a small box. He sat down and opened it and looked at it for a long time. For the first time since he'd met Siena again the dull ache of need and the emotions she caused within him seemed to dissipate.

Eventually he pulled out a drawer and put the box in it, a sense of resolve filling his belly. It was the same sense he'd felt when he'd laid eyes on Siena for the first time in five years, except this time the resolve came with a lot of fear, and not a sense of incipient triumph.

He had to acknowledge, ruefully, that he'd felt many things in the last tumultuous couple of months, and triumph had figured only fleetingly.

A week later

It was Friday evening and Siena was leaving work. Andreas's driver was waiting for her outside the office and she got into the back of the car. Andreas had called earlier to say he'd been held up in Paris, asking if she would come to meet him if he arranged transport. Siena had said yes.

So now she was being taken to his private plane, which would take her to Paris. Trepidation filled her. She wasn't sure what it would be like to be in Paris with Andreas now... He'd been in a strange mood all week. Monosyllabic and yet staring at her intensely if she caught him looking. It made her nervous, and Siena had a very poisonous suspicion that perhaps Andreas wasn't quite done with torturing her. Perhaps he was going to call time on their relationship in Paris, where it had all started?

And yet the other night he'd surprised her by asking her abruptly why she loved the birdcage necklace so much. She'd answered huskily that to her it symbolised freedom. She'd felt silly, and Andreas hadn't mentioned it again.

At night, when they'd made love, it had felt as if there was some added urgency. Siena had felt even more shattered after each time. Last night she'd been aghast to realise she'd been moved to tears, and had quickly got up to go to the bathroom, terrified Andreas would notice…

Siena knew she wouldn't be able to take it for much longer. Being with Andreas was tearing her apart. Perhaps Paris was the place where *she* should end it once and for all if he didn't?

When she got to Paris her heart was heavy and the weather matched her mood: grey and stormy. The hotel was busy, and with a lurch Siena recognised that it must be the weekend of the debutante ball as she saw harassed-looking mothers with spoilt-looking teenagers.

Surely, she thought to herself wildly, Andreas wouldn't be so cruel…

But then he was there, striding towards her, and everything in Siena's world shrank to him. She was in so much trouble. He kissed her, but it was perfunctory, and with a grimace he cast a glance to the young debs and their entourages of stylists and hair and make-up people.

'I'd forgotten the ball was this weekend…'

Relief flooded Siena and she felt a little weak.

Andreas was saying now, 'I've booked dinner. We'll leave in an hour. I just have some things to finish and I'll meet you in the room.'

Siena went up and tried to calm her fractured nerves after seeing the debs and being back here again. *Still* Andreas's mistress. She forced herself to have a relaxing bath, weary after her week in the office but still exultant to be working.

When Andreas arrived he was in a smart black suit, open shirt, and she had dressed in a gold brocade shift dress.

Solicitously Andreas took her arm and led her out to the lift, down to the lobby, and then into his car. He was so silent that Siena asked nervously, 'Penny for them?'

He turned to look at her blankly for a second, a million miles away, and then focused. He smiled tightly. 'Nothing important.'

He looked away again. Siena's sense of foreboding increased.

They were taken to a new restaurant on the top floor of a famous art gallery with grand views over Paris. The Eiffel Tower was so close Siena felt as if they could touch it. They were finishing their meal before Siena realised that they'd had the most innocuous of conversations. Touching on lots, but nothing really. As if they hardly knew each other.

The bill arrived and suddenly Siena felt as if something was slipping out of her grasp. A panicky sensation gripped her, but now Andreas was standing and they were leaving... She took his hand and thought guiltily that if he didn't say anything neither would she.

Andreas didn't make conversation in the car on the way back—again—and Siena was quiet too, not knowing what to say in this weird, heavy silence. When they got back to the hotel one of the duty managers rushed up to Andreas with a worried look.

After a brief, terse conversation Andreas turned to Siena, 'One of the guests at the ball has had a heart attack. I need to make sure everything is being attended to.'

Siena put a hand on his arm. 'I'll come with you if you like?'

Andreas looked at her and his eyes seemed to blaze with something undefinable. But then he said, 'No, you should go to bed. I'll see you in the morning.'

Siena watched him stride away, so tall and proud, master of the domain from where once *she'd* had him cast out. She felt a sense of futility. It would always be between them. Insurmountable.

After Siena had got into bed she tried to stay awake for a long time, in case she heard Andreas return, but sleep claimed her. When she did wake she was groggy, and it felt as if it was still dark outside.

Andreas was saying, 'Siena… I need you to get up… I've laid out some clothes for you.'

Siena sat up woozily and saw Andreas straighten.

'I'll wait for you outside.'

He was dressed in jeans and a light sweater. She saw a pile of clothes on the end of the bed—jeans and a similar sweater for her, and a jacket. He was walking out of the room.

Feeling dazed and confused, wondering if she was dreaming, Siena got up and quickly dressed. She looked outside for a second and saw that it was close to dawn. Where had Andreas been all night?

Pulling her hair back into a knot, she emerged and saw Andreas standing with his back to her in the salon. He turned when she walked in and even now, half-asleep, he took her breath away. His jaw was stubbled.

'Where were you?' she asked huskily.

'Nowhere important. Caught up with the guests. I want to take you somewhere…'

He came and took her by the hand. There was such an intensity to his expression that Siena couldn't decipher it, so she just said, 'Okay.'

When they were in the lift on the way down Andreas looked ahead and didn't say anything. Siena tried to stop her mind from leaping to all sorts of scenarios. She was waking up now, and as they walked through the hushed and quiet lobby she had a painful sense of *déjà-vu*. She thought of another dawn morning, five years ago. Of the turmoil in her heart and head as she'd walked out, unseeing, straight into Andreas's chest.

They walked around the corner of the hotel, intensifying Siena's sense of *déjà-vu,* and then she saw the huge gleaming motorbike. Siena blinked. Maybe she *was* dreaming.

Andreas was letting her hand go and taking out a helmet. When he drew her close to put it on her head Siena knew this was no dream. She couldn't decipher the expression on Andreas's face. It was forbidding. Then he was putting on his own helmet and lifting one leg over to straddle the bike.

He showed her where to put her foot, and with her hand on his shoulder to balance Siena swung her leg over the bike, sliding down into the seat behind Andreas, her front snug against his back.

He lifted up and pushed down and the bike roared to life, shattering the peace of the morning. Andreas reached back and pulled one of Siena's arms around his waist, and then the other one, showing her where to hold him. Her heart was thumping and she knew she was definitely awake as the bike straightened and they took off.

Unbelievably, it was Siena's first time on a motorbike, and she instinctively tightened her arms around Andreas's waist. It was exhilarating—the wind whipping past them, feeling the bike dip dangerously as Andreas took the corners.

When they stopped at a red light he turned his head and said above the noise, 'Okay?'

Siena nodded and then shouted, 'Yes!' when she realised he couldn't see her. And then they were off again.

Siena felt as if they were the only two people in the world as the faintest of pink streaks lined the dawn sky. Only a handful of cars passed them by.

Siena looked at the closed-up shops and bars that only hours before would have been teeming with people. The Eiffel Tower appeared in the distance, grey and stoic in the dawning light, bare of its glittering night-time façade. Siena preferred it like that.

They wound their way through the streets and Siena noticed that they were starting to go uphill. And then she saw the huge white shape of the Sacré Coeur in the distance. Through a series of winding, increasingly narrow streets they got closer and closer, until Andreas brought the bike to a stop under some trees.

He got off and removed his helmet, still with that enigmatic look on his face.

Siena pulled her helmet off and asked, 'Why are we here?'

Andreas took her helmet and said, 'Not yet. Another couple of minutes.'

He put the helmets away and pocketed the keys. He held out his hand. Siena put her hand in his and let him lead her up a path and through a small wooded area until the iconic church loomed above them, stately and awe-inspiring.

They were already quite high up, and Andreas led the way onward until they reached the steps outside the main doors. Siena turned around and saw the whole of Paris laid out in front of them, jaw-dropping in its beauty. She'd seen this view before but never like this, at dawn, without hordes of tourists, and with a dusky mist making everything seem hazy and dreamlike.

There was just one other couple. The woman was wearing what had to be her boyfriend's dinner jacket over a long dress and they were arm in arm, leaning over the balustrade that looked out over the ascent from the hill. They were too engrossed to notice Siena and Andreas.

'Let's sit.'

Siena looked to see Andreas indicate the steps. They sat down. He muttered something that Siena couldn't make out and then said, 'It's too cold.'

The stone *was* cold, but Siena wouldn't have swapped it for the world. 'No, it's fine... Andreas, why are we here?'

For the first time Siena noticed that Andreas was avoiding her eye and then she looked more closely. Her heart lurched. She might almost say that he looked nervous... He seemed to take a deep breath, and then he turned to look at her. The tortured expression on his face nearly took her breath away. Then he took her hands in his and she didn't say anything.

He looked down for a moment, and then back up. Siena had never seen him hesitant like this, and her heart beat fast.

'That morning...the morning after...when you came out of the hotel and I got on my bike and left...this is where I came. I came to this exact spot and sat on these steps and I looked out over this view and I cursed you.' Andreas gripped her hands tight, as if to reassure her, and then he continued.

'But mostly I cursed myself for being so stupid... You see, I thought *I* was the fool, to have been seduced by you. I thought you were like those other debutantes. Worldly-wise and experienced. Spoilt and bored.'

Siena tried to speak, familiar pain gripping her. 'Andreas—'

He shook his head. 'No. Let me speak, okay?'

Siena's heart lurched and she nodded. Andreas looked impossibly young at that moment.

'From the moment I saw you in that room I wanted you. When the opportunity came to be alone with you I jumped at it. And you were nothing like I'd expected. You were sweet and funny, so sexy and innocent.'

His mouth twisted. 'And yet those were all the very things I thought you'd fabricated when you stood at your father's side and denounced me. When his men took me outside I felt I deserved a beating for having been so duped... When I was called into my boss's office I lashed out at you—you received the full brunt of my pain. You see, I was arrogant enough to believe that no woman could enthral me. I wasn't going to have my head turned so easily. I'd vowed to get out of my small town and make something of myself. I wasn't going to get caught up in suffocating domesticity like my father had and waste my life…and I wasn't going to fall in love with some girl only to find out she didn't love me, as my friend Spiro did to his tragic cost. Yet within minutes of setting eyes on you you'd turned me inside out and I didn't even know it.'

Siena wasn't sure if she was breathing. His eyes burned like two dark sapphires.

'After what happened I put you down as a rich, cold-hearted bitch. But I couldn't stop thinking about you. I wanted out of my world and into your world so badly. I wanted to be able to stand in front of you some day and show you that I wasn't nothing. Prove that you had wanted me. You heard that conversation with my boss, didn't you?'

Siena's eyes were locked on Andreas. Slowly she nodded, and whispered, 'I went looking for you. I wanted to apologise, to explain.'

Andreas's mouth thinned. 'I probably wouldn't have believed you—just like I never gave you the chance to speak the next morning.'

Siena's hands tightened in his. Her voice was pained. 'You had to *leave* Europe. *I* did that to you.'

Andreas extricated one hand and lifted it to tuck some wayward hair behind Siena's ear. He smiled. 'Yes, and it was probably the best thing that could have happened to me. I got to America fired up with ambition and anger and energy. I caught Ruben's eye…and the rest is history. If that night hadn't happened and I'd stayed here I might be lucky enough to be managing that hotel now. I certainly wouldn't *own* it… I don't think I even knew my own potential until I went abroad.'

Siena said fiercely, 'You would have succeeded, no matter what.'

Andreas's hand cupped her jaw and he said seriously,

'Would it even mattter to you if I was just the manager of some middle-of-the-road hotel?'

Siena's heart stopped for a second and then galloped on. She shook her head and said honestly, 'No, not in the slightest.'

Andreas's fingers dropped from her chin and he took her hand again. He looked pained. 'There's something I should have said to you long before now...when you asked me if I wanted children...'

Siena remembered what he'd said that night and started to speak, not wanting to be reminded, but Andreas squeezed her hand.

'No. It was unforgivable and cruel, what I said. You touched a nerve and I lashed out. And I'm sorry. You didn't deserve it. You are not a cold-hearted tease. Any child would be lucky to have you as its mother, Siena.'

Siena felt tears prickle and blinked rapidly. His apology was profound, and she couldn't speak, so she just nodded in acknowledgement. Andreas drew in a shaky breath and reached into the pocket of his jeans to take something out. And then he got down on one knee before her, with the whole of Paris bathed in dawn light behind him.

Her eyes grew huge as she saw that he held a small black velvet box. His hands were shaking.

He looked at her and admitted, 'I can't believe I'm doing this... I always associated this with the death of ambition and success. I had a horror of somehow ending up back in my home town, having nothing. I thought my father had sacrificed too much by not taking up a college scholarship, by getting my mother pregnant and then marrying her having baby after baby. Staying stuck.'

'But your parents...' Siena said softly, still moved by his apology, trying not to let her heart jump out of her chest as she thought about that box. 'They created something wonderful. And if you hadn't had that secure foundation you might never have believed you *could* escape.'

Andreas smiled wryly. 'I know...*now.*' His smile faded slightly. 'When you admitted to me how you felt about meeting my family...my mother...I knew I had to stop fighting it. That I had to stop trying to box you into a place that made it easier for me to deal with you... I tried to make you admit you hated it, but that was only to bolster my own pathetic determination to avoid looking at how it made me feel. The fact is, going home with you...it made all those demons run away. I saw only love and affection. The security. And I felt for the first time as if I could be part of it and not be consumed by it.'

Siena looked from the box to Andreas. He was still on his knees. 'Andreas...?'

He opened the box and Siena looked down to see a beautiful vintage ring nestled in silk folds. It had one large round diamond at its centre, in an Art Deco setting, and was surrounded by small sapphires on either side. It was ornate, but simple, and Siena guessed very old.

Andreas sounded husky. 'I know you said you never wanted another piece of jewelry, but this was my grandmother's engagement ring. My mother gave it to me for my future wife when I was eighteen and heading off to Athens to work for the first time. I resented the implication that I would have to get married. I hated it and everything it symbolised and I vowed that it would be a cold day in hell before I gave it to anyone. Consequently it's languished at the back of many safes over the years—until this week. When I took it out and got it cleaned. Because I'd finally met the one person I could contemplate giving it to.'

Siena felt slightly numbed. Andreas held the ring up now, out of the box, and took her hand. She could feel him trembling—or maybe it was her trembling.

'Siena DePiero...will you do me the honour of becoming

my wife? Because you're in my head and my heart and my soul, and you have been for five years—ever since I first saw you. First you were a fascination, then you became an obsession, and now…I love you. The thought of you being in this world but not with me is more terrifying than anything I've ever known. So, please…will you marry me?'

Siena opened her mouth but all that came out was a sob. Her heart felt as if it was cracking open. Tears blurred her vision. She tried to speak through the vast ball of emotion making her chest full.

'I…' She couldn't do it. She put her hand to her mouth, trying to contain what she felt.

She saw the look on Andreas's face—stark sudden pain as it leached of colour. He thought she was saying *no*. Siena put her trembling hands around Andreas's face and looked at him, fought to contain her emotion just for a moment.

'Yes…Andreas Xenakis…I will marry you.' She drew in a great shuddering breath. 'I love you so much I don't ever want to live without you.'

That was all she could manage before she put her arms around his neck and noisy sobs erupted. His hand was on her back, soothing until the sobs stopped and she could draw back. Siena didn't care how she looked. Andreas was smiling at her as he'd smiled a long time ago, with no shadows of the past between them. Just love.

He took her hand and slid the ring onto her finger. It fitted perfectly and she looked at it in shock, still slightly disbelieving. She looked into his eyes. Her breath hitched. 'That morning…when you left on your bike…I wanted to go with you.'

Andreas smiled and ran his finger down her cheek. 'I wanted to take you with me, even as I cursed you.'

'I wish you had,' Siena whispered, emotional as she thought of the wasted years.

'Your sister,' Andreas reminded her ruefully.

Siena smiled too, a little sadly. 'Yes…my sister.'

Andreas moved back onto the steps beside her and held her face in his hands. 'Serena is being looked after and she will be okay, I promise you. Here and now is for *us*. This is where we start…and go on.'

Siena looked at him, her smile growing, joy replacing the feeling of regret. 'Yes, my love.'

And then, after kissing her soundly, he drew her between his legs, wrapped his arms around her and together they watched the most beautiful city in the world emerge from the dawn light into a new day.

EPILOGUE

TWO AND A HALF years later Siena stood under the shade of a tree on the corner of the square near Andreas's parents' house. It was a fiesta day: long trestle tables were laid out, heaving with food and drink, and Andreas's extended family were milling around, children running between people's legs, causing mayhem and laughter. Flowers bloomed from every possible place.

Siena could see the bright blonde head of her sister Serena, where she sat at one of the tables. Just then Andreas's mother came past and bent to kiss her head affectionately.

When Serena had been discharged from the clinic they had brought her here and she had moved in with Andreas's parents. Receiving the unconditional maternal love that Andreas's mother lavished on everyone had done more for Serena than any amount of drugs and therapy.

They'd just bought her an apartment in Athens and she was starting a job. Every day she got stronger and better, surrounded by people who loved her.

Once Serena had been strong enough Andreas had set up a meeting between them and their brother Rocco. It had been very emotional. Rocco had regretted his harshness on meeting Siena for the first time. But now they had a half-brother, a niece and a nephew, and Siena had a best friend in Gracie, his wife. The only reason they weren't here today was because Gracie's brother was getting married in London.

Siena's eyes didn't have to search far to find the centre of her universe. Her husband and her eighteen-month-old son, Spiro, their two dark heads close together.

She could see Andreas start to look around, searching for her. She recognized that possessive look of impatience so well, and it sent thrills deep into her abdomen, where she harboured the secret of a new life unfolding.

She put her hand there for a moment, relishing the moment she would tell him later, and Andreas's head turned as he found her. Siena smiled and swallowed her emotion, and walked forward into the loving embrace of her family.

* * * * *

MILLS & BOON®

Mills & Boon have been at the heart of romance since 1908... and while the fashions may have changed, one thing remains the same: from pulse-pounding passion to the gentlest caress, we're always known how to bring romance alive.

Now, we're delighted to present you with these irresistible illustrations, inspired by the vintage glamour of our covers. So indulge your wildest dreams and unleash your imagination as we present the most iconic Mills & Boon moments of the last century.

Visit **www.millsandboon.co.uk/ArtofRomance** to order yours!